I'm losing her! Sara thought in panic. *She's going to waft right out of this room!*

'But that's the wonderful thing about *fiction*,' Sara said. 'You can rewrite it and rewrite it until it satisfies you. *You* have control.' When the woman did not turn back, Sara continued, 'Unlike real life, which can be so obstinately uncooperative.'

She had said the right thing. Fanny looked back at Sara, studied her face in silence, moved just a few inches towards her.

'Someone as young and lovely as you can't have found life to be "obstinately uncooperative"?' she said, her voice challenging.

'Oh, but I have,' Sara told her. She dropped her eyes. How much would she tell this woman? Her own personal despair washed over her briefly and she shook herself. She must be professional. 'I have,' she repeated.

MORNING

Nancy Thayer

SPHERE BOOKS LIMITED

SPHERE BOOKS LTD

Published by the Penguin Group
27 Wrights Lane, London w8 5tz, England
Viking Penguin Inc., 40 West 23rd Street, New York, New York 10010, USA
Penguin Books Australia Ltd, Ringwood, Victoria, Australia
Penguin Books Canada Ltd, 2801 John Street, Markham, Ontario, Canada l3r 1b4
Penguin Books (NZ) Ltd, 182–190 Wairau Road, Auckland 10, New Zealand

Penguin Books Ltd, Registered Offices: Harmondsworth, Middlesex, England

First published in Great Britain by Hamish Hamilton Ltd; 1988
Published by Sphere Books Ltd, 1989
1 3 5 7 9 10 8 6 4 2
Copyright © 1987 by Nancy Thayer
All rights reserved

Printed and bound in Great Britain by
Richard Clay Ltd, Bungay, Suffolk

For Julian Bach

I would like to express my appreciation to the Mugar Memorial Library, in particular to the staff of Special Collections, for their assistance in directing me to the following sources: Sir James G. Frazer, *The Golden Bough* (New York: Macmillan, 1950); Dorothy Jacob, *Cures and Curses* (New York: Taplinger, 1967); Paul Ghalioungui, *The House of Life* (Amsterdam: B. M. Israel, 1973); M. Ester Harding, *Woman's Mysteries* (New York: G. P. Putnam's Sons, 1971); Angus McLaren, *Reproductive Rituals* (London: Methuen, 1984); Audrey L. Meany, *Anglo-Saxon Amulets and Curing Stones* (Oxford, England: BAR British Series 96, 1981); and Elwood B. Trigg and D. Phil, *Gypsy Demons and Divinities*. The quotations pertaining to fertility rites were taken from these books (listed in the order in which the quotations appear).

CHAPTER ONE

When she awoke, his hand was already under her nightgown, on her breast.

'Steve,' she said, stretching, rolling her body to face him.

'Good morning,' he said. 'Sara.' He spoke into her neck, her name coming on his breath as if it were a word of praise, or need. He lifted her nightgown higher, so that it bunched up around her hips.

'Wait,' Sara said, 'bathroom.'

She rose, shivering in the cold house, and hurried off. She hurried back, not pausing even to brush her teeth. They were so married, they were like animals. Every bodily smell was aphrodisiacal. She wore perfume now only to treat herself; for Steve she washed off all scent but her own.

The bed with its homely flannel sheets was deep and warm and receptive. Once under the covers, she raised her arms to pull her nightgown over her head and off. She tossed it onto the floor. Steve already had his T-shirt off, and she nuzzled against his chest, foraging into his prickly hairs, his sweet sweaty smells. Foraging – to search for what one needs – and she found it, and raised herself up over her husband. With his hands he pulled the sheet up around her back and shoulders, holding it there to keep off the chill until she grew hot from her laboring against him and with one quick movement shoved it away. When finally she fell against him, he pulled the covers up again, and stroked her back beneath the warm quilt as she calmed down. Around her forehead her hair and even behind her kneecaps her skin was sticky with sweat.

Between her legs she was sopping, and she lay against her husband, so intimately, as close to him as his skin, and yet in her own female way as far away from him as the moon, thinking of those fluids now, almost *listening* to those fluids: his, and hers, from this morning's love – and what else? What else.

While Steve showered, she made breakfast for him, eggs and bacon and toast and honey, because he worked as a carpenter and needed the calories. There had been a frost last night, but golden chrysanthemums and a few pale, summer-pink roses still bobbed brightly against the stone wall at the back of their yard. The five maples that towered along the fenceline blazed, but beneath them summer's pink impatiens broke upward through the russet leaves that layered the ground. All that triumphant, spectacular nature made Sara smile. She thought she had a secret.

She had turned up the thermostat when she came downstairs and now the furnace came on, filling the kitchen with warmth as the coffeepot filled the air with its tantalizing aroma. She inhaled deeply. God, she was such an aroma-nut she should hunt for truffles like a pig. Or root around for drugs at airports. She laughed out loud at the thought.

'What's so funny?' Steve asked, coming into the kitchen, all fresh and clean, his blond hair still damp.

Her heart kicked like the furnace, with a forceful thump, just to see him. After two years of marriage, the sight of him still moved her to her depths.

'Oh, nothing. Everything. It's such a beautiful day,' she said, going to him for a hug.

'You're such a beautiful lay,' he said.

They sat across from each other at the kitchen table. Another ordinary day, Sara thought, smiling to herself – but then again, maybe not. She looked down at her lonely cup of coffee and pitiful grapefruit half, then over at Steve's abundant plate where salty bacon curled seductively, waving at her. She grabbed up a letter she'd tossed onto the table the day before and began to read it again, just to keep her hands off that bacon.

'Whmmph?' Steve asked, his mouth full.

'A letter from Julia,' Sara said. Julia was her best friend, her direct line from Boston, her safety valve and counselor. 'Listen to this, I meant to read it to you Saturday when it arrived. She's such a nut. She's been digging little tidbits up for me from the BU library. This is from Frazer's *Golden Bough*.

'"In the county of Bekes, in Hungary, barren women are fertilized by being struck with a stick which has first been used to separate pairing dogs."'

'Charming image,' Steve said, grinning, 'but hardly practical.'

'I don't know,' Sara said laughing. 'There are lots of dogs on Nantucket.'

'And I'd have to beat you with a stick which has separated the mating dogs? Sounds a little kinky to me.' Steve paused, then grinned across the table at her. 'All right, I'll do it. I think I could really get into it.'

'Oh, great,' Sara replied.

Steve rose and pulled his grubby red vest over his tattered but clean flannel shirt. 'I've got to go now or I'll be late.' He leaned over and nuzzled the back of Sara's neck. 'Sorry I can't stay here and beat you with my stick.'

Sara turned in her chair and their lips met. They smiled at each other when he straightened.

'See you later,' he said. Then, at the door, he paused. 'Meet me at the Atlantic Café tonight about five, okay? It's Mick's birthday and the group's going to get together.'

'Oh, sure,' Sara said, feigning enthusiasm. 'Fine. Well – do you want me to pick up a present for Mick? Something funny?'

'I don't think so, hon. Mick will be happy if we just sing happy birthday and buy him a few beers.'

'All right. See you then.' Sara looked back down at Julia's letter.

'Of course you're feeling crazy,' Julia had written. 'If you didn't feel crazy now, I'd think you really were. I mean, in the first place, you gave up all the power and prestige and a CARPETED OFFICE and your name carved in wood on your door at Walpole and James to follow your true love, just like Annie Oakley in a dinghy, across the ocean to live on an island that has fewer people than a shopping mall parking lot. And

3

Nantucket is Steve's territory – nobody knows you and *everyone* knows Steve – some quite a bit better than others, which has got to be a little wearing now and then. Now you say you want an instant baby? I don't know. I think this calls for one of our all-night alcoholic powwows in front of my fireplace. Perhaps all that sea air has clogged your brain. Though you know I wish you well.'

Something about her friend's letter irritated Sara. 'That's not fair!' she said aloud, to Julia, who was at this moment across the ocean in her Black Bay apartment getting poshed up for a day at her art gallery on Newberry Street. 'One year is not exactly *instant*!'

Sara tossed the letter aside and rose, restless with her thoughts. Children had been in their plans from the start. When she and Steve moved to Nantucket a year ago, they bought a house with an extra bedroom – for the children. Sara had been glad to give up her position at Walpole and James and start free-lance editing because she knew that kind of work would be more suited to a life with children. Julia knew all that. She knew Sara's life every step of the way. 'Instant baby' was really not fair.

It was true, though, that it had never occurred to Sara that there wouldn't be an instant baby – not after all the years she had spent guarding against one. The first few months, she had been just simply amazed, each time her period started, as if something really bizarre had happened.

When the sixth month of not using birth control and still not getting pregnant rolled around, Sara had become scientific and efficient. She went to see a gynecologist. He had laughed at her worries – actually laughed. 'You've only been trying six months,' he said after giving her a pelvic exam. 'The average time – *the average* – it takes a woman to get pregnant is three and a half months. That includes all the young teenagers who get knocked up just thinking about sex. You're a perfectly healthy young woman, you're only thirty-four, you've got lots of time. Just go home and relax and screw a lot.'

Sara had been shocked that a doctor would say 'screw'. Now, six months later, when she was beginning to worry about herself, she wondered if her reaction to the word 'screw' hadn't been puritanical, indicating some deep inner prudishness that was keeping her from getting pregnant. She'd have to mention that to Julia. Or was she overanalyzing?

If only Julia were here, where she could talk with her every day. Sara was certain that she and Steve were as close as any man and woman could be, but he couldn't talk about the juicy female things that she talked about with her women friends in Boston. And he seemed baffled by her increasing fears about her fertility. Well, she was baffled, too. Fate before had always been so kind. Her achievements had not been effortless – she had always worked hard – but she had never before met with this kind of repeated failure.

Perhaps at the very grown-up and accomplished age of thirty-four there was something basic about procreating that Sara needed to learn. Something along the lines of the old wives' tales that Julia was beginning to jokingly send. Sara longed for a good woman friend here in Nantucket, someone she could call every day to confide in, without worrying about long distance phone bills. Steve had plenty of friends here, and they all had wives, except for Mick, who was the eternal bachelor of the group. And she liked the wives – but felt shut out by them. They were part of a network of friends who had known each other for years and years, and when Steve returned to this island, where he had grown up, he slipped right back into place; he had always been one of them. Everyone was pleasant to Sara, but she was kept at arm's length. The people who chose to live year-round on this island thirty miles away from the mainland were independent and inner directed; they were strong, but hard to get to know.

And of course, it was Sara's fault, too. Her work was so solitary, requiring long hours of silence. For days on end she had no need to leave her house – really, she had no need to even get out of her robe. She would curl up on the sofa or sit at the dining room table and edit gothic romances until, when she raised her head, she saw that the sun had sunk and the day had gone. And she was shy. She did not know how to force her way into the intimate center of the group. They seemed so complete without her. They shared memories and jokes and references she couldn't understand. Mostly it was four other couples and Mick the bachelor, who with Steve made an even ten, a sort of tacit closed set involved in an old island square dance of friendship. She did not know the steps. She was the outsider, stumbling at the rim. The longer she felt left out, the more she longed not to long to be included; perhaps that was perverse of her. Perhaps she had too much pride.

Perhaps everything was intertwined? All the couples but one had children, and over the past two years Sara had heard the wives announcing helplessly, 'Oh, Lord, I'm pregnant, I don't even know how it happened!' She knew how the group gossiped, how secrets were eagerly carried from person to person like treasure – she knew she could not bear it if these people knew that she was trying to get pregnant and failing. Again: her pride. Still, she had gone off-island to Hyannis to see the gynecologist six months ago. Rumors flew around the small community as abundantly as the sea gulls circling the sky, and she did not want a Nantucket doctor or nurse to mention her problem to someone who would mention it to someone else – it meant too much to her.

In the first year of their marriage, like many lucky couples, Steve and Sara experienced that drawing together of spirit and mind and body that made them feel there was something basic about their love, something elemental and rare, like the birth of twins. It was as if they had thought they were separate entities, but in their marriage realized they were truly two halves of a whole, as in turning, the moon shows its bright and dark sides joined. Now there was a fissure in that whole, a hairline crack running between them, so small still that they scarcely noticed it was there.

They had not spoken of this. Sara was aware of it only because she realized that for the first time since her marriage to Steve she was relying heavily on Julia for sympathy and comfort and support. Perhaps it helped that Julia was not so close to the problem and could not be hurt by Sara's infertility. Julia helped Sara put it all in perspective – gorgeous Julia, who had her own problem, her own secret – she was having an affair with a married man, she was passionately in love with that married man, who had some power and fame in the state. The last thing in the world Julia wanted was to get pregnant, and the easiest thing in the world Julia did was laugh, so she was able to put Sara's plight in perspective for her. Thank God for Julia, Sara thought. And for Sara's sister, Ellie, who lived in the Midwest and who was a nurse. Ellie was married, a mother, and sensible; she relayed relevant scientific tidbits about fertility to Sara just as Julia had begun, in her own wacky way, to send unscientific ones. With these two on her side, how could she fail?

Perhaps she hadn't failed. Perhaps – for it was the twenty-ninth day – Sara hurried into the bathroom and checked. No blood! Looking at herself in the mirror, she grinned gleefully, then cringed, once again regretting the haircut she had just gotten. She was getting superstitious. She was really getting nuts. First the weight, and then the hair, and now look at her.

Six months ago, after the off-island doctor had told her to relax, Ellie had told Sara about a study about women joggers who had trouble getting pregnant, who even stopped having periods. So Sara had stopped exercising and watching her diet – it made sense in a sappy way – what baby would want to nestle in a bunch of bones? A plump and cushiony body seemed much more the sort of place for a baby to nest and grow. Over the past six months, Sara had gained fifteen pounds. Soft depths. She felt good – but she looked different, and now she thought perhaps she had gone too far.

And the haircut – that had been even crazier. For years Sara had worn her thick blond hair in a simple style, parted in the middle, sleekly falling on each side to slant gently under just at chin level. She had always known she was pretty, and had chosen that severe style because she thought it made her look serious, intelligent, sensible, not given to vanity, the way an editor should look.

But a few weeks ago at a group get-together, she had heard Carole Clark announce that she was pregnant. 'God, I never should have had my hair cut,' Carole had said, laughing. 'Every time I get my hair cut, I get pregnant!'

Well, Sara had thought, *hmmmmm*. There *was* a connection between hair and power – look at Samson and Delilah! After waiting for two weeks, so that no one might suspect what she was doing (she was that paranoid these days), she had gone to a local hairdresser and had her hair chopped very short. She said she wanted a 'modern' look, not punk, but chic.

When Julia saw her on a recent visit, she told Sara she looked like Boy George. Steve had jokingly asked if she was going to start wearing chains of safety pins in one ear. It was not a successful haircut; it was just too drastic.

On the other hand, perhaps it *was* a successful haircut. It was the twenty-ninth day and she hadn't started her period. If she were pregnant, she wouldn't care what her hair looked like!

Her stomach was swelling outward the way it always did just before her period – she couldn't ignore that. So maybe she wasn't pregnant. And her breasts were sore. That, Ellie said, could mean anything either way.

Sara looked up from her stomach to see her face in her mirror. Her blond hair was sticking up and out all over. 'You're losing your mind,' she said to herself. 'Get to work.'

After her marriage, after blissful months of painting woodwork and matching napkins to placemats, Sara had grown bored and had called on her old boss at Walpole and James for help. Donald James had gladly sent her work. In the past year she had edited a no-sugar-or-salt-or-alcohol cookbook, a nonfiction book about the slaughter of seals and whales, and a dreary novel about the end of the world. Jokingly, she had said to Donald, 'Cheerful stuff you're giving me to fill my days with,' and he had replied, 'Cheerful? You want cheerful?' And he had given another Boston publishing house her name, more in jest than anything else.

Heartways House, with a millionth the prestige of Walpole and James, but with more than five times the sales, specialized in paperback romances, the sort of books Sara had never even read before. To her surprise she found it a treat, like eating junk food, to edit these books, and for the past few months she had spent her days reading about lust, revenge, lace-covered bodices, heroines running from castles, dark-eyed mysterious men. The endings were all predictable – but at this point in her life she appreciated that.

Her workroom was the living room (while the spare bedroom sat waiting for its baby). The manuscripts and notebooks and pencils were stacked neatly on a shelf in the bookcase. With a fresh cup of coffee on the table next to her, and an afghan pulled up over her knees, she settled down with the latest gothic from Heartways House. It was a lazy way to work, cozying up on the sofa, still in her nightgown and warm pink robe, but she loved it. No intrusions, no interruptions, no other people scurrying down a hallway outside the office, laughing, calling out, luring her mind from her work – just the warm silence of her house. Sunlight slanted through the windows, making a crazy quilt of dark and light squares on the faded ruby and azure Oriental carpet. Her body was still: no signs. She bent to her work.

Seraphina stood panting next to the mammoth wooden doors that led to the turret. The heavy brass keys were in her hand.

'Seraphina,' Errol called, 'my darling! Let me out!'

Seraphina shuddered as fear and desire passed through her slender body like a flame. Should she let Errol out? Or should she run and fetch Jean-Paul? Which man was the murderer? Which man should she trust?

Oh, for heaven's sake, Seraphina, let poor old Errol out, Sara thought, sighing. *We all know he's the hero; he's the one who's got all the money and will inherit the castle.*

After a few more paragraphs (during which Seraphina let Errol out of the turret) Sara looked up, away from the manuscript. She stared out of the window at the blue sky, but didn't really see it. She was wondering whether when Seraphina and Errol got married they would have any trouble conceiving. *That* was the real mystery, the real adventure, Sara thought, getting a baby. But no, Seraphina would get

9

pregnant right away and deliver a healthy baby boy, just like Princess Di. For some people it was as easy as slipping down a slide.

She forced herself back to the manuscript. She had to be attentive, even with this writer, who was usually meticulous. Did she feel anything? Any twinge anywhere? No.

She forced herself to concentrate.

Errol, much to Seraphina's (and Sara's) surprise, once out of the turret, tied poor Seraphina up with rope and gagged her with his ascot, inflicting light bruises (and copping some feels, though the writer didn't quite put it that way) as he did. Sara's interest was whetted. She had been sure Errol was the good guy. She turned the page.

When I was twelve, I raised my own herd of polled registered Hereford for a 4-H project. I had five heifers who were old enough to be bred and to calve that year. I loved those heifers. I had a name for each of them. My father gave me one side of the barn just for them and I kept their stalls full of straw so fresh and golden that a princess could easily have spun it into gold; when the sun slanted in through the high loft door, the dust motes drifted down onto that straw and onto the backs of my cows like more gold, golden coins; you could almost hear it chiming as it fell.

All animals, if loved personally and often, respond. So it came to be that every evening when I went out to the barnyard to call the cows home from the pasture, clanking the bucket of grain against the great round metal water trough and making triumphant gonglike dinner-bell sounds ring out, those five cows came running in from wherever they were. Really running. Father said he'd never seen anything like it. My brother, who was sometimes home from college, talked to us about Pavlov and stimulus-response. Whatever it was, when I called my cows in the evening, they came, knowing they would get a nice big helping of sweet ground corn and part of a bale of hay. Later, when they had been bred and were big with their calves, I would laugh to see them come running up, their enormous bellies swaying above their slender legs. It was as if all the maiden ladies at our church had suddenly run out together into the street, their flowered pillbox hats bobbing, their pocketbooks and huge corseted bosoms and hips and stomachs swinging gently above their tapered ankles and dainty tiny feet. My shy-eyed cows did have that air of refinement about them.

Sara picked up the next manuscript sheet. Seraphina was there, twisting and writhing, her bosom heaving under delicate lace. Errol had left her shut in the turret.

Sara looked back at the page she had just read. How had this realistic little memoir about cows got into the middle of the romance novel? Had Heartways House mixed up two manuscripts? But what would Heartways House, which published only romance novels and a few spy and adventure stories, be doing with a realistic piece? Perhaps one of the editors was reading it for a friend.

Sara set the page about the cows aside. She'd rather read about that than old Errol and Seraphina, she thought. *Seraphina*, really, what a hokey name.

Before she read on, she treated herself to another trip to the bathroom. Her heart leapt: still no blood.

That evening, her work done, Sara stood in the bedroom, looking at herself in the full-length mirror that hung on the closet door. She had pulled up her newest pair of jeans – size fourteen. My God, she had never worn size fourteen before in her life, she was getting to be an absolute WHALE. And today the jeans would not quite fit. They were too big and loose on her legs, but she could not zip them up around her stomach and waist.

Despair beckoned. All day long she had hoped, but this was one of the unmistakable signs that her period was about to start – this swollen stomach that bulged out in front of her like a mock pregnancy. In a few days, after she had gone through the heaviest flow, her emptied body would suddenly slip back into shape, her stomach would tighten, all of its own accord, and she would look normal again, if not terribly slim, at least not bloated. But for now, she was stuck with the silhouette of a kangaroo. Still – her period hadn't started . . .

Bending over to tug off her jeans, she smiled at her tummy. 'Hi,' she said. 'Anybody home?' Then, optimistic, she dressed in a long denim skirt and several bright baggy shirts, grateful that the layered look was in. She pulled on knee-high red boots, brushed her hair up and out, and put on dangling earrings that her mother would have scorned as being fit only for gypsies. Throwing on her red wool cape, she went out into the evening, to walk to the Atlantic Café to meet her husband.

It was not quite five o'clock, not yet dark. This was a mild November so far, and the air was gentle, the wind low. One of the pleasures of living on Nantucket was that one could walk to almost any spot in the village, along streets that were as charming as a dream. Pleasant Street curved before her like a scene from a European fairy tale, brick mansions with their walled gardens and winding stone paths next to snug cottages with blue doors and window boxes still spilling over with flowers. The lamplights and shop lights glowed golden across the cobblestones as she turned down Main Street, where, this time of year, she saw more people walking their dogs than driving cars. She slipped into the Hub to see what new magazines were in, then wandered on down to the Atlantic Café.

The group was already there, laughing, at several tables they had pushed together; Sara eyed them with nervous uncertainty.

'Hi, Sara!' Carole Clark called. 'Sit here!' She beckoned, indicating a chair between her and Steve.

As Sara squeezed into place, Steve pulled her to him. 'Hi, babe,' he said, nuzzling her ear. His skin was silk over steel; he was as strong as a lumberjack but he looked like a lawyer with his thick blond hair and perfectly regular features.

'Ahh, don't give me that crap, he's a scumbag!' Mick roared from across the table, and Steve released Sara and turned back to a discussion of a local real estate agent.

Sara ordered a glass of white wine, then settled back to watch and listen, trying to keep a smile on her face. At least, she thought, relaxing, at least, *thank God*, The Virgin wasn't here tonight.

The Virgin was Sara's secret nickname for Mary Bennett, a woman Sara's age who had been Steve's serious girlfriend for years. They had broken up just a few months before Steve and Sara met. Now Steve was married to Sara and Mary was married to Bill Bennett, but Mary never let a meeting pass by without referring in as many ways as possible to the old days when she and Steve were lovers.

'Remember – he was that guy who sang folk songs at that beach party at Cisco?' she would say to Steve. 'That party where we slipped off and –' Mary would stop talking and just grin.

'Oh, yeah, I remember that guy,' Steve would say, not returning Mary's conspirator's smile.

Or, 'Steve, where did you get those turquoise and silver earrings you gave me for Christmas a while ago?' she would ask, right in front of Sara and Mary's husband, Bill.

Steve, embarrassed, uncomfortable, and aware of Sara's feelings about Mary, would mutter, 'Oh, I don't remember, Mary. That was so long ago.'

'Not *so* long ago,' she would say with a smug smile.

The first few months Sara had lived on the island, Mary had been openly, if sneakily, hostile to her. If they passed each other on the street, Mary would look the other way, or, if Sara spoke first, Mary would only look at her, unspeaking, sometimes with contemptuous surprise on her face as if she were thinking 'Who is this dreadful person and why is she talking to me?' – sometimes with simple blank dislike. She had pretended for a long time not to remember Sara's name: 'Hi, Shari,' or 'Hi, Susie,' she would say when she found it necessary to acknowledge Sara's presence.

In defense, Sara came up with a nickname of her own for Mary: The Virgin, because even when taunting Sara, wide-eyed Mary looked and acted as pure and perfect and maternal and loving as a saint. Mary had the sweetest face on earth, heart shaped, with a pointed chin and huge soft brown eyes. She had lots of long curling brown hair that framed her face and feathered around her head and shoulders like a halo. She spoke in a high, breathy, little-girl's voice with never a hint of harshness or sarcasm, so that her question, 'It *is* Susie, isn't it?' seemed as innocent as an angel's.

Everyone else seemed to adore Mary. Four years ago, when Steve and Sara were living together in Boston, Mary had married Bill Bennett, a tall handsome angry man who wanted to be a novelist. Mary devoted her life to helping him; she supported them entirely by running a day-care center in her home. It was no wonder everyone adored her; she took care of everyone's children with love and tenderness and sympathy and everlasting patience. 'Mary's just incredible,' people were constantly saying. 'I don't know how I'd live without her.'

Sara wondered if no one else noticed that Mary, in spite of her goody-goody act and her sweet childish nature and great rolling cow eyes, wore the most revealing clothes of any woman on the island. Pretending to poverty (Steve told Sara there was money in Mary's family), Mary wore nothing but jeans and T-shirts or turtlenecks or sweaters. She never wore a bra, and every sweater or top she ever wore was so tight on her that her breasts and nipples were outlined with great clarity. She might as well have worn a shirt with 'Hey! Look! Great breasts!' and arrows pointing which way to look. Her jeans were always skin tight. She had two children, one three, one almost two, and until recently she had nursed the baby, pulling up her shirt in front of anyone and everyone, exposing her large full breasts. Once Sara had noticed Steve watching Mary nurse; she had then looked at Mary and, startled, had received a look from her that was full of smugness and scorn. 'I was his first love, he'll always be fascinated by me,' Mary seemed to say with every glance at Sara.

It had been later that night, back at home, only a few months ago, when Sara had lost her temper and stormed at Steve, 'I hate her! I hate being around her!' Steve had pulled into himself as he often did when she was upset. He was calm and hated fights. (One evening Sara had yelled at him, 'Oh,

14

you drive me crazy – you're so – so *blond*!' 'But Sara,' Steve had replied, baffled, 'you're blond, too.' That was true, but Sara felt that she was blond like Charo, every now and then erupting into a tumult of shaking ruffles, screeching so wildly in her passions that she cruised right through her anger into a foreign language – at times she was sure it must seem that way to Steve.) As their marriage unfolded, she had tried to be more reasonable in her angers, but that night Sara had been driven past reason.

'I saw you looking at Mary's breasts. God, can't you understand how hard it is for me to live here with you, with you looking at your old lover's breasts? How would you like it if I sat around with David Larkin looking at my breasts!'

'She was nursing a baby,' Steve had sighed.

'That's beside the point!' Sara had cried, lying. For of course it hadn't been beside the point at all: there Sara was, starting her period after seven months of trying to get pregnant, and there Mary was, Steve's old girlfriend, nursing her *second* child. If Steve had married Mary, he would have children by now. Surely that thought had occurred to him, although he would never be able to be so unkind as to speak it aloud.

'The point is,' Sara had gone on, 'that you are living here with your old friends, seeing your old lover all the time, *looking* at her, talking with her about old times. And Christ, she's always kissing you!'

'She's always kissing everyone,' Steve said. 'That's just the way she is.'

'Oh, you know what I mean, Steve. She's always acting like the two of you share some big secret.'

'I know what you mean,' Steve had said, weary, 'but I think you're exaggerating it. Mary's just one of those super-friendly people. I don't love her anymore, Sara. I love you. And she's not interested in me, she's married to Bill, they've got kids, she's working her ass off to support the family so he can write. Don't get paranoid.'

'Oh, right. *Paranoid*,' Sara had sniffed, going cold and sarcastic. 'Mary's perfect, just friendly, and *I'm* paranoid.'

'Well, you are,' Steve said. 'You know I don't care a thing about her.'

'I just wish David lived here, I just wish I ran into my old lover every single damned day of the year, I wish he were kissing me every time we saw each other – then we'd see about paranoia.'

'Look, what can I do?' Steve had asked unhappily. 'She and Bill are part of the group. They're friends with everyone I'm friends with. I can't avoid them.'

'No,' Sara had agreed. 'So for the rest of my life I've got to live with the knowledge that you'll be seeing your first love all the time – and God knows how many times you run into her when you're off by yourself.'

'Oh, Sara –'

'Oh, Sara nothing.' No wonder you were longing to move back to the island. The place where you and your lover had such wonderful times –'

'Sara, come on,' Steve had said, trying to take her in his arms.

But she had been in a fury then, feeling trapped, and angry because no one could understand how it was for her – and jealous, jealous beyond words that Mary had children and Sara had only this week of cramping womb and flowing wasted blood.

She had pulled away from Steve. She had gone into their guest bedroom, and lay on the bed, sobbing.

At last Steve had come in. He had sat down next to her on the bed and put his hands on her shoulders. 'Sara, I hate it that you're so upset,' he said. 'Listen, we can always move back to Boston. I wouldn't mind at all. We could buy a place outside Boston, in the country, you could go back to work for Donald James . . .'

Slowly becoming sane again, Sara remembered all the cocktail parties for authors she had gone to, all the authors she had picked up at the airport for her boss, all the handsome men who wrote or edited or published or worked somehow in the field and who had flirted with her or complimented her or somehow passed through her life vividly enough to remind her that she was a sexually attractive young woman. Steve had

16

never been jealous of those parties she had gone to by herself, of those men she had 'had to' eat dinner with or somehow entertain. He had never accused her of anything during all those associations with all those men. She knew he loved her as much as she loved him. She really did know that.

'Oh, Steve,' she had wailed. 'I'm so ashamed. I know you love me. I know I'm acting like a bitch. I'm just so jealous, so jealous of the way she looks at you, of what she is always trying to imply.'

'She means nothing to me, I promise you. I was the one who broke up with her, if it's any comfort to you.' (It was – great comfort.) 'I'd kept going with her for months just out of habit. She's really not that interesting, if you really knew her, Sara. She's – oh, Sara, I never would have *married* her.'

Sara had turned over, scooted across the bed, snuggled into Steve's arms. 'You would never have married anyone but me,' she told him.

'That's right,' he said. 'That's absolutely right.'

They had not discussed Mary after that, but Sara could tell whenever the gang was together that Steve was doing his best to deflect Mary's attentions.

Now he sat, his arm flung casually across the back of Sara's chair, a beer in his other hand, involved in a conversation with Mick and the other guys about football.

'Listen,' Carole Clark said, touching Sara's arm, 'are you guys going off-island for Thanksgiving?'

'No,' Sara answered. 'We'll stay here. My family's all back in the Midwest and Steve's parents are in Florida.'

'Great,' Carole said. 'Then you and Steve can spend Thanksgiving with all of us. If you want to, I mean. The gang usually gets together at someone's house every year for Thanksgiving and every couple brings something and it's a huge feast. It's going to be at my house this year. I'm doing the turkey and the stuffing, and everyone else is bringing the rest.' Carole paused. 'I know it's late asking you, but, um, we weren't sure you'd want to come. I mean, we'll all have our kids there, so there'll be about a thousand children, and the noise level – well, you know, it won't exactly be elegant.'

'It sounds *wonderful*!' Sara exclaimed. Conflicting emotions battled inside her: she was delighted that Carole had asked them, but terrified at her words. Did Carole think she was too cold, too unaffectionate to enjoy little children? Was Sara secretly flawed and could everyone else sense it?

Carole was rattling on now, about what the others were bringing, wine and sweet potatoes and pumpkin pie and vegetables – what would Sara like to bring? Did she have any speciality? Sara roused herself and began discussing favorite recipes. Annie Danforth made her husband trade places with her so she could join in the conversation. Sara liked Annie – partly, admittedly, because Annie was in her early thirties and had no children yet – but also because she was a nice, intelligent woman. This evening was the first time Sara had had a chance to spend any length of time getting to know Carole and Anne, and with a beer inside her and the talk flowing so naturally around her, she began to have a warming sense of things being all right with the world.

'Hi, everybody!' came a high sweet breathless greeting.

Sara looked up and inwardly groaned: it was The Virgin, at last blessing them with her presence.

'Sorry, I'm so late, I had some little kiddies stay late – you know, Mandy's children – she's in the hospital and Greg couldn't get off work sooner.'

As she talked, Mary slipped off her thrift shop tweed man's coat and pulled a muffler from around her neck. She was wearing jeans, knee-high boots, a green turtleneck sweater as tight as skin. *Well*, Sara thought sardonically, *we can all see that you haven't lost or gained an ounce this week.*

'I told Bill he just had to stay home with our kiddies tonight,' Mary was saying, her breathless voice making everything she said of immense importance. 'I've been with children all day and need a little adult time! And we couldn't get a sitter. But I can't stay long, just one beer, and I want to hear how you all are!'

Mary slipped her slender hips into a chair between Annie Danforth and Pete Clark.

'Your Jeremy was so cute today!' Mary exclaimed, turning

18

to Carole and back to Pete. She began a detailed account of something the Clarks' three-year-old had done, and the Clarks listened, rapt. Sara watched, thinking that there must be nothing as enthralling as stories about one's children being clever.

Sara leaned back in her chair and sipped her beer. People started talking in small groups around the table again, about football, or what had happened at work, or the selectman's meeting the night before. Keeping a pleasant alert look on her face, Sara surreptitiously listened to her insides: what was going on? She wasn't cramping yet. Nothing seemed to be happening. She leaned forward, put her elbows on the table, smiled at nothing and everything. Would the time come when Mary would say, 'Oh, Sara, your baby did the cutest thing today!'?

'Sara,' Mary said suddenly, leaning forward across the table toward Sara, 'I've been wanting to ask you something.' Her voice was low and secretive. 'Now you go on and talk to the guys,' she ordered Pete Clark. 'This is just for us women!'

Pete smiled and turned away. Mary leaned even farther forward, her face all sweet friendship.

Sara thought: *Maybe she's nice after all, just spacey, maybe I've been imagining everything.* She was, in spite of herself, pleased to be singled out by Mary, who usually ignored her, pleased to have Mary treating her like a friend.

'What have you been wanting to ask?' Sara smiled and leaned forward, too. Between her and Mary, Annie and Carole sat watching.

'Well – I suppose this is really pretty presumptuous of me – probably I shouldn't say this – but you know I've just been *so curious* for weeks now I'm going crazy – Sara, are you pregnant? Or have you just gained a lot of weight?'

'Oh, God,' Sara said, and for a brief second that was all she *could* say. 'Oh, have I gained *that* much weight? I'd better go on a diet. No, I'm not pregnant, Mary. I guess I've just let myself go since we moved to the island. You know I do free-lance editing, which means sitting around a lot – and I tend to eat when I'm sitting around reading – and in Boston when I worked for the publishing house I had to walk a lot more, around the office and around the city and so on – and here I just don't get that much exercise –' She was blithering, she knew it, she couldn't stop herself, she was trying to put a wall of words between herself and Mary, spinning a cocoon of words to hide in.

'Oh, Sara,' Annie Danforth said, 'you don't look *pregnant*. I swear, Mary, you've got babies on the brain. Is that all you ever think about?'

'Well, can you blame me?' Mary laughed. 'That's all I see from morning to night. Don't get me wrong, Sara, I don't mean you look *fat* or anything, it's just that – well, you *have* gained some weight since you moved here, haven't you? And naturally, I just thought, I mean Steve's so . . .' She let her voice trail off. She smiled knowingly at Sara.

'I'm the one who looks pregnant!' Wade Danforth said, leaning into the conversation from the other side of Steve.

Sara cringed inwardly again, realizing that the entire table had heard Mary's question.

'Look at this!' Wade went on, patting his big belly. 'I'm the proud father of a six-pack of Michelob!'

'More like a case,' someone at the table said, laughing.

'That reminds me,' Carole said. 'Who's bringing the wine for Thanksgiving? And what shall we have for cocktails? Does someone want to do mulled wine or something? I really don't want *beer* at our Thanksgiving dinner.'

'Hey, why not? I'm not coming if we can't have beer,' Wade yelled.

'Don't be such a peasant,' Annie told him. 'One night a year you can try for a little class.'

The conversation flowed on again past Sara. *Now am I paranoid or was Mary being intentionally cruel*, she wondered, *and if she was being cruel, well, why?* Next to her, Steve was deep in a discussion about building codes on the island; she knew he had been oblivious to Mary's question. She wished Julia were here – she could envision how Julia would squint her eyes, and mouth 'What a bitch!' across the table to Sara.

No. What Sara wished, more than anything, was that in a

few weeks she would say, laughing, to Mary, 'You know, when you asked me if I was pregnant that night at the Atlantic Café? And I said no? Well – guess what? – I was! But I didn't know it yet!'

Sara smiled, lost for a moment in this reverie of her triumph, telling the woman about it with a hushed voice, an amused but smug expression. Then it would be all right, then she would be able to handle Mary, then she could handle everything.

When the group finally dispersed, Sara and Steve walked together through the darkened autumn night, and after the noise the silence swirled around them as if enclosing them in an iridescent shell. Steve put his arms around her and pulled her against him. She leaned her head on his shoulder as she walked. They entered their house and soon were naked together, delving deeper into the intimate whorls of their love. Sara's veins seemed to flow with gratitude, with honey and delirious joy and gratitude. She and Steve were one; and with the logic of such strong love and such a complete marriage, their joining would make three. A baby. Their baby. She could almost see its creamy skin and tiny limbs. She could almost feel its fragile breath.

But when she rose from her bed she found that once again their baby was not there.

CHAPTER TWO

Morning.

Sara was brought to consciousness by a click from the bed-side radio.

'. . . a beautiful morning. The weather report for the Cape and islands in just a moment. But first a warning to all you turkeys out there, in case you forgot, tomorrow's Thanks-giving!'

She reached over to her bedside table, moving as little as possible, and picked up the small plastic blue-and-white case that held the basal thermometer. She put it in her mouth, feeling the brief bite of cold glass under her tongue, then looked at the digital clock on the bedside clock radio, 7:01. She had to keep the thermometer in her mouth for exactly five minutes. The instructions that came with the thermometer specified that she use it before rising from bed, even before going to the bathroom, because any activity might raise her temperature a few crucial points and throw off her chart. So she lay still, obedient.

Beside her, Steve groaned and pulled his pillow over his head. A few measures of music blared from the radio, inter-rupted by the disc jockey's jovial patter.

'The first caller to tell me the name of this song wins two free tickets to the Cape Movie Mart! Come on out there, you guys, this is an easy one.'

Mouth pursed around the thermometer, Sara drifted on the sounds of the music, an easy-listening tribute to an artist with a difficult vision, a man too beautiful for this world. The DJ shouted cheerfully the instant the record stopped. *He must do cocaine or at least drink eighty cups of coffee to be so energetic at this time of day*, Sara thought.

'Hello, dear!' the DJ said to his caller. 'What's your guess?'

' "Starry Starry Night"?' a young girl asked.

'Sorry, hon, that's close, but no cigar,' the DJ said.

'Just a moment,' the girl cried. Muffled shrieks came over the phone. 'I meant "VINCENT"!' she said.

'That's right!' the DJ shouted, as thrilled as if the girl had just unlocked the door to eternal life. 'You're absolutely right! "Vincent" by Don McLean. You've won two free tickets to the movies, sweetheart. And I'll tell you what. If you can tell me who the song's about, I'll throw in another ticket.'

Sara smiled, thinking of sunflowers, impressionism, severed ears.

'Vincent *Price*!' the girl replied triumphantly.

Sara took the thermometer from her mouth as she exploded into laughter. She looked at the clock — it was all right, five minutes had passed. Switching off the radio, she retrieved the thermometer from the blankets and rose from bed.

Tying her pink robe around her, sliding her feet into fleece-lined slippers, she hurried downstairs. By now she had a little ritual set up (and there was some comfort in rituals). She turned up the thermostat, started the coffee water perking, quickly used the bathroom, then took her chart from its special drawer in the kitchen and sat down at the table with it. Holding the thermometer to the light, as meticulous as a scientist with a test tube of radioactive particles, she squinted to steady her vision, and read the morning's news.

98.4. Well, that was just fine. She rose to get a cup of coffee, then sat back down to complete the rite.

It *was* a beautiful morning, still warm, and foggy, the windows filled with a shimmering gentle silver light. From Brant Point the foghorn lowed slowly and long, like some great stupid animal lost in the mist. Sara smiled, liking this, liking the sense of something out there waiting in the unseen world. Spreading her chart before her on the table, she took a pencil and put a dot just where the date column met the temperature. She drew a line connecting yesterday's dot with today's. Her chart reminded her of a child's dot-to-dot game, which, when finished, would reveal a picture of a duck or a Christmas tree. Would her chart, when finished, reveal signs

23

of a completed embryo? Was this the ritual that would conjure up her child?

Certainly it had to be better than Julia's latest lunatic suggestion, which had come in last week's mail.

To Promote Breeding

Let the party take of the syrup of stinking orach a spoonful night and morning. Then as follows: take three pints of good ale, boil it in the piths of three ox-backs, half a handful of clary, a handful of nepp (nepata) a quarter of a pound of dates stoned sliced and the pith taken out; a handful of raisins of the sun stoned; three whole nutmegs pricked full of holes. Boil all these till half be wasted. Strain it out and drink a small wineglass at your going to bed as long as it lasts. Accompanying not with your husband during the time or sometime before. Be very careful and let nothing disquiet you. Take Sherpherd's Purse a good handful and boil it in a pint of milk till half be consumed and drink it off.

'I've looked up these weird things in the dictionary,' Julia had written on an attached sheet. 'Guess what? You can get them – or improvise.'

At first Sara had laughed, then frowned. Why not? If it worked well enough in ancient times that they wrote it down, perhaps there really was something to it. So, feeling like a witch or an escapee from the nearest mental asylum, she had made her own brew, using boiled ale, store-bought cans of oxtail soup, sage, dates and raisins Cuisinarted to mush, catnip, and nutmeg. It had tasted absolutely foul. She couldn't even drink it, and its taste and smell discouraged her completely from trying to improvise on a 'stinking orach'.

The thermometer was Ellie's suggestion. Two weeks ago, when The Virgin snidely asked Sara if she was pregnant and she had gone home to discover that she was not, she had called her sister in despair.

'Get a basal thermometer,' Ellie ordered. 'And use it for at least three months to get some idea of the day you ovulate.'

'Three months!' Sara cried, amazed. Three months seemed like an eternity to her. She wanted to be pregnant NOW.

'You see, a thermometer can't tell you when you're going to ovulate,' Ellie said. 'It can only tell you when you *have* ovulated. When your temperature rises, you've ovulated. After you've used it for a few months, you'll have a pretty good idea if you ovulate regularly and on just what day. Then be sure to make love on the day you ovulate, and bingo!'

'Oh,' Sara moaned, cramping and dejected and indulging in her sister's concern, 'I wish I could just go bingo without all this stuff. I'm beginning to get all obsessed with it, you know. I don't understand why I'm not getting pregnant easily, naturally, just like everyone else.'

'Give me a break, everyone else!' Ellie said. 'Everyone else is having problems, too. Why do you think people invented gadgets like this thermometer in the first place? It wasn't dreamed up yesterday just for you.'

'Thank heaven you're there,' Sara said. 'I don't know what I'd do without you. No one else seems to understand how I feel. Julia thinks I'm a complete can of mixed nuts for even wanting to get pregnant, and Steve has enough to deal with when I'm in my premenstrual madness without any added gloominess. And Mother – do you know what Mother said when she called and I was all upset because my period had started? She said, "That's all right, dear, I've already got a grandchild. Don't worry about it."'

'Oh, Mother!' Ellie said, and both sisters burst out laughing.

Sara and Ellie's mother, Monica, had never been interested in the nitty-gritty of mothering. When Ellie told Monica two years before that she was going to have a baby in January, Monica had hung up and scheduled herself on a three-month cruise around the Caribbean. Sara and Ellie didn't mind – Monica had paid her dues, they knew; she had been a good mother and a devoted wife who had nursed her husband through a lingering and difficult death. She deserved some fun.

And it did help Sara to know that there was at least one

person in her life whom she wasn't letting down by not getting pregnant. Sara often envisioned herself as one of those insane seabirds squawking and flapping and splatting around in the unchartable seas of procreation, while Steve remained walrus-like, lazily lolling around on the sand, content to let the sea of sexual chance wash up and around him as it pleased. He smiled through his mustache, grandly comfortable, watching Sara sputter and flip in her fury that she had failed once again. 'Aren't you sad that I'm not pregnant?' she would screech at Steve, and he would reply, affable and placid, 'No, of course not. We'll just try again next time.' But she was suspicious. She knew he wanted a child.

She knew her in-laws wanted a child, too. They had never said anything, but they didn't have to, certain things in the world didn't have to be *said*. Clark and Caroline Kendall, Steve's parents, were as nice as humanized teddy bears. Now retired, they wintered in Florida and spent the five good warm-weather months in their house in Nantucket. They would never pressure Sara about anything: but Steve was their only child. No words had to be spoken.

Perhaps this was the month she would succeed. The thermometer was her magic wand. Today was the eighteenth day of her cycle, and according to her chart, she had ovulated on the fifteenth day. That was when her temperature rose from 97.5 to 98.2 – a good, clear, obvious jump of seven tenths of a degree.

That morning Sara had been triumphant. 'Hey, good for you, body!' she had said, her heart leaping with hope. She could almost *feel* that microscopic egg peeking out, looking for its lover. She had raced back from the bathroom into the bedroom and awakened Steve.

'Today's the day!' she had whispered, snuggling close to her husband and caressing him.

'Every day's the day with you, babe,' Steve had grinned, turning toward her.

Afterward, he had gotten up and dressed and left her there swooning under the covers. She was as lazily satiated as a bear who had just devoured a honeypot. Also, she didn't want to move around; she didn't want gravity to pull the semen down, away from her eager egg.

Today her temperature was still high, 98.4. The basal temperature dropped at the beginning of menstruation. But the eighteenth day was really too early for any indication of anything. Her temperature wouldn't start to drop – if it was going to – for about a week.

Sara looked down at her chart. Dutifully, according to instructions, she had circled each point on the chart whenever she and Steve had had intercourse. Now those circled dots looked back at her like so many googly eyes, like groups of nippled breasts. She was nuts. She was obsessed. She was sleepy. She and Steve had stayed awake late last night, partying with friends, then sitting up watching and laughing at an old horror movie. She had had only six hours of sleep. She should go back to bed or she'd be cranky all day.

But first she sat a bit longer, in the silvery silence of the kitchen, studying the chart, as if it could tell her something now, as if she could read her fortune there among the leaps and dips of the penciled dots, which formed mysterious and meaningful constellations, like those of the stars.

Wednesday morning, the day before Thanksgiving, Sara's temperature was still at 98.4. She kissed Steve good-bye, poured herself a fresh cup of coffee, then curled up on the sofa with the Seraphina manuscript. Poor old Seraphina was locked in a dark underground passageway, wearing only a see-through nightgown and the obligatory sweeping cape. Sara yawned.

My mother often said that she knew early on that I was lost to the farm, that she knew when I was only six years old. It was a winter day, when the snow was piled like walls around the house and school was canceled and the white air was filled with the lowing of hungry cows and the answering growl of tractors plowing paths to the barns.

I was in my bedroom, playing school. Four dolls were lined up on the floor and I stood across from them, wearing a flowered flannel dress my mother had hand-smocked across the bodice, matching ribbons around my pigtails, and my mother's high-heeled dress shoes over my thick white socks. I was writing on a chalk-board, pretending to be a teacher.

Mother stood in the door watching, unobserved, silent, until I wrote on the board: 1 plus 1 equals 4.

'Jenny!' she cried, interrupting me. 'Why did you write one plus one equal four? You know better than that! Don't you?'

I turned to her, exasperated. 'Oh, Mother, of course I know that one plus one equal two. Everyone knows that. But I just get so *bored* with the same answer all the time.'

Then Mother knew I was lost to the farm. For although nature plays her tricks on farmers to keep them in a state of constant and anxious uncertainty – will an early frost kill the crops, will a drought kill the crops, will a flood kill the crops? – the daily life of a farmer is based on repetition. The cows, chickens, pigs, sheep, must be fed twice a day, at regular times, or there will be no milk, no eggs, no bacon, no lamb: those animals are the farmer's household gods and offerings must be made regularly, sacrifices in the name of life. There are days when the work seems holy, the simple act of scatter-ing corn filled with a pagan and Christian grace, when the cow's steamy breath rises out hot and high on a snowy day like ghosts, like the Holy Ghost. But there are also days when the same acts seem only drudgery, dulling to the spirit and senses and the stupid cows knock against each other greedily and shit on the clean golden straw you have just pitched down from the loft. Then the doves fly cooing upward across the shaft of light and their cry is a knife in the heart, a reverberating yearning: *There must be more. But where? But where?*

Sara turned the page; there was no more about Jenny. Just sexy Seraphina calling out for Errol.

'Oh, no!' she cried aloud, for it was Jenny she wanted to

know about. She flipped through the manuscript, skimming over the pages until she found what she wanted: another section about Jenny.

Heat hurts. If you put your hand on the red burner of an electric stove, that heat hurts so much that you instinctively draw that hand away. When I was sixteen, we had a summer in Kansas that was as hot as the burner of a stove, and the sun coiled red above us every day, relentless in its burning. It hurt to go outside, and air-conditioned tractors had not been invented yet – not that we could have afforded one. Our farm unraveled around our weathered house, rows and rows of plowed and planted land turning to dust, the hidden seeds crumbling. Even the messy cottonwoods, planted along the fencelines to act as windbreaks for the fields, began to wither and dry up, their leaves turning cracked and then brown. The grass around the house crackled and exploded with angry grasshoppers and crickets as we walked on it, and the well went low, so that what water we rationed out tasted old and rusty.

The coolest place in the house was the basement, where we had several cots, a card table with a shortwave radio, and stacks of canned foods, all in preparation for an imminent tornado or Russian bombing. We owned one old pickup truck and couldn't afford to drive frivolously, so I wasn't able to visit friends – but then, I had no friends to visit. At sixteen I had become both 'intellectual' and sexual, in ways my classmates were not prepared for. I didn't want to get married and have babies and my own farm like the other girls at my four-county school – I wanted to get out and travel and drink champagne and write novels. I liked learning. I wanted to go to college. I had become a freak in my own town.

So when I wasn't helping with chores I was alone, in the cool dark basement, reading. Until the middle of July, when I put on my best clothes and packed my mother's cardboard suitcase and was sent to the 'camp for academically talented children' to which I had won a scholarship. When the principal had called me into his office at the end of the school year to tell me I had won the scholarship, I had thought: this is the beginning of my real life.

And I was right, although not in the way I imagined.

The camp was in western Massachusetts. I hadn't been out of Kansas before, I hadn't even been to Kansas City. I had spent weekends or summer days at various Girl Scout camps in the area, and so my idea of a 'camp' included sleeping bags, wienie roasts, and hiking boots to protect you from snakebite.

The 'camp' was on the campus of a boys' preparatory school that was not in session in the summer. The buildings were more beautiful than anything I had ever seen. It all looked like what books had told me castles were like. The rolling grounds with groves of green hardwoods and pastel-flowering bushes were as amazing to me as miracles. As I walked to the room I had been assigned, I tried to adjust my expectations to fit this idea of a 'camp', but no one had explained it to me and I was only sixteen – there was only so much I could imagine.

I shared the room, at first, with Olivia DeWitt, from Connecticut, the tiredest girl I had ever seen. Her face had no animation. She moved languorously, dropping her clothes here, there, dropping herself finally onto the bed.

'I like your necklace,' I said in my midwestern friendly way, wanting to make her like me.

'Why do you call it a nicklace?' she asked, so bored she could hardly speak the words.

Olivia had brought her tennis racket. I had not. I had never played tennis. She had brought her black riding boots. I had not. I rode, but western style, on heavy roping saddles on farm horses. Olivia's parents were at their 'summer home' – so were mine, but theirs was the same as their winter home, it was their only home, and they were working like slaves there, sweat and dirt drying in brown lines in my father's red burned neck, into my mother's chafed hands. Olivia sailed. I did not.

I walked with Olivia to the auditorium for orientation; we didn't speak. I was afraid to be ridiculed again for my accent. I don't know why she didn't speak. She seemed too tired to have anything to say, but once inside she waved to some girls she knew, and she hurried off to sit with them, leaving me alone.

Thus openly abandoned, I walked down the aisle, telling myself that everyone here must feel uncomfortable this first day.

'Hi,' someone said. 'Sit here.'

I looked to see the green-gold eyes of Jeremy Gardner smiling upon me. He was the tallest, handsomest, blondest, most magical boy I had ever seen.

I sat down next to him, my heart thumping so hard I was afraid he'd hear it. He told me he was in the math section, I told him I was in creative writing and literature. He said he was from Connecticut; I said I was from Kansas. He asked me if I'd like to take a walk with him after dinner. I said I would. Then the headmaster started speaking and we had to stop talking, but we kept looking at each other sideways, then smiling. For the first time in my life, I was in love. So many new emotions, so fast.

That afternoon the entire group had to trail around with the athletic director to see the camp. The mornings were given over to classwork in our various specialties; the afternoons were free for study or sports. There was a pond, a stable, a tennis court, a soccer field. After lectures on good sportsmanship, we were sent to our rooms to get ready for the evening meal.

Olivia moved slowly, but was gone from our room before I was ready, and when I entered the dining hall, she was already seated at a table in the middle of the group of girls from the auditorium. I moved toward the table.

31

'Sorry,' a dark-haired girl said, pushing the chair so it slanted against the table. 'I'm saving this for a friend.'

I moved to the end of the table.

'Sorry,' a blonde said. 'I'm saving this for a friend.'

I turned, feeling my face reddening, and looked as well as I could with my downcast eyes around the dining hall. There were two other tables; one full of boys, Jeremy Gardner included, all of them horsing around. And the other table, which was obviously where I belonged.

Obviously, because at that moment Mr McCausland, the headmaster, touched my arm.

'Why don't you sit at that table, Miss White?' he asked. 'That's where the other midwesterners are.'

The other 'midwesterners' were Trudy, a shy pretty girl from Indiana; Allen, a boy with bottle-opener teeth from Nebraska; Larry, a boy from Oregon, who could have been handsome were it not for a case of red-and-black screaming acne; Odessa, from Mississippi; George, from Arizona; and Hilda, a terrified, six-foot-tall cornfed Amazon of a girl from Iowa.

Sitting down next to them that first day, introducing myself, I thought in a panic: My God, we're all Outsiders. This is the Outsiders' table. I babbled and smiled and hoped that perhaps we could somehow all find a way to cohere into a group as happy and superior as those at the other tables. But this was not to happen; we were doomed from the start. We knew we were Outsiders. Hilda and Trudy were sitting next to each other, already partners against the world; they formed a bond early and never let anyone else in. Odessa, whom I sat next to and tried to be friends with, was, I soon came to discover, a real intellectual, also poor, also ambitious, and she had little time for fun. We Outsiders always ate together, but other than that were not a real group – which was really all right with me. I only wanted to be with Jeremy.

My life quickly fell into a pattern. Classes in the morning, swimming with the Outsiders in the pond in the afternoon – we didn't know how to play tennis, and I didn't like to ride because I didn't do it properly, the English way. Dinner with the Outsiders, and then the evenings, which were sometimes filled with lectures on wildlife or astronomy walks, and sometimes left open. Then all the students would gather in the cleared dining hall to watch a movie or dance or just talk.

That was when I got to be with Jeremy. I will always believe that he really did like me, liked *me*. He liked hearing me talk about our farm and the animals, cows, horses, dogs, cats, hens, geese. My pet rabbits. His parents had an apartment in New York City, but he had lived most of his life at boarding schools and summer camps. He loved animals but had never been able to have a pet. It was an old story about a rich boy: his parents never spent any time with him. They sent him away as much as possible. Much later, I was to think back on that time and wonder if Jeremy had been drawn to me because in my voluptuousness I seemed maternal, and certainly I was more responsive than the other girls there. More corny. He was a handsome rich boy but he needed something from me. And God knows I needed anything he could give me during those six weeks when I lived among strangers.

It was on the very first night that I knew I would always be among strangers there. During our painful dinner I tried to chat and laugh with the other Outsiders, tried to pretend that we hadn't been ostracized, that we weren't different. I heard my silly voice trilling out far too loudly, carrying raucously through the dining hall, and I knew I was overdoing it and couldn't stop myself. The girls at the other table laughed low, as if humming. The only person at my table who tried to join in my pitiful ruse was acned Larry, and he was very nice. Still there was at our table such an aroma of sweating misery that it tainted the food we ate. Now I suppose we were only victims of some adult's theory of 'geographical distribution', just as black children were victims of busing twenty years later.

Jeremy Gardner left the dining hall, punching another guy in the shoulder as he went, but not without looking over at me and mouthing, 'See you later!' I threw him a smile, pretending that I was having a wonderful time. At last, when I had sat through the meal for what I considered a decent amount of time, I sprang from my untouched food and my untouchable clan and headed for the bathroom.

The girls' rooms were on the second floor of the building, and so was the large many-stalled bathroom we all shared. I raced for a stall and entered, locking the door, grateful for privacy. I was cramping with a fierce attack of diarrhea brought on by nothing I had eaten. As I sat there, wracked with every kind of torment, I heard the doors open and the eastern girls come in, their assured voices floating unabashed in the air.

'. . . Jeremy can't possibly like her. It's just her big tits.'

'Tits, my dear, UDDERS!'

A scream of laughter. 'She is such a cow.'

'I think she's beautiful. Like Elizabeth Taylor.'

'Oh, God, I suppose, but her "beauty" is so tacky.'

'I think you'll discover, darling, that what you call tacky is what men like.'

'Exactly.'

More laughter.

I was bent double in my stall, trying not to make any noise that would embarrass me and make them aware of my presence. All around me doors slammed, toilets flushed, girls laughed.

'I don't think Jean has anything to worry about. I can't imagine that he'd ever be unfaithful to Jean.'

'Still, perhaps we should write her?'

On this note, they left. I sat in my stall, paralyzed, really ill. I tried to console myself, to do what my mother would tell me to do: to 'be sensible'. It wasn't that those girls disliked me, it was that they were championing a friend, I told myself. And no one likes a girl who steals someone else's guy. I tried not to take it personally.

But it was a very personal summer. Everything came close, too close. All the other Outsiders were in math or sciences; I was the only literature Outsider, and so I walked from my room or the dining hall to the classroom and back to my room alone, and while the group of eastern girls who walked in a cluster just in front or behind me were not within touching distance, their presence pressed in on me like the Kansas heat. My face burned. I would shrivel into myself, wishing I could pull my ears right into my head so that I wouldn't hear the low hum of their laughter, their whispers, which I was sure were all about me. I would carry my books against my chest, my arms crossed over my books hard, trying to crush my offending bosom flat. Olivia DeWitt spent every evening until lights-out in the other girls' rooms; at lights-out she'd run into our room, jump into bed, and go to sleep without a word to me. Her absolute avoidance of me was as vivid and visceral as insults or blows, and I lay quaking in my bed, sick at my stomach, as if physically attacked.

But what came closest that summer was Jeremy Gardner. That summer I wrote for my class a short story about a woman who wore around her neck a heart-shaped locket with an intricate design like an arabesque on the front. If one looked closely, he could see that the design was really a keyhole, and in truth the locket was her heart and she was living her life waiting to meet the man who carried in the lapel of his jacket a small gold key. That key would unlock her heart and the man and woman would know they were meant for each other, had been sent to each other by Fate. But no one came to the town where the woman lived, and no one wore jackets, let alone anything extraordinary in their lapels. So the woman traveled, saved her money, took jobs that would enable her to travel and to live among men who wore jackets. Still she did not meet the man with the key to her heart. And it embarrassed her so, as she grew older, to wear that heart-shaped locket, and it kept her from knowing other men. Finally, when she turned thirty (which to me at sixteen seemed infinitely far away), she gave up in despair and went to a jeweler to have the locket and chain broken, and her neck was free. As she turned to leave, a wonderfully handsome man entered. He had a gold key in his lapel. The woman cried '*Oh!*' and smiled at him. She almost threw herself on him. The man looked at her face, then looked down at her neck, and, as it was bare, his face went blank and he walked on past her without speaking.

It was a foolish story but not without its humble truths, and no one knows how it is that with one glance a boy can break through into a girl's heart. Jeremy and I might as well have worn locket and key, for we responded to each other on sight and when we were together we were complete and satisfied. In spite of our different interests, we were intellectual comrades, and I told him about the symmetry of poetry; he told me about the symmetry of math. We both felt separated, apart from our families and peers, different. We could put on a good show, but we were lonely most of the time, even with others. Together, we were blissfully content.

Every night after lights-out we would sneak out of our rooms and walk down to the pond together. It was really the only way we could be together for any amount of uninterrupted time. We would hold hands as we walked, and we would talk about everything, and finally we would lie on the grass by the pond and hold each other and kiss. That was all. We did not make love. Jeremy didn't insist, although we lay on top of each other and pressed against each other, wanting to make love. He told me he loved me and that he wanted to work out a way so we could see each other after camp ended. I told him I loved him. Jeremy Gardner came closest to me that summer of all the things in the world, and I could bear the daytime, when I was with the Outsiders or walking alone, surrounded by the hot whispers of the eastern girls.

The third week I was at the camp, an eastern girl named Dottie Collier became friendly with me. She was in the writing and literature class and she wasn't stupid; after I had read aloud my story about the locket, she approached me, smiling. 'That was a really good story,' she said. She left the classroom with me, and walked and talked with me as we went down the hall to lunch. She asked me to sit next to her at the table with the eastern girls. The others ignored me, but Dottie kept talking to me – we were telling each other about our favorite novels, and in that were caught up in a spell.

Dottie wanted to be a writer, too. When we had a chance, we told each other the plots of the novels we would like to write, but there was never enough time, camp was always so regimented and busy, with classes in the morning and sports and homework in the afternoon. I was surprised but thrilled when Dottie suggested that she trade rooms with Olivia so we could talk to each other during the free part of the evenings and after lights-out. Olivia was glad to trade, and from then on, how delicious camp was! Still I swam in the afternoon with the Outsiders or played bumbling games of volleyball with my breasts thumping against my chest; but I had the nights to look forward to, talking in my room with Dottie, then sneaking out much later to meet Jeremy.

'Jenny?' she would whisper, when I came sneaking back into the room. 'Are you all right?'

'Oh, yes,' I would sigh. 'Did I wake you up?'

'No, no, I've been awake. I worry about you, you know. You know how boys are – you aren't letting him *do* anything, are you? I mean – you aren't *doing it*, are you?'

37

Dottie's voice was so warm, she was so concerned. I was wrapped in bliss.

'Of course we're not doing it,' I said, sliding out of my clothes and into bed.

'Well, girls can get pregnant so easily, and boys just slip away,' Dottie said.

'That won't happen to me,' I promised. 'I'm not a fool.'

But I was. I lay awake, in my joy telling Dottie everything, telling her that Jeremy was going to help me find ways to apply to eastern colleges, to get scholarships, that he was going to write me, that he was going to try to come to visit me at my farm on his school vacation that fall. The night after Jeremy told me that, and I in turn confided it to Dottie, I met Jeremy at the pond as usual. We lay together, wrapped in each other, rapt in each other, and so we did not hear Mr McCausland, the headmaster of the camp, approach.

'Mr Gardner,' he said. '*Miss White.*'

We rose awkwardly, adjusting our clothes, shaking, the warmth of our bodies disappearing in the sudden numbing cold of fear.

'You will follow me back to the hall,' he said.

We followed in silence, walking back through long grass that tickled my legs as foolishly as it had done when we walked earlier, arm in arm, down to the pond.

'Mr Gardner, you will go to your room. I'll deal with you later.'

Jeremy obeyed. He was pale, looking down, and so our eyes did not meet.

'Miss White, you will go to your room and pack. Tomorrow morning our van will drive you to the airport. You may consider yourself expelled. You know our policies. We do not allow girls who let themselves behave wantonly to remain at our camp. I will of course of necessity write to your parents and your school authorities about your actions here.'

There was no compassion in his voice. I did not argue.

It was the best I could do not to weep before him. I walked, stiff-backed, to my room. How could I tell Dottie? I was so ashamed.

But Dottie was not in our room when I entered. It was after lights-out, and she was not in our room. There was not a trace of her, all her clothes were gone, and she had not left me a note.

I did not go to sleep that night. I sat up all night long, packing, smoking every cigarette in the contraband pack I had hidden under my mattress, which Dottie and I had often shared during our late-night talks. It did not take an 'academically talented' person to guess how it was the headmaster knew why and where to look for Jeremy and me.

The cabdriver came for me the following morning. He carried my luggage, and I followed behind him, walking down the dormitory halls and into the foyer of the school. Wide double doors gave off the foyer to the dining room, and clustered in that doorway were a variety of students. At the front, lounging against the doorframes and each other, arms folded, eyes drooping with smugness, were the eastern girls. Dottie was with them and she looked right at me with a triumphant smirk on her face. She would be the heroine with her group now; first a spy, then the instrument of my departure, saving Jeremy for Jean.

Behind the eastern girls, weaving and jumping and looking like general fools in order to make themselves seen by me, were the Outsiders. They called and waved; Larry, who was tall, called that he would write me.

I did not wave back. I did not cry or smile or let any expression cross my face. I had learned how to do that at camp. I just kept walking, through the foyer that expanded with Einsteinian magnificence, until it almost echoed around me. All those eyes burned me so that I felt I was walking through flames. But I did not faint. And I did not catch any sight of Jeremy.

Later, the film *The Wizard of Oz* would capture with

39

bizarre accuracy just what it was like for me to return to Kansas after my stay at the eastern camp: it was like going from dazzling technicolor back to black and white and gray. Dust and heat and empty spaces, loneliness. My parents and the principal of the school were incredibly kind and understanding. They blamed Jeremy Gardner as much as me for our escapades, and took a compassionate view of what we had done – and really, we had done so little. The principal of the school did not enter my scandal onto my school records, and he kept the information to himself, something of a miracle in our small gossiping community.

I spent the rest of the summer in our basement, reading and writing. Jeremy Gardner wrote to me when camp was over; he had been allowed to stay at camp, because his father knew the headmaster. At first his letters were passionate and full of promises, and he did try to help me get back east; he sent me catalog after catalog about eastern colleges and scholarships. But we were so young. I was so poor. The distance between us was so great. Once school started, our letters tapered off and finally stopped.

What I learned on my summer vacation. I could have knocked my English teacher's hat off with an honest essay. For this is what I learned on my summer vacation that year: that I had some power over boys because of my looks and my body. That if I was to get anywhere in my life – away from the dust and emptiness of our Kansas farm – I had to use that power, for there was little charity in the world, and no equality. And finally, most important, that I could trust men, to a certain extent, because of my power, but never females: females betrayed, smiled and lied and conned and betrayed worse than any man. I knew I never would have a female as a friend again in my life.

Sara rose and carried the manuscript box to the dining room table. Turning on the chandelier so that its light would blend with the sunlight to illuminate the pages clearly, she carefully went through the manuscript, page by page. Two hundred and five pages of Seraphina and Errol (Errol *had* turned out to be the hero, after all, and the author had left them in a passionate embrace waiting for the priest to arrive to marry them). Only about fifteen pages of Jenny. Yet it was Jenny, not Seraphina, who sprang alive from the paper. Where had Jenny come from? Who had written about Jenny? Those pages had a ring of autobiographical truth about them – but so did any good novel written in the first person.

Sara gathered together the fifteen pages of Jenny material and studied them. She compared them to the Seraphina story – almost certainly the two stories had come from the same word processor. At least the typeface was the same, the margins, the weight and color of paper. It seemed that the same person had written them both and somehow gotten the two stories mixed up. Sara looked back at the title page. Could someone who called herself Aurora Dawn actually have written the Jenny material? God, Aurora Dawn.

Sara went to the kitchen phone and dialed Linda Oldham, the senior editor and president of Heartways House. Linda was an older woman, brisk and businesslike, who had been placed in charge of the publishing firm three years ago and had methodically and efficiently drawn up the plans that she thought would make the company a financial success. Basically, her motto was: Give the public what it wants. The public of Heartways House was women, women longing for romance, and Linda had set forth guidelines for romantic novels that would bear the heart-shaped HH insignia, and ruthlessly saw to it that her authors stuck to those guidelines. During the past two years that Sara had done editing for Heartways House, she had never before had occasion to discuss anything as maverick as these pages with her boss. Sara realized her heart was thumping as she began to speak: all her editorial instincts told her that the Jenny book could be good; she must handle it with care.

'Linda, I've got a question,' Sara said cautiously, when Linda's brusque hello came over the phone.

'Shoot,' Linda replied.

'It's about an author of yours. I'm editing one of her romances now. *Desperate Dangerous Desire*. Aurora Dawn.'

'Oh, yes, Aurora Dawn,' Linda said. 'She's one of our old-timers. Turns out one of those babies every six months. People gobble them up like candy.'

'Well – well, have you read anything else she's written? I'm asking because there's some other material mixed up in the romance manuscript I'm editing now. It looks like material for another book, a memoir perhaps, or a realistic novel. It's really good stuff, and I'd like to see more of it.'

'Heartways wouldn't be interested in a memoir, honey,' Linda said. 'You know that. Don't waste your time.'

'Oh, I know Heartways wouldn't want it,' Sara pressed on. 'But it's so interesting – *I'd* like to read more of it. Perhaps encourage her to finish it, to take it to another house.'

Linda was silent a moment. 'What's it about, this other book?' she asked.

'I'm not sure,' Sara began. 'About a young girl growing up on a farm in Kansas –'

Linda's laughter exploded over the phone. 'Honey,' she said, 'the last thing *anyone* in publishing is interested in is a farm in Kansas. Good God. You know what people want. They want "Dynasty". They want castles and diamonds and yachts. Jesus, not a farm in Kansas. I suppose she writes about cows?'

'Well, yes,' Sara said.

Linda laughed again. Then, calming down, she said, 'Now what was your question?'

Sara paused. 'Well, I wondered if you could give me Aurora Dawn's address or phone number. I'd like to get in touch with her. I'd like to read the rest of the farm book and encourage her to publish it – with another house, of course – if the rest is as good as this.'

'All right,' Linda said. 'I'll tell Maxine to give you the author's phone number. She lives in Cambridge. But listen, tell her not to get so carried away with her cows that she forgets to write her romances. She's a money-maker for us, you know.' Linda laughed again, then said, 'I'll put you on hold a minute, then transfer you to Maxine. By the way, are you through editing *Desperate Dangerous Desire*? We've got it scheduled to come back from you this week.'

'Yes, yes, I'll have it in the mail today,' Sara promised.

A moment later Maxine came on the line and gave Sara Aurora Dawn's name, address, and phone number in Cambridge. The writer's real name was Fanny Anderson. Fanny, Sara thought, it was not so far a change from Fanny to Jenny. Fanny was an old-fashioned name. Dialing the number, Sara wondered how old Fanny Anderson was, what she was like – if she was the original beautiful Jenny from Kansas or only her creator.

A woman with an Irish accent answered. 'Mrs Anderson is not at home,' she told Sara. 'May I take a message?'

'Yes, please.' Sara was frustrated, so near to talking to the author of Jenny, and yet so far. 'Tell her that Sara Kendall called, from Nantucket. Tell her that I've been editing her book and I want to talk with her about the Jenny pages. Tell her I used to work for Donald James. Tell her – oh, perhaps I should just call her back. When will she be in?'

'I'm not sure,' the woman said. 'I'll take your number and have her call you.' Her voice was old.

Discouraged, Sara gave the woman her number and hung up.

She went back to the dining room table and stacked the manuscript neatly back in its box, keeping the Jenny pages out. She stretched and looked at her watch. Just after one o'clock – and here she was, still in her robe. What a luxurious way to work. But now was that wrenching time of day when she had to pull herself away from the enveloping fantasy of the books she edited into the messy reality of life. She wandered into the kitchen and turned on the oven.

Dutch apple pie, she thought, yum. Tomorrow was Thanksgiving and she had been assigned to take dessert to the party at Carole Clark's house – where everyone in the group would be gathered, including Mary.

Well, she had this much to thank Mary for – The Virgin's

'innocent' question about her weight had spurred her into action and for two weeks now she had been dieting and exercising again. Already she looked different: better, slimmer, tighter. She could get back into some of her favorite clothes. And she'd found a new way to style her hair. She brushed the bangs forward and the sides back; it was a pretty look, less punk. She was pleased with her hair now, and with her temperature, with everything. Everything in the world seemed possible.

Sara turned the radio on to the classical music station and sliced apples and rolled pie crust dough to Vivaldi's *Four Seasons*. While the pies baked, filling the house with the fragrance of cinnamon and sugar and apples, she showered and dressed – the size-fourteen jeans were too loose for her now. Hoorah. She took the pies out of the oven and admired the perfectly fluted crusts, then, on the spur of the moment, picked up the phone and once again dialed Fanny Anderson's number. It was just after three-thirty in the afternoon, a decent time to call.

Again, the Irishwoman's cold hello. But this time, 'Just a moment, please, I'll get Mrs Anderson for you.'

And then, softly, 'Hello? This is Fanny Anderson.'

'Oh, Mrs Anderson,' Sara said. 'This is Sara Kendall, calling from Nantucket. I'm a free-lance editor for Heartways House. I've been editing your *Desperate Dangerous Desire*. But I worked for several years as Donald James's assistant at Walpole and James, so I've had quite a bit of experience in editing – all kinds of books. And I'm calling because I found some pages in your romance novel that didn't fit. The pages were about a girl named Jenny . . .' Sara let her voice trail off. Before she plunged boldly into suggesting that Fanny Anderson work on a Jenny novel, she needed to hear more from that woman than just hello.

'Oh, yes,' Fanny Anderson said. Her voice was soft and lilting, with a slight drawl that Sara assumed had lasted from her Kansas days. 'I was wondering where those pages were. I didn't realize –' She didn't finish her sentence.

'Well,' Sara said, 'I called you because I wanted to tell you how much I enjoyed the Jenny pages. I thought they were wonderfully well written, and Jenny is fascinating. I'm so curious about what happens to her. And so I thought I'd call and see if perhaps you are working on this as a novel, and if so, how far you've gotten, and if you need an editor, and also, perhaps, well, it's possible that Donald James might be interested in seeing the story. Although I haven't of course talked with him about it yet.'

For a long moment there was silence. Then Fanny Anderson spoke, her voice softer than before. 'I didn't intend for anyone to read my Jenny pages yet,' she said. 'Not just yet. This is all most confusing. I'm not sure just what to say. I really hadn't meant for anyone to read that particular piece yet.'

'Oh,' Sara said, disappointed. The woman seemed so hesitant, so unsure. 'Well, there were about fifteen pages mixed up with the romance novel,' she said. 'And I couldn't keep from reading them – as I said, they were wonderful.'

'You really liked them?' Fanny asked.

'Very much. *Very much.*'

'Well, my goodness,' Fanny said. 'This is just so very – perplexing. I don't know what to say. I think I need to have some time to think about all this. You see, I was really writing the Jenny pages just for myself, although of course I can't say I didn't have the thought of a novel about Jenny in my mind. But I really wasn't ready for anyone to read it. Yet here it turns out you already have read some of it – and liked it – it seems just a little bit like Fate, doesn't it?' Fanny laughed, huskily, softly. 'We writers are so superstitious, you know. We rely on Fate so much it's really foolish. But it does seem – I was trying to decide what to work on next. Whether to start another romance novel, or whether to really settle down with Jenny . . . and now here's your phone call. And you say you worked with Donald James?'

'Yes.'

'Well. My. That's quite impressive. Oh, dear, I don't know what to do.'

After a moment Sara asked, 'Well, do you have any more written about Jenny? That I perhaps could see?'

Silence. A long silence. Then, softly, 'Yes. Yes, in fact I do have quite a lot more written.'

'I'd love to see it,' Sara pressed.

'I just don't know,' Fanny replied. 'I just don't know. I hadn't even thought about showing it to anyone yet. You see, I *care* about this novel, quite a lot.'

It was then that Sara felt certain that the Jenny pages were a memoir as much as a novel. But she said, 'I can understand that. Writing this kind of a novel must be much more difficult than writing a romance novel where it's easy to stay within certain limitations. The Jenny novel is much more risky.'

'Yes,' Fanny replied, her voice warm with approval. 'Yes, that's it, you see.' Then she was silent again.

'I wonder,' Sara said. 'I wonder if I could come up to Cambridge and see you. Perhaps meet you for a drink or take you to lunch or somehow just sit and talk with you about this.'

Silence.

'Please understand,' Sara said, 'I'm a free-lance editor. I can't promise anything. And I don't have any hidden motive for doing this, I just really am intrigued by your Jenny. I would like to see it become published, and, well, all my editorial instincts have been aroused. I think the Jenny book could be very exciting.'

'I just don't know,' Fanny said. 'It's lovely of you to say all these things, very kind of you –'

'Oh, it's not *kindness* –' Sara interrupted.

'– but I just don't know,' Fanny finished.

'Well, I've got to come up to Boston early in December – to do some Christmas shopping,' Sara said, inventing an excuse on the spot. 'Nantucket's so small, you know. No big stores. Perhaps when I come up I could come see you for just a little while and we could discuss this.'

Silence. Then, 'Tell me about yourself,' Fanny said, her soft voice firm.

'Oh,' Sara said, thrown by the question. 'Well. I'm thirty-four years old, I'm married to a carpenter, we've lived here on Nantucket for two years and lived in the Boston area before. I went to Williams College and then worked with Donald James

46

for about eight years . . . I have no children. I love editing, but my husband was raised on Nantucket and wanted to live here, and so we thought we'd try it. I like editing romance novels, but I also like editing, um, more serious work.'

'Are you very pretty?'

Surprised, Sara said honestly, 'Well, I suppose so. Well, perhaps not *very* pretty, but certainly pretty.'

'Beautiful?'

'Oh, no, not beautiful. Well, my husband thinks I am, I suppose, at least I hope he does, at least he says he does, and that's what counts . . .'

'And when you go out of the house, when you walk down the street, when you meet people?'

'Yes?' Sara asked, not sure what the woman was driving at.

'Do you always find you make an *impression*?'

'Why, no, I don't think so,' Sara replied. She was puzzled. 'I suppose sometimes I do. But most of the time I think I look just like anyone else. You know, we're pretty casual down here.'

'You don't seem overly burdened with vanity,' Fanny Anderson said.

'No,' Sara replied. 'No, I don't think I am.' She laughed. 'I've never had any reason to be "overly burdened" with it.' Then, suddenly flashing on what it was Fanny wanted to know, she said, 'I've never been as beautiful as Jenny, for example. I've never had to give any care about a gift of beauty. But I've had enough so that I could understand her, I think.'

'Yes,' Fanny said. 'I see. What, more precisely, do you look like?'

'Well – I'm about five foot seven. I have blue eyes, blond hair – which I've just had cut very short. I never was "cute" but I suppose I always was pretty. I think I look more intelligent than anything else, in spite of the fact that I'm blonde. I mean blondes are supposed to look cute and sexy and dumb, the stereotype, that is. And I'm a little overweight now, I find I go up and down with weight.'

'Yes, weight can be a problem, can't it?' Fanny said.

Sara waited. She wondered if she had somehow passed whatever test it was the other woman had just given her.

But Fanny only said, 'Well, my. This is very interesting. I must say I am pleased that you like my Jenny pages. It encourages me. Still –'

'I would love to come talk with you about it,' Sara said, determined to pin down this elusive woman.

'Let me think about it,' Fanny Anderson said. 'Why don't you give me your phone number, and your name again so I can write it down, and I'll think about it and call you back.'

Sara tried to keep the disappointment from her voice as she gave her the information. Yet when she finally hung up, she found she was smiling with anticipation. She had found something, the real thing, she was sure of it, she had found a true eccentric who was writing a truly good book. She felt like Sherlock Holmes on the trail of a culprit, Madame Curie in her laboratory – she was close to a discovery of some importance, and now waiting was a necessary part of the process that would lead to a triumph in her life. She felt sure of this, as if she had been granted a vision.

CHAPTER THREE

Sara had always thought of Thanksgiving as a formal occasion, involving polished silver, the best china, and a flower-embellished table. As a child, she had been expected to make an attempt at good manners and solemnity as soon as she was old enough to hold a fork. It was boring, but there had been the triumph of knowing that her younger or more boisterous cousins were relegated to the playroom with a sitter.

This Thanksgiving had all the formality of a football stadium during a Super Bowl. Mick had brought in his contribution: a case of Michelob and his color TV, which he set up in the living room next to the Clarks' TV, so the men could watch two football games at the same time. While the women put steaming bowls and the burnished turkey on the dining room table, Jeremy Clark and Blaise Bennett, both three, ran under the table and underfoot, throwing a tiny football and tackling each other, while two-year-old Heather Bennett toddled after them, screaming at the top of her lungs, waving her chubby arms, tripping over her own feet, already a great little cheerleader. Dinner was served buffet style, and for a few brief moments relative silence reigned while the men ate, but now they had finished dessert and had settled down to serious TV watching, which seemed to necessitate clapping, cursing, and yelling. The women hissed and booed at the men for a while, then gathered in the kitchen with the door shut, ostensibly to do the dishes, but really to get down to some good gossip.

Sara leaned against the kitchen door. Annie Danforth had put an Irish coffee in their hands, and in the heat and the laughter and the informality of the kitchen, Sara began to feel at home.

'I don't know what to do. Alison Wellington hasn't paid me

for baby-sitting her kids for four months now,' Mary said. She was seated at the kitchen table, covering dishes with foil.

'Don't baby-sit her kids anymore till she pays you,' Carole Clark said. She was drying the glasses Jamie Jones was washing.

'What can I do, lock my door against her? She works, you know,' Mary protested.

'She was *always* that way, always!' Annie Danforth said, 'Remember in Girl Scouts? Even in Brownies, for heaven's sake! She *never* paid her dues. NEVER.'

'Well, she says it's not her fault,' Mary said. 'She says her husband takes her paycheck and keeps it and doles money out to her.'

'Yeah, and if you believe that, let me sell you a used car,' Carole said. 'Mary, remember when our senior class went on the trip to Washington, D.C.? And she said she lost her wallet and we all had to chip in so she'd have spending money?'

Leaning against the door, Sara watched, fascinated by the gossip about the legendarily skinflint Alison Wellington, envious of the other women's shared history and the ease with which they worked together. She wished there was something she could do to help – she didn't want them saying later, 'Did you see the way Sara Kendall just stood there, not lifting a finger, like she thought she was some kind of queen?' But she didn't know what to do. The women seemed as organized as a hive of bees; she didn't know where to jump in.

Then from the living room came the sound of a crying baby. Jamie Jones, who was struggling with a crusted scalloped potatoes pan, looked over her shoulder.

'Damn!' Jamie said. 'She always does that. Just when my hands are wet. I've got to feed her. I know that cry, and it's been four hours. Would someone get her for me while I finish this pan?'

It was only natural for Sara, the only woman doing nothing, to say, casually, 'I'll get her, Jamie.' No one fainted from shock, so she turned from the kitchen, her heart racing. She had really had so little to do with babies before. She wasn't even sure how to carry one.

But Sheldon handed his daughter over to Sara at once. 'She's soaking,' he said, his eyes fixed on the television – it was first and goal – 'You'll have to change her.'

'Um,' Sara began, slightly alarmed.

'The diaper bag's in the guest bedroom upstairs,' Sheldon said. Then, as his team scored, '*All right!*' he yelled, and left her to her fate.

The baby cradled carefully in her arms, Sara left the living room full of yelling, clapping, stomping men, and made her way through marauding children up the stairs. The little girl wailed and thrashed her legs and arms determinedly, hitting Sara in the chin and chest. Sara was amazed at the strength of this six-month-old, at the difficulty she was having holding her as she twisted in her arms.

'Sssh, sssh, there, there,' she said. 'You're okay, sweetie,' she said, looking down at the baby, who had a pink ribbon tied around a whale's spout of dark hair. She gave the baby a big smile.

'*Aaaaaaaaah!*' the baby screamed, her face contorted.

In the bedroom, things only got worse. Sara had never changed a baby before, but would rather die than admit that to any of the other women. And surely she could do it, she was not an idiot, it was not that hard.

But the baby girl was enraged now because she was hungry and wet, because she didn't know this stranger, because this woman was handling her with clumsiness instead of the rapid efficiency she was used to from her mother. Sara gently put the baby down on the bed and unsnapped her terry cloth jumper. She pulled at the tape holding the wet diaper together, then stood a moment wondering what to do with the diaper. She couldn't put it down on the bed, it was so wet it would soil the quilt, she couldn't leave the baby to cross the room and put the diaper in the wastebasket. Her hesitation made the little girl furious. The baby kicked her fat bare thighs as if she were in a bike race, and her cries became frantic screams. Sara might as well have been pinching her.

Sara bent over the baby, her face growing hot with shame and frustration – and to her absolute horror, with anger: how *could* this baby embarrass her this way? She was doing her best.

'Sssh. Sssh. You're all right, little Rosemary. I know you want your dinner. Let's just change your diaper. Just give me one more minute, please,' she whispered at the screaming child.

But little Rosemary flailed her arms and legs and twisted her body, turning over, so that Sara had to get hold of the chubby little creature and turn her back over on top of the dry diaper. This made the baby even madder, and her screams would have drowned out a fire engine's. Sara's heart was thudding and her hands moved like great clumsy wooden sticks.

Suddenly, flashing across the room, an angel of mercy to the rescue of a tortured child, came The Virgin Mary. She grabbed up the distressed baby and held her against her chest, whispering in her ear. She stroked the back of her head. The baby's bare bottom hung down over her arm.

Sara hoped the baby would shit on Mary's sweater.

But of course Rosemary didn't. Instead, leaning back and looking up, she saw a face she recognized – Mary baby-sat for Rosemary – and, comforted, her cries began to ease.

'Poor baby, poor wittle ba,' Mary said. 'Aren't you a foolish ba?' She jiggled the baby, smiled at her. As the baby calmed, Mary looked at Sara. 'It sounded like you were sticking pins in her,' she said to Sara, grinning.

'I don't think she likes having her diaper changed,' Sara said, although that was not what she thought – she thought that there was something so unnatural about her, so *unmotherly* about her, that the baby had instinctively reacted with fear. Was that possible? She wouldn't ask The Virgin.

Now Mary ignored Sara. 'But we have to have our diaper changed if we want our bobble,' she said, lowering the baby back onto the bed. She reached out – it was as if Mary had eyes on the side of her head, for she managed to keep both eyes on the baby's, smiling, and at the same time see and grasp a rattle, which she presented to the baby with a flourish. 'Now oo just play with this little ba, and Mary will get Rosemary all bootiful so oo can have oor din-din.'

52

Oh, dear, am I going to have to talk that way if I have a child? Sara wondered. Then, heart sinking, she though: *Maybe I can't have a child simply because I'm not capable of talking that way. I just don't have the right instincts.*

Faster than a speeding bullet, Mary diapered the child and whisked her out of the room, saying not another word to Sara.

Sara followed Mary down the stairs and into the kitchen, searching for just the right words to explain what had happened. The words wouldn't come. Her mind was a blank. *I'm so glad I'm an editor*, Sara thought wryly, *it's such a help in my life*.

Jamie was seated at the round oak kitchen table. She reached for Rosemary, brought the baby to her unbuttoned blouse, and watched for a few seconds while the baby began to nurse greedily. She looked back up at Sara, smiling. 'I'm sorry she gave you such a bad time,' she said. 'She's at that shitty stage they call "making strange". She sees a new face and freaks. It's so fucking embarrassing. Sheldon's parents came over last week to visit and she screamed at them every time they came near her. I wanted to kill the little monster. Great for keeping pleasant relationships.'

'I remember when Jeremy was that way,' Carole said, leaning against the refrigerator. 'I couldn't get through the grocery store with him. Every time some little old lady coochie-cooed at him he yelled his head off. I had to leave him at home just to get the shopping done. And it went on for *weeks*,' she added ominously.

'Aren't you a terrible little troublemaker,' Jamie said to her daughter, her voice thick with love, her eyes gleaming with pride. The baby suckled happily.

Sara sank down in a chair and listened while the other women talked about babies. At last Annie Danforth started talking about Christmas. Sara relaxed, until the children, exhausted from the celebration, began to fight at high volume and without mercy. Mothers scattered into the dining room to gather up their tired broods; it was time to leave.

Carole Clark slid up against Sara. 'Would you guys drive Mick home?' she whispered. 'He's a little on the drunken side.'

In fact Mick was a lot on the drunken side, but he was a jolly, hearty drunk. He was hard at work now trying to get into his overcoat. 'The Patriots lost, but what the hell, right?' he yelled.

'What the hell!' Steve yelled back, cuffing his friend. He grinned at Sara. 'I'll go up and get our coats,' he said.

Sara leaned against the wall in the front hall, as Mick replayed the last quarter of the game.

'The referee made the wrong call, but what the hell, right?' Mick asked her.

'Right,' Sara replied. Other couples brushed past, going up the stairs and down again with their arms full of coats, carrying children and foil-covered pans of food out the front door, hugging and calling to each other.

'The Patriots are the number-one team, right?' Mick yelled.

'Right!' Sara yelled back, though by now Mick was pacing the hallway and addressing his remarks to a seemingly large imaginary audience.

'We're going to go *all the way, right?*' Mick yelled.

'*Right!*' Sara yelled back. 'I'm going to go see where Steve is, I thought he was getting our coats,' Sara told him, in a normal tone of voice. 'I'll be right back.' She hurried up the carpeted stairs.

Steve was in the guest bedroom, their coats in his arms.

Mary Bennett was the only other person there. She was seated on the bed, leaning back against the headboard. Her expression was serious. So was Steve's. When Sara entered the room, there was that quality of silence that indicates the interruption of an intimate moment.

A spark of fantasy exploded in Sara's mind: she would look with frigid arrogance at her husband, walk without a word from the room, drive home, pack, leave him forever.

Instead, she said, as normally as possible, 'Oh, I thought you couldn't find the coats. Ready? We've got to get Mick home before he passes out.'

'Sure,' Steve said. 'I'm ready.'

Sara crossed the room, stood close to her husband, smiled.

54

'Help me?' she asked, and he held her coat for her to slide into. She smiled sweetly at Mary. 'Bye,' she said.

'Bye,' Mary replied, her face surly.

Silently, smiling to the death, Sara followed Steve down the stairs. Jamie Jones was at the doorway talking to Carole Clark. '. . . see you Tuesday night as usual?' Jamie said, *sotto voce*. She looked guiltily at Sara.

'Sure. I'll call you,' Carole told her friend, and they hugged. When Carole turned to Sara, it seemed there was an artificial brightness about her smile.

Now what's going on? Sara thought. *Am I truly paranoid or did those two not want me to hear their plans?* But the awkwardness of the moment passed as she and Steve guided Mick out the door and into their car.

Mick babbled all the way home about his beloved Patriots, giving Sara plenty of time to stew in her own suspicions. *If I wanted to, I could work up a really good case of self-pity*, she thought. The baby didn't like her, Jamie and Carole were doing something from which they definitely but guiltily wanted to exclude her – and, worst of all, her husband had just been involved in some sort of heavy-duty discussion with his old girlfriend. *This isn't Thanksgiving*, Sara told herself, *this is Halloween.*

Steve wrestled Mick out of the car and into his apartment, then got back into their car for the drive home.

'Mick's really soused this time. He's going to feel awful in the morning,' Steve said.

'What was your little conference with Mary all about?' Sara asked, trying to keep her voice normal.

'What little conference?' Steve answered innocently.

Sara studied her husband as he drove. He kept his profile to her, concentrating as if he were steering the car through a raging blizzard.

'Oh, come on, Steve,' she said.

Steve was silent for a while. Then he said, 'Nothing, really. It was nothing, Sara.'

She waited, her eyes lasering into Steve's stubborn head. Finally she turned away and sat in a deadly silence, letting her anger fill the car like a perfume. When they got home, she slammed from the car and into the house and up to their bedroom in one sweep of fury.

I will not have a baby, I will not stay on Nantucket, I will not stay married! Sara thought as she yanked off her silk blouse and skirt. *I will go back to Walpole and James, I'll take hundreds of lovers, Julia and I will live together, eating salad, drinking chablis, we'll go on vacations together and pick up and discard men like playthings!* She pulled her flannel nightgown over her head.

'Yeah, you really look like a vamp,' she said to her reflection in the mirror. She sank down on the bed in misery.

The door opened and Steve came in. He sat down on the bed next to Sara. 'All right,' he said. 'I will tell you every word. Okay?'

Sara did not look at her husband. Did not speak.

'Mary asked me if I was happy. I said yes. Very. She said, "That's too bad, because I'm not." I said I was sorry to hear it. She said, "How sorry?" I said, "Not *that* sorry,' and grinned at her. I mean I didn't want to insult her, Sara.'

'What did she say then?' Sara asked.

Steve hesitated. 'She said, "Now I'm even more unhappy."'

'That bitch!' Sara said in a steady voice. 'She wants you back, doesn't she?'

'I don't know what she wants, Sara. I really don't. And I'm sorry if she's not happy, but I really don't care.'

Sara looked at Steve. 'You were up there for a long time.'

'Yeah, well, lots of people were up there. We were all stumbling around the bedroom getting our coats and stuff. I was alone with Mary for only a few minutes. I swear it, Sara. Nothing happened. Nothing else was said.'

Sara looked at Steve searchingly. 'Steve, don't you know how I hate this? I hate having to play the jealous wife. I hate being an interrogator. This all just makes me feel sick.'

Steve pulled her against him. He spoke into her hair. 'Hey, Sara,' he said. 'You know you don't have to worry. You know how it is between you and me. We're married. I love you. And

56

I don't feel anything for Mary at all – except maybe pity. She doesn't just come on to me, you know, she flirts with all the guys. I don't know what her problem is with Bill, but he's such an arrogant bastard I'm not surprised she's unhappy. I guess I'm sorry she's unhappy. I'd be sorry if anyone I know was unhappy. But that's all. And you know that. Come on.'

As Steve spoke, he caressed Sara, gently, in the ways he knew so well would please her. Sara hid her face in Steve's shirt, smiling with pleasure, allowing herself to be cajoled back to reality: Steve there next to her, handsome, loving, there were his hands on her body, here was his mouth on her mouth. They made love for a long time, talking to each other, watching each other as they moved together in the light. They fell asleep with their clothes tossed on the floor and the light still on.

At the end of the first week of December, Sara received two packets in the mail. She read the one from Julia first. It was a Xeroxed page from a textbook, with the pertinent parts highlined and embellished by Julia with a number of arrows, stars, and obscenely illustrative cartoons.

Prospective mothers wishing to ascertain their ability to conceive submitted to *tests of fertility*. A group of tests relied upon the assumed existence in fertile women of free passages between the genital tract and the rest of the body, that allowed substances introduced per vaginam to reach the breath and the various systems. Thus, if the propositus vomited after sitting on date flour mixed with beer, she could conceive and the number of vomits indicated the number of children she would have (K.27). She could also conceive if she had borborygmi (C,V) or passed urine with faeces or wind after genital fumigation (B. vs., 1, 7–9); but if she vomited, she would not (C,V). A test that acquired some fame later with Hippocrates (Aph., V, LIX) and the Arabs (Demiry) consisted in smelling for garlic or onion in the breath after introducing it per vaginam, a principle recently revived in Speck's test of injecting phenolphthalein in utero and testing for it in the urine.

Julia had stapled a small bulb of garlic to the letter.
'Great,' Sara said aloud. 'Thanks a lot.'

It was a rainy Saturday, cold and comfortless, and Sara was grousing around the house in an especially nasty mood: she could tell that her period, in spite of the thermometer, was going to start tomorrow. Her breasts were sore and swollen, her stomach had developed a life of its own, bulging out before her in its evil little parody of pregnancy, and her back was beginning to cramp. For most of this day she had soldiered on, cleaning the house and going through the exercise routine that had helped her get her body back in shape, but now it was three-thirty, a dimming December hour on a dreary day, and Sara was tempted to wallow in her despair.

She was glad the mail had come. She reread the sheet Julia had sent, and looked seriously at the garlic bulb a moment, considering. How did one get hold of date flour? If she mixed it with beer – and *sat on it?* In her mind she could almost hear Julia's laughter. Sara laughed in response. She might be crazy, but she wasn't going to sit on flour mixed with beer – or on this garlic. Tossing the letter with the other mail for Steve to see, Sara opened the packet from Fanny Anderson.

Dear Mrs Kendall, [the accompanying note on heavy creamy bond writing paper read]

Because of your kindness I am taking the liberty of sending you some more pages from my Jenny manuscript. Please don't feel obliged to like them or even to read them. I am hard at work on another Aurora Dawn book and have little time even to think of the Jenny pages. But since you went to the trouble of calling . . .

With very best wishes,
Fanny Anderson

Thirty pages of Jenny! Sara looked at the packet as if it were a box of chocolates. *This* was the cure she needed; her work, some good book to dig into with all her talent and abilities. She brewed herself a pot of decaffeinated coffee (in deference to her premenstrual insanity; caffeine was supposed to aggravate P M S), and settled down to work.

At seventeen I was caught up in a maelstrom of desires. I *wanted*. What I wanted seemed infinite and nameless. I loved many things with intensity – with such a great intensity that, having felt that love, it seemed I had given love sufficient for eternity and must move on to other things or die of boredom.

I loved my parents and our farm, the Kansas skies, the free far windy sweep of land, but I wanted *more*. I had been dating for a year an 'older' man, Will Hofnegle, a farmer across the county who at twenty-two had inherited his parents' large farm. He was a good and gentle man who worked hard on his land and yet had the energy and insight to care for me as I was. He rode horseback with me; but he also listened to me read my stories aloud; he gave me picture books about Paris and Rome. He understood what I wanted. I would have been desperately lonely in Kansas without him, for I had no other friends, no one else who understood my love for literature and my desire to escape into a more literary world.

Will's life was full of physical beauty – his horses, Herefords, spaniels, barns and stables, rich rolling fields, which were much more productive than ours; and he was tall and handsome and moved through his life with a loping unhurried grace. He offered himself and his farm to me, he offered to marry me, and did not take it as an insult when I told him I had to try to get out for a while. He told me he would always be there for me if I needed him.

I won a scholarship to the University of Kansas. I wanted to go east to college – perhaps I still had fantasies of dramatic reunion with Jeremy Gardner – perhaps I simply just wanted to go east, to get away. But my parents couldn't afford to send me anywhere else, and I was told I should feel lucky to have a scholarship. Everyone told me I should be grateful to be going off to college, but even before I got there, I wanted *more*.

It was probably predictable that I immediately became obsessed with Henry Cook, the instructor of the required freshman art appreciation course. He was from the East. Little else mattered. He wore cashmere sweaters, tweed jackets, elegant loafers made of leather that looked and felt like silk, and there was something about him – his accent? the way he cut his hair? – that reminded me of Jeremy Gardner on a basic, physical level.

The other students at the college seemed gushily naive, too easy to please, silly. In contrast, Henry was handsome, nervous, even tormented, like a powerful energetic neurotic thoroughbred trembling with the need to run. And he became my conveyance; I became his jockey. I became his master – but, strangely enough, never his mistress, although his hope for that was the whip in my hands.

For I continued to be lucky with my looks. I knew this; I exploited myself – what else did I have to work with? I had waist-length black curling hair, which I tied up with blue ribbons to bring out the blue of my eyes. I had very pale skin that blushed rosily when I was happy or excited, and long legs, a slender waist, and what I learned over and over again was a spectacular bosom. Before I went to college, I spent hours in front of the mirror admiring myself, criticizing myself, deciding just how to improve myself, and every admiring look I received I took as proof and omen: use this to live your life.

Still, I do not know how I had the courage, the sheer brashness to pursue Henry as I did then: it was desperation, all desperation. I was wild with need. Henry came from an old eastern moneyed family, never mind that he was dark and handsome and thin; he could have been a fat dwarf from an old eastern moneyed family and I would have been crazed for him. My needs and his insecurities fit together perfectly.

Henry wanted to be an artist. His family insisted that art was frivolous and would not support him in his attempts to paint. They said he was, at twenty-seven, too young to know what he wanted in life, and that he would not get his inheritance until he got a 'real job'. Over the bronze-bright autumn semester, I spent time with Henry, first over coffee in the student union, then over wine in his apartment. Never in bed: that was how I tempted him. I discovered that although his family was cutting him off from the real money, he was still receiving income from a trust his grandmother had set up for him, which his parents could not touch. After I recovered from the shock of it – that he was given more money than my family with all their labors had ever earned and he considered that money 'nothing', I grew even harder within myself and more ambitious. Why did a fool like Henry have so much when my hardworking parents had so little? There was no justice in the world – none given – so I must take and wreak and wrestle what justice I could.

You must paint, I told Henry, you are an artist, you must not waste yourself here. You should go to Paris and paint, it's 1950, that's where the artists are. I believe in you, Henry, I will go with you, I will encourage you, I will help you be brave.

So we went. What a flurry it caused! What telegrams and phone calls from his parents, his sister, his brother, his uncles, the head of the university art department! I loved it. My own parents and Will did not seem surprised when I told them, and they all wished me well. I loved Paris. Stone and river, cathedrals and cafés, lovers kissing openly in the streets, and everyone openly admiring me, blowing kisses at me as I walked past. We took a small apartment in a crooked building in the Latin Quarter. We drank Pernod at Les Deux Magots, we ate at La Coupole, I read Hemingway and Stein and Camus and Genet, Henry argued art with other painters, other painters taught me to speak a decent French and promised me that if I would only let them, they could teach me the language of love. I remained a virgin. It was one of my powers. It made Henry crazy for me. But I did not love Henry – I was so young, I loved only myself, I loved others loving me, I wanted everyone to love me. I was so young, so vain, so naive: I thought the lust of men was love.

The phone rang, jolting Sara back into the present. Sears had an order of vacuum cleaner bags in for her. She put the receiver back and stood a moment, staring at the phone. How brave Jenny was, how determined – she went out and got what she wanted! At seventeen she had had the courage and the spunk to get herself all the way to Paris. She had not waited passively for Fate; she had manipulated Fate. Jenny thought of life as a malleable object, a ball of clay she could pummel and mold; Sara had for too long thought of life as a great wind that blew her helplessly in any direction. She could change her mind; she would change. She would put her feet down, grab hold, be bold. There were things she could do to get what she wanted, and now she would do them. As soon as she had finished reading the Jenny pages.

'You may go in now,' the nurse said.

Sara walked into the gynecologist's office, and her first thought on seeing Dr Hiram Crochett was *Thank God he's not young and handsome.*

Julia had recommended him; she promised that he was grand-fatherly, kind but brilliant, the best in his field. 'A gynecologist named Crochett?' Julia had howled with laughter. 'He'd have to be fabulous to make up for that name!'

Sara liked Dr Crochett on sight. He was short, slightly homely, with a gently sagging, wrinkled face, and eyes myopically huge behind glasses. He had curly salt-and-pepper hair, a bristly mustache, a kind smile. He was slightly overweight – Ah, good, Sara thought, relaxing. He must have to deal with the little greeds and inadequacies of his body, too. He must have learned compassion.

He was wearing a white lab jacket over his day clothes, and had a stethoscope hanging around his neck. His office was paneled in oak with pictures of newborn babies on every wall. He shook Sara's hand when she entered, a courtesy Sara appreciated, then indicated a chair. Then he sat at his desk just across from her and studied the form she had just filled out, which the nurse had handed him on a clipboard.

That form: how reassuring. It was like being in school again and taking a test to which she was certain she knew all the right answers. She was healthy, Steve was healthy, their parents were healthy. Sara's father had died of cancer that was particular to males. Sara and Steve had no allergies, asthma, heart problems, ulcers, kidney stones, VD, arthritis, anemia, hepatitis, tuberculosis, history of mental illness. They had health insurance. If there was an intelligence looking down at the available gene pools on earth, undoubtedly that intelligence could see how superior theirs was. This test rated an A.

If that had anything to do with anything.

Dr Crochett lifted his head and looked at Sara. 'You have written here, next to "reason for visit", "desire to get pregnant".'

Sara cleared her throat. This was difficult. 'Well, I probably should have written infertility. But I couldn't put that down in black and white. It would have seemed so definite. So – *final*.'

Dr Crochett smiled and leaned back in his chair. 'You have been trying to get pregnant for how long?'

'Just over a year now. Thirteen months.'

'Your periods are regular?'

'Yes. Very. Every twenty-nine days.'

'Have you ever been pregnant before?'

63

'No.'

'So you have never had an abortion.'

'No.'

'Has your husband ever impregnated a woman before, to your knowledge?'

'No.'

'What has been your usual method of birth control in the past?'

'Diaphragm and condoms.'

'Did you ever take the pill?'

'No. Never. My sister told me not to. She's a nurse.'

'Ah. I see you've come from Nantucket. A lovely place to live. I used to summer there as a child.'

'Yes,' Sara agreed. Then, realizing he was waiting for something, she told him, 'There are no gynecologists on the island. Only general practitioners. And . . . it's a very small place in the winter. And I'm a very, well, I don't think *neurotically* private person, but a very private person. If I did go to a doctor on the island about this . . . problem . . . well, I know some of the nurses . . . everyone on the island would know in a matter of minutes. Small-town living. That would make it even harder on me.'

'Of course it would,' Dr Crochett said. 'This can be such an emotional issue, can't it? You did the right thing, coming to me. The GPs would have sent you to a specialist anyway. What are your periods like?'

'Heavy. I mean the flow is heavy. The first few days. Then it tapers off and is light. I go seven days, but the first three days are the really terrible ones. I have cramps. And I get chilled and depressed and ravenous and nutty before my period. I go insane.'

Dr Crochett smiled. 'Good old PMS,' he said. 'We're just now beginning to learn about it. Well, you seem healthy enough, normal.'

'Do you think I am too old?' Sara asked.

Dr Crochett laughed. He had a good hearty laugh, throwing back his head. 'No, my dear, I certainly do not! You are' – he consulted his form – 'thirty-four. That's a perfect time to get pregnant. Why, I have women in their early forties getting pregnant. No, you are not too old.'

'I brought this,' Sara said, reaching into her purse and handing him her temperature chart.

The doctor took it and studied it, then handed it back. 'So far, so good,' he said. 'One month doesn't tell us much, you know. You'll have to keep that up for several months if you want accuracy. How often do you and your husband have intercourse?'

As often as possible, Sara thought, and stifled a smile. 'Um, perhaps four times a week.'

'Fine,' Dr Crochett said. He stood up. 'Let's take a look at you, shall we? I notice you had a Pap smear seven months ago. You don't need another one so soon. But I want to do a pelvic, to see if everything's in the right place.'

The examining room was cheerful, with flowery wallpaper and more pictures of babies. After undressing in the bathroom and putting on a paper robe, Sara lay down on the table with her feet in metal stirrups, her knees drawn up. She had always hated this part, the feeling of vulnerability, the exposure. She had asked for it, but her body informed her mind that as far as it was concerned, she was being violated. Her muscles tensed.

Dr Crochett pulled on rubber gloves and put his hand inside her. 'I had a patient once,' he said, 'who tried for three years to get pregnant. She finally made it. She really wanted that baby. When it came time for her to deliver, I met her at the hospital, lifted her gown, and saw that she had had her pubic hair shaved into the shape of a heart all around her vagina.' He laughed a booming laugh.

Sara laughed politely, thinking that all sounded a little bizarre, but the image flashed before her mind and then the doctor was dropping the paper sheet between her legs. So soon the examination was over.

'That's fine. You can sit up now. Why don't you get dressed and come back to my office? We'll make a plan of attack.'

In the office, Dr Crochett said, 'You're fine. All the right equipment in all the right places. Perhaps a slight case of endometriosis, but I can't tell much.'

'What's that?' Sara asked, alarmed.

'Endometriosis — briefly, it's tissue that forms in the abdominal cavity. It can cause painful intercourse if it's bad enough. It often occurs in women as they grow older and haven't had children. Interestingly enough, the cure for it is pregnancy. But that's something we'll check into later, if necessary. There are some other things we can do first, some tests we can do right away that will tell us a lot. Where are you now in your cycle?'

'I'm on the tenth day,' Sara said.

'That's great!' Dr Crochett said, so enthusiastically that Sara almost jumped. 'Now let's see,' he went on, musing aloud, 'you probably ovulate on the fifteenth day. By the way — keep on taking your temperature. That chart will be very helpful after a few more months.'

A few more months, Sara thought. *Here we go again.* How wonderful it would have been to come here and have a gynecologist wave a magic wand so that she would go home and get pregnant immediately. The thought of having to go through *a few more months* of waiting and hoping and being disappointed made her spirits plunge.

'Now,' Dr Crochett was going on cheerfully, 'I want to do a postcoital on you. I can tell a lot from that. Cut through some steps. And I want to do it just before you ovulate. Now, can you come back here on the fifteenth day? Let's see, that puts us on December twenty-three. Well, close to Christmas, hmm? The last day I'll be in the office. You and your husband will have to have intercourse on the twenty-second of December. Then I'll need to examine you first thing in the morning. Can you arrange that?'

'Will you need my husband here, too?' Sara asked.

'No, that won't be necessary. Either the two of you can come up to Boston for the night, then you come see me in the morning, or, if you want, you can have intercourse on Nantucket on the twenty-second and fly up here on the morning of the twenty-third. Whichever you wish. The important thing is that you do have intercourse then and that you get your body in here to me as soon as possible after that.'

Sara thought a moment. The twenty-second was the night of Jamie and Sheldon's Christmas party. And Steve had to work on the twenty-third. But she could fly up.

'Yes,' she said. 'I can do it.'

'Fine,' Dr Crochett said. 'We'll schedule an early-morning appointment with my secretary – and pray for clear weather. I know what those Nantucket fogs can be like.'

'Yes,' Sara said, suddenly worried. She hadn't thought about the weather not cooperating. And this could be such a difficult time of the year.

'Don't look so troubled,' Dr Crochett said. 'You're a young, healthy woman. Your body seems to be in good shape. You'll get pregnant.'

'I hope so,' Sara said. She rose and followed the doctor from his office into the reception room and made an appointment for the morning of the twenty-third.

'Oh, and here!' Dr Crochett said. He scribbled something on a pad and handed it to her. 'I want you to get this prescription filled. It's for multivitamins. We've found that women who take these for a few months before they get pregnant have a smaller incidence of babies with spina bifida. See you soon!'

Then he was gone, back into his office. Sara looked at the piece of paper in her hand, his indecipherable scribbling black and definite on the page. *Magic pills*, she thought, *just what I wanted, a prescription for magic pills.*

Buttoning her coat against the chill as she stepped out of the office into the day, Sara felt buoyant. She felt she had done the absolutely right thing, had set something in motion, and somehow begun a chain of events that would lead to her pregnancy. Dr Crochett's optimism was infectious. He had given her body his seal of approval; maybe that was all she needed, maybe she only needed this bit of authoritative go-ahead to get pregnant. Certainly she felt more fertile now; she felt wonderful.

Dr Crochett's office was in a brownstone in Brookline; Sara took a cab from there to Fanny Anderson's house in Cambridge.

She was going to do something she had never done before,

something aggressive and pushy – but what else could she do? She was so frustrated.

During the past week, after finishing the Jenny material that Fanny Anderson had sent her, Sara had tried at least fifteen times by telephone to reach Fanny Anderson. Each time she had been thwarted by the same person, Fanny's housekeeper or maid, who always said, in a cold hostile voice, 'Mrs Anderson is not available at the moment.'

'Well, could you please ask her to call me?' Sara had asked, politely at first, then, as the days passed and her calls were not returned, with increasing anger.

'I'll give Mrs Anderson your message,' the woman said, and hung up before Sara could say another thing.

Sara was beginning to envision the housekeeper as some kind of awful tyrant, some jealous jailer, who saw Sara as an enemy, an intruder to be fended off. Certainly she sounded that way on the phone. Perhaps she was the writer's lover? A neurotic lesbian, afraid to let any other woman come in contact with Fanny Anderson? In any case, it was strange and maddening, how the woman with her cold, thin voice refused to put Sara through to Fanny. Sara remembered Fanny's voice, by contrast so warm and soft and welcoming, so *personal*. And Fanny *had* sent her more of the Jenny pages, so she wanted to keep in touch with Sara. Something odd was going on, and Sara wanted to know what it was. More, she wanted to try to persuade Fanny to finish this book, she wanted to help her to shape it, she wanted to be a real editor in a way she seldom had been before.

So, once she had made the appointment with a gynecologist in Boston, she tried Fanny Anderson's number once again, and after she once again received the same response, the cold, hostile 'Mrs Anderson is not available at the moment. I'll give her your message,' Sara had written a letter.

Dear Fanny Anderson,

I have tried numerous times over the past week to reach you, day and night, but the person who answers

68

your phone seems unwilling to let me speak to you and since you have not returned my calls, I'm afraid you haven't gotten my messages.

I would like very much to talk with you about the Jenny book. I've finished reading the pages you sent me, and they are wonderful. Jenny is a fascinating person, and your writing style is at once elegant and intimate. I want to read more! And I know that many others will want to read this book, and will love it.

I have to come to Boston for medical purposes on December 19th, a Thursday. I would like to stop by your house around two-thirty, to see you and return the material you sent to me, and I hope, to pick up more. And if possible, I would very much like to sit down and talk with you about what you're writing. I don't know your writing schedule, but I promise I won't take up too much of your time. Perhaps on Thursday we could meet briefly and then set up another time for a longer talk about your book. I would be very grateful if you could afford me just a few minutes in your day.

With very best wishes,
Sara Kendall

There, Sara had thought, *that should do it*. She had praised the book, she was offering to make the trip from Nantucket to Cambridge, she was practically groveling. If only she could get past the dreadful housekeeper, or lover, or envious spinster aunt, or whatever she was.

Fanny Anderson's house was a tall old Victorian set behind a wrought iron fence, graced with towering ancient maple trees that arched and draped their naked winter limbs over and in front of their house like giant garlands. The windows were long and narrow and shuttered. Stained glass glittered on either side of the massive oak door.

The woman who opened the door to Sara's knock was so much like Sara's mental image of her that Sara almost gasped. A woman in her fifties, perhaps, she had dark hair pulled back into a bun, and forbidding brown eyes set in a wrinkled somber face. She was wearing a drab brown wool dress and the heavy brown laced shoes of a woman who has no claim to vanity.

Jesus, Sara thought, but gave her most winning smile. 'Hello,' she said confidently, 'I'm Sara Kendall. I've been corresponding with Mrs Anderson – ' She stopped a moment, waiting. Surely this woman couldn't be Fanny Anderson? When the woman showed no change of expression, Sara pressed on, –'and I have some material that I'd like to return to her.' She nodded down at the packet in her arms. 'I wrote Mrs Anderson a note last week, telling her I would be in town and would like to see her – is she in?'

'Mrs Anderson is not available,' the woman said.

Oh, no, Sara thought, and nearly burst into tears. 'Well, I could wait,' she said. 'If she's out. Or if she's writing and might be available later. I could wait, or I could come back later today.'

'Mrs Anderson will not be available today,' the woman said coldly.

Angered, Sara frowned. 'Oh, *really*,' she said. 'You mean she will not be available at any time today, not free for even a moment?'

'Mrs Anderson is indisposed,' the woman said.

Well, Sara thought, *I can't argue with that. I can't protest that she's not sick. Indisposed, what an old-fashioned word.*

'Well,' Sara went on, conceding defeat, 'would you please give her this package? It contains some writing of hers, and a few notes I've made. And would you please tell her I stopped by? And that I would like to hear from her as soon as possible?'

'Very well,' the woman said, and took the manila envelope. 'Good day,' she said, and shut the thick oak door in Sara's face.

'You old harridan,' Sara said aloud, with quiet rage. 'You Nazi.'

She turned and traced her steps back down the winding slate walk, out of the wrought iron gates to the street. She had dismissed the cab. That was all right, she could walk to Harvard Square from here, then get a cab to the airport.

On impulse, she turned and looked back up at the Victorian house. She saw, on the second floor, a woman looking down at her through parted heavy drapery. It was not the woman who had answered the door – this woman's face was fuller – but that was the only judgment Sara's mind could make before the woman, seeing Sara's gaze, drew back, disappearing from view.

My God, Sara thought, *I wonder what's going on?* She stood a few more minutes, watching, but the woman did not appear again. Then, shivering, for it was a cold day, Sara turned her back on Fanny Anderson's house and walked toward Harvard Square.

CHAPTER FOUR

Morning.

An amazing morning, really. It was barely nine-thirty, and here Sara was, not curled up in her robe with a manuscript in her lap, but lying back on a medical table in a white paper gown with her legs drawn up and her knees spread apart.

She had been so tense about it all. Last night at the Jones's Christmas Party she had hardly been able to hear people talk, so obsessed was she with thoughts of what had to be done later that night and early the next day. What if the weather turned bad, if it snowed or got foggy. Or what if the plane crashed? Or if the cabdriver had an accident? Last night, the more she thought about it, the more impossible it seemed that she would actually make it from the island thirty miles out at sea into the civilized serenity of Dr Crochett's office.

But here she was. Everything had gone smoothly. They had made love last night, and Steve had driven her to the airport this morning, and the plane hadn't crashed, nor had the taxi, and there had been no fog, or snow. In fact it was very mild for the twenty-third of December. It might easily have been April.

Sara closed her eyes and relaxed against the table. She was tired. She had awakened very early in the morning, around four o'clock, afraid that the alarm – which had never failed before – would, for some reason, not go off on time. When it did go off, she was lying in bed rigidly, staring at it, waiting for it, and so certain that it wouldn't go off that when the buzz came, she jumped, startled.

She had taken her temperature at exactly the right time, and noted what it was; she would write it down on the chart tonight. She wouldn't forget what it was; it had skyrocketed, up eight points.

'Sara! Get up! Get in here, *quick*!'

She raised her head, puzzled. Was that Dr Crochett calling her? He had done something between her legs that took only a few seconds, and then rushed out of the room. She had lain there, expecting him to come back. Instead, here was his voice again, urgent, excited.

She got herself off the table, and pulled on her panties, and clutching her gown around her she peeked out from the doorway of the examining room.

Dr Crochett was standing in the hall. He gestured to her to come to him. 'Hurry!' he said. 'I've got something to show you!'

He looked a bit like the mad scientist this morning, his white lab coat unbuttoned and hanging unevenly, his hair slightly mussed. Sara went down the hall and into a small laboratory.

Dr Crochett took her arm and led her over to a computer. 'Look!' he said, triumphantly, indicating a small microscope. 'Just look at that!'

Sara bent over the microscope. For a moment she could see nothing. Then she saw them, a swarm of tiny sperm swimming around like maniacs, their tiny tails wiggling.

'Wow,' Sara said. 'They look just like what the textbooks say they look like. This is amazing.' And in that moment she had much more faith in all the outer world with its technological paraphernalia. For there they really were, *sperm*, Steve's sperm, miniature tadpoles, fat round heads, wriggling tails, zipping around the slide with determined energy.

'So!' Dr Crochett said. 'This is great, isn't it! You should be very happy. Your husband's got plenty of sperm – look at all those little critters. *And* your mucus is compatible with his sperm. Another point in your favor.'

Sara looked up at Dr Crochett, who was beaming as proudly as if he had just that moment created the sperm himself. She couldn't help but feel fond of him. 'Do you mean there was a chance that it might not be?' she asked.

'Oh, yes, oh, yes, indeed,' Dr Crochett said. 'It happens quite often. Sometimes the woman's mucus kills off the sperm!

Quite a problem, you can imagine. But not in your case. Now – *watch*.'

He picked up the specimen slide and held it over the flame of a cigarette lighter. '*Aha!*' he said, 'just look at that!'

Sara couldn't help smiling. He was so excited, She looked, not certain what she was supposed to see. But she did see it, clearly, how the mucus from her body dried into a delicate, intricate fern pattern on the glass slide.

'Do you see that? That fern pattern? That's a sign that you're ovulating today! Hurry home now and have intercourse – you're ovulating today. This is the proof. And your husband has plenty of sperm and your mucus is compatible. All points in your favor.'

Sara smiled, elated. She was going to get pregnant today, she felt it, she felt as inspired as a sinner at a revival meeting; she had just been saved by the evangelist. 'Yes, yes, all right, thank you,' she said.

'Now look,' Dr Crochett said, his voice slowing a little, 'if you don't get pregnant this month, call me right away. Then I want to schedule a uterotubalgram. Don't be alarmed, it's just a little test to see if your Fallopian tubes are blocked.'

'Blocked? But – how?' Sara asked.

'Oh easily, with anything. Happens all the time. Sometimes a bit of menstrual matter attaches itself to the Fallopian tube at the wrong place, then the eggs can't get down from the tube into the uterus. And if that's the problem, the solution is easy, because when we run the dye through it blows the tube clean. This procedure can be therapeutic as well as diagnostic.'

'Well,' Sara said. 'Hmm.' She was trying to envision all that he was telling her, her Fallopian tubes, and a procedure that would clear them.

'Don't worry, don't even think about it, the uterotubalgram is just another step, but we many not even have to take it. Just think about going home and having intercourse. Today. And listen,' he said, leaning forward, smiling, giving her this one last gift, 'you know, quite often when I take the mucus from a woman's body, that procedure in itself makes pregnancy a

74

little more possible. Because I opened the cervix slightly, it makes it possible for those little devils to swim right up there and – WHAM! You might be getting pregnant right now!'

Instantly Sara was covered with goose bumps. She might be getting pregnant right now. Oh, God, wouldn't it be wonderful?

'Thank you,' she said. If she was pregnant she would come back to his office and fall on her knees and kiss his feet. She would bring him gifts. She would name her child after him. What was his first name? Hiram. Well, maybe she wouldn't do *that*. 'Thank you,' she said again.

'Well, well, we'll see what we see. You call me, either way. All right?'

'All right,' Sara agreed.

Now she hated parting from the doctor, hated going from the lab room to the reception room where other patients sat waiting. She felt that if she could only stay at his side, soaking in his enthusiasm, his optimism, she would effortlessly swell outward with pregnancy. She sat down a moment in the waiting room, pulling her knee socks up inside her high boots, then just sitting a moment, thinking. So many terms had been thrown around this morning, and Dr Crochett spoke with such intimate familiarity about the mysterious movements of minute things: sperm, tubes, eggs. All those reproductive objects that she had read about but never really paid much attention to before, because they had been no more relevant to her than the existence of another galaxy of stars.

But now. Now. She might be getting pregnant even now.

She wanted to sit there in his room all day waiting, all month waiting, not moving, willing it to happen, as if the combination of his energy and her desire would make her wish come true.

She had intended to do some last-minute Christmas shopping in Boston, but really she had gotten everything already, and she wanted to be back on Nantucket, back at home, like a bird ready to sit on the eggs in her nest. She would not try to go to Fanny Anderson's house today – she had not heard from her, and was miffed. And she did not want to encounter the dragon lady, she did not want to have any negative experience today. She wanted to stay in this happy, hopeful state.

Steve picked her up at the airport when the heavy old P B A D C-3 clucked down at eleven-thirty. Only eleven-thirty, and so much had happened. As she came toward him where he stood waiting for her at the gate, looking ruggedly sexual in his weathered work clothes, her heart swelled with love for him. Look at that man! He was so handsome, so good. He should have a son. She ran toward him, threw her arms around him, and kissed him as passionately as if they had been parted for months instead of a morning.

'Hey.' Steve laughed, pulling away, embarrassed a little by her display. 'You okay?'

'I'm fine,' she said. 'I'm great. Come on, I'll tell you about it in the car.'

As they drove back to the heart of town, Sara described the doctor and his procedure. Steve listened intently.

'So,' he said, very quietly, 'so it seems I'm okay then. That . . . I've got enough . . .' He didn't finish the sentence.

Sara studied her husband's face. He was driving the car very seriously, not looking at her. *Oh*, she thought, *of course. Of course he would worry about that.* Although it had never really occurred to her that it could be his body at fault.

'Oh, Steve,' she said, laughing, and imitated Carl Sagan's enunciation about stars, 'you've got *b*illions and *b*illions and *b*illions of sperm; I saw them swimming around, I really did. It is amazing,' she went on, 'what science can do. I mean, they tell you in text-books that all these teeny-weeny things are going on inside your body, but it's hard to believe.'

'Teeny-weeny,' Steve said, grinning. 'There's a textbook term.'

She laughed from relief because he was kidding her, he was back to normal, he was relaxed. He was fine.

So now, she thought, sobering, now they had to see if she was just as fine.

At their house, Steve stopped the car but kept the motor running. 'I've got to get right back to work, babe,' he said, running his hand along the back of her neck, gently rubbing. 'Will you be okay?'

'Sure,' Sara said, smiling. 'I've never felt better.'

'Well, I'm sorry you have to do all this running around. I hope you know I appreciate it. All you're doing. The flying and the examinations and all.'

'Oh, Steve.' Sara leaned across the seat to hug him. She knew how hard it was for him to say something like that. 'I love you.'

'I love you. See you tonight.'

'Yeah. You bet you'll see me tonight,' she grinned.

Once in the house Sara hung up her coat, then sank down on the sofa to think. She realized then how tired she was, and leaned back on the pillows and instantly fell asleep.

She awoke to the sound of the mail thumping on the floor through the slot in the door. She looked at her watch; it was just after two. She stretched. She looked down at her stomach. She smiled. Maybe she had been so tired, had fallen asleep like that, because she was already pregnant?

After daydreaming awhile she rose and crossed the living room to the hallway to see what the mail had brought. Some Christmas cards, some bills, a magazine, and another manila envelope from Fanny Anderson.

Dear Sara Kendall, [again the dark-blue gracefully round handwriting on heavy cream-colored stationery]

I understand that you have been trying to reach me and I'm so very sorry if I've caused you any inconvenience. I haven't been well lately and have needed to envelop myself in a cocoon of complete peace and quiet. I hope you will forgive me for not seeing you when you stopped by the other day and also for not answering any of your phone calls. It is just that I have been ill, and need to put my health first these days.

77

But also please believe me, I am very grateful for your appreciation of my Jenny pages, and your encouragement means a great deal to me, more than you could ever know, more than I could ever express. And the notes you sent me with my last pages – marvelous! So helpful. You are a gifted editor. You are perhaps the perfect editor for me.

So please bear with me, if you will. I would love to meet you personally when I am better. Until then, I have sent you some more of the Jenny pages. Again let me say that you mustn't feel obligated to read them or to like them. But your criticism is immensely helpful, immensely appreciated.

Happy Holidays to you and yours. Perhaps we can talk after the new year.

With warm regards,
Fanny Anderson

Sara looked through the envelope. This package was thicker than the others: fifty pages. She read the first page. It was a continuation of the Jenny story, picking up where the last page had left off, with Jenny sitting in a café at Montmartre, plotting to leave Henry Cook, whose love, if it could be called that, had become oppressive.

Sara was hungry. She made herself a thick sandwich and a pot of tea with lots of sugar and milk and settled down to read.

I found a small *pension* to stay in. The room was five floors up, and tiny and bare, with just a steel cot and a cheap dresser and a rickety chair, but it was clean. The WC was three floors down. I moved in with all I possessed – the clothes I had brought with me when I ran away with Henry – and began life modeling for artists. But it was difficult. The artists pressed me to sleep with them. They insulted me when I refused. I thought I was so sophisticated – why couldn't I sleep with Henry?

Many times I tried, only to find myself fighting, scratching, sobbing, running away, ending up on a strange street at two in the morning wrapped only in a blanket, shaking with fear. Henry first told me I was delicate. When he got tired of my evasions, he changed his mind. He told me I was crazy. Perhaps I was. Such a simple thing, to lose one's virginity, and I had thought myself so adult, so hard. But I was afraid, and even more, I did not love Henry. Over the months we had lived together in Paris I had gotten to know him too well to love him. He was a spoiled rich boy. And he was not a good artist. But I did not want to leave Paris – some of the painters had become my friends. I wanted to stay in Paris, but not with Henry.

When finally I had very little money left, not more than a week's worth to live on, Henry Cook discovered my hiding place. He had seen an oil painting of me, nude, and assumed I had slept with the painter, after months of refusing to sleep with him. He broke into my tiny room, he called me names, he raged at me, and then he beat me. Not terribly, but enough to hurt me and to frighten me.

I wired Will Hofnegle: Please send me the money to get home. I need to see you. Please don't tell my parents.

Will sent me the money immediately. I took an Air France flight to New York, then a Braniff flight to Kansas City. When Will met me at the airport, my left eye was still swollen and discolored and my body was bruised. Will looked so handsome to me, so tall, so strong, so gentle, that I wept to see him and could not understand how I ever could have left him.

He drove me down to the Flint Hills in Kansas, where his farmhouse sat in the midst of his thousand acres. His red-and-white Hereford cows grazed on green pastures; it was April. The sun slanted generously across the land, the wind swept through the undulating hills, making the grasses wave, a sea of glowing emerald. His spaniel and her puppies ran out to greet me.

I stayed with Will. He became my lover. That was what I had wanted, what I had always wanted. How simple the right thing can be. Will was a wonderful lover, all I had ever dreamed of.

I called my parents and reunited with them but refused to come home, insisting on living with Will, even though we were not married. This upset my parents terribly and opened a breach between us. It was all right for me to run off to Paris, but it shamed them that I was living out of wedlock with a man in my home country. I could not explain myself to them. I did not have to explain myself to Will; he did not propose marriage to me. He did not even ask how long I was planning to stay.

And I didn't stay long; I left the next January. I loved Will, but the Kansas winter, with its walls of snow and howling winds and frozen landscape, as dead as the moon, made me wild. I felt trapped. I had to get away. Will gave me some money. He had plenty of money. He did not try to make me feel indebted; he did not try to make me stay. He did not judge me. He did not ask, 'What are you searching for?'

I was nineteen. I flew back to Paris. It was winter there too, but spring was nearer, the weather was not so savage, and did not matter so much in the city. The streets of Paris, the clamor, the clothes, the art, the arches, the artists! Now I was ready in every way for the complexity of this place. Within a few days I had become the lover of a young French painter who called himself, simply, Lalo. I lived with Lalo, posed for him, sat in the café with him, watching spring come in Paris. Once again there were people to see me, and I liked that. I needed the men to whistle and wink and stare and approach, I needed the envious glances of women. Cows could not appreciate my beauty, but Parisians could.

I lived with Lalo for almost a year, then left him for another painter, Jean-Paul. He was more intellectual, more interesting, there was more to him than just good looks, and after a year I went with him and a group of his artist friends to Mexico. We rented an old rundown *hacienda* outside the small town of Guanajuato. Seven of us, seven artists.

For I became an 'artist', too; I decided to write poetry. Sometimes, I would recite my poetry aloud while Phillippe, one of the gay artists, accompanied me on the flute. Artists from other colonies in Mexico came to visit, and we seven bought a dilapidated van and drove through the mountainous, barren, rocky Mexican countryside to visit other colonies. People began to hear about us, to study us! Journalists came down, sweating in their wrinkled city suits to admire us in our loose bright-colored cottons, bare skins, and sandals. The day came when I read about myself in a prestigious American periodical. There was an article on artists in Mexico, and I was listed as one of the group that was becoming known as 'The Seven', I was very happy. This was what I had meant to happen in my life. I only wished they had taken photographs.

It did not cost much to live in Mexico, but it cost something. One of the members of our group had some money, enough to fill our most minimal needs. But eventually I began to want more, some pretty clothes, some bangles. It was chic then to be Bohemian and shabby, but I longed for lovely clothes. For decorative combs to hold back my hair. For the cheap flashy rings from the Guanajuato marketplace. I began to write poetry more seriously, and then short pieces, articles, short stories, fantasy stories, and sent them off to various magazines. My poetry was rejected, as was everything else for a very long time, but at last a short article sold, a mixture of fact and fantasy about an artistic colony in Mexico. I was elated. Now my life was real.

I insisted then that I have a separate bedroom in the

old *hacienda* so that I could write whenever the mood struck. My small success had made Jean-Paul angry and jealous. And it was becoming obvious to us both that although I was his lover, I did not love him. Restless times fell upon The Seven, everyone changed partners, everyone slept with everyone else, or tried to – even the gay couple did their best. A period of discontent set in. Bottles were thrown in anger, voices were raised, dishes smashed, clothes torn. Nothing else I wrote was accepted for publication.

Five years of my life had passed. I had thought I had caught hold of a comet that might carry me into the heavens, but so soon it seemed to be fizzling. I was not as happy with my new lover, François, as I had been with Jean-Paul. My beauty was taken for granted among the five I lived with.

The next time we drove in our van to visit another artists' colony I packed my few belongings. And stayed with the people we had gone to visit. This was easy for me; I was so beautiful, and there were many men. This group was British; they served tea in china cups on the hottest day. These people, too, were trying to be artistic and Bohemian – and they were artistic – but were so tidy and refined and reserved and brittle that they could never be truly Bohemian. But because they were British, they were exotic to me, and I stayed with them, moving from man to man, for four years.

But then it was 1960 and the times were changing. Now England was the place to be. Perhaps that was why I fell so hopelessly in love with Cecil Randolph. Or perhaps I would have loved him anyway. He was a newcomer to the British artistic colony and had come during the time when I (luckily) had fought with my current lover and moved into a room of my own. Cecil wasn't an artist as much as a connoisseur. He had come to visit his younger brother George. The moment he walked into the room, I was enthralled. Much later I would realize that Cecil was a slimmer, more erect, more sophisticated, more haughty version of Will Hof-negle. But then I did not see the resemblance. I saw only the long narrow nose, the cold pale blue eyes, the aristo-cratic lean height of the man. Perhaps one really loves only different versions of the same man all one's life. Perhaps not. The truth was that I had not loved any man with my heart since Will, but I did fall in love with Cecil – I fell dangerously, helplessly, my wings melted, absolutely everything changed, like Icarus soaring too close to the sun.

But if I was smitten, I was also twenty-eight, and had learned a few things. I did not let Cecil see how attracted I was. On the contrary, I was evasive and cool, pretend-ing that I was absorbed in my writing. Cecil became attracted to me, and eventually we became lovers. We were so opposite – I so hot, he so cold – that we were magnetic together. Except for Will, it was the only really passionately sexual love affair I had been involved in, and with Cecil I was the one who loved more, who needed more, so my love was more painful, and so seemed more deep.

Cecil didn't care much for Mexico. He wanted to go back to England, and he asked me to come with him. He lived in a vast stone manor house in Sussex and in an apartment off Bayswater Road in London. He often went to visit his parents, who lived in an even larger manor house in the Cotswolds (he drove me by it once and pointed it out) and in a flat in London. I never met his parents, even though I lived with Cecil for five years. All along I was aware that although Cecil was truly in love with me, he found me just not quite right, this American girl he had discovered living with artistic loose-ness in Mexico. I couldn't understand his friends, nor did they like me; they were so reserved, like artifacts of people. Each time Cecil had a house party at the manor, I was aware of the women's unspoken scorn and the men's kinder condescension. 'Good' women did not live openly, then, unmarried, with men. When I walked, in a satin dress, through a blazingly lighted ballroom at one of Cecil's parties, it was if I were accompanied by the ghost of my sixteen-year-old self, the girl who had all unwittingly and without intent attracted the ardor of Jeremy Gardner and the dry-ice disdain of the eastern girls. Now I was surrounded by the ultimate 'eastern' girls, and again I walked through flames.

I was without female friends. I had never wanted a girlfriend. I had vowed never to trust one. No doubt I created my own shell for protection, but it walled me in as much as it walled others out. I had no one to talk to and no one who could help me understand a thing. All I could use at that time was my physical beauty – and so I used it. When artists asked to paint me, I posed for them. That at least gave me some kind of social contact.

And finally, in desperation, afraid I could lose Cecil's love, I let myself be painted nude, Rubens-style, reclining on a chaise, satin pillows all around me, fat grapes in a bowl on the table in front of me, my hair tousled over my shoulders, over the pillows, my cheeks flushed. It was a message to Cecil: 'Don't forget how beautiful I am!' But I knew at once, on seeing Cecil's face as he unveiled the portrait, that I had done the wrong thing. This was too sensual, too blatant a presentation of myself: one did not do this sort of thing. It made me seem common, and compared to Cecil I was common, at least according to the standards of the rigid British class system.

Did I think I could really disguise the Kansas farmgirl in my own voluptuous flesh? I tried. And when Cecil and I were alone together, everything was perfect. Then we seemed two of a kind. Cecil was interested in the farmers who tenanted great parts of his land or who owned adjoining land, and this was something I knew about and could share with him, something I could even occasionally advise him on. Together we rode over fallow fields, discussing the best future use of those

84

fields, or attended local farm meetings to fight for the best pollution control of the local streams, or stayed up all night together watching Cecil's prize field trial bitch give birth to healthy pups. Then I would forget that we weren't married; I would feel that we had become as one; I was happy and knew Cecil was happy, too. We were both readers – he loved non-fiction and history, and I loved fiction and poetry – so when we weren't outside in the fields, we were inside by the fire, reading and interrupting each other to read aloud a fortunate phrase. When other people weren't around, our union was complete; but we could not always live in our own isolated world.

After we had been together for almost five years, Cecil came to me one day and said, 'My parents tell me I must get married.'

For one brief moment my heart leapt up. I thought he was proposing. But then I read his face – how exquisitely embarrassed he was, how miserable, I said nothing. At least, I would later tell myself, at least I had that to pride myself on – I had held back from my instinctive response to jump up and throw my arms around my lover, crying, 'Darling!' I had sat there, frozen, watching. I had learned that much from the British.

For of course his parents had not just told Cecil that he must get married, but that he must get married to a certain woman, a second cousin. Their affiliation would join and enlarge their estates. It might as well have been feudal times.

'Well,' I said, 'then I must pack and leave. Today.'

With great dignity and reserve I rose from my chair and crossed the room. All my life had led to this point, this act of dignity. At least I hoped it looked like dignity; really, it was a state of shock that made me so still.

When I looked back, I saw something I had never thought I would see: Cecil, seated, weeping into his hands, his shoulders shaking with grief. I was unbearably touched. But I knew enough not to go back,

85

not to embrace him, not to console him. I knew he
would soon rise and wipe his eyes and go on with his
life. Cecil would marry. What would I do?

I went to London, numbed. I had met many interesting people through Cecil, and I was able to get a job as
an assistant to the articles editor on a glossy ladies'
magazine. Again, it helped that I was beautiful. I was
too voluptuously built to model – Twiggy was now the
rage – but I was photographed everywhere, at parties
and nightclubs and theatre gatherings. Bewildered by
Cecil's desertion of me, which, when all was said and
done, no matter how important his parents and class
and station in life, had been cruel and callous, I began
seriously to sleep around. To sleep with men not for
love or romance or even pleasure but for reasons that
had to do with crasser things, with power and ambition
and acquisitiveness.

Perhaps it mattered that, when I knew Cecil was going
to marry someone else, I had called Will Hofnegle. I
wanted to know how he was, I said, thinking that perhaps he would fly to me now, or ask me to come home
to him, for a while, for consolation. But Will was married. He had two children. He was very happy, how was
I? Oh, very happy, I told him. And thought: what had I
expected? That he would wait for me all his life? That
after fourteen years he would still be true to me, pining
for me?

For it was true, fourteen years had passed.

I was older.

I was alone.

I had awakened from a dream of life.

So I lived in a frenzy of activity. I slept with several
men on any given day. I had so many clothes and
changed so many times I had to hire a maid to keep
them hung up (Cecil had given me a considerable sum
of money on our parting and, not proud, needing to
survive, I had taken it). I now had 'friends', women I
lunched and gossiped with, women I worked with on the

ladies magazine, women I talked clothes with. We were all 'darling' to each other, we were all 'divine'. What we lacked in depth we made up for in movement: I lunched, I dined, I danced, I flirted, I shopped, I made love, I laughed about my lovers with my 'friends', I had a wonderful time. London was swinging then, and I swung.

Carnaby Street, the Beatles, X-T-C, the Rolling Stones, now and then a champagne supper on the lawn at Glyndebourne, drinking all night at the Playhouse, my picture in the society section of the best papers and occasionally in both literary reviews and cheap tabloids. Younger and younger men, richer and richer men.

Then it was 1972 and I was thirty-nine.

There Jenny's story ended.

'*Aaah!*' Sara cried aloud, frustrated. She wanted to read more, to know what happened. If she had known Jenny as a living person, she probably would have disliked her – would have seen her as selfish and arrogant. But as Sara read these pages she felt as if she were looking through a kaleidoscope that flashed beautiful patterns, and now and then suddenly flared away to reveal a small, clear heartbreaking gem of truth. What would happen to Jenny when she no longer could protect herself from others with her swirling colors? What kind of woman was really hidden back in the necessary dazzle?

Sara spent the afternoon at the dining room table, bent over the Jenny pages, making notes, then typing a long letter to Fanny Anderson. What a book this could be, she thought. With a little shaping, a little editing, what a successful book this could be.

Julia flew down from Boston on the afternoon of the twenty-fourth to spend Christmas with them. The two friends sat drinking champagne in the living room, waiting for Steve to come home from work. The windows framed a sky deepening into indigo; Sara did not turn on the lamps, so that they could enjoy the flickering lights of the enormous wood fire she had built and the tiny, brilliant, jewellike lights on the Christmas tree.

'Here,' Julia said, handing Sara a small silver package. 'Open this now.'

'I thought we'd wait until later to open gifts,' Sara said, surprised.

'This isn't a Christmas gift. And it's just for you. I think Steve might be – embarrassed about it.'

Sara opened the silver package and lifted out a tiny crescent moon that hung from a clear plastic thread that was so slender it was almost invisible. The moon was made of glass, so that as Sara held it dangling from her hand it caught all the lights from the room and spun and glittered, throwing spangles on the wall.

'It's beautiful,' Sara said. 'We'll put it on the tree.'

'No, silly,' Julia said. 'Read the note.'

Sara unfolded the paper that Julia had put at the bottom of the box. She read:

'"When, however, a childless woman wants a baby she exposes herself to the light of the new moon or makes offerings to the moon and invokes its aid."'

'I don't think you'd always be able to "expose yourself" to a new moon,' Julia, 'so I thought perhaps this would do.'

'Oh, it's beautiful Julia, and it's magical. How could it not be? Look at it!' Sara twirled the slender thread and the moon whirled and threw off light. 'I'll hang it above our bed!'

She leaned over and kissed Julia and hugged her. *I'm lucky*, she thought, *I have Steve. Poor Julia.*

Julia called the stretch between Christmas Eve and New Year's 'The Suicide Season' because her lover spent every minute of this time in the bosom of his family. After the first of the year, after the family festivities and the two-week family trip to the house on St Martin, her lover came back to her with the desperate and complimentary greed of a drowning man coming up for air. But these few days were sacrosanct, the time he was a good father, a good son and son-in-law – and a good husband. The presents – diamonds, flowers, chocolates, more diamonds – that he lavished on Julia on the third December could not make up for the two weeks of pain that followed.

'Why do you stay with him?' Sara asked Julia. It was the afternoon of Christmas Day; Steve was home reading by the fire, enjoying a day of luxurious laziness; the two women were walking at Surfside Beach. The day was surprisingly mild and gentle, the waves frothing up playfully, nipping at their ankles.

'Why do you want to get pregnant?' Julia countered, weaving away from the foam to keep her feet dry. She was wearing the silver fox coat her lover had given her and a green scarf over her wildly abundant red hair.

'My desire is reasonable,' Sara said. 'Women get pregnant. Husbands and wives have babies. That's what people do.'

'Well, men get divorced and marry the women they really love,' Julia said. 'My desire is just as reasonable as yours!' She kicked a shell away from her path.

Sara studied her friend's face – what she could see of it, for Julia was staring ahead defiantly as if looking into her future. Sara had tried, over the past three years, to talk Julia out of her affair, which seemed to Sara self-defeating and doomed. But Julia was obsessed.

'We're obsessed, you know,' she said to Julia.

'I know,' Julia said. 'Believe me, do I ever know.'

'What gets me is the waiting,' Sara said. 'You wouldn't *believe* how long the days take to pass. I seem to spend my life *waiting* – waiting to ovulate, waiting to see if I'm pregnant, waiting for my damned period to be over so I can wait to ovulate again, and the days just crawl by.'

'I know,' Julia said. 'I know that, too. When Perry is with his wife, nothing I do will make time pass quickly, and I've tried everything.'

'How did this happen to us?' Sara asked. 'We are two intelligent, capable, dynamic women. How did we get to the place in our lives where all we can do is wait?'

'I don't know, honey. I've asked myself that a million times,' Julia said. 'At least you've got your work.'

'Ha!' Sara yelled. 'All I can do there is wait, too! That damned Fanny Anderson, she's so *frustrating*! I would love to get to work on her book, but I can't get in touch with her, she just won't talk on the phone or see me or anything!'

'She sounds crazy,' Julia said.

'Oh, we're all crazy,' Sara moaned. She ran ahead of Julia, dancing away from the jagged surge of waves. She ran back and grabbed Julia by the shoulders. 'You don't understand,' she said. 'I really am going crazy. I really am obsessed. I'm turning into some kind of maniac. All the time after I've *ovulated* all I'm *really* doing is listening to my body for some kind of sign. Every *minute* I'm thinking, "Do my breasts sting? Am I getting cramps? Am I sick at my stomach?" I analyze everything! At first it wasn't so bad, but each month I don't get pregnant I get more strung out.'

'You'll never get pregnant that way,' Julia said, looking Sara in the eye.

Sara flung herself away from her friend. 'Oh great, thanks a lot, that's just what I needed to hear!'

'Well, it's true,' Julia said. 'Sara, you need to relax.'

'Julia, you need to find a man who's not married,' Sara said.

The two friends glared at each other, bristling. Then Julia grinned, 'I will if you will,' she said, and they hugged each other and laughed wryly and turned around to walk back down the beach, two hopeless cases at the edge of the careless waves.

January third was a cold bright day, a day for movement. Julia had gone back to Boston and her lover, Steve had gone back to work, and Sara had decided to take charge of her life. She was going to *move on*. She was going to drop this elusive Jenny business and get back to work on some other books.

She dialed Fanny Anderson's number one last time. This time she would tell the old bitch who answered to tell Fanny Anderson that she was going to drop the book completely if she continued to be put off in this way. Really, she was a *professional*, there was no need for her to be chasing after her in this way, if Fanny Anderson didn't care enough about her own work to even *talk* to Sara about it . . .

'Hello?' A soft, hesitant voice came over the phone.

'Hello? Mrs Anderson?' Sara stammered, caught off-guard, not certain now that she had dialed the right number.

'Yes. This is Mrs Anderson.' Such a soft voice.

'Oh! Oh, well, Mrs Anderson, this is Sara Kendall. I'm calling because – well, I hope you received your material back with my comments.' She couldn't help herself, she had to try one last time.

'Yes. Yes, I did, thank you.'

'Well, I hope you understood from my letter how excited I am about this book. I would very much like to show what you've done to Donald James. And I'd like it very much if I could come see you sometime and sit down with you and discuss the book in detail. Or, if you'd prefer, you could come here. Nantucket is a beautiful place, even in the winter.'

There was a long silence.

'Mrs Anderson?' Sara asked at last, for the silence was so complete that she could not even hear the other woman's breath.

'I don't believe I could come there. I don't travel very much anymore, you see.'

'Then I'd be glad to come to you,' Sara said.

'There's another thing,' Mrs Anderson said, then paused. 'I'm not quite sure just how to put this. But – well, you must understand, I don't usually *see* the people I work with. After all, it's really not necessary, is it? I mean, there is the telephone, there are letters, there is the mail. With Heartways House, for example, my goodness, I must have written ten or twelve novels for them now, and I haven't met a soul there. Miss Oldham doesn't seem to mind. I do believe that early on she asked me for lunch or drinks a few times, but I was always unable to make such arrangements, and we have continued over the years to have a very satisfactory relationship without meeting even once.'

Now Sara was quiet. 'Well,' she said finally. 'Well, you see, the Jenny novel is such a different kind than the ones you've been writing for Heartways House. Those have a formula, a pattern, and if the writer sticks with that, there's not much an editor needs to do, except watch for inconsistencies in timing, for example, or check to be sure the hero has aquamarine eyes all the way through. But the Jenny novel is quite different. It doesn't fall into any category, any formula. It is romantic, in a way, but the writing is different, so it wouldn't be a romantic novel. It would be –'

'Yes, yes, my dear I do understand all that. The difference between my little romances and this novel.' This time Mary could almost hear Fanny Anderson smile.

'They you understand how a different kind of editing needs to be done on the Jenny book. I suppose I could write you a long letter telling you my ideas, but I've always found that a dialogue, a give-and-take of ideas, is much more helpful for both the writer and the editor. And it saves so much time.'

'Well, as for time,' Fanny Anderson said softly, 'I'm not in any particular hurry to have this little book published. I've had it in mind for so long.'

Sara went silent again. 'Disregarding time, then,' she went on, 'it still would be helpful if we could sit down together. I would love to edit this book, and to be honest, I think it would be a real feather in my cap. It might be helpful if we could discuss what exactly you want the book to be seen as, and how I could help you make it so. It wouldn't take long. Just an hour or two.'

'Yes,' Fanny Anderson said. 'Yes, I do understand.'

Sara waited.

Silence.

'Yes, very well,' Fanny said. 'Let's do that.'

'Wonderful!' Sara said. 'Shall we set a date now?'

'Oh, well, I don't have my calendar right here next to me. Perhaps I could have your number and call you back,' Fanny Anderson said.

'I'd be glad to come tomorrow,' Sara offered.

'Yes, but I believe I'm busy tomorrow,' Fanny said. 'It really would be better if I call you back.'

Sara gave the woman her number, refraining from pointing

out that she had given it before both on the telephone and in letters. She kept her voice courteous. She tried not to be pushy. But she was afraid, when she hung up, that she wouldn't hear from Fanny again for a long time, if ever.

That night Sara had to admit to herself that her breasts were sore.

The next day Fanny Anderson did not call. And when Sara looked at herself sideways in the mirror, she could see the old familiar pouching of her stomach. Her breasts were very sore, and she awoke and went through the day in a state of barely controllable madness. Mad in both meanings of the word – insane and angry, so angry at Fate that she wanted to hit out, to hurt back, to destroy. She drank wine with lunch, but that didn't help. She took a long walk, even though the weather had turned very cold, but that didn't help – except to make her so exhausted that her fury died down into a low-burning self-hatred.

When Steve came home that night, she could scarcely speak. She was not angry at him, it was not his fault that she wasn't pregnant – he had *b*illions and *b*illions of healthy sperm – no; it was her fault. She kept away from him with the wisdom of a wounded animal, knowing that because she was wounded, she would strike out at any kind hand that tried to touch her.

After dinner, she said, 'Steve? I'm going to start my period tomorrow. I can tell.'

'Oh, honey, I'm sorry,' he said. He rose from the table, came around, bent down, and hugged her. 'I know how disappointed you are. I am, too. But listen, we're both young and healthy. There's no hurry. If it doesn't happen this month, it'll happen next month, or the month after that. And I love you, however you are, whatever happens. You know that, don't you?'

He turned her face to him, so he could look into her eyes.

'You know I love you, don't you, Sara?' he asked again, smiling.

Sara could scarcely trust herself to speak. She could see that he loved her. She knew that he loved her, that he understood as well as any man could what she was going through. That he was doing the best he could to help her.

Sara went into the bathroom and ran a tub of steaming water. She sat there, weeping in a fury. Oh, wasn't Steve a nice husband! Oh, what an understanding husband. Oh, he said he loved her. Oh, he was such an optimist. Didn't this touch him at all? Didn't this touch him *at all*? Why wasn't he weeping and sick with misery because once again they had missed, they were not going to have a baby? Why was he so cheerful, so calm? Didn't he have any *FEELINGS*?

There he was, the perfect husband, and here she sat in the tub, not pregnant, the imperfect wife. The flawed wife. The inferior wife. The rapidly-mentally-deteriorating wife.

She wanted to go break all the dishes over his perfect, understanding, optimistic, loving, helpful head.

Instead, she sat in the tub for an hour, until she had really exhausted herself and had no more tears. Then she put on her warmest nightgown and robe, and drank warm milk with two aspirin, and watched television until it was time to go to bed.

Then, so soon, it was morning. And she could tell instantly, the way her gown stuck to her legs, that her period had started again.

CHAPTER FIVE

Morning.

Winter sun hit the yellow stone of the old Boston building and filled the foyer with such bright warmth that Sara felt she was entering a cube of light. The carpet was blue. On the wall in the entrance hall was a large glass-cased black board listing, alphabetically, the various offices in this building.

She looked at the sheet of paper Dr Crochett's office had sent along to her: she wanted Foster, Larch, Wang and Sikes.

F L W S Radiology Associates.

Sara smiled. She could see herself reflected dimly in the glass of the office listing: a young woman, the collar of her red cape turned up against the January cold, her cheeks flushed. That was not the cold; it was excitement, optimism, hope.

She was going to have her 'tubes blown out'. Horrid phrase. Yet Dr Crochett had told her that this procedure was both diagnostic and therapeutic. Wisely scheduled after she had finished her period yet before she ovulated, this procedure could clear out any tissue that might be blocking the way of her egg getting down from the ovary through the Fallopian tube and into her uterus. This procedure might clear the path. Twenty percent of all women who had this done got pregnant that very month.

So!

Sara had flown to Boston (and again the plane did not crash!) and taken a taxi to this clinic, situated near one of Boston's major hospitals. Her appointment was for ten-thirty. It was only ten-fifteen; but she had not wanted to be late.

She found the correct door and entered the F L W S waiting room. A young woman smiled at her from behind a desk. Sara crossed the room, spoke to her, took the forms offered, hung her coat up on the coatrack.

She sat down in one of the blue plaid chairs that were scattered around the room in little groups, took a deep breath, and looked around her. There were five other women in the room, women of different ages. They did not look up at her.

Sara looked down at the sheet of paper the woman had given her, telling her to give it to the nurse when her turn came. The sheet said, simply:

Uterotubalgram
Ultrasound
Mammogram

On her sheet, 'Uterotubalgram' was circled with blue ink.

Shit, Sara thought, her heart jumping. She looked up again, studying the women around her. She had forgotten that there were worse things in the world than not getting pregnant, that there were dangers lurking in one's own body, cruel treacheries, cancers and cysts and tumors, an entire range of problems that no one ever asked for, that everyone feared. Suddenly she felt so frivolous being here, so foolish. Why should she have anyone mess around with her perfectly good body? Why should she take up the time and place when some other women, seriously ill, was waiting to know the results of a much more important test?

She almost left. But she didn't, she stayed sitting, her mind racing, and now all the frightening negative words came flooding back around her, the little scary bombs other women she had spoken with had unwittingly dropped all around the field of her consciousness.

When she told her mother she was going to have a uterotubalgram, her mother had said, 'Oh, dear. Did they tell you how much it's going to hurt? I had a friend . . .' and began to relay such a gruesome tale of pain and incompetence that Sara had had to ask her mother to be quiet. 'Oh, that was foolish of me,' her mother had said. 'I didn't mean to scare you. I'm sure things have changed for the better by now.'

When she told her sister, Ellie had said, 'Great. I'm glad you're doing it. And it won't hurt as much as everyone says.'

'What do you mean?' Sara had sputtered. 'Dr Crochett said there should be some discomfort, but no real pain. Or at least nothing that lasts very long, only for a few seconds.'

'Oh, that's right,' Ellie said, lying so sincerely that only a sister could hear. 'I must have been thinking of another procedure.'

When she told Julia, Julia had said only, 'I'll meet you at the doctor's office. What time do you have to be there?'

'What have you heard about this?' Sara demanded, suspicious.

'Not a thing,' Julia said silkily. 'I just love the pleasure of your company.'

Now here Julia was, hurrying into the doctor's office, giving Sara a quick kiss, sitting down next to her. 'You look great!' she said. 'We'll have lunch when it's over and I'll take you to the airport. Now listen, I've got a new joke. A super-rich woman donates a lot of money to a hospital for a maternity wing. So one day she comes to see the wing and the doctors and nurses fall all over themselves because she's Mrs Moneybags. They show her all the new babies and they hand her one baby and she looks at it and coos and goos and they hand her another newborn baby and she coos and goos, and they hand her another one. She looks at this one, turns it this way and that, and finally says, "Doctors, there's something wrong with this baby. This baby just doesn't look quite right." The doctors say, "Oh, no, we're really proud of that baby. That baby is a test-tube baby!" And she hands the baby back and says, "That proves it. I've always said spare the rod and spoil the child."'

'Oooh.' Sara laughed, aware of the eyes of the other patients. 'That's truly horrible, Julia.'

'Mrs Kendall?' A nurse with a light blue cardigan over her white uniform stood in a doorway, a piece of paper in her hand. 'Would you come with me?'

Sara dutifully followed. The nurse was young, with blond hair that had been overbleached and overblown and stuck out stiffly from her head like seagrass. But she was pleasant enough; she smiled when she showed Sara a curtained cubicle, and said, 'Take everything off from the waist down. Put the paper gown on. You can leave your blouse and sweater on. I'll come back for you in a minute.'

In a changing room much like one in any department store, except that the mirror on the wall was small, reflecting only Sara'a face, Sara stepped out of the lower half of her clothes. She looked at herself in the strange mirror, studying her face. The stark haircut was growing out and looked softer now. In this light she looked quite young and pretty – and healthy. Absolutely capable of having a baby.

She had just sat down on the little wooden bench in the changing room when the nurse returned.

'Would you follow me, please?' she asked, and briskly led the way out of the changing area and down a hallway into a small laboratory room.

'Now,' she said, efficiently, 'you just lie down here. Put your feet here. Your legs need to be up. Good. Now scoot down. Way down. Your bottom should be way down here. That's fine. You're getting a uterotubalgram, right?'

'Right,' Sara said. 'Does it hurt?'

'Oh, it depends,' the nurse said, bustling around, arranging the paper sheet over Sara's naked lower body. 'Sometimes it does. But not for long. And usually not worse than a really severe menstrual cramp. It depends on the person.'

A flare of fear shot up inside Sara then, surprising her. She had experienced so little pain in her life, really, she had never even had a broken bone, and the only time she had been in the hospital was when she was very young, having her tonsils out. What a lucky life she had led until now!

The doctor came in then, whisking through the door as quickly as someone on his way to catch a plane. He walked past Sara without even glancing at her, pulled up a stool, and seated himself at the foot of the table, between her spread knees. Sara caught a glimpse of black-rimmed glasses. The man's expression was grim.

Isn't he even going to say hello? Sara wondered. There had to be some kind of protocol for this procedure. Even if he never saw her again – and he probably never would – still he was going to be doing some of the most intimate things she had ever had done to her body. Not even Steve had seen her so gracelessly, helplessly exposed.

The nurse said something to the doctor that Sara didn't catch. Her heart was pounding suddenly, so loudly that it seemed to be blocking out other sounds.

'I'm a little nervous,' she said quietly.

'I'm just going to put a speculum inside you now,' the doctor said suddenly. 'It won't hurt.'

He bent forward. Sara felt vaguely the intrusion of metal into her vagina. She shifted uncomfortably. She could see the top of the doctor's head; his hair was white, and he was wearing a short-sleeved blue smock. He must do this all day, Sara thought with amazement. That man must spend all day looking up women's vaginas. What an odd way to live.

She had almost relaxed when, suddenly, with a grunt of disgust, the doctor pulled his instruments out of Sara's body and pushed himself away from her. His face was grim, contemptuous, even repelled.

Oh, my God, Sara thought. What was wrong? What was wrong with her? Did she smell? Had he seen something unexpectedly repulsive inside her? Was there something terribly wrong with her body?

The doctor said a few brief brusque words to the nurse and left the room.

Sara raised herself up on the table. 'My God,' she said, 'what's wrong?'

The nurse patted her shoulder and smiled. 'It's all right,' she said. 'You just haven't completely finished menstruating yet. We can't do the procedure today. You'll have to come back tomorrow.'

'But – I don't understand,' Sara said.

'Here,' the nurse said, helping Sara off the table. 'Let me show you back to the changing room and then we can make an appointment for your tomorrow.'

'But, please,' Sara said. 'Wait a minute. I still don't understand.'

Now the nurse turned to Sara, slightly impatient. 'He was

going to blow dye up inside you,' she said. 'But you still have some slight show of blood. That means there might be some capillaries open inside your uterus, and the blood could get in and . . . cause a problem.'

Sara was horrified. 'A problem?' she said. 'But . . . I was told this procedure wasn't dangerous.'

'It's not,' the nurse said. 'Not if it's done on the right day. This is the wrong day. But you can come back tomorrow and it will be fine. You wrote down that you're on the ninth day of your cycle. That's correct, isn't it?'

Sara, who had spent more time counting the days in her menstrual cycle than an accountant would spend preparing for an I R S audit, suddenly went blank. 'I – I think so,' she said. Seeing the look of impatience on the nurse's face, she said, more firmly, 'I'm sure of it, yes. Absolutely sure.'

'Well, then, come back tomorrow. We'll do it tomorrow.'

'Is there something wrong with me that I still have some blood inside? That I still have capillaries open?' Sara asked. All sorts of fears and worries were popping up in her mind. She saw now that she had not properly considered the intricacies of her body, had not thought of all the tiny parts inside her, which could be harmed if a mistake was made. For some reason, she began to shake.

'No, no, you're fine,' the nurse said, distracted now, ready to get on with another patient. She led Sara to the changing room and vanished.

Sara dressed with trembling hands, her thoughts racing. It was all so new, so unfamiliar, this reproductive business. She had assumed – now she didn't know why – that Dr Crochett would be doing everything to her, that he would be her doctor with every procedure. And that would have been all right. She trusted him, she had talked with him, he had looked at her – he had *seen* her. He was a human being who saw her as another human being with a specific problem he could help solve. He had discussed her problem with understanding and even with enthusiasm.

She couldn't expect that of everyone, after all. These other doctors didn't have time to be human, with all the women waiting nervously for all the tests they needed done. As she left her curtained cubicle, she passed one of the other women, an older woman who looked almost in shock, so white was her face, so wide were her eyes with terror. The other woman looked at Sara and then quickly away, and in that brief second of contact Sara saw tears glaze the other woman's eyes. Oh, there was life-and-death business going on here, there was a necessity for speed, no wonder the doctor had been disgruntled with her body, her healthy body taking up time when it wasn't ready.

Still. Still, that doctor could have said hello, Sara thought.

She went back through the door from the hallway into the reception room.

Julia was reading an old *People* magazine. As soon as she saw Sara, she rose, dropped the magazine, and in a flash had crossed the room and wrapped her arms around her.

'Are you okay? How do you feel, sweetie? Do you want to sit down? I didn't want to tell you before you went through with it, but it's hellish, isn't it?'

Sara pulled away from Julia. 'I didn't have it done,' she said.

Julia dropped her arms. 'Why not?'

Sara explained. 'I've got to come back tomorrow,' she added.

'Great. You can stay with me,' Julia said. 'We'll play today, and I'll bring you back here tomorrow, then drive you to the airport.'

Sara saw the receptionist eyeing Julia and smiled to herself. If opulent Julia had been lying on that table, the doctor would have spoken to *her*! She made an appointment for the next day, then left the office and the yellow building.

Julia drove her to her apartment in Marlborough Street, where they talked until Sara could call Steve, at home for lunch, to tell him what had happened. Then, on an impulse, she dialed Fanny Anderson's number. The dragon lady answered, and said, as Sara had known she would, that the author was not available. She took the number Sara gave her but did not assure her that the writer would call.

Sara sat in Julia's living room after Julia had gone back to work and thought about the morning at the doctor's office. She thought about how Julia had rushed to console her when she saw her, and began to wonder how much this tube-blowing business was going to hurt. She put her hands on her lower abdomen. What if the doctor, careless, uncaring, made a mistake? It could happen. Mistakes happened all the time. And underneath the comfortable pillowy covering of her skin lay all those tiny little functioning parts with their own terribly specific duties: passageways, tubes, arteries, receptacles, infinitesimal in size, immense in importance.

How easy it would be to damage such delicate, microscopic tissue.

One fraction of a centimeter's slip with a knife –

Or dye or air blown with too much force, blasting a tube into fragments –

Sara jumped up. She had to stop thinking this way. It was foolish, self-defeating.

She dialed Donald James. He was delighted to hear from her and asked her to join him for a drink that evening. He was a confirmed bachelor, too fastidious to be even gay, and absolutely not a person to engage in discussions about sex, babies, and bodies. This would be good for her.

She spent the rest of the afternoon staring at television shows she never watched at home, waiting for Fanny Anderson to call.

Fanny Anderson did not call.

At five she took a cab to the Ritz and met Donald James. It was wonderful being with her old boss again, hearing all the literary gossip, talking about books. And it was a great consolation to know that he wanted her back anytime because he missed her, *her*, Sara, not a woman capable or incapable of reproduction, but a woman who was a good editor and an intelligent friend.

Later, at dinner at the Harvard Club with Julia, she continued to forget her fears and fantasies. The one time she attempted to move their conversation onto the particularly maudlin track she had become so fond of, Julia had quickly gotten them off it.

'Do you know,' Sara had confided, ever-so-slightly drunk on two vodka tonics and half a bottle of wine, 'Dr Crochett told me that the trip all those little sperm have to make to get from the vagina into the Fallopian tube to get to the egg is equal to a trip that a man would have to make if he *jogged* all the way from Boston to Detroit?'

'My God,' Julia said, seeming properly impressed. 'Just think of that. All that effort, and then to end up in Detroit.'

Of course Sara had to laugh at that, and Julia, seizing her opportunity, began to regale Sara with every dirty joke she had heard in the last six months. It was incongruous, sitting in the dignified serenity of the Harvard Club dining room with the pianist playing Mozart to the genteel accompaniment of silver against china, to hear the vulgar jokes Julia had to tell. But it took Sara's mind off her worries, and before she knew it she was back in Julia's apartment, passing out on the fold-out sofa bed.

And then it was morning.

Her appointment was for nine-thirty. Sara drank two cups of coffee and three glasses of water – all the alcohol of the evening before had helped her fall asleep, but had also de-hydrated her. She put on the clothes she had worn the previous day, and Julia, dressed in supple black Ultrasuede and pearls, drove her back to the yellow-stoned clinic.

'Shall I tell you some more dirty jokes?' Julia asked as they waited in the reception room.

'My God, can you possibly know any more?' Sara asked, laughing. But her heart was pounding. Today she was more nervous than yesterday. When the nurse called her name and led her into the changing room, she began to tremble. She had had too much time to think about it. Today she knew too much – and too little.

A different nurse, an older woman, led her into the narrow room where the table and equipment sat coldly waiting. Sara licked her lips. Like a good child, she hoisted herself up on to the table and lay down, her legs spread apart, her bottom scooted down to the end of the table so that she knew she made, from a certain angle, a giant *M*, with the crevice of her crotch leading into the cave of her body, centred at the fork of the *M*.

That place, that delicate spot, which so few had ever touched, which Steve touched only with gentleness and reverence and lust and love . . . now it was exposed to bright light and a stranger's judgment, all hairy and homely, like a shy night creature that, trapped in the light of day, becomes paralyzed.

She was still new enough to marriage with Steve to base much of her love there, in that low space between her legs, beneath her skin. She loved lying with Steve against her, his penis in that moist iridescent shell-pink passageway, and all the most profound pleasures of her life pulsing there. That was the true heart of her body and her life.

But now she knew that furled passageway led to more secrets, secrets she could only imagine, something more serious than the pleasures of sex, something even homelier and more regal: the beet-red womb rooted deep within, life's home.

And what else? She was so ignorant. Her ovaries, her tubes, those mute accessories that she had carried with her all her life, uncaring. They were up inside her, too, under her dumb friendly tummy. Were they at fault? Was something wrong? Could they be cured? Or were they simply on a slower schedule than Sara's — was she rushing them? Would this intrusion damage them, offend them, cause them to withdraw deeper into their wordless dark world?

The door opened. A man came in. It was not the doctor of the previous day. This one was taller, and younger. He was wearing a blue smock, gray flannels.

As his colleague had done the day before, he passed down the length of the table without looking at Sara's face, without speaking to her, and he pulled up the stool, positioning himself between Sara's naked spread legs. He grunted orders to the nurse.

'I'm nervous,' Sara said. 'I hope this doesn't hurt.'

No one answered. Sara couldn't believe it. No one replied. She glared at the nurse, who smiled briefly at Sara.

'I'm going to blow dye into your tubes to see if they're open,' the doctor said suddenly, and without warning began to insert items into Sara's vagina. 'It won't take long and it will tell us if your Fallopian tubes are open for the eggs to get down into the uterus.' He seemed to be reciting the words wearily, by rote, an automaton who had done this procedure so often he had become mechanical in its performance. 'Okay, let's go,' he said to the nurse.

The nurse approached Sara and said, 'We're going to take an X ray now. Hold your breath. Don't breathe again until I tell you.'

Dutifully Sara held her breath. She felt the mute blunt movement of hard metal inside her and then a hot cramp of pain shot through her lower abdomen.

'You can breathe,' the nurse called from somewhere in the room. She disappeared, came back. 'Here,' she said to the doctor.

'Mmmm,' the doctor grumbled to the nurse. To Sara he said, 'The dye has gone through your right side but not your left. We're going to do it again.'

What does that mean? Sara wondered. Would they have to use more force? It had hurt only briefly the first time — would it hurt longer this time? And why was only one tube open, was something wrong with her? She began to shake. 'I really am getting nervous,' she said. 'I have a friend out there, do you suppose she could come in and hold my hand?'

'Won't be necessary, we'll be through in a minute,' the doctor said.

'I'm feeling a little dizzy,' Sara said. 'And — it's strange, my hands feel all tingling. My head's tingling, too.'

'Oh, Christ, she's hyperventilating,' the doctor said to the nurse. 'Give her some smelling salts.'

'Smelling salts?' Sara asked aloud. She felt like Alice in Wonderland, with everything getting curiouser and curiouser. She thought only old ladies with 'the vapors' used smelling salts; she didn't know they were even in use anymore. 'What will smelling salts do?' she asked.

'They'll just shock you a little,' the nurse said.

Sara jumped at that. *Shock.* She thought of electric shock. She didn't want to be *shocked.*

'I don't want smelling salts,' Sara said firmly.

'You'll have them whether you want them or not,' the doctor said brusquely.

Sara nearly rose off the table. Only the knowledge that her lower body was filled with metal tools and God knew what else – she didn't! – kept her from getting up and walking out. How dare he speak to her that way! What was his problem? What kind of doctor would speak that way to a patient? By coming here, by lying down on his table, she had given him the power to perform a certain procedure on her – she had not thought she was also giving him the power to tyrannize her.

In her rage, she burst into tears.

The nurse approached Sara and said quietly, 'I'm just going to wave these over you quickly, you'll just get a little smell of ammonia, it will just be a little shock, nothing that will hurt you, just enough to clear your head.'

The nurse waved the salts at such a distance from Sara's face that the sharp and not unpleasant odor was more tantalizing than shocking. Sara took a deep breath.

'I'm all right now,' she said, but she was still trembling with anger.

'Let's get this over with,' the doctor said.

Sara glared at him, but of course he could not see her glare; his head was bent between her legs.

'We're going to do another X ray,' the nurse said. 'Hold your breath. Don't breathe until I tell you.'

Sara held her breath. Once again a sharp pain bit into her abdomen, more forcefully this time, so that she felt her body naturally, automatically recoiling, contracting at the pain. But it didn't last long, it really was no worse than a menstrual cramp – she had had much worse cramps than this.

'You can breathe now,' the nurse said. She disappeared from Sara's side, reappeared holding some slides for the doctor to see.

The doctor removed his equipment from Sara's body and rose. 'Your left tube is blocked,' he said and walked past her to the door.

'Wait!' Sara called. She twisted on the table to look at the man. 'Can't you – can't you do the procedure again to open the tube up? I thought that was why I was here, so that you can open up my tubes if they're blocked. I want to get pregnant,' she admitted.

'You can get pregnant. You've got one working tube. You can talk to your doctor about it,' the doctor said, and left the room.

'Are you all right?' the nurse said, hurrying to Sara as she pulled herself into a sitting position and swung her legs around to the side of the table. 'Don't try to walk just yet, not till you're sure you're not dizzy.'

'I'm not dizzy, I'm confused,' Sara said. 'Why couldn't he – he was in and out of here so fast. He didn't explain – I didn't have time to understand. I don't understand. If I've got one tube blocked, why that means that I've only got six months a year when I can get pregnant. Right? Don't the ovaries alternate in producing eggs?'

'Well, that's what we used to think,' the nurse said. 'But now I guess the theory is that we don't know. Sometimes the right ovary can produce the eggs for months at a time, sometimes the left. They don't automatically alternate every month.'

'Then – then that means that my left ovary might be producing the egg but it can't ever get down because that tube's blocked,' Sara said. 'Oh, can't the doctor come back and open up my left tube?'

'No, dear, it would be too uncomfortable for you,' the nurse said. 'He did as much as he could today. Now we need to get you moving along. Can you stand?'

Sara was almost in tears again. She was sure the doctor had left her with one tube blocked because she had been such a cowardly patient.

Somehow she knew she had failed. Somehow she failed again, to do what was necessary to get pregnant. If only she had been calmer, braver. She could not bear this kind of judgment, it was a judgment that cast a shadow over her entire life.

'Could I please speak to the doctor?' Sara asked.

'He's busy,' the nurse said. 'Your gynecologist will explain things to you.' Her impassive face made it clear that she didn't want to discuss anything with Sara. She took Sara by the arm and led her back to the changing room. 'You can pay the bill at the desk before you leave,' she said.

Sara changed back into her street clothes and found her own way out to the waiting room. She smiled at Julia, spoke with the receptionist, and calmly left the office. Not until she was seated in Julia's red convertible did she burst into tears again.

'It was so humiliating,' she cried. 'It was so awful. *I* was so awful. Such a coward.'

'What happened, honey?' Julia asked. She started the car so the engine could warm them up as they sat.

Sara explained what had happened.

'Doctors can be such insensitive assholes,' Julia said. 'There should be a law: no man can put his head between a woman's legs without first introducing himself.'

Sara laughed. 'True. But I still feel at fault. I don't know why, but I got spooked. I suddenly got scared, started shaking, got all nervous –'

'I'd love to stick some metal up that guy's penis and see how calm he'd act,' Julia said.

Sara smiled. 'So would I, actually,' she said. She sat a moment, envisioning – the power of it, to be probing into someone's delicate sexual and reproductive organs. 'Julia,' she went on, 'do you think I'm not a *natural* woman?'

Julia burst out laughing. 'Yeah,' she said. 'I think you're synthetic.'

'No, really,' Sara pressed on. 'I haven't gotten pregnant easily, I can't even have an examination easily. Maybe I'm secretly frigid. Do you know even Queen Elizabeth gave birth in less than a year after her marriage?'

'What does Queen Elizabeth have to do with this?' Julia asked.

'I mean – she appears so proper, but –'

'Oh, honey, sexual passion and love have nothing to do with reproduction. Women get pregnant when they're raped by maniacs. The body is just so perverse. Everyone's is. You're a natural woman, for heaven's sake. I'll tell you what you are, though, that's hurting you, you're getting paranoid about all this. You're putting too much on yourself. Why are you doing all this cha-cha-ing around to the doctors? Why not just relax and enjoy yourself? You're young. You'll get pregnant eventually. Why not go off to some desert island this winter with your yummy husband and fuck your head off? I mean, I've heard the harder you try to get pregnant, the less it happens.'

'I've heard that, too,' Sara said. 'Perhaps you're right. I don't know. I know I'm not keen to see any other doctor for a while. Although Dr Crochett's nice enough.'

'Well, you ought to tell him about your experience at the clinic,' Julia said. 'That shithead shouldn't be allowed to get away with brutalizing women like that.'

'You're right. I'll tell Dr Crochett,' Sara said.

But she knew she wouldn't be able to do that. What if Dr Crochett and the laboratory doctor were best friends? Certainly they knew each other, Dr Crochett had sent her there. What if she complained and Dr Crochett talked to the lab doc and said that Sara was a recalcitrant patient? What if Dr Crochett decided there was no use treating her, since she freaked out at the slightest operation?

Sara leaned her head against the car window and closed her eyes. Suddenly she was overcome with exhaustion. It was all so complicated, this trying to get pregnant – all so *unnecessarily* complicated! Her anger made her feel weighted down, the situation made her feel helpless. She wanted to sleep.

'I'll get you to the airport,' Julia said now. 'We'll have some coffee while we wait for your plane.' Without waiting for a reply, she put the car into gear and pulled away.

Steve met her at the Nantucket airport. During the flight Sara had decided how much – or how little – she would tell Steve about her experience. She wanted so desperately for her getting pregnant to be a joyous occasion, an event of love and delight. She did not want to drag it down with dreary tales. She did not want to appear dreary to her husband – it would be too much for any man to have to bear, to have a wife who was not only infertile but also cowardly and gloomy.

And, at the sight of her husband, her spirits lifted. Oh, she loved him so much! And it was such good luck that they had found each other in this world, such good luck to have every day with each other. Steve crossed the small airport waiting room in three strides and encompassed her in a bear hug. He smelled of fresh air and sawdust and sweat. He was delicious, he was wonderful, he loved her, she was safely home in his arms, everything was possible.

As Steve drove her back to their house, she chattered about Julia and her escapades, and Donald James's gossip, and gave him only a superficial and cheered-up version of her visit to the lab.

'So what happens next?' Steve asked. 'I mean, if you've got one tube blocked?'

'I don't know,' Sara answered. 'I have to talk to Dr Crochett. He did tell me that twenty percent of all women who have this procedure get pregnant that month. It's supposed to be therapeutic as well as diagnostic.'

'Well,' Steve said, and took Sara's hand. 'That's good news.' He looked at her and smiled. 'Thanks for doing all this stuff,' he said.

'Sure.' She smiled back.

It was Steve's lunch hour, and once at home they heated up a can of chili, covered it with grated cheese, and sat companionably together in the kitchen. They talked about their past day apart and Sara was in two worlds at once; part of her aware of the thick pad between her legs at this unusual time of the month; she was bleeding slightly from the morning's procedure. She didn't want to mention this to Steve; it wasn't the right sort of thing to discuss over a meal, and she didn't want to seem to be asking for pity. But she could not escape her awareness of it, of how her lower body felt, of all she had been through that morning, of the things she had left unsaid.

Steve leaned back in his chair. He studied Sara; she could tell something was up.

'Yesss?' she asked. Perhaps he was thinking of going to bed

right now. God, she hoped not, she really wouldn't enjoy it right now. But she knew that at least one tube was open . . .

Steve grinned. 'What would you think about going to New Orleans for the Super Bowl? It would be expensive, but how many times do you get to see the Patriots play in the Super Bowl? Several of the guys have been talking about going – I think it would be a lot of fun. What do you think?'

Sara looked across the table at her husband, who was tipped back in his chair, his arms stretched up so that his hands were crossed behind his head. He was wearing grubby old work jeans that were more brown than blue now and several plaid flannel shirts under a torn wool sweater. Through all the layers of clothing his healthy muscles and strong frame showed; his body looked as thick and hard and impermeable as steel. Like Superwoman, she could see through those clothes to the flat stomach, the tight muscles that lay under his hairy chest and abdomen.

'Oh, yes, the Super Bowl!' Sara said, and suddenly, to her suprise as much as Steve's, she was in a rage. 'Well, why not? Why not spend time and money to watch a bunch of men smashing into each other? You can't really hurt *men*, can you? Not where it counts. Their private parts will be protected, you can count on it. No matter how they bash each other around, they'll still be able to make babies. No one's going to fool with their penises!'

Steve looked at Sara as if she had just lost her mind.

'Sara,' he said with concern, 'what are you talking about?'

Sara looked at her husband in dismay. What *had* she been talking about? She lowered her head into her hands, hiding her face, which contorted now as she began to cry. Steve rose, came around behind her chair, put his hands on her shoulders.

'Sara?' he asked.

'Oh, Steve,' she sobbed, 'it was so awful. It was frightening and humiliating and unpleasant and you talk about the Super Bowl.'

Steve tried to embrace her, but she remained rigid, crying into her hands.

'I didn't know,' he said. 'I didn't know. You didn't tell me. You seemed okay.'

'Well I am *okay*,' Sara said. 'And it wasn't anything *drastic*, it wasn't *that* bad. And I had to do it, all by myself, I had to lie there with a strange man doing things to my . . . and you weren't even thinking of me, you were out in the fresh air, building houses, talking to your friends about the goddamned Super Bowl!'

'Well of course I was thinking about you,' Steve said. 'Sara, of course I thought about you this morning. You know that. But you sounded fine when I spoke with you yesterday, and you told me before you went up that it was going to be a piece of cake. Those were your exact words, remember, "a piece of cake".'

'Well, I was wrong,' Sara said. 'And if you'd had any imagination, any *sensitivity* – I mean, I told you what they were going to do, I told you they were going to force dye through my Fallopian tubes. You might have thought about it a little, that it would be unpleasant for me, that it might hurt.'

'Well, I'm sorry,' Steve said, rubbing her back and shoulders. 'I didn't mean to be callous.'

'Oh, I know.' Sara sighed, wiping her tears with her hands. 'I know you didn't. And I'm sorry to blow up at you. I think I'm getting mad at you because of the way the two doctors treated me. They were so brusque and insensitive. They made me feel like – a piece of meat.'

'I'm sorry,' Steve said again. 'I wish I could have been there to help you.'

'And I wish, I really wish, that you had to bear just some of the bother of this!' Sara said. 'I think that if you just had to, oh, say, go have some strange woman handle your penis, look at it, stick something in it, decide whether it was a *good* penis or not, then you'd understand a little more.'

Steve's hands stopped caressing her back. Sara could feel how startled he was at her words, how he had withdrawn from her, puzzled by her anger.

'Well, Sara, it's not my fault that the human reproductive system is the way it is,' Steve said. He crossed back to his chair and sat down. His expression was bleak.

He thinks that what I've just said to him is horrible, Sara thought. She felt she had overstepped some boundary in their marriage. She felt he would never understand how it was for her, that no man could ever understand how it was for women. There he sat with his intact and solid body, insulted by the mere thought of someone messing around with *his* reproductive organ.

She felt that the gap between men and women was so huge that she would never have the energy to imagine crossing it again. Often she had thought of herself and Steve as one. But now she knew that was only a foolish illusion.

'I've got to get back to work,' Steve said, breaking into her thoughts.

'All right,' Sara said. 'I'll see you tonight.'

She sat at the table, head in her hands, while he put on his coat and cap and gloves. She did not raise her head for a good-bye kiss, and he did not come to kiss her but went wordlessly out the door, which he pulled shut firmly behind him.

'Oh, honey,' Ellie said. 'Oh, sweetie.'

Even though it was the middle of the day, and prime-time rates were in effect, Sara had dialed her sister when she heard Steve pull away in their Jeep. She needed desperately to talk. She told Ellie about the procedure and then about how oddly she had reacted, first trying to persuade Steve that everything had been easy and fine, and then, to her consternation, lashing out at him for what wasn't his fault.

'I think I'm going nuts,' Sara said. 'I'm certainly acting nutty. But, Ellie, sometimes I feel that I'm ready to *explode*. I can't seem to get control over anything. Everything in my life seems so *stuck*. I can't get pregnant, and I can't get this infuriating Fanny Anderson to even talk to me on the phone. I can't get anything to work for me. My life is just stalled.'

'Now look,' Ellie said, 'you're getting everything confused. This book business has nothing to do with getting pregnant. They are both frustrating problems, but they are not related. You're making yourself crazy connecting the two this way.'

'I know,' Sara said. 'I know.'

'Listen,' Ellie said, 'will you listen to me, please? I'm just a nurse, but I do know something about all this. Sara, we don't have any idea how much fertility or infertility is affected by stress. And you've put yourself under heavy-duty stress. Especially by thinking of your work and your body as the same sort of general thing, you're working yourself right into a kind of trap. You really have to relax.'

'Oh, Ellie,' Sara said, 'I know that. I've read that. I've heard that. But how do I *relax*? All I can think about is getting pregnant.'

'Well, let's consider the possibilities. First of all, you're only thirty-four. You've got a good eight years to get pregnant. You're healthy, Steve's healthy; you two have just gotten a late start, and it takes a little longer to get pregnant when you're older. I know you can't forget about it now that you want it so much. But perhaps you can think of some ways not to focus on it so much. When you were in your twenties, there was so much you wanted to do, enjoyed doing. You liked to travel, you liked to swim and ski and horseback ride . . . Why don't you and Steve take a vacation? Not a vacation to get pregnant, but one to enjoy yourselves. Doing things you really love to do.'

'We don't have a whole lot of money,' Sara began.

'My darling, you have more money now than you will after you have children, believe me,' Ellie said. 'You will get pregnant, you know, and the day will come when you'll wish you had the freedom you have now. When you'll be stuck at home with a sick kid and you'll wish you and Steve had done something slightly glamorous and exciting.'

'Well,' Sara agreed, 'we could use a vacation. We could use some time together *not* thinking about a baby. And I could use some time *not* waiting for Fanny Anderson to call.'

'Well, then,' Ellie said. 'Why not? Do something wonderful together, something you both would like. You might surprise yourself and get pregnant.'

'Oh, Ellie, what would I do without you?' Sara asked.

'I can't imagine,' Ellie said. 'You'd probably just have to be locked away somewhere.'

The sisters laughed. Ellie changed the subject, to tell Sara about a problem she was having with her supervisor. Sara forced herself to concentrate: *I've got to stop dwelling on my problems*, she told herself. *I've got to relax.*

When Steve came home that night, Sara had filled the house with the aroma of garlic and parsley as she made linguine with clam sauce, one of Steve's favorite meals. She felt shy when her husband came in the door, and she could tell by the way he looked at her, holding himself tensely, slightly wary, that he was shy, too. For one long moment she was unsure of herself. Then, 'Hi, sweetie,' she said, just at the moment that Steve said, 'Hi, sweetie,' and they grinned, amused at themselves, and in a flash were in each other's arms. All anger, all embarrassment disappeared, replaced by a wonderful mutual flow of comfort and content that rapidly brought on lust. They went to bed before they ate.

When they went back to bed later that night, they lay for a long time, holding each other and talking.

'Baby, baby, I didn't mean to upset you, I didn't mean to be insensitive,' Steve said. He held Sara nestled against him, and he softly massaged the back of her neck and head; it was a wonderfully soothing thing for him to do. Sara thought she would purr from it. 'There's just so much stuff I don't know about it all,' he said. 'And you seem so easy with it.'

Sara smiled into her husband's chest. *Now*, in this dark room, warmed and comforted by her husband's words and touch, the obsession faded, relaxed, so that she knew that what was real and good and important in her life was all here, all now, in this room, in this bed. Steve's touch, and his words, which she could feel spoken, his warm breath rustling her hair, made her feel cherished.

Sara wrapped her arms around Steve and snuggled close to him, chest and pelvis pressed against his, her head bent and nuzzling against his shoulder. Oh, *this* was what it was all about, this was what the world was about, this was what men and women were all about. Not just a sexual love, though that, of course, but this love that included it all: parent and child, brother and sister, man and wife, excitement and content. He was everything to her, and she was everything to him. She had forgotten this, and it was deeply sweet to remember.

The next day they made reservations on a super-saver flight to Jamaica. They would leave in two weeks and spend ten days there. Steve could easily take the time off from his job, for January and February were slow months for carpenters. And Sara wasn't editing another book yet. She decided to devote the two weeks to getting her body in shape for a bikini.

Five days before they left, while Sara was scrutinizing herself in the bedroom mirror, trying to decide if she really could walk around in front of strangers with so much flesh exposed, the phone rang.

'Hello, Sara? This is Fanny Anderson,' the soft lilting voice said.

Sara plopped down on the bed, amazed. She had not tried to reach the author for weeks. She had really given up hope.

'Oh, yes, how are you?' Sara asked.

'Oh, I'm well, thank you,' Fanny replied. 'I've been writing, and I think I'm just about through with my Jenny book. But I can see where it would be of great help to have an editor at this stage. And your letters have been so kind, and you do seem to understand just what I'm attempting here. I was wondering if perhaps you would like to come for a visit, in the near future, as you had suggested.'

Sara's heart jumped. She almost couldn't believe what she was hearing. 'Why, of course,' she said. 'I'd be glad to come anytime. I'm delighted.'

'Well, then,' Fanny said, 'when shall we schedule this?'

'Why I could come tomorrow,' Sara said. 'Or the next day or the day after that.'

There was a silence then, one so long and profound that Sara thought perhaps they had been disconnected.

'Hello?' Sara said. 'Hello?'

'I'm here,' Fanny said, her voice faint. 'Yes. All right. Do come tomorrow.'

CHAPTER SIX

It had been months since she had worn this suit, a sleekly cut chocolate-brown tweed, expensive, elegant, even glamorous. She was wearing an ivory silk blouse with lace jabot and cuffs and her killer boots, dark supple leather with heels so high she could never wear them on Nantucket's cobblestone streets. But she was in Boston now, in a taxi on the way to Fanny Anderson's house in Cambridge, her leather portfolio in her hand, and she felt better than she had in weeks. This was the moment she had been waiting for. Here the taxi was in front of the house. There were the wrought iron gates, the sinuous slate walk, the forbidding oak door.

If the housekeeper didn't let her in this time, she'd torch the place.

She had scarcely lifted the brass knocker when the door was opened by the vampire housekeeper.

'Mrs Kendall?' the woman said. 'Come in. May I take your coat? Mrs Anderson is waiting for you.'

Sara caught only a glimpse of the vast formal foyer – a large statue of Venus on a pedestal, a high Chinese vase full of reeds and grasses, an ornate mahogany staircase winding to the second floor – before the housekeeper escorted her into another room. Without saying another word, the woman pulled the door shut behind Sara and vanished.

For a moment Sara thought she was alone in the room, and was glad for this, because it would take a few moments for her eyes to adjust to the light. It was another dazzling winter day, cold and brilliant, but this room was as dark and hot as a tropical jungle. Rhomboids and diamonds of ruby and blue slanted from the stained-glass windows across the Oriental rugs that were layered over a thick carpet of deep turquoise pile. The other windows were covered with peacock blue velvet draperies that swagged and sloped heavily from the high windows to the floor, managing with their graceful weight to obscure more light than they let in. A wood fire flared and crackled from a vast blue-veined marble fireplace that ran across one wall of the room. Above the fireplace hung an oil painting of a nude woman, a breathtakingly beautiful nude woman. This painting was lighted by a small picture lamp just above it. The paneled walls were painted in a turquoise blue and were hung with oil paintings of beautiful women; the same beautiful woman, Sara realized. They had to be paintings of Fanny Anderson at different stages of her life, by different painters. Oh, Fanny Anderson had to be Jenny.

Sara took a step farther into the room. 'Hello?' she said. The room was very large, and all the blues in the dim light made it seem dusky, shadowy, mysterious. The flickering light of the fire helped her to make out shapes of furniture, deep sofas, great soft chairs, the gleaming brass of fireplace equipment, tables covered with books and china figurines.

'Hello?' she said again, and this time was answered by a deep bestial sound, a woof.

Then she realized that the sofas and chairs were occupied by several large and amiable-looking spaniels. A fat, long-haired white cat observed Sara lazily from a deep, velvet-cushioned window seat. Two other cats dozed by the hearth. There were at least six animals in the room.

But where was Fanny Anderson?

Sara advanced cautiously. Her eyes were becoming adjusted to the dim and fluttering light, and she was not quite so disoriented. A dog, almost as large as a deer but white with three large black spots, opened her mouth in a wide yawn, then folded herself back down and dozed off in a blue wing chair.

The housekeeper had said, 'Mrs Anderson is waiting for you.' But where?

Then, at the far wall of the room, a door opened and a woman entered.

'Mrs Kendall?' she said, and the lilt in her voice told Sara that at last she was to meet Fanny Anderson.

'Yes, I'm Sara Kendall. Hello,' Sara said, crossing the room, holding out her hand.

She's decorated this room to show off her eyes was Sara's first thought, for Fanny Anderson's eyes were a luminous turquoise blue. Sara's second thought was: *My God, how beautiful she is.*

Fanny Anderson was perhaps five foot eight, just a bit taller than Sara. She was wearing a deep blue mohair dress with a high neck, the long sleeves puffed gracefully at the top, the cut plain, simple, so that the soft material slid over her voluptuous body. Her heavy dark hair, streaked with white like whipped cream through chocolate, swooped low over one eye, then was swept back and coiled in an elaborate twist at the back of her head. She was wearing pearl earrings and a long string of pearls. Her perfume, something Sara did not recognize, gently drifted through the blue air.

She was somewhere in her fifties, Sara thought, for the telltale signs were there, the wrinkles around her eyes and along the jaw-line, the sag at the chin. No, she did not look young. But she was stunning all the same.

'I'm *so* glad to meet you,' Fanny Anderson said. 'You look just like Princess Di.'

'Oh, my!' Sara said, laughing. 'No one has ever told me that before! It must be my haircut.'

'No, but really,' Fanny said, her voice seductive, her head cocked slightly to one side as she studied Sara, 'really there is a resemblance. The same golden hair, and your aristocratic carriage – and the enchanting surprise of a sweet smile. Really very much like Princess Di.'

'Well,' Sara said, flustered, not sure how to deal with such a barrage of compliments, 'I believe I'm carrying a little more weight than Princess Di.'

'Ah, yes, she has gotten so scrawny, hasn't she,' Fanny Anderson said. 'It's a pity. So unfeminine. You're right not to let yourself get that way. You look so much more luscious.'

'Thank you,' Sara said, smiling, completely confused. She had never been complimented so extravagantly and outrageously before. Why was the woman doing this? In a flash, Sara realized that the woman wanted to be flattered just as excessively. No doubt she was used to it and thought that just in case her guest didn't have the sense to begin their association in just such pleasant way, she would take the lead.

'Coming from you, this is true praise indeed,' Sara said, sincerely, 'since you are so remarkably beautiful. It must be wonderful to be so beautiful.' She paused, then, still going on intuition, she said, 'You know, I have to say this – now that I see you, I know you must be Jenny.'

To her surprise, a shadow of displeasure fell across the woman's face. She turned aside. 'Oh, no, my dear, oh, my, no,' Fanny Anderson said. 'No, I'm not Jenny. How could you think that? Jenny is young, you know, I am old.'

'But eventually Jenny must have gotten old, too. I mean, what are her choices? One either must get old – or die!' Sara said, smiling, trying for a light note, glib in her confusion.

Fanny Anderson gave Sara a long look. 'Perhaps in her case one is the other,' she said.

'What?' Sara asked, startled.

Fanny reached out to a table and adjusted the angle of a porcelain bowl, turning her back to Sara as she did so. 'That's exactly the problem, isn't it?' she said, her voice so low that Sara could scarcely hear her. She drifted slowly back toward the door at the far end of the room, touching the back of a chair, straightening a picture. 'The end of Jenny's life,' she said, talking to herself more than to Sara. 'I can't seem to get it right.'

I'm losing her! Sara thought in a panic. *She's going to waft right out of this room!*

'But that's the wonderful thing about *fiction*,' Sara said. 'You can rewrite it and rewrite it until it satisfies you. *You* have control.' When the woman did not turn back, Sara continued, 'Unlike real life, which can be so obstinately uncooperative.'

She had said the right thing. Fanny looked back at Sara, studied her face in silence, moved just a few inches toward her.

'Someone as young and lovely as you can't have found life to be "obstinately uncooperative"?' she said, her voice challenging.

'Oh, but I have,' Sara told her. She dropped her eyes. How much would she tell this woman? Her own personal despair washed over her briefly and she shook herself. She must be professional. 'I have,' she repeated.

'Let's have some tea,' Fanny said. Her voice was warm now, and she moved quickly across the room. 'Please,' she said, indicating a sofa. 'Sit down.'

Sara settled into one of the two fat curving deep sofas that faced each other in front of the fireplace. On a low table between the two sofas were pens and pencils, clean lined paper, and a manuscript. *So she was planning to work today*, Sara thought. Still she was cautious, and felt as if she were on trial. There was a maze the writer wanted her to find her way through in order to gain admission to her confidence. Sara sat quietly, waiting, when she really wanted to grab the manuscript and see what the rest of the Jenny pages held.

Fanny rang a small silver bell and immediately the woman in brown opened the living room door.

'Yes, madam?' she asked, her face expressionless.

So she is the housekeeper, Sara thought. *She is only the housekeeper, not a lover or a jailer.*

'We'll take our tea in here, Eloise,' Fanny said. 'Thank you, dear.'

Sara hid a smile. Well, perhaps the woman was a housekeeper and a lover, or a friend. There were all kinds of strange relationships in the world.

Eloise returned at once with the tea cart, which held a sterling silver tea service and a silver platter full of delicate pastries full of cheese or chocolate or fruit. She wheeled the cart to the sofas in front of the fire, then quietly left, closing the door behind her. The room came alive then with interested animals who stretched and loped or slunk across the room to gather close to their mistress, staring with adoring and imploring eyes.

'You have such lovely animals,' Sara said.

'Oh, yes, I know,' Fanny agreed. 'They are such a joy. Such a constant pleasure. And so nonjudgmental.' She leaned forward to stroke the fat white cat, who arched her back to receive the caress. Fanny looked up at Sara. 'Isn't she a beauty? And do you know, she is thirteen years old. It is amazing, isn't it? Really, I have so often thought that life would be immeasurably happier for human beings if they only had fur.'

Sara stared at her hostess, smiling politely, thinking, *Now what do I say to that?* It was obvious from the temperature of the room that Fanny liked to be warm; fur would keep one warm.

'Then, you see,' Fanny went on, 'our age wouldn't show. Our wrinkles and sags would be hidden. Not until we were *truly* old would we have physical signs of aging. We would be beautiful until we were simply too decrepit to move or eat or see. We would not have to go through any part of the humiliating, crippling metamorphosis we have to go through. We would not have to waste our time fighting it off, holding it back. We could have *years* more of love and pleasure.'

'Mmm, yes, I see,' Sara said. 'Then we wouldn't have to bother with makeup. When I think of the time I spend trying to camouflage shadows or wrinkles –' She knew she was only echoing her hostess's thoughts, but she wasn't quite sure what this conversation was about. More and more she was certain that Fanny and Jenny were intertwined and that if she wanted to publish the Jenny book, she had to win Fanny's trust.

Fanny poured tea as they talked, and put some pastries on Sara's plate. They spoke in low voices of the psychology and paraphernalia of beauty. In her lilting, beguiling voice, Fanny spoke about salons and treatments and potions from Europe. She was like a witch speaking of spells. Sara sipped the tea, listened, absent-mindedly stroking the silky back of a dog who had come to sit with his head on her knee. It was so warm in the room, the light so dim and flickering.

'I've been having trouble with my weight recently,' Sara said. Then, with a sense of release, she said it all. 'I'm eating from frustration, I think. You see, I've been trying to get pregnant for quite a while now, and it just isn't happening.'

'Aaah,' Fanny said. 'That is how you know about life's obstinate uncooperativeness.'

'Yes,' Sara said. 'Yes, I am learning that lesson well.'

'Have you seen a doctor about it?' Fanny asked.

Sara found she wanted to confide in Fanny. As she spoke, Fanny watched her carefully, with sympathy. From time to time she slipped bits of cheese or pastry to the various animals around her until finally they were satisfied and lay back down on the sofas or on the floor next to the two women, so that the air was filled with the sounds of firewood crackling and animals purring or snoring.

Sara gave herself over to her problem; she told everything, and she cried. It was when she felt the tears on her cheeks that she pulled herself together with a little shudder of embarrassment: what was she doing? This was no way to edit a book or gain a writer's trust in her intelligence!

'Excuse me,' she said, 'but I need to use a bathroom. I need to wash my face.'

'Of course, my dear,' Fanny said. She rang the silver bell and Eloise appeared immediately. 'Would you please show Sara to the powder room?' she asked.

Sara followed the housekeeper out of the blue room and into the central hall, which seemed blindingly bright by contrast. Beneath the winding stairs was tucked a half bath, all pink and gold and clean. Sara splashed cold water on her face and hands. She looked at her watch: she had been here almost two hours. What an extraordinary morning it was. She was not certain what even had happened in that warm blue room. She splashed more cold water on her face, then looked at herself in the mirror. *You are letting your obsession with getting pregnant ruin your life*, she said to herself, squinting meanly at her reflection. She took a deep breath and turned, determined to get the author back to the track of her novel.

But when she returned to the warm, large living room, she found her hostess standing back by the door at the far end of the room.

'I've gotten tired,' Fanny said. 'It's unfortunate, but I do tire so easily. I so seldom see people.'

'Oh!' Sara exclaimed, disappointed.

'Please,' Fanny said, holding out her hand. 'I want you to understand. This meeting was very important to me, and I want you to know that now I an convinced that you and I can work together on the Jenny novel. To be blunt, I like you, Sara. I think we are compatible. I would be grateful if you would take the manuscript – the one there, on the table – back to Nantucket with you and read it, and then come back here and talk with me about it. In depth.'

Sara stared at her, still uncertain. She was glad to hear what Fanny was saying, but she hated to be dismissed so soon.

'Please,' Fanny said. 'Take the manuscript. And whenever you have finished reading it, come back to me. I promise you that whenever you want to, I will see you here. I will work with you. I promise you that. But I am very tired now. I must rest.'

There was nothing Sara could do but to cross the room and pick up the manuscript, then, cradling it as carefully as if it were a newborn child, she said good-bye to Fanny Anderson and left the room.

On the flight home from Kingston to Boston, Sara smiled most of the way. It had been a good vacation; it had been a time together that they needed. There had been no appointments to keep, no phone calls from bosses or friends, no mail. It had been sunny and hot and easy, and they had made love, ridden bikes, made love, gone scuba diving, and swimming, made love, drunk technicolor alcoholic drinks. And they had talked, about what they wanted in life, what they hoped the future would hold – and then, as if they had never spoken of all this before, of their pasts, of family crises and high school embarrassments and college triumphs. All these words had looped and laced through the invisible web of their marriage, making it stronger and more elaborate.

And then, Sara had met Morris Newhouse.

Thank God she had met Morris Newhouse. Now she didn't feel so freakish and alone.

She had noticed the couple the very first morning at the hotel. Or rather, she had noticed the woman. The husband had been rather anonymous-looking, slight and tidy in a perfectly groomed, expensively dressed way. He was of the type she and Steve called 'the brown men', men with brown hair and eyes and suits and attaché cases who worked in New York at important but unexciting jobs.

But his wife was something else. She was almost six feet tall and exquisitely slender, with fine long bones. Her thick black hair was pulled back off her face into a high ponytail; on her this teenage hairdo looked sophisticated. She needed no makeup on her olive skin; she tanned beautifully. And her eyes were large and slanted, a startling dark brown. She was exotic-looking and elegant beyond words. Heads turned when she walked by. Later, when Mary saw the woman come down to the beach in her white string bikini, she said to Steve, 'That's not fair.' For the woman's body made a Barbie doll look like a Russian peasant.

Sara had no desire to get to know this gorgeous creature and secretly told herself the woman must be dumb, or mean, or something. But the two couples kept running into each other on the beach, in the hotel lobby, at the marketplace, and out of politeness they always smiled and said hello. The third night there, the four of them entered the hotel bar at the same time and ended up sitting together.

Kip and Morris Newhouse. Kip was a partner in a large investment and stockbroking firm in New York. He was as stuffy as he looked, but as they got to know him, they realized that he was also intelligent and kind. Morris was a potter — sometimes. She hadn't worked for the past five years, not since they'd had their babies. She showed Sara and Steve pictures of their five-year-old son and three-year-old daughter, lovely storybook children. This was the first time the Newhouses had been away, alone together, without the children. They missed them.

Oh, God, Sara thought, oh, God, of course this perfect woman would have perfect children. That night she was still hoping not to start her period, but her stomach was bloated and her breasts were sore and she was easily irritable: she wanted to scream at this beautiful woman, she wanted to throw her drink in her wonderful face.

For the rest of their stay, Sara tried to avoid the couple,

especially after she started her period. She just didn't think she could bear it.

But on the seventh day there, Steve wanted to try deep-sea fishing and Sara, uncomfortable and soggy with her period, wasn't interested. Somehow, in the easy way things are often done on vacation, it was decided that Steve and Kip would go on the fishing trip while Sara and Morris lay on the beach and sunned themselves.

And on the beach, Morris and Sara began to talk. Sara confided that she was having her period, and it always made her grumpy, and Morris said, 'Oh, God, I know. I always turn into a maniac when I get my period. And before I had my children – well, my periods used to make me nearly suicidal. It took me five years to get pregnant, you see.'

'Really?' Sara asked. She turned on her side and stared at Morris, who had suddenly, with her admission, transformed herself from a beautiful woman into a fascinating one. *Really?*

Sara confided her problem to Morris with grateful eagerness –for Morris was a stranger who did not judge her and who would probably never see her again. For her part, Morris seemed glad to relive her own difficulties before an appreciative audience, in the way a traveler likes to tell of an adventure he was forced to endure and came away from scarred but alive.

They had a late lunch and spent the afternoon near the hotel pool, under a striped umbrella, drinking Mai Tais and talking and laughing.

Morris had taken her temperature and kept a chart for fourteen months. During that time, she and her husband had to have sex on the eleventh, thirteenth, fifteenth, and seventeenth days, every month. It got so that they almost dreaded making love. Certainly it became a duty. Then, immediately after sex, Morris had to flip her bottom up in the air and manoeuver her body into a position much like the Yoga Plow, holding her hips up high and her legs stretched down so that her feet rested on either side of her head. She had to stay that way for twenty minutes. She tried to get Kip to talk to her, but he almost always fell asleep. Finally they moved a television into the room so she would have something to help her pass those twenty minutes. In the winter they liked the bedroom cold, but with her bottom in the air she couldn't manage to keep it covered and warm; if Kip pulled the covers up over her, it also smothered her because her bottom was so near her head. Both women collapsed with laughter – and Sara laughed aloud on the plane, just thinking of that elegant woman in such a position.

Morris had had to do another embarrassing and bizarre thing. Her doctor was an old-fashioned one who has started practicing during World War II. He held with old practices, but he did have a high record of success. So she had done what he told her; she had had him perform a culdoscopy. Drugged into a zombielike state, Morris had had to kneel on a table, with her head down against the table and her legs spread and her bottom high in the air so that the doctor could insert a culdoscope into her vagina and look through it into her abdominal cavity with magnifying mirrors to see if she had endometriosis. Afterward, it seemed to take forever for the drugs to wear off; she had been nauseated and spaced-out.

None of the procedures revealed anything. There seemed to be no reason for her infertility. She had a D & C, she took various drugs, and she did not get pregnant. Instead, she said, she 'got weird'. She began to hate every woman she knew who had a child. In department stores, in grocery stores, she would see a woman with a baby in a cart or in her arms and she would be filled with such anger, such hatred, that she would have to leave the store, leave her cart full of groceries, or risk hitting the woman – it was that bad, her fists would clench and she would want to hit, to *hurt* any woman who had a baby.

People kept telling her to 'relax'. This only made her more insane. At last she and Kip took a six-month trip around the world, which he could afford to do only by quitting his firm. But he did it; money was not their problem. She did not get pregnant.

They went back to New York, Kip joined a new firm and

worked hard, she worked hard as a potter. There was nothing else for them that could be done medically. There was no explanation. She was not resigned; she was still frantic and depressed and greedy for a child. And one month, and she had no idea why *that* month, she missed her period. After five years, she was pregnant.

Sara loved knowing all this, and that night in bed she had told Steve. It gave her such courage to know about Morris, to know all she had been through, and how even medical science had failed, and how, after all, she had gotten pregnant. It gave Sara hope. And it made her laugh, which was a real gift. The thought of Morris – elegant, exquisite Morris – spending night after night with her bottom above her head put things into a better perspective for her. Things did not seem quite so gloomy and impossible, after all.

Sara took comfort in the fact that she was not alone. She was, in fact, in good company.

She kept Morris in mind when she called Dr Crochett her first afternoon home. By now he had been able to see the results of her uterotubalgram.

'You've got one tube blocked, Sara,' he told her. 'I've seen the X rays; the dye came through the right side but not on the left.'

'I – um – I was disappointed with the doctor,' she said, feeling brave. 'He didn't stop to explain anything to me. And I wish he had gone ahead and done the procedure the third time. Perhaps that would have opened the tube. I wouldn't have minded the discomfort.'

'My dear Sara,' Dr Crochett said, 'if the doctor had put the dye through the third time, he would have had to use more force, and you would have experienced something much stronger than discomfort. No, he did what he could. Now it's time to schedule you for a laparoscopy. This is a procedure that requires day surgery in the hospital. I'll do a small incision in your abdomen, insert a laparoscope and look around to see if you have serious endometriosis. Find out what's blocking that tube of yours. If you do have endometriosis, I'll want to do a laparotomy; I'll open you up and clean you out. Then, of course, you'll have a longer hospital stay, probably about five days.'

'Good Lord,' Sara said. 'Does this require general anesthesia?'

'Yes,' the doctor replied. 'Which means some discomfort. And, of course, if you have the laparotomy, you'll have scars from the incision. But nothing you won't be able to hide under a bikini.'

'Oh,' Sara said. 'This seems like such a serious thing to do.'

'Well, you don't have to do it right away,' Dr Crochett said. 'No one is eager to have general anesthesia. You can wait as long as you want. You may not have endometriosis. But we've determined that your husband is okay, your mucus and his are compatible, you're ovulating, and you have one tube blocked. This seems like a reasonable next step. But we can do it whenever you want. Why don't you think about it? Talk with your husband about it. We can wait as long as you'd like.'

'Fine,' Sara said. 'I'll call you back.'

Steve was at work. The house was silent and bright with winter sun reflecting off layers of snow that glittered from lawns and along tree branches and rooftops. Sara sat thinking.

She had to admit it to herself: she was afraid of general anesthesia. She had heard too many horror stories; she was afraid she would die from it. Not wake up. Or have brain damage. The longer she sat thinking, the more frightened she got.

She knew she couldn't do it, not just yet. And really, why should she? Look at all that Morris had gone through, only to finally get pregnant for no real reason at all. And she wanted to edit Fanny Anderson's book, there was that, too, to be responsible for its seeing the light of day. If she went into the hospital, she couldn't work. If she went into the hospital and died – no. She just couldn't schedule it, not yet. She would give herself another month or two. Why not? Perhaps if she became truly engrossed with the Jenny book, so that she wasn't always thinking about getting pregnant, she would get pregnant. And it really would be better, from a financial point of view, if she edited another book or two and saved up some more money before she went into the expense of surgery and a hospital stay.

When Steve came home, she explained to him all that the doctor had said and explained her thoughts to him, including her feeling of fear.

'Well, let's wait, then, Sara,' he said. 'I don't want you to have to do anything you don't want to. I admit, if it were my body going under a knife, I'd hesitate, too. Let's give ourselves some more time. After all, we've got years ahead of us.'

'Oh, Steve, I do love you,' she said, and hugged him. She felt she had just been given a reprieve.

All right, body, she secretly said to herself, *I'm not going to subject you to surgery just yet. So why don't you get busy and cooperate and get pregnant and we won't have to do surgery at all?* She wondered if anyone else spoke to her body in quite the same way she had come to speak to hers, as if it were a willful and cunning and traitorous child.

Winter had hit the coast in earnest now. It was too dangerous to fly in the tiny planes that serviced Nantucket through the high winds and thick fogs or snow-laden clouds. Sara had no choice but to take the six-thirty ferry over to Hyannis, where she rented a car to drive to Cambridge.

Sitting on the ferry, Fanny's manuscript in her lap, Sara leaned her head against the window. Today the sea shimmered like a dream, with snow spiraling down onto the peaks of ice-blue waves and the wind whipping the flakes toward the window, then tossing them away in a flurry. That was the way Sara felt: spirited, energetic, swirling enthusiastically through time. Her energy was high.

She had agreed to edit another romance novel for Heartways House so that she would have additional money for the surgery. She had actively tried to become a more integral part of Steve's Nantucket group; just this week she had had the group, including The Virgin and her grumpy husband, over for a lasagna dinner followed by a boisterous game of Trivial Pursuit. She had made an appointment to talk to Donald James about Fanny Anderson's book.

And now she was going back to see Fanny. Fanny had kept her word. As soon as Sara had returned from Jamaica and done the work she needed on the Jenny pages, she had called Fanny, and Fanny had said, at once, 'Yes, dear, of course, come tomorrow.'

The final section of the Jenny novel began in London in the early seventies, back in a world full of men and champagne and dangerous parties. The first few pages were fine, although Sara noticed something that had not been included in the novel before: every time Fanny mentioned a new man that Jenny was involved with, she mentioned the man's age, and the men were all in their twenties. Sara made a mental note to ask Fanny about this. Undoubtedly she wanted to prove a point – that Jenny was so beautiful and exciting that she could attract men ten and twenty years younger than she. But it made the writing stilted: 'Jasper Kitteredge, who was only twenty-two, crossed the ballroom toward Jenny with the assurance and determination of a much older man' 'Jenny returned from her ride just as the Wharton's new guest was arriving. From the high back of the black thoroughbred jumper she looked down at Stephen Matte, who was twenty-four years old, just stepping out of his sleek low Aston-Martin.'

We'll have to do something about this, Sara thought. *Eventually*.

The end of the novel was surprisingly bleak.

One night at a dinner party, I looked around the elegant dining room table and realized that I had slept with every man seated there. I excused myself, saying I had a sudden headache, and left the room and the party. I knew I had to change my life, and I did, on the first opportunity offered to me. An American banker, fifteen years older than I, visiting London and not aware of my past, became smitten with me and asked me to marry him. I did not love him, but I was not certain of my capabilities for love any more. And he offered me the security I needed. So I went back with him to the United States, where he set me up in a fine old house in a fine old city. He provided me with every luxury, and we were compatible. It was not unpleasant. My husband worshiped me – but I was uncomfortable with this worship, which I knew was based on my looks, my fading, failing beauty. It was a relief when he died from a heart attack at the age of sixty. It was a relief to be left alone, with enough money to provide a secure hiding place, a place where I could remain comfortable and solitary, with no one to watch me age.

I had come a long way from the Kansas farm where my parents knelt and lifted and strained in the dirt in their ceaseless task of renewing the earth and its animals, a necessary ritual with the stately repetitions of a dance. Often I sit remembering that farm, those tasks, the people I loved (who are dead now), and I also remember that the only sound of appreciation for their performance was the heartless crack of applause when a thundercloud rolled its lightning overhead. And I remember that the only gold that was tossed to those slavish dancers was the gold of sunlight that fell like glittering coins through the well of the barn where it disappeared among the soiled straw, never to be touched, never to be picked up and carried off to buy them freedom. I had realized early in life that the gold in that place was only an illusion.

So I had done this much: I had escaped. I had freed myself from a repetitious drudgery, I had seen places in the world where real gold rimmed the plates and paintings and limbs of women. I have possessed real gold myself. I have been admired and adored by many – I had given happiness to many. I had loved and been loved. I judge my life to have been entirely satisfactory. I see years ahead during which I will be able to sit here alone, remembering the freedom, the gold, the far countries, the lovers and their gifts.

It is only sometimes, when the sunlight steals across my room to strike a spark against a prism in a chandelier so that the air trembles with the possibilities of more radiance than I had guessed at, when I feel just as I felt as a young girl, hearing the doves cry out in the barn as the sun sliced golden through the everyday air:

There must be more. But where?

But where?

Sara was not satisfied with the way the novel ended. When she was once again seated in the hot blue living room, with the assorted animals, whom she was coming to learn to know by name, snuffling and purring around her, and Fanny seated across from her in the embracing depths of the sofa, she at first spoke of other things, trying to find just the right moment to give Fanny her criticisms – hoping that the inscrutable and moody Fanny would not take offense. Once again the stoney-faced Eloise brought them a cart laden with delicacies and a sterling silver pot of smoky Lapsang Souchong tea. Once again Sara spoke first of herself: her meeting with Morris, her doctor's advice, her fear of surgery.

'Some women actually love being in the hospital, being fussed over and lifted and lowered and rearranged, but others, like you and me, hate it,' Fanny said. 'I think it's losing control we're afraid of.'

'I think it's *death* I'm afraid of!' Sara laughed. 'I have so much I want to do in this world, and the thought that one careless slip –' She couldn't continue.

'I know,' Fanny said. 'Really I do. And I sympathize. If it weren't for that fear, that a surgeon would have some fatal moment of stupidity, I'm sure I would have had several face-lifts by now. Not to mention having everything else lifted, too.' She laughed. 'But really, Sara, you know these things are safe. And it sounds as though you really need this procedure. Especially if you have one tube blocked. I think you should go ahead and do it. Soon. Really I do.'

Sara smiled at Fanny and raised her cup in a sort of toast and sipped her tea. *All right*, she thought to herself, *if you can tell me what to do with my body, I can certainly tell you what to do with your book!*

'All right,' she said, smiling but serious. 'I'll make the

appointment as soon as I get home. It shouldn't put me out of commission for too long. You know I'm longing to get this book to Donald James, and he's wild to see it.' She opened her notebook. It was difficult making out the print in the dim blue light of the room. 'Do you think we could have more lights on?' she asked.

'Oh, well, electric lights make everything so garish, I always think,' Fanny replied. 'It *is* daytime. I'm sure we've sufficient light to read by.'

This time there was no mistaking the will of iron cloaked in the lilting luscious voice. *For God's sake, what vanity!* Sara thought impatiently. *We'll both lose our eyesight just to keep it dark enough in here to hide her wrinkles.* But she smiled and said, 'Yes, you're right. This is fine.'

For a few moments Sara pretended to study her notes. Really she was searching for just the right words to say. If Fanny shied away from light on her face, how would she handle the harsh light of judgment on her book? At last Sara stared at the author. She took a deep breath.

'Is this a novel?' she asked.

Fanny, who now held the fat cat and was stroking it, looked up at Sara, startled. 'What do you mean?'

'I mean, is this *fiction*?' Sara pressed, her judgment making her bold.

'Why yes, my dear, I thought you understood that absolutely,' Fanny said. 'Of course it is fiction.'

'Then you must change it,' Sara said. 'You can't do this to your readers. You make us care so much about Jenny, you make us curious, you take us through her life, where so much happens, until we are longing for her to be happy, to be loved and to honestly give love back. You can't let her end up this way. You can't let the last relationship of her life be the sort of marriage you describe. And then such bitter loneliness.'

For a moment Fanny did not speak. Sara was silent, too, biting her tongue, refusing to take back what she had said.

'The requisite happy ending,' Fanny said at last, sighing.

'In this novel it is fitting,' Sara said.

'But it would not be true.'

'What "truths" do you care about, Fanny?' Sara asked. 'A novel is fiction, but it must contain truths. It must seem real. I can believe Jenny's life up to a point. She was a prisoner of her insecurities and her beauty, but she has been brave enough to get herself away from the farm and to other countries, she has had the courage to lead an interesting life. It isn't believable that she would settle at last for a loveless marriage and then loneliness. Don't you see? It's not real.'

'But it's very real,' Fanny insisted. 'Jenny has no choice, at last. She got old, you see.'

'But what is she at the end of the novel? Only about fifty years old!' Sara protested. 'Are you saying that once women turn fifty their lives are over? No men will love them? That's ridiculous! Steve will love me when I'm fifty, I'm sure of it. And I'll love him, even though he'll probably be bald and have a paunch. People might be attracted to each other at first because of looks, but real love isn't so superficial.'

Fanny smiled. 'You are so passionate about this,' she said.

'And another thing,' Sara pressed on. 'Her writing. All through her life she writes. In Mexico she wanted to be a writer, she even managed to get things published. In England she worked as an assistant on a fine magazine. She cared about writing, she was not just a beautiful face and body. What happened to that side of Jenny? I really can't imagine her, no matter how much money she has, just curling up in a hole forever. She would be so bored.'

Fanny ran her fingers across her forehead in a light, obscuring gesture. 'Yes,' she said softly. 'I do see that. I can do that for Jenny.'

'And friends!' Sara continued. 'After all these years, Fanny, Jenny should have some friends.'

'Then you've missed the point completely,' Fanny said, her face changing, her voice becoming harsh. 'Jenny never really had friends. She didn't know how to have friends –'

'Couldn't she make friends? *One* friend?'

Fanny rose, took up the poker, and fussed with the fire in what seemed to Sara an attempt to hide her agitation. At last she turned back. 'I have had trouble all along with the ending of this novel,' she said. 'I have felt like a fortune-teller who suddenly has lost the ability to see through the crystal ball. I've had sleepless nights about this, I assure you. Sara, I want to trust your instincts, but I cannot go against my own.'

Sara gave the writer time to collect herself. Fanny's hands were shaking slightly now, her mouth was working.

'Novels can be revised,' Sara said quietly. 'Even lives can suddenly, at the last hour, change.'

Fanny looked at Sara. 'Yes,' she said finally. 'Yes, that's true.' She sat down, took up her notebook and pen. 'Very well. Jenny can have her work, and that in turn can give her friends. That is plausible, isn't it. *True?*' Now she was almost smiling.

'Yes,' Sara answered, smiling back.

Fanny scribbled on her pad. She looked up at Sara and said, 'That's the difference between life and fiction, isn't it? Jenny can have whatever life I give her.'

After her meeting with Fanny Sara had run over to the CVS pharmacy in Harvard Square. She carried her purchase, hidden in a brown paper bag, as protectively as if it were jewels, back to Nantucket.

It was the meeting with Fanny that had given her the courage to do this. She understood Fanny's hesitation about meddling in something that should happen naturally. For Fanny it was writing; for Sara, it was getting pregnant. Part of Sara still believed that because she and Steve loved each other so much, and loved making love with each other so much, a natural and even inevitable consequence would be pregnancy. But perhaps the natural needed a little help – and that was just what she thought she had in her brown paper bag.

It helped that she had been in Cambridge today so that she could buy the item at a pharmacy where no one she knew would see. In December, when she had the prescription for prenatal vitamins filled on Nantucket, the little white-haired old lady behind the counter, the pharmacist's wife, had embarrassed Sara so terribly she had nearly fled from the store.

'How far along are you, dear?' she had asked, as she came

shuffling out from the back room with Sara's prescription vitamins.

Sara had stared at the woman, trying to decide what to say. At that moment, she heard the front door of the pharmacy open and close. She heard female voices. She did not turn to look. If that was part of the group, she would die on the spot!

'When is your baby due?' the old lady repeated, in the ringing tones of the slightly deaf.

'Oh, oh, I'm not pregnant,' Sara said. She threw the old lady a blinding smile, as if pregnancy were the last thing on her mind.

'But these are *prenatal* vitamins,' the old lady yelled. 'They're expensive! If you're not pregnant, you don't need such expensive vitamins.'

'Could I please have them?' Sara asked quietly, not smiling.

'Of course,' the old lady said, and exchanged the package for Sara's money. Sara hurried from the store, glancing quickly at the two women – she didn't know them, had never seen them before, thank heavens.

But this item she had bought in the blissful anonymity of Harvard Square. No one knew she had it, not even Steve. Well, Ellie knew, for she had recommended it. And Sara felt good about it – felt smug. Here was the combination of science and magic she had been wishing for.

CHAPTER SEVEN

Seven o'clock in the morning.

Again.

Sara had been waking up at seven o'clock every single day for centuries, it seemed.

Steve moaned and turned on his side, pulled most of the covers with him. Sara reached for the thermometer and put it in her mouth. The five minutes took forever to pass. There was something urgent she needed to do.

At last she rose from the bed, slipped the thermometer into its blue case, pulled on her robe, and hurried into the bathroom, putting the thermometer on her plexiglass table next to the accompanying chart and pen.

And there was the kit in all its blue-and-white plastic glory.

Usually the little table held crystal decanters full of pastel bath oils, Royal Doulton china dishes full of scalloped soaps, perfumes, dusting powders, body lotions. All that had been pushed aside, jumbled up in a corner to make room for her new treasures: the thermometer, and now this kit.

It was an ovulation-indicator kit. Ellie had called to tell her about it. The thermometer, Ellie had said, only told a woman when she *had* ovulated. This kit would tell a woman just before she ovulated that she was going to, so there wasn't the chance of missing the day as there was with the thermometer.

She had been using the kit for several days now. She had the routine down pat. She took the small plastic cup and crouched over it, urinating, grinning as she did so, thinking to herself: *I'm mad, I'm mad, I'm the mad scientist.* She set the cup on the table and hurriedly washed her hands.

With a clean medicine dropper, she took some of the urine from the cup and put it into a tiny tube already containing a clear liquid. Then she had to wait for fifteen minutes. She looked at her watch. It was ten minutes after seven. She had to time this portion of the test very carefully.

While she waited, she noted her temperature – the same as the day before – and marked its spot on the temperature chart. She was beginning to see the black line that recorded her temperature as an endless repetitive road to nowhere. For five months now it had jigged and jagged along, rising when she ovulated, only to plunge when she started her period. If she was to get pregnant, the temperature would stay high, would not take that dreadful fall that carried her emotions with it. Ellie had reassured Sara that she should take great comfort from the chart: it proved that she was ovulating regularly, that her system was functioning nicely.

'But not nicely enough!' Sara had replied.

Today was the fifteenth day of her cycle. Today her temperature should have risen, but it hadn't. What did that mean? Sara sat on the carpeted bathroom floor and leaned back against the tiled wall, closing her eyes for a moment. The ovulation-indicator kit said that the day she ovulated her urine specimen would turn bright blue and that the change on that day from the color on previous days would be the most extreme. She kept the color of her tests, rated from one to six, on another chart. So far, each day for the past four days, her urine had remained a frustratingly clear color that scarcely deserved a one on the chart.

'Oh, body,' Sara said aloud, 'come on!'

She looked at her watch. Ten more minutes to wait. She raced out to get the letter she'd received from Julia yesterday, and brought it back with her to the bathroom. Eight minutes left. She sat down on the floor, leaned against the wall.

'At last!' Julia had written in her fat loping scrawl. 'I've found it! The advice you've been waiting for! Oh, what would you do without me? I really can't imagine. Now it's up to you to find a spell for me to use to get Perry away from his clam-trap wife!'

Paper-clipped to the note was a Xeroxed page from a book devoted completely to ancient reproductive rituals. Sara checked her watch. Five minutes to wait. She read.

Whether or not the woman was fertile could be tested; for example, by watering corn with her urine. If it grew she was not barren. If it did not, a variety of remedies were at hand to increase her fecundity. Sea holly was recommended by Elizabeth Okeover; nutmeg would 'help conception and strengthen nature', asserted Miss Springatt; sitting over hot fumes of catmint was suggested by several authors. Anything that warmed and invigorated such as brandy and hot baths found favour. Nicholas Culpeper, self-proclaimed student in physick and astrology, provided in his *Directory for Midwives* (1656) typically elaborate instructions on how to aid conception. In addition to good diet and exercise he recommended wearing amulets such as a lodestone or the heart of a quail; drinking potions of eringo, peony and satyrion; eating 'fruitful' creatures such as crabs, lobsters and prawns; and consuming concoctions of the dried and powdered wombs of hares, the brains of sparrows and the pizzles of wolves.

'Darling, I'm combing the stores of Boston to find you some hare wombs and wolf pizzle!' Julia had scribbled on the bottom of the note.

If she finds it, I'll use it! Sara thought. And why not. Here she was, sitting on the bathroom floor in her robe. She hadn't combed her hair or brushed her teeth. She had taken her temperature and peed into a plastic cup. She felt like some superstitious primitive native waiting for a cloud to pass over a mountain, giving her a sign. And she wanted a baby so much she would go to a witch doctor or drink pizzle of wolf – she would do anything!

The time was up. Sara rose, took a tiny plastic stick and dipped it into the tube holding her urine and the solution. Now she had to wait five minutes more. She brushed her teeth and combed her hair. Now she looked civilized even if she was acting like a heathen.

According to the instructions, she had to rinse the dipstick under cold water to the count of ten, then put it in yet another little tube of another solution and swivel it back and forth. She did this, almost holding her breath as she concentrated.

When she put her stick into the tube and stirred, the solution turned a beautiful bright turquoise blue. In one day the color had dramatically jumped from one on the chart to six. This was the day she was ovulating!

She hurried into her bedroom. Steve was up, standing near the dresser. He had his jeans on and was pulling a T-shirt on over his head. Sara went to him and put her arms around him.

'Good morning,' he said, head coming out through the neck of the shirt.

'Take off that shirt,' Sara said. 'Take off your clothes. Get back in bed.'

In March, the weather settled down. Way down. The swirling white energy of winter whisked back up into the heavens and hid behind a thick cloud of gray that hung over the island and coast for days at a time, dimming the sun, coating the air with a gray monotone as gloomy and dispiriting at the soiled slush that still edged the streets.

Sara had never been happier. Her instincts had been right: Donald James had read the first half of the Jenny novel and called her the moment he had finished the last word. He wanted it. He wanted to come out with it in January and to do all sorts of publicity that writers would usually beg for. This set off a chain of work for Sara – just the sort of work she loved. She went to Boston to meet with Fanny Anderson's agent, Clayton Hughes, and was not surprised to find that Clayton had never met Fanny in person but had always spoken with her on the phone. Donald James offered Fanny a good advance for the book and offered Sara a good fee to edit it. Now she could afford the laparoscopy, but couldn't imagine where she would find the time to take three weeks or three days out of her life. She was doing what she felt she had been born to do.

She spoke with Fanny daily on the phone, and traveled to Boston to work with her for two days a week. To save on traveling time, she spent nights in Boston with Julia; they went out to dinner and sat up late discussing the eccentricities of life over brandy or Bailey's. Clayton Hughes called Sara with the news that the British rights to the Jenny novel had been sold for a wonderful sum. Sara tried to get Fanny to go out to dinner to celebrate, but Fanny steadfastly refused to leave the house. So Sara brought champagne, which they drank from platinum-rimmed crystal in the hot blue shadowy living room.

The novel was to be called, simply, *Jenny's Book*. Fanny could not bring herself to let Jenny end up living happily with a man she loved, but she did give Jenny a job with a literary review in Boston, which in turn gave her prestige and colleagues and friends. At the end of the novel, Jenny lived by herself but led an active life in Boston's intellectual world, going to book publication parties and gallery openings and concerts and ballets. Her friends were poets and critics and artists and professors. This was the life she had escaped Kansas for so long ago.

Sara was pleased with the way the book ended. She sat with the pages of the manuscript in her hand, feeling a sense of pride in what she had helped Fanny to do. Her period had started and she held on to the manuscript and stared into space, wishing that life could be revised as easily as a book.

Steve's parents moved back to their Nantucket house from Florida at the end of April, and came to dinner at Sara and Steve's the night after they arrived.

It was warm enough that they had opened the windows, and the fragrant spring air wafted through the house, slipping past the curtains, puffing at the candle flame. Sara had served a leg of lamb with garlic, and asparagus, and fresh raspberries for desert, and the four sat content around the dining room table, idly gossiping over their liqueurs. Caroline admired the needlepoint pillow Sara had finally finished and offered to help Sara make a set of needlepoint covers for the dining room chairs — if Sara didn't think it was too intrusive of her. They spoke of patterns, colors, materials, and Sara snuggled her chin into her hand, leaning her elbow on the table, relaxed, wishing she could have shared the same kind of moment with her own mother. Then Caroline changed the subject, and for Sara it was as if the older woman had abruptly pulled a gun and shot her in the stomach.

'What am I saying?' Caroline said. 'Sofa pillows! I'll have so much sewing to do in the next few months. Erica Evans's daughter is pregnant, and I promised to knit a blanket and a layette for the baby. And you know – Steve, did you know? The Anderson girl is pregnant!'

'Donna Anderson?' Steve asked. 'Are you sure? She just got married last month.'

Caroline laughed. 'Well, newlyweds,' she said. 'Yes, I saw her on Main Street today. The baby is due exactly nine months from their wedding date.' She turned back to Sara. 'Donna Anderson was Steve's first girlfriend. Or the first *I* knew about. When he was thirteen. Lovely girl.'

'Yeah, lovely, and thick as a brick,' Steve grinned.

'Well, she'll make a wonderful mother, she's got such a calm way about her,' Caroline went on. 'And more than half of our friends in Florida have become grandparents this year, or are about to be.'

'Caroline, my love, you are as subtle as a tank,' Clark said, leaning back in his chair and laughing.

'Why, what do you mean?' Caroline asked, eyes wide, all innocence.

Steve was laughing, too. 'Mother's forte,' he said to Sara. 'The indirect approach. I think she learned it from the Chinese torture experts.'

'Oh, Stevie, how can you say such things?' Caroline said, affecting pique but enjoying her son's teasing.

'Look, Mom,' Steve said. 'Sara and I want to have children. And we will, someday. But right now we're doing exactly what we want to do, Sara's busy editing a great new book, and there's a lot of work I want to do on the house before we even think of having children.'

'Well, that's good to know,' Clark said, his voice booming. 'I have to confess I'm eager to have a grandchild.'

'Yes, dear, and you know it isn't good to wait *too* long,'

Caroline said. 'You know, the older women get, the more difficulty there is in the entire childbirth business, the more likely birth defects are. Why, a friend of ours in Florida has a daughter who waited until she was thirty-five to start her family, and she had one miscarriage after another and then carried a baby nine months only to have it stillborn. So many older mothers have Down's syndrome babies.'

Sara looked across the table at Steve. *Read my mind*, she thought. *If you don't get your mother to shut up I will rise from the table like the Devil Incarnate and spit fire at you all.*

'Okay, Mom, okay.' Steve laughed, holding up his hands. 'Let's change the subject to something cheerful like traveling to Europe.'

'Traveling to Europe! My goodness, who would want to do that these days? With all the terrorists and bombs!' Caroline said.

Steve and Clark burst out laughing.

Sara rose to clear the table. She took her time in the kitchen, rinsing and stacking the dishes. Trying to regain some composure.

Oh, I didn't know, she thought. *I should have guessed, but I didn't know for sure. How much they both want grandchildren. How much it means to them.*

She was so grateful to Steve for not mentioning the problem they were having conceiving; she knew she could not bear their pity, their concern – their scrutiny. She could not bear to have his parents think she was a failure, a defective woman, to wish Steve had married some other woman, the dumb productive Donna. My God, why was it that all Steve's old girlfriends got pregnant as easily as rabbits?

'Sara?' Steve called. 'Do you want some help?'

She realized she had been hiding in the kitchen too long. 'No, no, I'll be right there,' she called.

It took all her strength to pull her mouth out of the downward curve it had been tugged into by her despair. More and more she felt on the verge of losing control. Sometimes she was afraid she would do something violent and dreadful.

She knew she would start her period again tomorrow. In

spite of the ovulation test. The sides of her breasts were heavy. She had stained a little. She had cramps. And she was pre-menstrually nutty. And now, and now she felt that the burden of her in-laws' desires had been injected into her like a gas that was pushing against her skin, her rib cage, her brain, causing such an excruciating pressure that she wanted to scream from it. *I can't bear it anymore!* she cried silently.

But she closed the dishwasher door, and turned off the hot water, and dried her hands and went back into the dining room to chat with her family.

That night, when she crawled into bed with Steve, she snuggled up next to him and stroked his arm. 'Thanks,' she said. 'Thanks a lot. For protecting me tonight.'

'Huh?' Steve said. 'What are you talking about?'

Their eyes met.

'I mean with your parents. For protecting me from – from their knowing that I'm having trouble getting pregnant. I don't think I could stand it if they knew.'

'Oh, Sara,' Steve sighed, and she could tell he was almost exasperated. 'I wasn't *protecting* you. That didn't even enter my mind. I just said what I meant, what I think, that we want children, and we'll have them sooner or later. That's the truth.'

'*Maybe*,' Sara said. 'Oh, Steve, I'm sure I'm going to start my period again. I'm sure I'm not pregnant again.'

'Well, that's all right,' Steve said. 'I've said it before, we've got lots of time to try.'

'Steve,' Sara said, pulling away from him in order to get a clearer look at his face, 'be truthful. Aren't you upset about this? I mean that I'm not getting pregnant after all these months? Aren't you secretly upset?'

'No,' Steve said. 'I'm not.'

'Oh, come on,' Sara said, pulling up to lean on one elbow, almost angry. 'Don't pull this macho stuff on me. It makes me feel awful, Steve, it makes me feel that I can't express all my sorrow to you because that forces you to play the optimist and keep your sorrow hidden in yourself.'

'Sara, I don't have any sorrow, for Christ's sake,' Steve said. He looked up at the ceiling, his jaw clenching the way it did when he was angry.

'None?' Sara pressed. 'None at all?'

'None at all. I've told you time after time. I love you, I love our life, if we have children, fine, and if we don't, fine. I'm sure we will have children, in time, I don't see what the rush is. I don't see why you get so upset and dramatic about it all.'

Sara lay on her back and stared at the ceiling, too.

'Men and women are so different,' she said, sighing.

'Yeah, well, it's a good thing,' Steve said, and turned toward her, grinning now. He began to unbutton her nightgown.

Sara wrapped her arms around him and kissed him. But she was thinking: *How can he do this? How can he be so untouched? How can he go from anger to sex in a second? I thought we were as close as two people could be, I thought we were practically one person. Oh, I've heard that crises often pull couples apart, oh, God, I don't want to lose what I have with him –*

Then her body interrupted her. *Shut up*, it told her. *Stop thinking. Enjoy what you can have with him right now, right now . . .*

And she obeyed.

Now Walpole and James had the finished plans of *Jenny's Book*, which was scheduled to go to the typesetter's in June. There was no business reason for Sara to go to Boston to visit Fanny, but she had become close to the woman and called her often, almost daily, to chat, and traveled up to spend the day with her every other week or so. It was soothing to sit in the dusky blue room where cats purred and dogs groaned in their sleep and the grisly Eloise wheeled in the tea cart laden with gourmet delights, then slipped, ghostlike, away.

Even when the weather grew warm and Sara found vases of daffodils, iris, tulips, here and there around the living room, the heavy peacock blue draperies were still kept closed to admit the least possible yellow spring light. In May a large embroidered floral tapestry on a dark wooden screen was placed in front of the fireplace, indicating that there was no more need for a fire, the season had changed. The flowers, the screen, brought a touch of reality to the room, which Sara began to feel was otherwise unconnected to the harsh outer world. She had a sense of being protected when she was in this room, of being able to *rest*, to drop her guard, to forget for just a while all her hopes and fears.

They talked about everything. Without ever actually announcing it, Fanny finally let it be understood that her life and Jenny's were the same. So they were able to talk about failed desires and unachieved longings, about old lovers, about moments of triumph and moments of despair.

Sara's period started again at the end of May. She had thought it would; there had been all the signs. Still, when she awoke on the morning of the twenty-ninth day to find that scarlet savagery of blood, she was wild with grief. Needing desperately to escape the house, where she could spend the day weeping, she called Fanny and asked if she could come to see her that day. Fanny said yes, and Sara was able to catch a plane and be at the writer's house by eleven.

She arrived to find that Fanny had asked Eloise to prepare a special little brunch to cheer her up. There were hot flaky croissants filled with chocolate or strawberry jam or cheese waiting on silver plates, bowls of fresh fruit, covered dishes of bacon and sausages and ham. And Fanny had asked Eloise to make ice drinks, which the housekeeper brought in tall crystal glasses with long silver spoons for stirring.

The drinks were Bloody Marys.

Sara sank down on the sofa and looked at the drink in her hand. She looked up at Fanny, questioning.

'Is something wrong?' Fanny asked. Then she exclaimed, 'Oh, my dear! How could I have been so stupid? Lord, Lord. Oh, Sara, I am so sorry, I didn't *think*. Or, rather, I did think, I was trying so hard to be helpful. When you called this morning and were so upset, I said to myself, now I must have something nice and delicious and *alcoholic* for Sara when she gets here, something soothing. And I always think of Bloody Marys as the drink to serve before noon. Oh, dear me, oh, my. Sara, let me have Eloise get you something else – some champagne? Oh, I don't know, what else does one drink in the morning? Sara, please, forgive me.'

Sara shook her head and smiled at Fanny. 'Oh, it's all right, don't be upset,' she said. She looked at her drink, which was so weak and orangeish-looking, nothing at all like the thick purple-tinged blood that was flowing from her now. 'It was kind of you to have all this waiting. And I'm always hungry when I'm in my period, and if I ever needed a drink, now's the time.' She sipped her Bloody Mary, then smiled again at Fanny. 'It's delicious,' she said.

'I'm a fool,' Fanny said. 'I really am an idiot.'

'No, it's fine, really,' Sara protested. 'My friend Julia – I've mentioned her to you – would roar with laughter over this.' Wanting to put her hostess at ease, she sipped her drink again, and again, making little humming noises of pleasure. And the drink was excellent, spicy and tangy and satisfying. In no time she had finished it and started another. Fanny urged her to eat some of the food, and Sara ate, but even so, the alcohol relaxed her inhibitions and she became openly emotional.

'It's unbelievable how my life has changed,' Sara said. 'I used to be an optimistic person, a rational person, calm and kind. Now I'm absolutely self-centred. All I think about is becoming pregnant and how I'm failing. The slightest thing can send me spinning off into a fury or a depression – an ad for diapers on television, a woman pushing a carriage. My God, Fanny, last week, when I was sure I was going to get my period, I was coming out of a store and I *knew* there was a woman pushing a stroller right behind me, I knew she had a shopping bag in one hand and was having trouble maneuvering the stroller, and I went out the door and let it slam behind me, I didn't hold the door for her, I didn't help her get the stroller out. I think I even wanted to hurt the woman or the baby somehow, letting the door slam behind me that way. You see, I'm going mad, I really am!'

'Oh, my dear,' Fanny said.

'And now my in-laws are on the island, and I can scarcely bear to speak to them!' Sara said. 'Every single time we get together, there's a sort of expectant pause, they sit there waiting, almost holding their breaths, as if they're thinking: *Today* Steve and Sara will tell us that Sara's pregnant. And Caroline calls me every day with a news bulletin about some other friend whose daughter or daughter-in-law is pregnant, and sometimes after I hang up I just sit and weep with despair. I hate letting them down so much. I'm letting everyone down, I'm failing everyone!'

'You're not failing me,' Fanny said. 'I don't give a damn if you get pregnant or not. Oh, that sounded cruel, I suppose. What I mean is that I hope you get what you want, I hope you get pregnant because it obviously means so much to you. I want you to be happy. But I think of you not as a potential mother but as a fabulous editor – and a dear friend.'

'Oh, I know,' Sara said. 'I know, and that helps, it helps so much. That's why I wanted to come here today, *needed* to come here. Here, I am Sara the editor, the friend, not the miserable unsuccessful baby-making machine. More and more, Fanny, I dream of escaping, of leaving everyone I know and love, because I am so tired of failing them and I know they'd be better off without me. I dream of just going off somewhere – England, perhaps, I could probably get work there – and not telling anyone where I am, divorcing Steve, never seeing him again, never seeing anyone again, never inflicting my barren self on those I love.'

Fanny looked at Sara. Today her white-streaked chocolate-brown hair was parted in the middle and swooped up and back like wings from her face. She was wearing a long-sleeved high-necked dress of flowered blue silk, and pearls. She was elegant, but now her small pointed chin trembled. 'Yes,' she said, in her lilting voice, 'I understand exactly how you feel. You may count on that. But, Sara, you pay a heavy price for isolating yourself from those who know and love you. I know.'

'You know?' Sara snapped, emboldened by the alcohol. 'How can you know? You told me you never wanted to have children!'

Fanny smiled, her eyelids lowered over her enormous blue eyes. 'That's not the only way to fail people. There are other ways.'

'How have you failed people?' Sara asked, aggressively. It was as if she were not to be denied her supremacy of self-pity.

'By not staying beautiful. By growing old.' Fanny's voice was low now, and she looked down at her hands, where jeweled rings sparkled among the wrinkles.

'What?' Sara demanded. 'What are you saying? In the first place, you *are* beautiful. In the second place, it's not your fault that you're growing older. Everyone grows older. You can't blame yourself for that.'

'Yes, I can,' Fanny said. 'Every bit as much as you can blame yourself for not getting pregnant.'

'But you're wrong!' Sara cried. 'Don't you see? Growing old is natural! Not getting pregnant is not natural!'

'I've never thought that what was *natural* played a very large part in our twentieth-century society,' Fanny said.

'Oh, Fanny,' Sara said impatiently. 'No one is going to blame you for getting older. No one is going to stop loving you because you've gotten older.'

'Aren't they?' Fanny asked, and looked Sara directly in the eye. 'Do you really think that if I went to Paris the young men would want to paint me nude now? Do you really think that when old friends see me, they don't have pity in their faces? Can you actually look at the paintings on these walls and then look at me and tell me there isn't an enormous change, one that causes *everyone* to treat me differently than they did when I was young?'

'But *love* isn't based just on looks,' Sara persisted. 'People will still love you even if you look older.'

'Then people will still love you even if you can't conceive,' Fanny replied.

Sara looked at Fanny. 'Yes,' she said, 'but in a different way.'

'Yes,' Fanny echoed Sara. 'In a different way.'

They sat in a slightly drunken silence, hearing the cars passing on Brattle Street, the cheerful repetitive chirping of birds. One of the dogs yawned and smacked its gums.

'I have not left this house for four years,' Fanny said, breaking the silence.

150

'Good God!'

'I can't bear to go out. I cannot bear to be anonymous on the streets.'

'You could hardly ever be *anonymous*!' Sara protested.

'Do you think the young men look at me?' Fanny said. 'Oh, I know that for a woman in her fifties I am *attractive* enough, like an old car that's been kept clean and has no dents or chipped paint. People are always *polite* to me. But do you think that I receive the same kind of glances and smiles and replies that I got even ten years ago? Sara, ten years ago, I could still make a man in his twenties stammer when he spoke to me.'

'But those are strangers!' Sara said.'What about the people who know you? Who care for you, the person under all that beauty?'

'You would be surprised how very few of those people there are,' Fanny said. 'And that's my fault. I know it. I forfeited many friendships to my vanity.' She paused, looked off into some secret distance of her own. Then, laughing, gesturing with her hand, as if pushing aside a curtain, she said, 'Well, can you imagine what I was like as a friend? Can you imagine that I ever let a girlfriend show up with a new handsome rich young man and didn't try in my own very subtle way to get that man for myself? Then, of course, once I had the man enamored of me, I grew bored with him. It's an old story, I'm not the only woman who ever spent her life that way. But it leaves one alone. You know, Sara, I've almost never had a woman friend who meant as much to me as you do. With whom I've spent so much enjoyable and intimate time.'

'There's Eloise,' Sara offered, touched and yet saddened by Fanny's confession.

'Eloise,' Fanny replied. 'Well, she is something different. Eloise *works* for me, you know. She has been with me for years now. She has her duties. She has a responsibility to me. She is paid quite handsomely for what she does. Not that she doesn't have some affection for me, as well, I suppose. I hope. Or perhaps not. Eloise sees me, you see, when I am – not in my best state. She protects me. I pay her for that. And she understands that she must be strict.'

Sara said nothing. She waited, hoping Fanny would explain more.

'Oh, my dear, look at you peering at me!' Fanny laughed. 'Don't worry, I'm not a madwoman or a nymphomaniac. I don't send Eloise out to procure young men for me, although don't think I haven't fantasized *that* now and then! No, it's very simply that when I am depressed, when I need to be alone, to hide in my bedroom and study, Eloise is there to keep intruders out. She does the shopping, answers the door and the phone, keeps the house, and even, when I'm especially bad, opens the mail. And – and so on.'

'What do you mean – especially bad?' Sara asked.

Fanny smiled. 'There are times,' she began, then paused. She began again. 'We females all have times when we cry and cannot stop, or wake up and cannot find the energy or the reason to get out of bed. Or feel we must take some definite action to end our lives. Sometimes this sort of thing just lasts a little longer for me than for most people, that's all.' She looked away. 'Oh, *you see*,' she said, her voice suddenly serious, 'there are days and days when I don't know how I'm going to go on with my life, Sara. When I am so lonely, when I long to be with people, and I know I can't go on living any longer in this solitude. That's when Eloise is necessary; she sees to it that, well, that I do go on living. It's not an easy job for her.'

'But you don't have to be so lonely,' Sara said weakly. 'Not someone like you.'

Fanny turned on Sara, angry now. 'You would advise that I join a bridge club? Attend church and do good deeds? Perhaps join a center for the elderly?'

'Fanny, for heaven's sake. I'm not thinking of anything like that. You could have lunch with Linda Oldham at Heartways House. She adores your work, she would love to take you out. And Donald James is longing to meet you. You could probably teach at one of the universities here, creative writing; the students would worship you, you could attend readings, you could give readings.'

'Don't you understand that I can't bear to have people see me as I've become?' Fanny said. She ran her hand across her forehead. 'Oh, no, you don't understand, of course you couldn't. You have no idea of how much I had and how much I've lost.'

'I think you're placing far too much emphasis on your looks,' Sara scolded. 'This is crazy. Life isn't just about how one *looks*.'

Fanny raised her head and smiled at Sara. It seemed her good humor had suddenly restored itself, but when she spoke her voice was cutting, 'Well, we all have our obsessions, don't we?'

Sara nodded bleakly. Was it possible that her obsession was as self-defeating and irrational as Fanny's? She didn't know; she couldn't decide, not with two Bloody Marys inside her before noon. And my God, she thought, my God. How terrible that this wonderful talented woman would hate herself so much that she would try to commit suicide, that she could not go out among people. What could she do about it? How could she help?

'But we have gotten too deathly dull!' Fanny exclaimed. 'You know, alcohol does have a depressing effect in the morning. We must cheer up. You must finish the story you were telling me when you had to leave last time. About the summer you and Julia spent in Europe after college.'

Sara took a deep breath. 'Well,' she began, 'we had Eurail passes –' At the back of her mind dark worries about Fanny clotted and surged just as the thick blood moved from her body, but she knew Fanny was right, there were times when the dark things must be ruthlessly shoved aside, the light forced in, or the spark of life would be extinguished.

In June and July, Sara and Steve had houseguests. Old college friends and their families. And Ellie and her husband, Jeff, and their two-year-old son. Secretly she hoped that being around her nephew for two weeks would trigger some hormonal release that would make her pregnant. Joey was a happy child who ran through life full-tilt. His affection for Sara and Steve was obvious, and by the end of his stay, he had established an early-morning habit of coming into their bedroom and rolling around like a puppy between them in their bed. Sara breathed in his fragrances – the sweet shampoo-smelling hair, the baby-powdered skin, and the dirty diaper. He snuggled against her and squealed with delight as she walked her fingers up his back – and she felt her body go warm and fluid with a special kind of love that was even a sort of lust.

Julia was their next guest, fortunately, because it was the end of July, and Sara's period was starting again. Ellie had tried to persuade Sara not to be afraid of the laparoscopy. But Sara hated the thought of hospitals, needles, losing consciousness, losing control. There were too many risks, no guarantees. She was afraid she would die.

'Just last month,' she said, 'there was a story in the news about a man who went to the dentist for oral surgery. He was terrified, but the dentist assured him he'd be all right. Well, the man was allergic to the anesthesia and died in the dentist's chair! He lost consciousness, he didn't have a chance.'

'But that's a freak accident,' Ellie insisted. 'That's a one-in-a-million event.'

Still, Sara protested, still, and she kept protesting. What about air bubbles in needles? She had seen people killed that way, sadistically, in movies. What about unclean instruments? What about all those incompetent doctors who were being sued for malpractice?

Julia agreed with Sara. A feminist, she believed that it was because most of the doctors were male that all the tests and operations for sterility were done on the females. Just as the contraceptive burden lay on women.

'What are the statistics on this operation?' Julia asked. 'Only about twenty percent of the women who have it get pregnant right afterward; they might have anyway. These quacks don't have any proof that the operation really helps. It's absolutely the old doctor-as-God routine, Sara; the old laying-on-of-hands bit.'

'Oh, Julia,' Sara said, sighing, 'I suppose you're right. Or maybe you're not. Damn, how I wish I knew what to do!'

Whenever Sara sat talking about blood and risk to Ellie or Julia, she went quiet if Steve came in. She changed the subject.

There was never a time that summer when she and Steve sat together, husband and wife, a couple united, and discussed their problem and Sara's fear. Sara knew she had discussed her desire for pregnancy and her fears and sorrows a hundred times more deeply with Ellie and Julia than she had with Steve. And this worried her, but she did not know how to change it. Steve was an easy man to be around, but he grew solemn and stiff when certain subjects were mentioned, even embarrassed. She did not want to seem to be ganging up on him with another woman.

And it was a busy time for Steve; in the summer carpenters worked long hours, trying to finish their work before bad weather set in. When he came home, he was tired and sweaty and wanted to relax. And Sara was aware that for her at least making love when she was ovulating had become tinged with an almost dreary sense of duty, and the times after she ovulated, when she thought intercourse might damage a possible pregnancy, were times when she felt more anxious than anything else.

On their bedroom dresser in a silver frame was an eight-by-ten photograph that Julia had taken at midnight, after a Christmas party three years before. Steve was sitting at one end of the sofa, Sara lay with her head in his lap. One of Steve's hands rested in her hair, the other on her rib cage, just under her breast. Thinking they were alone, Sara had reached up to stroke her husband's face. There was such concord between them. Such lust and depths and needs and generosity.

All that was in the snapshot. It made Sara's heart ache now to look at it, to remember that. For while they could not feel such abiding joy in each other every second – no one could – still, that had been the basis of their life together. Content, lust, love, harmony.

Now, was it gone? Now she remembered it, as if remembering a strain of music she had not recently heard. It was her fault, partly, even mostly; she had gotten into a state about her infertility and spent much of her time in grief or anger or bitterness or some sort of obsessional fit. But it was Steve's fault, too, a little. If Sara's anxieties and sorrows had swelled outward, filling the emotional atmosphere of their home with its tensions and glooms, just so had Steve withdrawn. It was all so subtle. He *seemed* just the same. But he had closed down from Sara, she could tell. She could not get him to admit that he ever, once, felt any sorrow or anger or anxiety about having or not having children. Now, all too often, when she tried to discuss it with him, he grew impatient, aloof. Sometimes it seemed to Sara that with every word she spoke, she shrank smaller and smaller, became a foolish child, while Steve grew taller and taller, quieter and quieter, until he towered above her, white and judgmental and bored, and she cowered beneath him, a quivering dwarf. She could not climb or squeeze into or even touch such a massive mountain of impassivity.

She knew that she had to do something, or better, *something had to happen*, or they would lose what they had together. They did not laugh so often in bed now. During the time she was ovulating, she insisted now that they make love with the lights off, to hide the fact that she could feel almost *nothing*, that her body was beginning to go numb. Other times, during her period and just afterward, when there was no chance she could get pregnant, she would be ravenous for him, she would pace the house, desiring him, needing him to come home, she would attack him when he came in the door, she would seduce him on the living room floor, and afterward, exhausted and replete, she would lie secretly thinking, *Thank God, thank God, it still works for me, I haven't lost all sexual desire*.

Sometimes, as they sat eating dinner together, or watching TV, or reading, Sara looked at Steve and thought how she loved him. She loved him without any reservation, past any hope of change, completely and irrevocably. She loved him with a passion that life might test but never destroy. She was deeply afraid that his silences, his independence, his gradual withdrawing from her, meant that he did not feel the same.

She was terrified that he was changing. She did not know what to do.

Mick drove the group crazy in the summer. He showed up at every get-together with a different girl, some rich college girl with a tan and a trust fund who was there for the summer to have fun and get laid. When Mick and one of his girls came around, everyone else felt suddenly shriveled with age and responsibility; they saw themselves trapped and dull and fat. And they were, compared to those gorgeous girls, who sometimes drove him to their parties in their Porsches, who came from the south and said that 'Daddy' was, oh, off in Italy now, or Daddy had taken Mummy on a cruise. On their own ship.

In August one of Mick's girls invited the gang to a party on her parents' yacht, which was anchored in Nantucket Harbor. It was as long as a battleship, with its own captain and butler and maids. Music of one's choice was piped into the bedrooms below, which were larger and more luxurious than the ones the group had in their houses. There were almonds coated in silver leaf for guests to munch on. Mick's girl had a thick braid of silver-and-gold hair that swung down to her waist. She wore a gold chain around her tanned, sleek ankle. She smiled with white teeth that would have dazzled any dentist. Her stomach was flat and she couldn't keep her hands off Mick. When the group went swimming together one Sunday afternoon, taking coolers of beers and sodas, she swam far out into the ocean, unafraid, and lost the top to her bikini, and didn't mind, but came casually, unaffectedly, out of the ocean, water dripping and glittering from her full, upward-pointing breasts. Men and women alike groaned aloud, with different kinds of envy.

Later, when Mick had gone off somewhere else with his Venus, the men played volleyball and the women sat in a cluster, watching their children make sand castles or wade in the surf. Here and there the youngest babies lay on beach blankets under umbrellas, naked, sucking bottles, their eyes closed, drowsy from the heat and bright light.

'I remember the days when my stomach was as flat as Mick's girlfriend's,' Jamie said, sighing. 'Never again.'

'Maybe Mick will knock her up,' Carole said with a nasty grin. 'Let's sneak into his house some night and poke holes in his condoms.'

'Nice talk,' Annie Danforth said, laughing. 'Listen, my

stomach isn't that flat and I haven't had any babies. Lord, my stomach wasn't that flat when I was eight!'

'We're the pizza generation,' Carole said. 'My parents told me that when they were growing up no one ate pizza. No one knew about it. I'm convinced that's the reason I'm chronically overweight.'

Mary had just covered her two-year-old daughter's bare skin with a light cotton blanket, shielding her from the sun's rays. Mary was wearing a bikini, her breasts swelling, so that the top looked several sizes too small. 'Well,' she said, smiling, 'I'm going to get to forget about dieting for a while. For the next few months I can get away with looking fat – I'm pregnant again.' She grinned at the group, triumphant.

There were squeals of surprise and pleasure.

'Mary! How great! When is the baby due?' Jamie asked.

'March,' Mary said. 'A nice little spring baby. It's about time, my other two have been early-winter ones. But I'm going to need some winter maternity clothes.'

Everyone talked at once, offering clothes, asking questions, everyone but Sara, who sat falsely smiling, shocked, caught in a rage of envy that made her feel wild. She had to use every bit of energy to control herself, to control her face, her voice, to hide her trembling.

Not fair! Not fair! Not fair! Not fair! something inside her was screaming. *Why does she get three babies and I get none?*

'Did you plan this baby?' Jamie asked Mary.

Mary laughed. 'Jamie, come on. Are you kidding me? I've never planned any baby. In fact they've *all* been accidents. I just *think* about sex and get pregnant.'

'You mean you get pregnant even if you use birth control?' Annie Danforth asked.

'The first time I was using a diaphragm, if you can believe it. I guess it was just worn out. It was super-old. And I took it out after about four hours; you're supposed to leave them in for six. But I was filled up with that spermicide goop. And Heather happened when I was nursing Blaise. They'll tell you you can't get pregnant when you're nursing, but believe me, you can. And with this one, I was using foam. I still don't know what happened. It's just the way I am, I'm just basically an old breeding sow, I guess.' Mary leaned back on her elbows, looking down at her stomach, which still stretched sleekly between the two tiny strips of bikini. She smiled, a smile Sara had seen often before on others, a smile that reeked of secret pleasure and superiority.

Sara sat in the sun and listened to the others talk. She could not rouse herself to join in the conversation. She could not trust her voice not to shake, giving away her emotional state. And what could she ask? What could she say?

How do you do it? she could ask. *Can you tell me how you do it? Could you loan me some of your power, some of your luck?*

The sun shone down on them all, on the men yelling and falling in the sand as their volleyball game got wilder, on the babies toddling and sleeping around the group of women, and on the women, who sat focused now on the new queen of their group, the one with the secret, the power, the age-old triumph, the unknown baby growing in her belly. The sun shone down hotly, making the ocean throw off shards of light that sliced at their eyes. It was a good excuse to put on sunglasses, and Sara slid hers on gratefully, glad to cover her eyes, which she felt must be vivid with pain. When she put her glasses on, she realized with a shock that her hands had gone icy cold.

That night she said to Steve as they lay together in bed, 'I'm going to go ahead and schedule that laparoscopy.'

They had already turned off the light, and she could not see his face, or he hers.

'Are you sure?' Steve asked, turning toward her, putting a hand on her shoulder.

'It's the end of August,' Sara said. 'I know I'm going to get my period tomorrow, for the twenty-first month since we stopped using birth control. I think I really should do it.' She kept her voice matter-of-fact and pleasant.

'But you told me you were afraid . . .' Steve let his voice trail off in a question.

'Well, I suppose I still am, a little. But Ellie promised me that I'll be okay, and she's a nurse. She says the risk of getting killed in a car accident on the way to the hospital is higher than the risk of anything happening in the hospital.'

'Well, don't feel like you have to do it,' Steve said. 'I don't want you to do anything you don't want to do.'

'Oh, I know,' Sara replied. She could feel his hand on her arm, he was kneading her arm, and she was grateful for this sign of concern. 'But I've been thinking, now that I'm through with *Jenny's Book*, and almost through editing another romance novel, we aren't rich, but we have enough money for the operation. So that's okay. And – and I just think it's time to schedule it. The doctor told me it has to be done between the time I've finished my period and before ovulating. So that they're sure when they cut into me that I'm not pregnant. I know they won't be able to schedule it this month, so I'll have a month to finish editing *Love's Golden Clasp* before I go. I feel good about it, Steve, really I do.'

That was a lie, of course. She did not feel good about it. She simply felt desperate, in a strangely numb way. It was as if that afternoon on the beach, when The Virgin made her announcement, something had happened to her, to her entire body and soul, that caused her to go cold, blankly cold, like something dead. And she carried death within her now, she was in her period, she did not carry life. It was a relief, this cold, this blankness, for the heat of grief was so searing, so painful. She felt her husband stroking her now, and wondered that he did not mention how cold she was, wondered why he did not pull his hand away in surprise. She knew he was making love to her, and she knew she was responding acceptably, but she felt nothing at all, nothing at all.

CHAPTER EIGHT

'You're in luck!' the nurse said, as cheerfully as if she were from 'Wheel of Fortune'. 'We can schedule you for a week from Wednesday. According to what you've just told me, that should be your twelfth day. You'll be through with your period, but you won't have ovulated then, right?'

The nurse babbled away at Sara. The operation would take place at Brigham and Women's Hospital on Wednesday. She would need to come into Boston on Tuesday to get consent forms at Dr Crochett's office and then have lab work done at the hospital. She would have a general anesthetic; the day before the operation she would have a consultation with the anesthesiologist. They would do a laparoscopy, with a possible laparotomy if she had endometriosis. They would do a tubal lavage and an endometrial biopsy. Possibly a D&C. If the doctor did only a laparoscopy, Sara could leave the hospital that day – probably. If he had to do a laparotomy, which required a major abdominal incision, she would be in the hospital for five days more and should plan on spending four weeks after that resting and recuperating. She should get her insurance information ready for the hospital. She should plan to have someone drive her home from the hospital, she would not be allowed to leave the hospital by herself.

Sara hung up the phone weak with terror. She did not know why it was that her sister loved hospitals, while she grew sick with fear at the thought of them, but it was an instinctive reaction she couldn't help. Perhaps it was that her imagination was too vivid and that she remembered every medical mistake mentioned on television or in the newspapers. Perhaps she had a basic mistrust of people and knew how easily even the most careful person could make mistakes. Perhaps it was simply that this was her phobia, almost everyone had at least one special fear. But there was no way to explain it away. She did not know how to handle it. She would go ahead with this surgery, she would not back down, but she would go into it filled with dread.

She called her sister. Ellie tried for a few minutes to be sympathetic and reassuring, but then interrupted herself. 'Oh, Sara,' she said, 'I'm so sorry, I've been waiting for the right time to tell you this and I just can't wait any longer – I'm pregnant again! I'm almost five months pregnant. Yes, I was pregnant when I was with you this summer, but I didn't want to tell you. I knew it would upset you.'

'Oh, that's wonderful, Ellie, that's wonderful. I'm so glad for you,' Sara said. It took all her energy to infuse her voice with enthusiasm. She was consumed with jealousy. It was as if something had just grasped her heart and twisted it.

'You should see Joey,' Ellie said. 'He's so adorable now that my tummy's sticking out. He goes around sticking his fat little tummy out and saying, "I've got a baby in my tummy just like Mommy!"'

Sara laughed dutifully. And, just as dutifully, Ellie turned the conversation back to Sara's operation and reassured her once again.

When Sara hung up, she went out the back door and stood for a moment in the dark yard, looking at the empty blue sky. *Why Ellie? Why not me?* she asked whatever force it was that ruled the day and night, that caused the patterns of seasons and constellations and birth and blood. But whatever force it was did not answer. Sara knew it would never answer her, and she felt rejected by it, ignored. She wanted to sink into the ground, crushed with shame.

That weekend Sara and Steve were invited to dinner at Steve's parents' house. They had decided to tell the older Kendalls about Sara's forthcoming operation – it would be too difficult to disguise what was going on, especially if Sara had to stay in the hospital for five days. And Steve was going to take three days off work to go up with Sara on Tuesday and come back with her on Thursday; or, if she had the laparotomy, would come back after five days to pick her up. Sara and Steve spoke to his parents daily when they were on Nantucket; they couldn't just disappear for a couple of days without worrying them.

Sara had a stiff drink before facing her in-laws with the news of her inability to get pregnant. She loved Clark and Caroline and knew they cared for her, but still she worried what their reactions would be – concern, pity, bewilderment? The reaction, to her surprise, was impatience, even anger, from Caroline.

As they sat in the living room, looking out at the Atlantic, Caroline Kendall became uncharacteristically bold.

'Sara, this is ridiculous!' she said. 'A young woman like you scheduling herself for surgery. Steven, how could you let her do such a thing? Really! You should never schedule surgery unless it's absolutely necessary! Unless it's a life-and-death matter! It's so dangerous! Besides, this is an issue for the Lord to handle, not for surgery. I'm sorry if you've had trouble getting pregnant, Sara, but really I think you're going about it the wrong way. Surgery! I think you should *relax*. Everyone knows if you just relax, you'll get pregnant. Relax and trust in the Lord. If He wills it, you'll have a baby, and if He doesn't, no amount of surgery will help. You should trust in the Lord.'

Sara was so shocked at her mother-in-law's outburst that her breath seemed knocked out of her. She looked at Steve; his jaw was clenched.

'Look, Mother,' he said, his voice hard and formal. 'There's no point in arguing about this. We've made up our minds. We've been trying for quite a while now, and since "the Lord" hasn't come through for us, we're going to try a little intelligent medical help. This is the twentieth century, you know.'

'How long have you been trying?' Caroline asked.

Oh, spare me this, spare me, Sara silently pleaded. Still she could not answer.

'Almost two years,' Steve said.

Caroline was obviously shocked by this news. 'Oh, dear,' she said, and looked at Sara quickly, as if trying to see through her clothes and skin into her flawed belly. Then she looked quickly away. 'Well,' she said, and then she was speechless. Her hands fluttered up to her hair and her eyes blinked, then her entire face sagged. It was as if suddenly it occurred to her that this was serious, this was final; she was not to be a grandmother; she was not to have a grandchild. Her face almost crumpled. 'I'd better go check the roast,' she said, her voice quavering.

The silence when Caroline left the room was more painful than her loud comments had been just moments before. Clark Kendall sat red-faced, uncomfortable with the entire subject, and Sara was close to weeping. How horrible to be such a daughter-in-law, who brought these kind people sad instead of joyful news.

Steve broke the silence. Sara sat looking out at the ocean, sipping her drink, sick with grief. Somehow they managed to smooth over the rift in the evening and the dinner went on well enough. Sara thought the worst was over.

But when she was in the kitchen, helping her mother-in-law with coffee and dessert, Caroline surprised her by grabbing Sara's hands in hers. She looked Sara in the eye.

'Sara, my dear,' she said, 'I can't let you go home without saying this to you. I've never wanted to be an intrusive mother-in-law, I've never wanted to interfere – and I think you'd agree that I really haven't been too nosy. And now I just have to say my piece or I won't rest.'

Sara smiled encouragingly. She could see in Caroline's face how upset she was.

'I know you think I'm old-fashioned,' Caroline said. 'And yet I think you would admit that Clark and I have a fine marriage, a happy marriage. Well, we have this happy marriage because he's the man and I'm the woman. What I mean is, he works, and I take care of the home. Sara, dear, if only you'd stop working, I'm sure you'd get pregnant. It just isn't *natural* for a woman to work as hard as you do.'

Oh, no, Sara thought. *Oh, please, not this.*

Sara gently pulled her hands away. 'Caroline,' she said, 'it's true that when I worked in Boston I was under some stress, or at least I worked hard, and my days – and nights – were very busy. But now I'm only working part-time, only free-lance editing, some days I work only a few hours, and some days not at all.'

'And many days you go to Boston,' Caroline said accusingly. 'It's not just the time, don't you see? It's your attitude. It's where your *heart* is at. Sara, to be honest, I'm not sure you *want* to have a baby. I'm afraid that in your heart of hearts you're afraid to have a baby because it would interfere with the work you think is so important to your life.'

'Oh, Caroline,' Sara said, both angry and hurt, 'that's not true. That's simply not true. I can't tell you how much I want a baby.'

'Then you should stop working and try to live like a real wife, a real woman,' Caroline said. 'If you're going to go on living as you have been, half woman, half man, why of course you'll never get pregnant.'

Sara felt sick with despair. What could she possibly say to this woman that would change her mind?

'Will you at least think about what I've said?' Caroline asked.

'Yes,' Sara replied. She began to place coffee cups and saucers and spoons on the tray. She wanted to get it over with, the dessert, the evening, the relationship, which was now ruined beyond repair. She had not known how Caroline felt about her working. She had been so naive, so simpleminded. Now her horrid infertility was stretching grim death-dealing coils to this part of her life, too. Where there had been trust, there was now distrust; where there had been friendship, there was now enmity. It she had been able to present her mother-in-law with a *fait accompli* — a pregnancy, a baby — then Caroline would have had no power, no right to criticize her working.

But as it was, who could say that she was not right?

During the drive home, Sara told Steve what Caroline had said.

'Oh, Sara, don't pay any attention to her,' Steve said. 'She's so old-fashioned.'

'But do you think she's right?' Sara pressed. 'Do *you* think she's right? That I'm not getting pregnant because I'm working? Do you think I'm too success oriented?'

'No, Sara,' Steve said. 'I think you're fine. I think you're wonderful. I think my mother is an old fogy who doesn't know when to keep her mouth shut.'

Sara looked at Steve, amazed. His tone of voice had been neutral, and so was his expression. But he never had criticized his mother before – Sara couldn't recall a time when he had ever spoken against her. She felt sick. Had she forced Steve to take sides with her against his mother?

Would there be no end to the damage her infertility could do?

It was a beautiful summer evening, warm and bright with moonlight. As they parked the car and walked to their house, they could hear laughter drifting from the backyards and patios of other houses. It seemed everyone else in the world was carefree and happy.

Sara went to the bathroom as soon as she was in the house. Her pad was soaked with blood. She sat looking at it, so rich and thick and red, so deep and huge that it spread across her life, blotting out life and joy.

She hated herself enough to do herself damage. She hated herself so much that if she could have done it with a simple word, she would have chosen to vanish from the earth. But it was not so simple, and so she put on a fresh sanitary napkin and got ready for bed – for *bed*, which once meant only joy and rest but now meant, at the best, confusion.

Ten days before her surgery, Sara ran away from home. That morning, Tuesday, September 12, was vivid with glancing lights, as if the buildings of Boston held separate suns that splattered silver from every skyscraper. The tiny whining plane that had carried Sara up the coast from Nantucket swooped low over Boston's glittering harbor and landed smoothly on a runway that unrolled before them like a sheet of aluminum foil. The taxi that carried Sara to her destination was new and smelled of leather and success and it ticked speedily away through tunnels and over bridges without a single hitch or pause, as if the world were efficient and new.

The Charles River sparkled, windows winked light, everything was clean and metallic and joggers slipped by effortlessly along the paths, propelled by their robot hearts.

Sara's heart was slick, too, her body sleek, she stepped from the taxi, admiring herself as she moved: such sophisticated high heels, patterned hose, slender figure in svelte suit. Her hair glittered all in a piece, like a helmet, and her face was flawless, a beautiful mask. She felt like a woman from the twenty-first century.

In the waiting room, she unbuttoned the camel suit jacket to reveal the blouse she was wearing, which in turned revealed her. It was a red silk blouse with full sleeves. She had turned the collar up high to further accentuate the way the neck plunged, unbuttoned, so that when she moved the rounded tops of her breasts were teasingly exposed. She knew what she was doing; she did not know what she was doing.

'Tell Mr Larkin that Sara Blackburn Kendall would like to see him,' she said to the secretary, and when the secretary asked politely if Mr Larkin was expecting her, she smiled arrogantly and said, 'No.'

The secretary spoke on the phone to David Larkin, and in a flash he was there, opening the door into his office, looking out at her, his face beaming with surprise and delight.

Her old lover. And it looked as if he still loved her. At least as if her presence, her simple presence, brought him pleasure.

'Hello, David,' she said, smiling. 'Do you have a minute?'

He was a successful architect, she knew that, and she knew he was a busy man, but she knew also that this was his own firm, he was his own boss. So she felt no qualms about bothering him at work; he couldn't get fired or hassled. She moved about, admiring the plush rug, the spotless glass-and-chrome furniture, the cool serene Japanese prints that adorned the otherwise bare walls. She was just as cool and serene as she talked to her old lover, her heart was as slick as the glass, as cold as the chrome, she enticed her old lover, she lured him. It had been a long time since she had done anything like this. It was like swimming after years away from the water; she slid through the morning like a seal in the sea. Cold was her element. But at least in some way, this way, she could still move, and her body still mattered, and had powers.

David took her to lunch. They had champagne. He told her about the condominiums he was designing and the wing for the university. She told him, at length, about *Jenny's Book*. He asked her if she would like to come to see his new apartment. She said she would.

His apartment was as sleekly modern as his office. There were pictures of a beautiful brunette all over the apartment, by his desk, by his bed, on the kitchen wall. David told her that her name was Cynthia and he thought they would be married. Sara thought, *Good, a challenge*. She needed a challenge, she needed to win a contest, she needed more proof that she existed, that her body worked.

'You've changed,' David told Sara as they sank down into his dark leather sofa. He had brewed strong coffee for them, insisting that they had both had more than enough champagne for the day. 'You're quite different.'

'Oh?' Sara laughed. 'Does that mean you don't like me?' She had taken off the jacket to her suit. She was aware of the way her breasts moved against the red silk of her blouse, and her perfume filled the air.

'Oh, Sara,' David said, a gentle chiding tone in his voice, 'you know I could never not like you. But I don't understand you. Perhaps it's just that it's been so long since I've seen you. Seven years? At least seven years.'

Yes, it had been seven years since they had been together. They had been lovers. They had almost married. They would have had a good marriage, two ambitious professional people with their work centered in Boston; they would have been chic and clever and successful together. Sara had broken off the relationship; she had stopped loving him. She had not stopped caring for him, but she had stopped loving him, and after she met Steve she realized she had never been wild for him, not in the way she was wild for Steve. She had always liked David, though, and had liked having him in love with her, for he was an intelligent, thoughtful, handsome man, compact and well dressed, and as kind as he was brilliant.

168

Now, looking at him, she saw signs of age — inevitable, of course. She was certain he could see them in her. His black hair was thinning, his immaculately clothed body had thickened slightly, and there were crow's-feet around his eyes. The skin on his hands had roughened. But still he had beautiful hands, supple, long-fingered pliant hands. And there were other parts of his body that were beautiful, that she had loved. Looking at him, she could easily remember his naked body. As she knew he could remember hers.

They had done things in bed with each other that all lovers do with one another. They had loved each other, but she had left him, unsatisfied. It had not been the right love for her. Still he was a desirable man, one of the most desirable men she had ever met. It mattered to her a great deal that he desire her, too, now, still, that he desire her enough to betray the brown-haired Cynthia.

Sara moved closer to David on the sofa. 'Sometimes it's easier to remember what happened seven years ago than it is to remember yesterday,' she said, smiling. 'The good memories last.' She reached out her hand. She touched his cheek.

David reached up and took her hand in his. 'Sara,' he said, 'what are you doing?'

'What do you think I'm doing?' she said, moving closer to him. Her breasts touched his arm.

'Is this what you want?' David asked, and put his arms around her, and kissed her.

She replied by putting her arms around him and kissing him back with a real but deflected passion, which like the light of the day around them came glancing off something else. She kissed him with great need.

'Oh, sweet Sara, you're still so sweet,' David murmured.

His hands were on her breasts, her waist, her stomach, her hips. He took off her clothes. He took off his clothes. He was lying on her on the sofa, both of them naked, his erect penis stabbing against her thigh as they manoeuvred together. She remembered how she had once teased him about being a gorilla because of the hair that ran down his back and his chest and stomach.

But when he tried to enter her, she twisted away with a cry. 'No, David. I can't!' she said.

'Sara,' David said. His voice was angry. 'For Christ's sake.'

'Oh, God, I'm so sorry,' Sara said, and to her surprise as much as his, burst into body-racking sobs.

David, always the gentleman, drew back immediately. The leather sofa squeaked vulgarly with their movements. 'Sara?' he asked.

And Sara, her white flesh vulnerable against the dark leather, pulled herself into a sitting position and looked at David with her wrecked tear-streaked face. 'Oh, David, would you hold me, please?' she begged. 'Would you help me?'

Puzzled, but kind – David was always so kind – he pulled her to him. He put his arms around her and pulled her over so that she sat on his lap, childlike, and he leaned back against the sofa and held her as if he were her father and she were his child. He held her and loved her as she was, naked, singular Sara. And at this kindness, Sara's heart burst through the cold walls that had entrapped it. She cried and cried, her tears and mascara streaking down David's naked shoulder, leaving trails of black. He held her, and smoothed her hair, and stroked her arm, and said nothing. Finally she was able to speak.

'Oh, David,' she said, 'I'm so sorry. I'm such a bitch. I'm such a failure. I'm a horrid bitch failure. I'm nothing, I'm not even a woman, you are so lucky I didn't marry you, I would only bring you misery, David, I'm cursed, or I am a curse, David, I wish I could die. I want to die.'

'Sssh, ssh,' David said. 'Don't say such things, Sara. They're not true.'

'David, I can't make a baby,' Sara said. She said this to his shoulder because it was too painful a thing to say while looking him in the face. 'I can't get pregnant. There's something wrong with me. I feel like such a piece of *trash*. I feel so worthless. As if Fate and God scorn me, disdain me, as if I don't matter to whatever force it is that brings life into the world. And I'm making everyone close to me miserable. Steve, his mother, his father – how they must secretly pity me and hate me and wish they could be free of me. David, I can't get a grasp on anything anymore. I can't see myself. I can't think straight. I don't feel like a woman. I don't feel feminine, *female*.'

'Oh, Sara, oh, sweet,' David said, soothing her. 'Sara, you are beautiful, you are a beautiful woman.'

'No,' Sara went on, 'you don't understand. I'm nothing. I am useless. And I'm so fucking helpless in all this! And it's all so unfair! David, I need a Kleenex.'

David rose, went into the other room, came back wearing a robe and carrying a box of tissues and a soft blanket. He waited until she had wiped her nose and eyes, then wrapped the blanket around her. He went into the kitchen, came back with hot coffee, which he had made sweet and strong and creamy.

Sara drank it, and the warmth of the blanket and the coffee soothed her. She leaned against a corner of the sofa and looked at David, whose dark eyes were sad and kind.

'I've got to go into the hospital,' she said, her voice calmer now. 'I've got to have an operation. A laparoscopy, possible laparotomy. They'll put needles in my veins and tubes in my mouth and drugs in my body. General anesthesia. They'll cut my stomach open with a knife. I'm terrified.'

'You never were good with blood, I recall,' David said lightly. 'Remember the night I sliced open my thumb when I was cooking you stir-fry?'

She smiled. 'No, I never was good with blood.' She sipped her coffee. 'David, do you know the worst thing about me? The very worst thing? Not just that I'm sterile, barren, useless. But I'm so full of anger, so full of a desire for revenge I can't believe it's me. David, I wake up in the middle of the night, thinking: I'm going to have this fucking operation, and I'm going to die on the operating table, and then Steve will be free, and his old girlfriend Mary will be there to console him in an instant, and they'll be in bed together within hours, poor Steve, he'll need solace, and then they'll get married and have children together. Sometimes I want to say to Steve, to *scream* at Steve, "Why don't we just get divorced? Then you can marry Mary and have kids and I won't have to die."'

'That's a horrible thing to think, Sara,' David said. 'You should be ashamed of yourself. I don't know Steve, but I can assure you that if you died his life would be ruined. If he lost you, his life would be absolutely ruined.'

Sara burst into fresh tears at David's words. 'Oh, David,' she sobbed. 'What am I going to do? This thing is taking over my life. It's warping everything.'

'Have you talked to Steve about all this?'

'I've tried. He won't talk. He keeps on being so fucking *cheerful* about it all, he won't admit he's feeling any strain, and yet I know he is. I can feel it. Things are different between us. And if I tell him how afraid I am of this operation, he'll tell me not to have it. But if I don't have it, I may not ever have a child. Hell, if I *do* have it, I may not ever have a child.'

'But you'll have Steve. And he'll have you. And, Sara, that's a lot. If you love each other, it's really everything.'

Sara looked at David. 'Not everything,' she said.

'Well, close enough,' he told her, smiling.

'You're such a nice man,' Sara said.

'Oh, yes, that's true, I am,' David said. His face took on a slightly angry cast, his voice became bitter. 'And I hope I've proved to you that you are feminine and desirable and . . . that your sexuality functions well enough to drive me crazy, even after all these years.'

'I'm sorry, David,' Sara said. 'I didn't mean to be – oh, I don't know. I need so much now, and I don't know how to get it. But you've helped me, in a lot of ways. I wish I could thank you.'

'Just give your poor husband a break,' David said. 'Just believe him. If he seems happy even if you don't have kids, then he probably is. You're a lot for any man, Sara. You're enough for any man, all by yourself. You don't need any attachments to make yourself worthwhile. To make yourself loved.'

Sara's eyes met David's and she smiled. 'You are so wonderful,' she said. 'You always were so wonderful.'

'I think you'd better get dressed,' David said, smiling back. 'I don't think you can trust my "wonderfulness" too far when you're sitting around wearing nothing but a blanket.'

Sara rose, pulling the blanket around her. 'Where did you say your bathroom was?' she asked. Gathering up her clothes, clutching the blanket to her, suddenly shy and embarrassed, she went across the room, down the hall, and into the bathroom to get dressed. When she came out, she found that David had dressed again, too, and was standing by the front door, jiggling his car keys in his hand.

'Where can I drop you?' he asked.

'You're angry with me, aren't you?' Sara said.

'I feel used,' David told her. 'I feel humiliated, like a naive little sophomore who's just made a fool of himself.'

'Oh, David, I never meant to make you feel that way. I never meant. I never thought ... well, that's it, isn't it, I didn't think of you, I was so selfish, I only thought of myself. But if it's any comfort, I don't feel like you've made a fool of yourself. I think you've been —'

'I know: *wonderful*,' David said. 'Sara, do me a favor? Don't come at me again like that unless you mean it. Unless you want me.'

He drove to the art gallery on Newberry Street where Julia worked, and Julia, surprised and delighted to see Sara, invited her to spend the night. They took wine and quiche Lorraine and fruit to Julia's apartment, got into their robes, and curled up on the couch to talk. Sara called Steve, told him she had had a good visit with Fanny Anderson, and that she would be home tomorrow. It was the first time in their marriage that she had really lied to him, and she felt sick with guilt. But Steve sounded his normal cheerful self, and she both loved him and felt irritated at him for that.

Sara told Julia everything: about Mary being pregnant again, effortlessly, about her mother-in-law's urging her to stop working, about her fear of the operation, about feeling more and more unreal, unworthy. She had woken up this morning knowing she must find someone who saw her for herself, not as a failed baby-making machine. She told Julia about her afternoon with David, and about his kindnesses. She felt so pressured and hurt by it all that she just wanted to escape, to run away somewhere — but where? And how could she, when she loved Steve?

Julia wore a heavy black silk Oriental robe embroidered with crimson birds, azure flowers, emerald leaves. Her thick red hair swirled around her head and over her shoulders. She was strangely silent when Sara finished, then got up and walked across the room, looked out the window, and came back and sat down.

'That's a shitty thing you did to David,' she said at last. 'Leading him on that way. I bet he felt like a fool.'

'Oh, Julia . . .' Sara began.

'Well, think how you would have felt if he had suddenly showed up to use you as an ego-testing ground. And Steve. What a thing to do to Steve! How would you like it if he went to his old girlfriend with his troubles?'

'He probably does, in his mind, at least!' Sara said. 'You think I don't imagine that he wishes he had married Mary, that he thinks about her when he sees her with her children?'

'Oh, shit, Sara,' Julia said. 'Steve loves you. And if he says he's not upset about having kids yet, then he's not. Steve's always told you the truth. You don't have any right to think such things about him. Listen. I think I'm getting mad at you. I love you, but I'm getting mad at you, too. I just can't stand to see you getting so soggy about everything. You aren't the tragic case you're building yourself up to be. You've got a fabulous husband who loves you. Do you have any idea how many women there are who would give all their teeth for what you have? Sara, you are *really lucky*. And you have work that you love and that has a good amount of glamour – how many women have that *and* someone they love who loves them? Maybe you won't get to have a baby instantly, or ever, maybe you won't get every single thing you want, but who does? That doesn't give you the right to get so fucking maudlin or to screw Steve around by going off and sexing up with your old lover. You would be in a *fury* if he did that to you. I can't believe you did it, I just can't. You're letting yourself get too spooked about this operation; everyone's told you you'll be fine, statistically you don't have a chance of *not* being fine. Be a big girl. No one's making you do it, you want to do it, you *aren't* going to die, you'll come out of it just fine, and you might get a nice little baby Steve or Sara out of it. So why not do it with some grace? And if you don't get pregnant, do that with some grace, too. For God's sake. Get your shit together.'

Julia was silent then, glaring at Sara. Sara glared back at Julia, amazed. Then both women grinned at each other.

'You look like an oracle in that robe,' Sara said at last. 'You look like, if I don't take your advice, you'll clap your hands and lightning and thunder will streak out from your fingers.'

'They will, too,' Julia said. She raised her hands dramatically, then let them fall in her lap. 'Oh, honey, what do I know?' She sighed. 'I just had to tell you how I feel about all this. But you know I am sorry you haven't gotten pregnant yet.'

'Well, I think what you said is right.' Sara stretched on the sofa. 'I am lucky. Sometimes it's easy to forget just how lucky I am. I think I'll feel luckier when I wake up from the operation – and even luckier when my in-laws go back to Florida and I don't have to get a daily neighborhood pregnancy report from Caroline. But you are right, Julia, I have been getting obsessed. It's just that not being obsessed when it's something that's going on with your own body is so hard. It's sort of like trying not to be in love with someone you're in love with who doesn't love you.'

'Or like being in love with a married man,' Julia said, smiling wryly.

'How is Perry?' Sara asked.

'How is he? He's with his wife tonight, that's how he is.' Julia sighed. 'Maybe *I* should go see David Larkin.'

'He's got the brown-haired Cynthia,' Sara said. 'And you're too tall for him.'

'No, I'm not. We're the same height. You just don't want me to have him.' Julia grinned. 'Oh, balls, Sara. In five years I'll be married to Perry and you'll be pushing three kids in a baby carriage, right? But for now we'd better go to bed. It's after midnight and I have to work tomorrow even if you don't.'

Sara watched Julia swank off in her opulent robe, her red hair swirling behind her. Julia had such energy, such force.

Sara wished her friend *were* an oracle, a magician, a witch, and could use her powers for Sara's sake. Although perhaps it was enough simply to have Julia as a friend; perhaps that was magic enough.

Sara arrived home the next morning to find Steve off at work, a note on the table telling her he loved her, and a packet from the Brigham and Women's Hospital lying in wait with the rest of the mail.

The packet held a preadmission guide, complete with maps of the city and surrounding area, floor plans of the hospital, and pictures of healthy patients smiling as they sat with needles in their veins and blood pressure cuffs around their upper arms.

A special sheet for day surgery patients had been included for Sara. She was *not* to eat or drink anything from midnight on the night before surgery, *not* to wear any makeup, hairpins, or fingernail polish (*Fingernail polish*! Sara thought. *Whyever not? How could it cause a problem?*), *not* to wear any jewelry, including rings. She looked down at her wedding ring. She had never taken if off. Would they make her take it off for surgery?

As she read the information about surgery, certain words jumped out at her and held her captive: 'anesthesia', 'intravenous', 'mask' – '*sleep*'. She could almost smell the acrid antiseptics she had inhaled as a child visiting the gruff and fractious doctor with his piercing needles, his total control over her helpless body.

Trying to counteract her fear, she made herself think of Julia. This morning when Julia drove her to the airport, she told Sara about a D & C she had had a few years ago. As she was being wheeled into the operating room, Julia had said to the anesthesiologist, a handsome smiling Oriental man, 'If I wake up with brain damage, I'll sue you.' And he had smiled ever more handsomely and said, with a lovely lilt to his voice, 'If you wake up with brain damage, you won't know.' Julia had thought that terrifically funny. Sara was not quite as amused. But she was determined to approach all this cheerfully, with, as Julia had said, 'grace'.

Steve was quiet when he came home from work, but that was often the case; he was working hard during the good weather. After dinner, to Sara's surprise, he said, 'Let's leave the dishes till later. It's still light out. Let's walk down to the Jetties and look at the water.'

'What a lovely idea,' Sara said. She stretched up on her tiptoes to kiss him, her clever husband. Her body, under her cotton slacks and sweater, was taut and healthy, her husband was tall and affectionate, the night was luminous and warm, promising eternal summer. How could she be unhappy?

The ocean was dappled with dark and silver blues. Far out, a white sailboat slipped like scissors through the waves. They sat in the sand, still warm from the day, and listened to the summer sounds: the gulls calling, the sea sighing, the laughter skating across the smooth water from sleek anchored yachts in the harbor. Sara stretched and leaned against Steve, rubbing her cheek into his chest.

'Mmmm,' she murmured, affectionate, in love.

'Sara,' Steve said, 'I need to talk to you.'

His tone of voice alerted her; something serious was going on. Her heart dropped like a rock in a shaft.

He was going to tell her he wanted a divorce. So he could marry someone else and have children. She knew it. She had been waiting for this.

For a moment she could not speak.

She pulled away from him. She did not look up at him. 'What is it?' she asked.

'I've been thinking about something for a while now,' Steve said. 'A major change in my life. Our lives. It's something I think I have to do. I can't go on any longer this way.'

So this was it. So this was how it was to happen. She could understand, she really could. She could understand, even forgive, there was nothing to forgive, he was doing only what any normal man would do, he *should* leave her, why would he want to stay? She would survive, she would go far away, she would never love again, she would be solitary and as cold as stone. Or maybe she wouldn't survive. She wrapped her arms around her knees, hugging herself protectively. She didn't speak. Couldn't.

'I want to go into business for myself,' Steve said. 'I'm tired of working for others. I know more than most of my bosses – about building, about architecture, about handling money, about dealing with people. And I know this island and I love it. I think if I set up my own contracting business, I could build some decent houses instead of the crap they're putting up these days. And maybe I could have some influence on what's going on. It would be an enormous change. If I left Mack's crew, I'd leave all the easy security. It would take some money to set up my own company, and it would take time before I could build up a reputation so that I could get jobs. The first few months I wouldn't have any idea how much money I'd make, and maybe I wouldn't make very much. We'd have to rely on your income to keep up the mortgage payments and so on. On the other hand, I've been saving up money for this, to carry us while I got started. And I could always hit up Dad for a loan. But it would mean a massive investment of my time as well as money, and I'd probably be anxious and busy at first – but then, I like the idea of that, not of being anxious, but of being busy, getting my own company organized . . . What do you think?'

'I think it's a wonderful idea!' Sara said honestly. 'Oh, Steve, I think it's a marvellous, exciting idea.'

'I called my lawyer yesterday. I've got an appointment with him tomorrow to find out about incorporating. Mick and Alex have already said they'd go to work for me if I set up on my own . . .'

Steve continued talking, his words coming fast with his excitement. Sara leaned against him again, smiling, listening. She was amazed – not that he wanted to go into business on his own, but that he was so very much engrossed with anything that didn't have to do with having children. It seemed really possible that he was not as caught up in the desperate desire as she was. At any rate, he was not thinking of leaving her, he was happy with her, he loved her.

Steve told her about the problems he had been having with his boss, about his sense of shame and anger at the shabbiness of the work they were doing, the corners they were cutting, the minor rules they were breaking. He told her what he hoped he could achieve with his own company. *My God*, Sara thought, *how have I let myself get so absorbed in my own problems? I didn't realize all this was going on.* For a long grand moment, she felt her heart swell out toward Steve so that she felt maternal toward him, protective, hopeful; *he* was the one she cared for most in the world, *he* was the one she wanted to help. After all, he was young, his life wasn't over yet, there were things he wanted to do. She did not have to stake the meaning of their lives on having children. She had forgotten this, or had not known it. It made everything more bearable.

Darkness dropped around them, bringing with it a gentle breeze. From across the water came an exotic almost-Oriental sound of wind chimes tinkling; it was the gentle clanging of wires and shrouds hitting the masts of the boats anchored in the harbor. The sand at their feet grew black. The sea disappeared into darkness, except for an occasional ruffle of wave that caught the slight moonlight for an instant. The breeze was cool. Summer was not eternal. Fall was coming. Changes were on the way. Sara and Steve rose and walked home through the easy streets, comforted by each other's presence in the dark and fluid night.

CHAPTER NINE

Morning.

They caught the six-thirty ferry. Today Sara would have lab tests done at the hospital. Tomorrow she would have surgery.

They had told Steve's boss and their friends, the people in their group, that they were gong to Boston for the rehearsal dinner and wedding of a friend of Sara's, a business colleague. Sara still was not on intimate terms with the women on Nantucket, so she knew no questions would be asked.

Now that they were actually on the way, Sara was relaxed. She had indulged herself one last time in maudlin self-dramatization; she had written Steve a long mushy good-bye letter and included it with a will (leaving Steve everything); both were in an envelope, lying on her side of the dresser where Steve could easily find it if he were to come home alone.

It was a pleasure to drive up over Cape Cod Canal and then along Route 3 to Boston. Already they could see the beginning of fall in the flame-tipped trees that bordered the road. The dunes and short scrubby trees that fought to grow on Nantucket and the Cape soon gave way to thick bushy evergreens and majestic maples, which in turn gave way to the splendid rampant Boston skyline.

Brigham and Women's Hospital was really a city all its own. The entrance to the day surgery unit was much like an airport terminal on a busy day; there was the same information desk with the same beleaguered woman answering the questions of lost souls; the same gift shop selling the same overpriced stuffed animals and anonymous kitsch; the same kind of crowd milling and surging through the echoing foyer, as if from one continent to another.

It took almost an hour for Sara and Steve to deal with the

first step: sitting in a cramped cubicle, they told a harassed secretary every sequence of numbers that had or ever would have any relevance to their lives. Birth dates. Social Security. Address. Phone. Health insurance policy number. Then they were sent off to give the hospital a check for fifteen hundred dollars, the deductible amount of Sara's health insurance.

They found the day surgery admissions room in the basement of the building. Here they were very organized. They presented Sara with a blue plastic card with her name and hospital account number stamped into it, a white file card telling her that her surgery would take place at eleven-thirty the next day and that she should be at the hospital no later than nine-thirty or she would be considered late and the surgery would be canceled, and several Xeroxed papers entitled 'Pre-Operative Instructions for Day Surgery Unit', 'Pre-Op Instructions for Diagnostic Laparoscopy', and 'Pre-Op Instructions, D & C'.

Sara and Steve sat in the crowded waiting room, waiting for the anesthetist to call her name. Steve looked at old magazines; Sara read the information she had been given. It all seemed very simple and straightforward, nothing to be alarmed about. And, she reasoned, if there were so many of these operations that material was Xeroxed to be distributed, they must be very common operations. Everything would be fine.

Finally her name was called, and she was sent down the hall to a small office where an anesthetist took her 'anesthesia history' and explained how the anesthesia would be administered. The anesthetist was a surprisingly beautiful young woman, even in her green scrubs with her hair stuck under what looked like a shower cap. She radiated health, and she had the longest, reddest fingernails Sara had ever seen.

'Do you have any questions?' she asked Sara.

To Sara's slight surprise (but then all this seemed unreal, and she felt so unaccountable, for on entering the hospital she had let go of certain inhibitions), Sara heard herself say, 'Yes, I do have a question. How did you get your nails so long? They're beautiful.'

The anesthetist laughed. 'Oh, they're fake,' she said. 'I had terrible nails, really, so I wear these. My eyelashes are fake, too.'

Surely, Sara thought as she walked back down the hall, surely something as dreadful as *death* couldn't exist side by side with that gorgeous woman with fake fingernails. She was extraordinarily cheered.

The lab tests were conducted in the Admitting Test Center. Sara gave them urine, asked Steve to hold her hand while the nurse took blood from her arm (it didn't hurt! She thanked the nurse, who looked amused by her gratitude), and had an electrocardiogram. When she lay down on the table for the E K G, her shirt and bra undone, exposing her bare breasts, she felt vulnerable for a moment, alarmed.

'Will this hurt?' she asked, looking at the funny little suction cups attached to myriad wires that the nurse was placing in semi-circles around her breasts.

'Honey,' the nurse said with what Sara recognized as a Jamaican lilt, 'when I get through doing this to you, you going to ask me to do it to you again.'

And it didn't hurt. It was over in a flash. The lab work was over – they were free to go.

The rest of the day flew by; they went to some bookstores in Cambridge, and to dinner at Pistachio's and a silly movie, then to the hotel to bed. Sara thought at first that she wouldn't be able to enjoy making love, that she would be too over-whelmed with emotion, thinking, 'This might be the last time I'll ever make love. Tomorrow I might die.' But all such thoughts vanished when she crawled into the hotel bed with Steve. It was fun to be in a strange bed with him, between crisp white sheets instead of their colored ones, fun to feel a little illicit; here they were just the two of them, together in an alien world. They made love for such a long time that Sara fell into a contented and exhausted sleep immediately afterward.

She awoke at six o'clock and couldn't get back to sleep. Two months ago she had had her thirty-fifth birthday. She felt so old, and so young. She slipped from the bed and into the bathroom to take a very long, very hot shower. She looked down at her naked body, which she had so often been so critical of. But it was a perfectly fine body, really, all of a piece, soft to the touch, but firm beneath. What would she look like after the surgery? Would Steve be grossed out by her scarred body? Really, she thought, they were living in a society that was too rational, too scientific. It would be better for everyone if some magic and ritual were included, too; if, for example, Steve also had to go through some procedure involving anesthesia and loss of consciousness and control and necessitating the slight scarring of his body. They they would be more of a couple, then he would understand her better because he would have been through similar experiences, then they would not be forced further apart by their differences. She was certain that she had read of such mirror behavior in primitive societies. She wished something like that could be done here and now, for more than anything else she was aware of the fact that when it came right down to it, she was going through it all alone.

She could not have anything to eat or drink. Not even a sip of water. She brushed her teeth carefully, using little water, spitting it all out, not swallowing a drop. She dressed – and undressed; for the nurses had warned her to take off her engagement and wedding rings. When her hands were bare, she felt sad; she had never taken her rings off before and it seemed wrong to do so, a violation.

She could not wear any makeup; another hospital rule. She peered in the mirror at her pale morning face, the eyes slightly puffy (they had had a lot of wine last night), the eyebrows too fine and light without pencilling; they seemed to blend into her skin, her six tiny pastel freckles jumping out across the bridge of her nose without powder to obscure them. She looked young and fragile: too young to die.

After she opened the door from the bathroom, fully dressed, ready to go to the hospital, the day blossomed before her with the startling rapidity of time-lapse photography. Steve dressed quickly, they drove to the hospital, they were in the waiting room. When her name was called, Sara was led to a woman's dressing room where she took off her clothes and put on a blue-and-white-striped gown with a blue-and-white-striped robe and squishy blue plastic foam slippers. She tied the robe tightly, thinking Steve might admire her slender waist, but when he saw her he said, 'Seersucker, huh. Pretty classy hospital.'

They sat together inside the day surgery unit, waiting for Sara's name to be called again. Nurses and doctors hurried past. Two healthy young men joked with each other from adjoining hospital beds. A pitiful-looking young woman pushing her I V pole with one hand and with a nurse on her other side holding her arm crept past them into the rest room. A man in a wheelchair, wearing a hat to obscure the fact that he had lost most of his hair, sat next to them, begging his wife to take him home, he did not want to face the treatment today. The day deepened around them.

At last a nurse came to get Sara. In front of the room full of people, Steve pulled Sara to him in a long embrace. 'I love you,' he whispered.

'I love you, Steve,' Sara replied.

The nurse led Sara to a barred hospital bed in the large open room and helped her climb in.

A tall young man approached, introducing himself as her anesthesiologist. Sara listened as he told her what they were going to do, nodding, not understanding a word. *I have already given up control*, she was thinking. *I would not any more jump from this bed and run away than stand up and curse in church. Even here, where I'm afraid I'll die, I'm polite and bound by etiquette. I could leave now if I wanted to; I'm not hampered. But I won't. I'll sit and smile at this guy, who, if he makes a mistake, could kill me or maim me, and I won't say any of the things I had planned to say, like 'Don't goof,' or even 'Please be careful.' I don't care that he's good-looking and might be judging me, I don't care if he sees my breasts or thinks my stomach's flabby. The world operates by a completely different set of rules here and I instinctively know them. I have already given up control.*

Dr Crochett appeared then, smiling, chatting, joking. 'Don't worry,' he said. 'I've already done two of these this morning, I've had plenty of practice.'

Sara was glad to see him, someone she *knew*, yet at the same time she felt estranged from him; he was part of *them*. She looked away while he put an IV in the vein of her left hand, surprised at how little it hurt, surprised to see the nurse still with her, on the other side of the bed.

Then she was being wheeled down the hallway and through a swinging door. She saw a sign, pointing in another direction, that said DELIVERY ROOM.

'I'd rather be going there,' she said.

'That's next time,' Dr Crochett told her.

She was helped from the rolling bed to the stationary table in the operating room. She felt drowsy, warm, and relaxed. Someone placed a mask over her mouth and nose; she was alert enough to mind.

'I don't like this mask,' Sara said.

'You'll be asleep in a few seconds,' the nurse said.

'I don't like losing control,' Sara said, for she could feel it going, or rather, feel herself going.

'Try counting backward from one hundred,' the anesthetist said.

'I really don't like this mask,' Sara said, and then, with complete awareness, but with no feeling of alarm, she felt herself go under.

'Hi,' someone said. Sara opened her eyes and saw that she was in the recovery room, blankets over her and a blurry nurse standing near her.

'Hi,' the nurse said again.

I'm alive, Sara thought. *I'm alive and I thought I'd jump for joy when I woke up, but I'm too drugged out.* She raised the blankets and lifted her gown and peered down at herself. There was an enormous Band-Aid just under her belly button and another one just above her pubic hair. *It's the same day; they didn't do a laparotomy*, she thought, and drifted off.

'Hi,' Dr Crochett said from the foot of the bed, 'You're just fine. A little endometriosis that I could take care of without a laparotomy, and we did a tubal lavage and you're all opened up. I did a D&C, too, so you're all squeaky clean. You're in great shape and ready to go.'

'You didn't do the laparotomy?' Sara asked.

'Didn't need to. You do not have severe endometriosis,' Dr Crochett said. 'I'll tell you more later. You won't remember anything I tell you now.'

'Oh,' Sara said. She watched the doctor rise into the air at her feet and slowly float along the ceiling away from her. It was amazing that he could do that, but she was too tired to watch.

A while later the nurse returned. 'Want to get up?'

'No,' Sara said. 'Never.' Vaguely, in the Sahara Desert of her mind, she remembered her sister's advice: the sooner you get up and walk around, move around, the sooner the effect of the drug dissipates.

But her sister hadn't told her that she would feel like this: overwhelmingly sick to her stomach. Her vision was murky with nausea. If she moved her head, bruise-colored waves splatted at her eyes. So how was she to move her body?

But the nurse was pulling back the covers and assisting her from the bed. Sara's robotlike body plopped down one leg, then the other, and the three of them, nurse, Sara, and the tall stainless steel I V pole, clunked along the floor away from the bed.

They had not really operated on Sara. They had really just beaten her up. They must have straightened up the bed so that she was strapped in standing position, and then taken turns beating her over and over again just under her rib cage. She was so sore there she could scarcely breathe.

'My abdomen hurts,' Sara said.

'That's right,' the nurse said. 'That's the carbon dioxide. They used it to blow up your abdomen so they wouldn't hit the bowel. It'll only last for a day or two.'

'If it lasts for a day or two, I won't last for a day or two,' Sara said.

The nurse giggled. 'You're doing just fine,' she assured Sara.

Together they shuffled and clunked their way across the

recovery room, covering entire inches in hours. Sara's head was thick, her abdomen and shoulders ached, and the nausea retreated slightly only to return in ever more violent waves.

'Why don't you just go in here and see what you can do?' the nurse suggested, guiding Sara into the same bathroom she had earlier in the day seen another woman enter. Vaguely she wondered if she looked as pathetic as that woman had.

Sara sank down on the toilet and looked at the pad she had automatically pulled down. It was soaked with blood. But she couldn't feel herself bleeding. She couldn't feel anything but nausea and the intense pressure from the gas on her rib cage. Through the vast wasteland of her mind came the knowledge that she was urinating.

When she had finished, she stood up shakily and washed her hands, careful not to get the I V tube on her left hand wet, then leaned on the sink, looking deep into the mirror to find her reflection. Yes, there she was. Alive, in a way. It was interesting that her face could look this way; at once pitiful and bland, like a piece of paper someone had stepped on. Slowly she reopened the bathroom door and wobbled back into the recovery room.

'Did you urinate?' the nurse asked.

'Yes,' Sara replied.

'You won't be needing this, then,' the nurse said. And she took away the I V and pole.

Sara felt bereft without the pole. It had given her something to hold on to. Now she slumped forward, in slow motion, knowing that sooner or later she would just sag right down to the floor.

'I wish you could make me feel better,' Sara said confidingly. 'I feel like shit.'

'Just sit down here awhile,' the nurse said. 'You'll be better soon. Why don't I bring you some crackers and a 7-UP.'

The nurse brought a little packet of saltine crackers and a cup of 7-UP.

'Would you like me to get your husband for you?' she asked.

'I really don't think so,' Sara replied. Surely the nausea

would pass in a while. She had with great effort managed to find the clock on the wall. She had even managed to decipher the time. It was three-fifteen. She was sure she would be better soon.

'Why don't I give you a shot of Compazine to help your stomach?' the nurse asked.

'Whatever,' Sara said. She was aware of the shot being administered in the way one is aware of a mosquito biting in a dream.

At four the nurse brought Steve in to her.

'She's doing just fine!' the nurse said cheerfully.

Sara looked up at Steve. She had not realized he was so tall. She had to crane her neck backward to look up at his face, which wavered before her thirty or forty feet in the air.

'Hi,' she said and leaned forward and vomited on his shoes.

This left her shaking with weakness, but amazingly clear-headed. She was aware suddenly of the nurses scurrying around, of people giving Steve paper towels, of Steve sitting down in the chair next to her to wipe off his shoes.

'I'm glad you wore your wing tips instead of your sneakers,' Sara managed to say. 'It would have soaked into your sneakers.'

'Do you feel better?' the nurse asked.

'A little,' Sara said to the nurse. To Steve she said, 'I didn't do that on purpose, you know.'

'I know,' Steve said. He put his hand on her shoulder. *Someone should tell him that his hand weighs as much as a car*, Sara thought. 'How are you?'

'Better,' Sara said. 'Alive at least.'

'I love you,' Steve said. 'I'm glad you're okay.'

'I love you, too,' Sara told him.

By four-thirty she was ready to leave. Steve drove her back to the hotel and Sara shuffled through the lobby and into the elevator. Steve opened the door, helped her take off her clothes and get into her nightgown, helped her get into bed. Her shoulders and abdomen were still pressured by the carbon dioxide, which in certain positions even made her wince. She arranged herself on several pillows, and lay there, fading into

188

and out of the evening. She was aware from time to time that Steve had left the room, had returned with a paper bag from Brigham's. She was aware that he was watching TV, eating, calling his parents, talking to her.

At last Steve turned off the television and the lights, undressed and crawled into bed with her. Vaguely Sara recalled the time she had called Dr Crochett in a panic to ask how long they would have to wait after her operation before making love. 'About two weeks if you have a laparotomy,' Dr Crochett had said. 'And if you just have the laparoscopy, the same night if you feel like it.'

'Yeah, *right*,' Sara said to Dr Crochett.

'Did you say something?' Steve asked.

'Good night,' Sara mumbled.

'Good night, Sara,' Steve said.

He leaned over to kiss her. His movements made the bed rock like a ship in a stormy sea. The slight touch of his lips set off waves of rolling thunder in her head and stomach. Finally he lay down and was quiet. He slept. Sara stayed in the position she had spent the evening in, propped against pillows – if she lay down the gas surged up into her shoulders and burned to get out. She was aware that she was listing sideways and that if she continued to fall she would have to make the monumental effort of righting herself or enduring pain. Her mind was stumblingly tackling this problem when she really fell, into the blessed black bliss of sleep.

Morning.

Glorious, ecstatic, celestial morning.

Sara woke up sane and whole and hungry. Ravenous. It had been thirty-six hours since she had eaten (the crackers and 7-UP didn't count, and anyway she had lost them on Steve's shoes).

Steve came out of the bathroom, trailing smells of soap and shaving cream. He was wearing slacks but no shoes or shirt, and when she saw his bare chest, all hairy and muscular, she felt the most delicious surge of lust pass through her.

'Oh, God!' she cried. 'I'm back to normal!'

Well, almost. In the bathroom she found that she was still bleeding slightly. She peeled back one of the bandages that covered her incision – which was torture, the hospital clearly had used Elmer's Glue to stick the bandages to her – and saw nothing very remarkable, only a messy wine-colored slit with plastic threads sticking out. Not very attractive, but on the other hand, nothing to get pitiful about. How pretty she looked, how young and fresh and healthy and whole.

And how beautiful this hotel room was with its geometric 1950s faded green-and-blue curtains and bedspreads, its chipped veneer bureaus and chairs. Oh, how wonderful the morning was with its heavy gray clouds scudding across the sky – life was grand! She was alive and well and *not nauseated*, and never again in her life would she complain about anything!

They dressed and went out for breakfast at a fancy hotel restaurant. Sara had scrambled eggs and sausages and country-fried potatoes and English muffins with piles of strawberry jam and butter and a tall glass of grapefruit juice. But first she had coffee, hot rich, dark coffee, thick with cream and sugar; it melted in her mouth like chocolate and expanded through her body like LSD. She didn't think she had ever been happier in her life.

Back home, the next day she awoke feeling truly normal – happy but not manic – and tired. She decided to spend the day in bed. She began reading a novel she had bought for just this day, and was delighted to see rain streaking down her bedroom windows, as if the weather were giving her approval to be lazy.

In the middle of the afternoon, the doorbell rang and she opened it to a florist delivering a magnificent arrangement of flowers that Fanny had sent. She put them on her bedside table where she could look at them, and then turned back to her novel. But now she could not concentrate. The flowers made her think of Fanny . . . something special about Fanny . . . she rose from bed and shuffled to the living room to get her Xeroxed copy of the manuscript of *Jenny's Book*. Back in bed, she leafed through the book, then stopped to read, carefully, the final two pages in Fanny's novel.

Some of us are meant to fight with Fate. Not that it's ever a fair fight, not that we can ever win completely, but the occasional triumphs we wrest away are so glowing, like golden trophies, like prizes we have never dreamed of, that finally, bad taken with the good, it is worth the effort.

And sometimes it is the fight itself that matters: the daily battle that makes our senses blaze.

The trick is to find the fight that belongs to you. In Kansas I knew even as a child I could never defeat the elements – that wind, killing frost, blistering heat, hateful air. The people who stayed to battle there I honor in my heart: they are mythic to me, humans who pit themselves against nature over and over again. They win simply because they stay to fight, their victories and defeats are often the same, their nobility becomes etched in the lines of their faces.

My battle was of a different sort. It is not over, nor will it be, until the day I die. I battle against elements almost as deadly as the Kansas weather – against dullness, stupidity, insensitivity – against nonsense. I would so much like for life to be comprised of something other than nonsense, and for people to be handsomer, more articulate, and kinder than they are. Also, of course, I would like them to admire me, I would always like that. Growing old, as I am, I am also growing, in my own way, more vain, and more demanding – imperious and difficult I have often been called.

But I have learned some things and in my wisdom feel superior enough to attempt to pass them on. As I grow closer to death, which if nothing else is the absence of the life I know, I have discovered the meaning of life. It resides in the books I love and the animals that surround me; in present friends and in memories of lovers and enemies, too; in silk, champagne, an applewood fire, and Mozart. It resides in what I can wrest from each day that I live.

It's here.

It's here.

'Well, Fanny,' Sara said aloud. She put the manuscript down on the bed beside her and spoke aloud to herself, to the air, the flowers, to Fanny's spirit. 'Good for you! You did it. You fought with Fate and won, and this book is your victory. And you know, it looks as if I'm meant to fight with Fate, too, I'm trying! I did have the operation, you know! I was terrified of it, but I did it, I did try to take control. But it's different for me. I've found the fight that belongs to me, but for me it's not the fight that matters – I want to win! I want the prize! I want a baby. And there's only so much *I* can do!'

Sara ran her hands over the manuscript. White paper, black print. It had taken Fanny a lifetime to accomplish this. Fanny's fight with Fate was all about creating, and so was Sara's, but in a different way. She had helped Fanny bring her book to the light of day, but it would take a different source of help for Sara and Steve to have a child. It would take that spark, that flash, that gift from nowhere seen, and Sara could have operations and use charts and pray, but still her Fate relied on more than determination and persistence; it relied on something beyond her control.

Still. Still, as Fanny said, the meaning of life was not about having babies, but in the present, in wresting what she could from each day she lived.

That night when Steve came home, he brought pizza, and chocolate chip cookies for dessert, and later they made love, gentle, careful, easy love. In the dark deep night Steve lay against her, Sara held him, he was inside her, she enclosed him, they were two halves of a whole, blended and blurred and complete. And Sara thought: *It's here. It's here.*

Dr Crochett had told Sara that many women got pregnant the first cycle after a laparoscopy, so when Sara's period started at the end of September she was nearly wild with surprise and grief. But when she called his office, he calmed her, 'No, no,' he said, 'this doesn't count, next month is the important cycle, not this month.' She hung up the phone, feeling foolish and weak with relief. She should have known; and after all, it would have been expecting a miracle for her to get pregnant right after the operation, because she had bled for almost a week. And she had taken strong antibiotics for two weeks in order to forestall any infection from the operation – that wouldn't have been good for a developing embryo. So it was all right that she wasn't pregnant. Logically it was all right.

She went to Boston to have the stitches removed. Dr Crochett pronounced her in great shape. 'Go home and get pregnant!' he said.

'Should I use the ovulation-indicator tests?' she asked him.

'No,' he said, 'don't bother with all that, don't even think about it. It will only get you nervous. Just have a great time with your husband. Make love a lot.'

It was the beginning of October. The days glowed. Sara took on as much editing as she could, needing to keep occupied and needing to replenish the money they had spent on the operation.

She spoke with Fanny on the phone several times a week – Fanny had received the galleys of her book for proofreading, and she was getting nervous about its publication. The book due was out in January; the earliest reviews would appear in December.

Caroline and Clark Kendall closed up their 'Sconset House and went back to Florida. Sara felt enormously (and guiltily) relieved to see them go.

The island emptied of tourists. Shops and stores and side-walks were no longer crowded. Steve had stopped working for Mack and, with two men working for him, had gone into business for himself. He was up and out early and home late and dirty and tired. But he was happy, and Sara was happy for him. And happy for herself.

They made love a lot that month. And it really was love. Sara stopped using the thermometer and didn't try to make love when she wasn't in the mood – but she was gratefully aware of the fact that they made love every night during the week she was to ovulate. After they made love, without even mention-ing it, she slipped a pillow under her hips, remembering how Morris Newhouse had held her bottom in the air to help the semen enter her uterus.

The last two weeks of October were golden. Sara biked every afternoon, luxuriating in the sun on her face; in the evenings she and Steve sat by the fire reading or talking. She started to needlepoint another pillow. She felt radiantly happy, in an almost sinfully contented domesticity.

Why was it that the group always got together on exactly the days that signs of her period began?

'I can't believe I'm so significant or wicked that the universe is conspiring against me this way!' Sara said aloud to the mirror as she got ready for the evening out. She was tense today, tense and worried, and she talked aloud to herself, chiding herself, cajoling herself, trying to control herself: if she didn't *think* her period was going to start, it wouldn't start. But there was no doubt that her stomach was bloated and swollen, her breasts were stinging, her spirits had plunged. And this afternoon, when she got out of the shower, she had been horrified to see a splot of blood on her ankle. At first she thought she had cut her leg somehow, then realized what it was, where it had come from.

'No,' she said. 'No. No.'

She had sunk down onto the floor, knocked out with dismay. Tomorrow was the twenty-ninth day. It looked as if she was going to start her period again. It looked as if she, unlike other women, was not going to be pregnant the first cycle after her laparoscopy. She sat on the bathroom floor, stunned, stupid, unable to think of a reason for getting up.

Finally she put her hand to her crotch, then pulled her fingers away and looked. No blood. No sign of blood. Perhaps – perhaps anything. *Oh, fuck*, Sara thought, perhaps anything at all. Ellie had said that quite often women still bled a little when they were pregnant, and that sometimes women even thought they had had their period when they were pregnant. She did not have to give up all hopes because of that spot of blood.

This thought gave her the courage to go on as normal. She

took her time in front of the mirror, putting on her makeup carefully, trying on various clothes. She wanted to get just the right look. Tonight there was a party at the Danforths' to celebrate Wade Danforth's birthday, which was today, and Sheldon Jones's birthday, which was tomorrow. It was a pot-luck dinner, everyone was bringing something, and there would be champagne, and since the Danforths' had a big house, there would be dancing. A real party. Sara felt that she had often dressed inappropriately for the group's get-to-gethers. She often wore a silk dress, which was what she would have worn in Boston, only to find that all the other women had worn jeans or slacks. Tonight she put on a huge loose almost-ankle-length cotton sweater dress she had ordered from Bloomingdale's. It was bright red and had big shoulder pads and a boat neck with a plunging V in the back. It was a great-looking dress, sloppy yet elegant, unstudied-looking. She put on a pair of long dangling gold-and-red earrings and lots of makeup.

'There,' she said to her reflection in the mirror, 'your body might be hopeless, but it still *looks* good.'

Steve whistled when he saw Sara. And he paid her his ultimate compliment, using the word she allowed herself to interpret in many ways, as 'gorgeous' or 'beautiful' or 'sexy.' He said, 'Hey, you look really nice.'

Sara smiled and kissed him, secretly wondering if he would ever in his life tell her she looked anything but nice.

Steve looked nice, too, after he had showered and put on chinos and a button-down shirt and a sweater. The heavy physical work he did kept him in great condition; his stomach was flat, his arms and legs were shapely with muscles. Sara loved the contrast of his civilized clothes on his prize-animal body. And he was so pleasant to be with these days, fun, relaxed, optimistic, and easygoing. She was more in love with her husband now, she knew, than she had been when they were married.

Wade Danforth had brought out all his old 1960s records and before long Wade and Annie were laughing and doing the old hand-jive to Bo Diddley. Sara took off her shoes and danced barefoot. She was glad to see that all the other women had worn dresses or sweaters and skirts. All except The Virgin, who was wearing her usual tight jeans and tighter sweater. The outfit looked strange on her now that she was four months pregnant and her tummy swelled outward just enough to make her look pudgy. Mary sat in the corner most of the evening, talking to friends, shaking her head when asked to dance. Sara noticed that Bill Bennett was paying no attention to his wife; but actually he seemed to be in one of his black moods, avoiding everyone and everything except the kitchen counter where the booze was. Now and then Sara thought about talking to him – after all, she was an editor and he was a writer – but he had never approached her on the subject. No, she wouldn't approach him; he was too scary, his dark moods emanating from him like a fog. She forgot about him and enjoyed herself, dancing with Steve and the other men, laughing and joking with the women, dancing again with Steve, drinking the champagne that had been brought for the birthdays.

She had enjoyed herself so much – and had had so much to drink – that when she went to the bathroom and saw that her pants were stained with a heavy flow of blood she felt only impatient, unreal. This hadn't really happened, her period hadn't really started, she didn't even believe it. She was at a party, everyone was happy, she was having fun. She wouldn't believe it, she wouldn't let it be. She left the bathroom without taking any precautions against getting blood on her clothing.

Coming down the hall from the bathroom, she was given a tunnel view of Mary Bennett, who was still seated in her corner of the living room, snuggled against the sofa.

Steve was sitting on the arm of the sofa, looking down at Mary. As Sara watched, Mary took Steve's hand and put it on her rounded stomach. She said something to him. Steve said something to her and smiled. With her hand, Mary moved Steve's hand upward so that while the greater part of it touched her stomach, part of his hand touched her large swollen breast.

Immediately Steve took his hand away.

Mary smiled at Steve, and Sara, still in the hallway, could

see the challenge in the smile. She was surprised that the sexual message Mary was transmitting hadn't made the entire group turn and stare at her in amazement.

Steve rose from the sofa and walked away.

Mary turned her head and saw Sara coming toward her. Mary's eyes narrowed like a cat's or a vampire's and she did not smile and she did not look away. *She is a witch*, Sara thought. *She is a witch and she is cursing me*. It seemed centuries before she arrived at the end of the hallway and entered the crowded living room.

Everyone was laughing, dancing, talking, but the magic had gone out of the party for Sara and it was with effort that she played her part. She danced until the stickiness between her legs made her realize she would embarrass herself if she didn't do something. She made her way back to Annie Danforth's bathroom. Locking the door behind her, she opened the big cupboard in the wall, looking for Tampax or a maxi-pad. She found both, and also found, with a frisson of delight, a First Response kit, a kit used to tell exactly when ovulation will occur.

So perhaps she wasn't alone. Perhaps Annie Danforth was having trouble getting pregnant, too. Annie was in her early thirties and had no children. She would have to have Annie to lunch; they could drink wine, get confidential. What a relief it would be to know one other woman who was having the same problem! A wave of real relief swept through Sara, counteracting the despair that was rising in her body like a well of tears. Someone else was having a problem. She was not unique, abnormal – she was not so terribly cursed or flawed.

Sara put Annie's things back in the cupboard. She washed her hands, combed her hair, refreshed her lipstick, stared at herself in the mirror. Did the pain show in her eyes?

When she came back into the living room, she found the party mellowing. Only Jamie and Sheldon were dancing. Everyone else was sitting now, sprawled on the floor or on the sofa and chairs, smoking cigarettes or pot, finishing beer or glasses of champagne. Everyone was there except Steve.

Sara went into the kitchen. No one was there. Even Bill Bennett had disappeared from his guard over the booze.

She went back into the living room, sank down next to Annie, and waited until she had finished talking with Carole to ask, 'Where's Steve?'

Annie yawned. 'I was supposed to tell you,' she said. 'He took Mary home.' Seeing the look of surprise on Sara's face, she went on, 'Where have you been? We've had quite a little drama in the past few minutes. Mary wanted to go home, I think, anyway she went into the kitchen and was talking to Bill, and the next thing we knew Bill was cursing and shouting and we all thought he was going to hit her or something. What an asshole he is. Anyway, he stomped out of here so fast he forgot his jacket. And then Mary asked Steve if he would drive her home; we saw Bill drive off in their car. Steve said he'd be right back.'

'Oh,' Sara said, feeling her voice come small and weak from her throat. 'I was in the bathroom. I guess, with the music I didn't hear –'

Carole leaned forward. 'I just hope Bill's not waiting at home when Mary gets there. He can be such a mean drunk.'

'No, it's early yet, he probably went off to a bar,' Annie said. 'At least I think that's his pattern. I don't think Mary's afraid of him. I don't think he's violent or anything. He just says such awful stuff. Poor Mary.'

Carole looked at her watch. 'You might think it's early, but I don't,' she said. 'We should go home, too.'

Sara looked at her watch. It was just after midnight. She had been in the bathroom for perhaps ten minutes, she thought – the Bennetts didn't live very far from here, no more than a five-minute drive. Steve should be back any minute.

Annie had risen to see Carole and Pete to the door. Other couples were getting ready to leave now. Women gathered casserole dishes and salad bowls. Sara watched from the sofa as the group clustered in the doorway and, couple by couple, disappeared into the night.

She was left alone with Annie and Wade. She did not need to look at her watch to know that Steve should be back by now.

'God, I'm beat, I'm going to turn in,' Wade said, stretching.

'Go ahead,' Annie said. 'I'm just going to clean up a bit.'

'Let me help,' Sara offered, glad for a chance to do something that would make the time pass, so that she wouldn't be sitting there awkwardly, abandoned. As she carried overflowing ashtrays and empty beer bottles into the kitchen, she thought about asking Annie about the ovulation test but decided against it; it was too late, they were too tired, Steve would surely be back any moment and their conversation would be interrupted. But what was Steve doing? Why wasn't he back? Damn, why wasn't he back?

A half hour passed intolerably slowly. The two women cleaned the living room, dining room, and kitchen, chatting all the while, dissembling. Just when Sara thought she could stand it no longer, that she would turn to Annie and let tears streak down her face while she bawled out her worst fears, there was a sound at the door and Steve came in.

'Hi,' he said. 'Where'd everybody go?'

'The clock struck twelve,' Annie said, grinning. 'They all turned into pumpkins.'

'What took you so long?' Sara asked, keeping her voice casual. She wanted to scream the words at him.

'Well, I had to take the baby-sitter home,' Steve said, 'and then I stayed a few minutes to talk to Mary. Poor kid. Bill has such a temper.'

'I know,' Annie said. 'Even when he's not in a bad mood he's scary. I don't think I've ever seen him be really pleasant.'

'I guess he thinks that artists are exempt from ordinary rules,' Steve said.

'Was he home? Is Mary going to be okay?' Annie asked.

'No, he wasn't home, and Mary said he probably wouldn't wander in until early in the morning. He's got drinking buddies he hangs out with. She's fine. She's not afraid of him, she just gets tired of him sometimes.'

On the way home in the car, Sara waited for Steve to say something else, to give her a fuller explanation. Surely he owed her that. He knew how she felt about Mary. And he had been gone a long time. But he said nothing. He drove in silence, occupied with his thoughts, and his silence was like fuel to the flame of anger that burned in Sara's stomach and finally blazed up when they entered the house.

'Did you kiss her?' Sara asked, her voice accusing and grim.

'What?' Steve asked, looking surprised.

'Oh, come off it,' Sara said. 'You heard me.' Cramps spread in waves across her body and down her thighs. She could feel the heavy blood pushing its swollen way through her. Just so was her anger mushrooming its way upward from her body, expanding into a black cloud of wrath she could no longer contain.

'No, I didn't kiss her. Jesus, Sara,' Steve said. He walked away from her, up the stairs to their bedroom.

Sara followed, feeling her body shaking with rage. 'Well, did you hold her? Comfort her? Did you "comfort" *poor Mary*?' Her voice was twisted with sarcasm.

Steve sat on the foot of the bed to take off his shoes. 'No, I didn't comfort her,' he said, his voice even and martyred. 'I did talk to her. I mostly listened to her. She's unhappy.'

'And she thinks you can make her happy. Right? Right?' Sara stood in the doorway, glaring at her husband. One part of her mind lifted up and away from her body, and, hovering somewhere in the north corner of their bedroom ceiling, stared down at Sara in amazement. Where did this harpy come from? What did she think she was doing?

'Sara, I'm tired. I wish you would just drop it,' Steve said.

'You go off and leave the party, leave me alone at the party, with all your friends knowing you've gone off with your old lover, you go off alone with her for over half an hour, and you want me to just act like nothing happened?' Sara said. Suddenly her anger became all confused with fear and she began to cry.

'Oh, Sara.' Steve sighed. 'I hate all this so much, don't you know it? I hate it when you're jealous. Why can't you trust me? Why can't you believe me? I love you. I don't love anyone else. I don't love Mary. I just feel incredibly sorry for her. But I wouldn't *do* anything with her. It's just stupid of you to be jealous this way.'

Sara crossed the room and sat on the bed, as far away from

Steve as she could get and still manage to find purchase. She huddled up against the headboard. 'I can't help being jealous,' she said. 'When I see the way she looks at you. I saw her with you tonight. The way she took your hand and put it on her stomach. The way you smiled at her. The way she smiled at you.' She looked up at Steve, who sat at the end of the bed, his elbows on his knees, his head lowered into his hands. She waited, but he said nothing. His silence goaded her on. 'Did you feel the baby move?' Sara asked accusingly. 'Did you like touching her? Did you wish she were your wife and that were your baby?'

Steve didn't answer. He only sat, head obscured in his hands.

Sara stared, tears streaking down her face. Then, startling herself, she grabbed a book from the bedside table and threw it across the room. It thudded against the wall and fell to the floor. 'God-damn it!' she screamed. 'If you're going to go off alone with your old lover, the least you can do is talk to me. If you want me, that is! If you don't, then at least have the decency to tell me. Or I swear I'll leave. I'll pack my bags and leave and you'll never see me again. That's what you would like, isn't it? Then you could be rid of me, and you could marry Mary and have babies with her. She could give you all the children you need.'

'Shut up, Sara,' Steve said. 'Please just shut up.'

Sara was so astonished that she did go quiet. Steve had never said anything like that before. She rose, went into the bathroom and changed her pad, which was soaked with blood, rinsed her face with cold water, trying to regain some kind of control, then calmly went back into the bedroom. She took her suitcase from the closet and opened it on the bed. She would leave him. It was all over. She couldn't believe it was happening.

'Sara,' Steve said. 'Look. There's something you should know. Christ, Sara, would you stop packing and sit down and listen to me?'

Sara looked at Steve. His face was strangely contorted. She didn't think she had ever seen him look quite so sickened. She sat down on the bed, looking at Steve, not touching him.

'When Mary and I were going together,' Steve began, then stopped. When he spoke again, his voice took on the cramped tone of a man holding back tears. 'When Mary and I were going together,' he said again, slowly, 'she knew I didn't want to marry her. I had told her, often, that I wasn't ready for that kind of commitment with her. I was always honest about that. You have to believe me. I never led her on. I told her I didn't love her anymore. But we kept on – going together – now and then, out of, oh, habit or convenience, I don't know. Anyway, I got her pregnant.'

Sara's heart was scalded with pain. The fire of all her anger turned back on her now and she burned at the stake of this new knowledge.

'It was an accident,' Steve was saying. 'On my part, at least. I mean, I thought she was using birth control. We had talked about it, and she didn't like me to use condoms; she said she would be responsible for it, she said she was on the pill. Then one day she came to me and said that she was pregnant, that she had done it on purpose, that she had been off the pill for months and hadn't told me, that she wanted to get pregnant, she knew she was trapping me, but she wanted to marry me, she loved me enough for both of us, it would work out.'

Grief, misery, anguish, jealousy burned through Sara, blistering and scorching her heart.

'I told her I wouldn't marry her.' Steve was silent awhile then. 'I told her I absolutely wouldn't marry her. I told her I didn't love her, that we didn't have that much in common, that I never wanted to touch her again now that she had tricked me – I said some pretty awful things to her that night. I called her a conniving stupid bitch, I called her . . . awful things. I told her I wouldn't marry her. That I didn't want to see her again. I told her the only thing I would do for her was to pay for an abortion.' Again, the silence. Then, his voice lowered, Steve went on. 'She went to Boston and had the abortion. I gave her the money for it. And I never spent any time with her alone after that – and then I met you. So you see, Sara, if I had wanted children so damned badly, I could have had them. But I wouldn't marry a woman just for children. I didn't marry you for children. I married you because I love you, because I want to spend my life with you, however it works out. I can't believe you could doubt that for a second. It makes me feel sick at my stomach when you say the things you say.'

'Oh, Steve,' Sara said, and moved across the bed, kneeling behind him. She wrapped her arms around him, leaned against his back and nuzzled her forehead against the back of his head. 'Oh, Steve, forgive me. I'm sorry. I'm sorry I'm so jealous. I didn't know. I didn't suspect. And I'm so nutty with not getting pregnant, it's turning me into a crazy woman. Steve, I'm starting my period *again*. And I feel like such a failure.'

To her wonder, she felt Steve's shoulders shaking. 'I sometimes think,' Steve said, and she realized that he was crying, 'I sometimes think it's my fault, Sara. Oh shit. I didn't want to have a child aborted. I felt like a monster. A murderer. But I couldn't marry Mary, it would have been hell for us both, it just wouldn't have worked. I didn't love her. But I didn't mean to get her pregnant, and I've always felt guilty that I was the cause of an abortion. And I sometimes think – that this is my punishment. That we can't have a baby, that I can't have a baby with the woman I love, because Fate, or something, God, whatever, is punishing me for causing an abortion.'

Sara could feel Steve's body shaking and tensing as he fought for control. She kept her arms wrapped around him. When she could find the power to speak, she said softly, 'Oh, Steve, it doesn't work that way. It really doesn't. You're not being punished. It's not your fault. It's not really my fault, either, it's not anybody's *fault*, it just is. Oh, Steve, I love you. Don't cry, oh, darling, don't be sad. You didn't do the wrong thing. You did the right thing. Steve, I'm so glad you told me all this, I know it was hard for you, but it will help me, don't you see how much it will really help me? I won't be jealous again like I was, I promise you that. It's made things clearer for me, it was all blurry and suspicious, you and Mary, but now I can understand. Oh, Steve,' she said.

203

After a while Steve pulled away and went into the bathroom. Sara caught a glimpse of his face, which was red and blotched with emotion and embarrassment. She turned off the lights and took off her clothes. When he came back, she reached for him as he got into bed and put her arms around him like a mother around a child. It seemed to Sara that she had never loved him so much and so completely.

At the same time, an evil demon of self-pity inside her taunted in a whining nasty tone: So you see? *He* can make babies. He has proof. You are the one who can't make babies. You are the one who is failing. Now you know beyond a shadow of a doubt.

CHAPTER TEN

In early November, Sara went up to Boston to meet with Linda Oldham of Heartways House. HH was starting a new line of romance novels, contemporary stories about women who had careers and talents and who would actually be allowed (although discreetly) to make love with a man instead of only panting and fainting and being fragile. Linda wanted Sara to oversee the series, and Sara agreed as long as she could stay in Nantucket. She would come in to the office at least twice a month for meetings. She would have a great pile of manuscripts to sort through and she would be in charge of setting down the guidelines for the series. It was a challenge for Sara, and she was excited about it; this was work she could believe in, for she did believe that the best world of all for women held both work and romance.

After meeting with Linda, she took a taxi to Cambridge and walked up the winding slate walk to Fanny Anderson's house. It had been a mild dry fall, so that the trees bristled and clicked with leaves that had become sere and crisp but had not yet fallen. Sara stood at the front door but did not knock. She looked around, at the gold chrysanthemums rimming the walls of the house, at the lawn sloping to the wrought-iron fence where leaves that had fallen caught in bunches between the rails. At one time, she had been slightly afraid of this house, and it had held an air of mystery for her. Then it had become a place that excited her, challenged her; and now it welcomed her, it held her own secrets as well as Fanny's.

Stone-faced Eloise opened the door when she finally knocked: this much had remained the same. The heavy blue curtains were pulled tightly shut in the living room, and a bright fire gleamed from the fireplace, filling the room with warmth and light. The cats were in their usual cold-weather spots, stretched in front of the fire. Fanny was on the sofa, her favourite spaniel next to her, its head in her lap. As Sara entered the room, she saw that Fanny was unusually agitated. Her smile trembled and she stroked the dog's head and ears with quick, nervous hands. *Oh-Oh*, Sara thought, *what could have gone wrong?*

At first they talked about the easy things, plans for Christmas and the weather, Sara's new job for Heartways House. But after Eloise had brought in the tea cart, Fanny said, 'Sara, dear, I have a problem.' Even in her distress her words came with the slow lilting ghost-of-a-Kansas drawl. 'Well,' she laughed, 'foolish me, I suppose most people wouldn't think of it as a problem. And that exacerbrates it.' She laughed again, stroking her spaniel's silky head. 'You see, I've had this letter,' she said. 'From England. From my publishers there. They say *Jenny's Book* has won an award. Quite a bit of money and a great deal of prestige. The Shelburne Prize.'

'Oh, my God, Fanny,' Sara said. 'That's absolutely fabulous. That's wonderful. Well, good Lord! How marvelous. The Shelburne Prize is really a feather in your cap.'

'Oh, yes, I know it is, I suppose,' Fanny said. 'But you see there *is* a problem. The letter states that in order to receive the award I have to attend an awards ceremony. I have to accept it personally and be prepared to give a small speech. In England. In January.'

'Well, you can do that!' Sara said. 'Good heavens, Fanny. England! The Shelburne Prize!'

Fanny stared at Sara. She opened her mouth to speak, then closed it and looked down at the dog in her lap. She stroked the dog in silence.

'You can't mean you're thinking of not going?' Sara asked, almost shrieking. 'Oh, Fanny!'

Fanny looked up. 'Well, my dear, I did tell you that I haven't left this house for four years. I have explained to you how I feel about going out. And this would be not only going *out* but going abroad. And going back. It is quite conceivable that I will run into people I used to know when I was in London. Old acquaintants, old colleagues – even old lovers. I really don't know if I can face all that.'

'Oh, Fanny, what nonsense,' Sara said. 'There isn't a writer on earth who wouldn't go to Hell and back to receive the Shelburne Prize, and you're only being asked to go to England. You have to go. You can't let your vanity get in the way here. Besides, you know that everyone else will have gotten older, too, if that's what you're worried about, but you will have the triumph because you've produced a book that's won the prize. Oh, Fanny, you have to go, I won't let you *not* go!'

Fanny smiled. 'I was hoping you would say something like that,' she said. 'Because, you see, my dear. I thought I probably *could* go – on the condition that you accompany me!'

Sara felt her jaw drop in surprise. One thought before all others leapt to mind.

Seeing Sara's expression, Fanny hastened to add, 'I would pay all your expenses, of course, air fare and hotel. I'll have loads of money and I wouldn't dream of asking you to go with me unless you would permit me to pay your expenses.'

'Oh, Fanny, that's so generous of you, and you know I would love to go with you, it's only that – exactly when is the ceremony? What dates in January do you have to be in London?'

Fanny reached for a letter lying on a table near the sofa. 'Around the middle of the month,' she said. 'January seventeenth is the date of the ceremony. My agent there said that she is going to try to set up some interviews and my publisher is giving me a publication party and so on, so that if I could be there for an entire week it would really be the best thing. The dates she suggests are January fifteenth to the twenty-first.'

By now Sara knew each phase of her menstrual cycle as well as her own name. Certainly she knew beyond any doubt that the week Fanny wanted her to go to London was the week in January when she would ovulate. The week when she should try to get pregnant.

She was now thirty-five. There was not that many months left in her life when she would ovulate, when she had a chance of getting pregnant.

But how could she *not* go with Fanny? She knew Fanny wouldn't go alone.

And perhaps she would be pregnant then. Perhaps by then it would all be settled.

'Of course I'll go,' Sara said. 'I'd love to go, Fanny. We'll have the time of our lives. My God, you're going to receive the Shelburne Prize. Do you have any idea how prestigious that is? How proud you should be of yourself? Oh, and Fanny, a week in London! We'll have the most wonderful time!'

Fanny's hands flew up to her hair. 'I've been thinking all night,' she said, 'whether I should put a rinse on my hair. There is so much white in it now. And I must go on a diet. And I suppose my clothes are hopelessly out of style – I suppose I should do some shopping . . .'

Sara laughed and leaned forward, talking to Fanny about her hair, her weight, her clothes. The Trip. The Prize. It was all so marvelous. In the back of her mind a thought ran like a song; Fanny is going to leave her house! After all these years of hiding!

And, further back, thrumming like a drumbeat, murmured the worry: You'll be missing a chance to get pregnant. You'll be giving up one month's chance to get pregnant. You'll be going to London during the time you ovulate. What do you think you're doing?

At the end of November, Sara's period started again. She could not believe it. She had done everything right this time, everything that could be done she had done. She was sickened with defeat. She did not know if she could get out of bed ever again. There seemed no reason to go on living.

She did get out of bed, finally, and spent the day in her robe, taking pills for her cramps, alternately drinking strong coffee, and white wine, trying to snap herself out of her misery, trying to stop crying. She called Dr Crochett, who said she must give herself a few more months before she tried anything else, such as progesterone or other medications or before they discussed something as expensive as *in vitro* fertilization. He told her tales of other patients who had not gotten pregnant for months, for years, and then who suddenly, for no reason at all, got pregnant. Sara realized that the doctor had been saying in his own words what everyone else had said to her: just relax.

In other words, there's nothing more we can do.

By late afternoon Sara was nearly hysterical with grief. When she turned on the television, hoping some talk show would distract her, she found herself bombarded with commercials for diapers. She turned off the TV and forced herself to dress and go for a walk. It was a cold day and windy, but sunny. She had gone no more than six blocks when she saw two different mothers with babies in carriages. She turned around and returned to the shelter of her house. At times like this it was very hard not to think that the world was mocking her, that the world hated her.

She fell on the bed, still in her coat and hat and gloves and sobbed. How had her life gotten into such a state? She had so blithely assumed that she and Steve would have children, when they married they had talked about having children and life, what LIFE was about, she had thought, was a family. She wanted to nurse a baby, to change a baby's diapers, to cuddle a baby, she wanted to read stories to a child, to comfort a sick child, to delight a child at Christmas. She wanted to share the joy of having a baby with Steve. She wanted to show Steve how much she loved him by having his baby. It was not fair, it was not right, it was not real! Their love was so good and strong and healthy and right that she should have gotten pregnant from the sheer force of their passion the first time around.

But she hadn't. And she wasn't pregnant. She felt useless and cursed and insane.

Just before Steve came home, she rose and washed her face and calmed down. Now that she knew how strongly he, too, wanted a child, and how he blamed himself for their failure, she felt it necessary to protect him, to play down her own disappointment. So she put on more mascara and she put on a loud rock 'n' roll record and she put on steaks to fry in butter and mushrooms and wine. She pretended to be optimistic even though her heart was breaking.

*

It was the middle of December. It was, in fact the middle of Sara's menstrual cycle; the fifteenth day, and The Day according to her test.

Outside, everything was dusted with a sugary sprinkling of snow. Inside, the house was clean and beautiful, for Sara had gotten creative and energetic with the Christmas decorations. Trying to keep active and optimistic, trying not to sink into a state of apathetic mourning, she had thrown herself into getting ready for Christmas with all the vigor she could muster. On Saturday night she and Steve were giving a huge Christmas party for the group and just about everyone else they knew on the island. Sara had brought an enormous tree with her from the mainland and had taken days trimming it with handmade cranberry and popcorn chains and red satin hearts and flashing stars made from mirrors and with the box of decorations that her mother had recently mailed to her, decorations that had been hung on the Christmas tree of her childhood. She had draped laurel on the staircase bannister and over the mantels in the living room and the dining room, and a wreath of native grasses and berries, tied with green velvet ribbon, hung in the kitchen window.

Because it was sunny and warm for this time of year, Steve had gotten up early and left to work on the house he was in charge of restoring. Sara had come from the bathroom, where she had just used the kit, to find him dressing. She almost said, *No!* You can't go now, you have to come back to bed first! But she knew he was concerned about getting work done on the house whenever the weather allowed them to work outdoors. She could wait until tonight. She just wished that the day would hurry. She felt her egg ticking inside her like a clock, saying Hurry, Hurry, fertilize me, before it's too late! She was nervous, impatient, even anxious. She could not let this day pass by without making love.

At least today was the day she had invited Annie Danforth for lunch. Sara set out quilted red placemats and matching napkins and put red tapers in the silver candlestick. She had made a quiche and a small salad and bought a nice white wine. This was the first time she had invited anyone to lunch on

Nantucket. She felt as young and excited as a child about to have a friend for a sleep-over.

Annie had a master's in English literature, but like many other women on the island – or any English major anywhere – she could not find a job that called for her particular qualifications. So she has started her own dressmaking and sewing business and was doing very well. But she loved to read and longed to talk about books and for the first part of the afternoon they indulged themselves in book talk. Sara was delighted, partly to find someone who loved books as much as she did, but also because she had wanted to put off any mention of children until late in their conversation so that she would not seem *too* interested in the subject.

'What luxury,' Annie said as Sara brought in a pot of strong tea to counteract the effects of the wine. Their dessert, raspberries in whipped cream flavoured with Chambord, waited before them in crystal bowls. Annie waved her hands, indicating the room around them, the world around them. 'This gorgeous day, and your house is so beautiful and this lunch is so good. And it's so peaceful here.'

'I know,' Sara said. 'It *is* peaceful. But that's partly because Steve and I don't have any children yet.' There, Sara thought, wasn't that a subtle enough nudge in the right direction?

'Do you and Steve want to have children?' Annie asked, stirring her tea.

'Mmm, I think so,' Sara said casually. She couldn't reveal her painful secret just yet. 'Do you and Wade?'

'Oh, we've always wanted to have a family,' Annie said. Her face grew serious. 'But we knew we had to save a little money first and get our lives organized! It took me a while to figure out what I was going to do here, since I couldn't use my English degree. And it's taken forever to get our house in shape. But Wade is thirty-three and I'm thirty-five. So we decided we'd better get started. It's such a hard decision to make.'

'I know,' Sara agreed. *Now*, she thought, *tell me what a surprise it was that you didn't get pregnant right away.*

'But we did make the decision, and I stopped using my

diaphragm. That was a whole *year* ago.' Annie looked into her tea. 'I guess we thought I'd get pregnant right away,' she said, her voice dropping. 'It's really been a hard year for us, because it didn't happen that way. I mean it didn't happen instantly like we thought it would.'

'I know,' Sara agreed. She almost added that she and Steve were having trouble, too, but Annie was engrossed in her own account. Sara listened, feeling the words come like balm over the wound of her lonely infertitlity.

'You wouldn't believe how hard something like this is on a marriage. I didn't think much about it for about six or seven months, although every month when my period started I was disappointed and then pretty upset. But then I know we're older and it probably does take longer. And the first few months we didn't pay any attention to the times when I might be fertile, I mean we just made love whenever we wanted to and didn't try on any certain day. But then I started reading up on how to get pregnant and sort of tried to maneuver Wade into bed on the right days. That was fun. But I still didn't get pregnant. You can't imagine how funny that made me feel.'

'Oh, I can imagine,' Sara said, sympathetically. She felt that when her turn came to talk, her sorrowful tale would rush from her like lava from a volcano, leaving her purged, cleansed, relieved, and fresh for a new beginning.

'Well, about two months ago I suggested to Wade that perhaps we should see a doctor because I wasn't getting pregnant. Man, you should have seen his reaction. Talk about macho defense mechanisms! He freaked. No way was he going to let a doctor fiddle around with his equipment! We had a terrible fight. The worst we've ever had. This fertility stuff really strikes at the deepest fears and feelings. God, I was really scared for a month. I thought our marriage might be ruined. I couldn't even get Wade to *talk* about it. I felt so lonely.'

'Oh, you should have called me,' Sara said, and almost began to say, 'because I've been going through the same thing.' But Annie kept on talking.

'So finally I bought this thing called an ovulation-response kit. It's sort of like a home chemistry unit, it tells you exactly the day you ovulate. You have to do a little test with your urine every morning during the middle of your cycle. Well, I used it, but I had to sneak around to do it because Wade would have hit the roof if he knew I was using it. Sometimes he's just such a caveman I can't believe it. Anyway, I did use it last month –' Annie raised her eyes and looked at Sara. Her smile was so radiant that it took Sara's breath away. She knew what Annie was going to say before she spoke. 'Sara, I'm pretty sure I'm pregnant! I haven't told anyone yet – I haven't even told Wade! Please don't tell anyone. I could be wrong. But I don't think so. My period's three weeks late.'

Sara smiled, and behind the facade of her smile her entire body switched into an alternative mode that focused on survival, evasion, and pretense. 'Annie, that's fabulous!' she said. 'Listen, since you used a home ovulation test kit, why don't you get one of those home pregnancy testing kits?'

'Oh, I have,' Annie said. 'I've used three of them. They've all said positive – I'm pregnant. God, I can't believe it. I have an appointment with the doctor on Friday. I want to be sure before I tell Wade. I don't want to be just maybe pregnant. I want to be *really* pregnant.'

'Oh, I'm sure you are,' Sara said. 'It sounds like it.'

'Well, my breasts are tingling at the nipples,' Annie said. 'And yesterday, while I was sewing? I just fell asleep. I've never done that before. I'm so tired and sleepy these days I can't seem to get anything done. That's not like me at all. And –'

Sara listened while Annie talked about the signs of her pregnancy and about when the baby would be due and about how she hoped it would be a boy for Wade's sake. Sara smiled and nodded and oohed and aahed, and thought: *Annie, you are so self-absorbed! Doesn't it occur to you to wonder why I brought this up? Or what I meant by all those 'I knows?'* But Sara knew that now she would never confide her own problems to Annie. She could not let Annie know that while she had gotten pregnant after using the test once, Sara hadn't gotten pregnant after using it several times, after a laparoscopy, after over two years of trying.

Annie kept on talking, but each word only pushed Sara further back into her own loneliness. Now she knew that every time she saw Annie, whose stomach would burgeon triumphantly with new life, with the real child she would be carrying, Sara would be made aware of the contrast between the two of them. She would be the failure.

What was happening? Why was this happening? Finally Annie left, and Sara, zombielike, cleared up after their lunch, then went to her bedroom and lay on the bed, stiff with self-hatred and confusion. She didn't deserve this; she could think of no awful thing she had done in her life that would have brought this on. But Fate was clearly turning its back on her, or worse, singling her out to curse. Her sister, Ellie, was pregnant for the second time. The Virgin, horrid Mary, was pregnant for the third time. The woman at the dry cleaner's was pregnant, a cashier at the grocery story was pregnant. And now Annie was pregnant. Now Steve and Sara would be the only couple in their group who didn't have a child. Why? How could this be explained? What could she do? *What could she do?*

Well, they could make love tonight. She was ovulating today. She had proof of that. She must hang on to that and be optimistic.

She really could not let herself sink into a bog of self-pity. She would be warm and loving to Steve when he came home tonight. Tonight could be the night.

But when Steve came home, he was tired and irritable. One of his workers hadn't shown up, and Steve thought they were falling behind schedule on the job. Sara served him a huge helping of lamb stew, which usually put him in a better mood but didn't work this evening. He was sullen as they ate, and responded to her cheerful chatting with monosyllables. Then, when she was in the kitchen, thinking that it was unfair of him to take his bad day out on her, Steve came into the kitchen with a sheaf of mail in his hands.

'Jesus Christ, Sara!' he said. 'I just looked at the Sears bill. And our MasterCharge and VISA. Have you gone mad?

Sara dried her hands and turned towards Steve. *Oh, Steve,*

she thought, trying to relay a silent message to him. *Let's not fight. Not tonight. We have to make love tonight.*

'It's Christmas,' she said. 'I got presents for everyone off-island, it's cheaper than here. We've got so many people to buy for – your mother and father, and my mother, and Ellie and her husband and Joey, and Julia and I always exchange gifts, and I wanted to get something for Fanny this year, she's become so special to me. And then I bought some specialty foods in Cambridge at Cardullo's for our party this weekend. I can't find anything like that here.'

'Well, God, Sara I just can't believe you spent so much! Jesus, look at these bills! As if we don't have enough to pay with our fuel bills in the winter.'

'Oh, Steve, it's not any more than we usually pay,' Sara said. 'It's just that it came all at once this year – the bills, I mean. Usually we don't get hit for it until January, or it's spread out over two or three months. I was just really organized this year and did all my shopping at once, and all the bills are coming at once.'

'Well, you should have consulted me before you spent so much money.'

'Oh, Steve,' Sara replied. 'Don't turn us into a cliché marriage with the husband telling the little wifey what she can and can't do. I bring in a good amount of money, you know, I work, too. I'll be paying half of those bills.'

'Yeah, but Sara, you know I'm strapped these days,' Steve said. He plunked down in a kitchen chair and tossed the mail with such angry energy that some of them flew across the table and onto the floor. 'I think you're really being inconsiderate. I'm not telling you what you can or can't do, but the least you could have done was to consult me.'

'But, Steve, you know how you hate buying Christmas presents,' Sara said. 'You're such an old Scrooge about it –'

'Oh, are we going to call names now? You're going to call me an old Scrooge? Because I think we have to watch our money? You don't want to get into the cliché of husband talking to wife about money, but you can call me names. Right? Right?' He was almost shouting at her.

'Steve,' Sara said, 'don't get so angry. Just because you've had a bad day at work, don't take it out on me.'

'And *you* don't try to get off the subject!' Steve said. 'I'm not crabbing about a bad day at work. I'm crabbing about these God-damned bills. Sara, you bought Joey about three hundred dollars worth of stuff!'

'Well, they were on sale,' Sara began. 'And they weren't just for Joey –' She turned away. How could she say what a pleasure it had been for her, to spend the afternoon in the toy department of the huge Sears store on the mainland. She had lingered over dolls with frilly dresses and fire trucks that pumped real water, overstuffed teddy bears with pink ribbons and dolls houses with miniature furniture. She had gazed with longing at the gaily colored educational toys that bloomed like huge plastic flowers in the baby section. She had wanted to buy every single item and take it home and give it to her own baby, her own little boy, her own little girl. She had bought presents for Joey, her nephew, and then, obsessed, she had bought presents for Ellie's new baby, which would be born in January. Tiny terry-cloth layette sets. Bath blanket and wash-cloth sets the color of a newborn chick. A silky quilt embroidered with bunnies and elephants and ducks and giraffes. An exquisite pure-white fleece winter blanket with a hood attached. Yes, she had gone mad. She had brought too much. But then, what was *too much* to welcome a new child into the world?

Yet she could understand Steve's point of view. She had been extravagant. She had spent too much. She had gone a little bit nuts. She had brought those things for herself, really. It had been worth three hundred dollars to spend that afternoon legitimately buying baby clothes and toys.

There was no way to explain all this to Steve without making them both even more miserable because they had no baby of their own.

'I'll pay for it myself,' she said calmly, not looking at him.

'Oh, Christ, Sara, why not just go ahead and cut my balls off,' Steve said.

Sara looked at him, shocked. He had never talked to her

216

this way before. But Steve was moving now, shoving his chair away from the table and stomping off into the other room. She heard him grab his coat and slam the front door. She heard the roar of the pickup truck as it went off into the night.

He had never done this sort of thing before. She had never done this sort of thing before. At the most, during their worst arguments, she was the one who left the room – but only the room. She had flung herself, weeping, from the living room, waiting for Steve to come find her, forlorn, on the bed. Sometimes he had come, sometimes not, and then she had had to swallow her pride and go back into the living room to start up the conversation again.

But she had never left the house during an argument, and neither had Steve. She felt sick at her stomach.

She picked up the bills that were scattered across the kitchen floor. They were pretty scary – the bills for Christmas presents; and she had charged the booze and food for the party on her MasterCard; and, mixed in with all the rest, they still owed a thousand dollars for her laparoscopy. At least Steve hadn't complained about that. He hadn't said that if she weren't such a failure as a woman they wouldn't have had to pay two thousand five hundred dollars in medical bills. And there were the ovulation test kits Sara had bought, thirty-five dollars apiece. That added up.

It all added up. It would be hard work fighting their way through the bills, paying them off. She should have been more frugal this year, knowing what a financial and emotional burden Steve's new business was on him. But they would come out all right, she was sure of that.

If only he would come home. Sara looked at her watch. It was almost nine-thirty. Her nerves jangled. Only two and a half hours before midnight! Only two and a half hours before the day she ovulated was over. He had to come home soon, they had to make up, they had to make love.

Needing to use up her frantic energy, she finished cleaning the kitchen. When, at ten o'clock, he still hadn't come home, she could only pace through the house. Where was he? Had he gone off to a bar for a beer? She would hate it if he did that, he never did that, it would be like telling the world they'd had a fight, it wasn't like Steve. But it wasn't like him to stomp out of the house like that, either.

At ten-thirty he came home; his face was somber and drawn.

'Where have you been?' Sara asked trying to sound worried but not nagging.

'I just drove to the beach and sat there listening to the radio and staring at the water,' Steve said. He walked through the hall, tossed his jacket on the stairs, and headed up the stairs to their bedroom. Sara followed.

Steve talked as he undressed for bed. *At least he's getting ready for bed!* Sara thought.

'I'm sorry I spoke to you that way,' Steve said. 'That was vulgar and crude of me.'

'I do understand about the money,' Sara said. 'I can see that I did spend too much. I'm sorry. But now that I'm working full-time for Heartways House –'

'But don't you see, Sara,' Steve said, 'it's not right for you to be paying more than half the bills. I can stand it that I'm not supporting you, I'm that liberated, but it just grates on me if you're going to be paying such a big portion of the bills, and spending so much money without consulting me, as if what I make doesn't matter.'

'Oh, Steve, I never meant for it to seem that way,' Sara said.

'I know you didn't. I know I'm overreacting about the money. But I've got expenses I didn't expect – the insurance premiums for the two men who are working for me are killing me. And the bookkeeping is a real pain in the ass. I've got to watch every cent we spend on this house, and if I make any mistakes, it comes right out of my own money. It's a lot harder than I thought it would be, having my own company. Sometimes I think I made a mistake.'

'Oh, Steve, you didn't, it's always more difficult when you start off,' Sara said. 'I'm sorry I spent so much. It was insensitive of me, right now when you've got so much on your mind. But it will be okay, Steve, really it will.'

Now, finally, Steve turned and embraced Sara. He held her to him and ran his hand over her hair. But it was only a gentle embrace, not a lustful one.

'God,' he said. 'I'm beat.'

He rose, went into the bathroom, came out, and crawled into bed. Sara went downstairs and turned off all the lights, then went back up the stairs, her mind churning. They had made up. But he didn't seem interested in making love. In the bathroom she deliberated. She could put on a sexy nightgown – but it was cold in their house at night in the winter; they purposely turned their thermostat way down. She always wore her cozy flannel night-gown Still . . . she put on a sexy skimpy gown.

Steve was lying with one arm flung over his eyes. He did not see her come through the bedroom. Sara got into bed next to him and wrapped her arms and legs around him. She cuddled up to him. She knew he must feel her body through the flimsy material of her gown.

Steve wrapped an arm around her and hugged her. 'I'm sorry Sara, I'm just no good tonight,' he said. 'I'm wiped out. I've got to get some sleep. I want to get up at six tomorrow. I've got to start getting out to the house earlier or we're going to be way behind schedule.'

But you have to make love to me tonight! Sara thought in horror. *You have to!*

She lay frozen while he reached out, turned off the light, then turned on his side, into the position he always chose for sleeping. His back was to her.

Sara lay still, but inside she was churning. She was insulted – didn't her practically naked body have any effect on him anymore? And more important – what was she going to do now? Should she say, Steve, you *have* to make love to me, I'm ovulating? That would be a real turn-on. But if she didn't get him to make love to her . . . She looked at the bedside clock. It was ten forty-three. The minutes were speeding away. What could she do? What should she do?

She heard Steve snoring next to her. Already he was in a deep sleep. He'd been falling asleep this way almost every night, exhausted from work. She knew she wouldn't wake him; she couldn't. It would be too crude, it would make it seem as if she thought of him only as a kind of stud who had to automatically perform and fertilize her. This was not a good time for her to push for anything now; he was already feeling too pressured.

Steve snored evenly, regularly, sleeping deeply. Sara lay next to him, painfully awake. What a day this had been: Annie Danforth's happy confession which had fallen like a bomb on Sara's hopes for a sympathetic friendship, and then the argument with Steve, and now this, her body waiting eagerly for something that would not happen. She lay awake deep into the night. She knew she would not get pregnant this month.

In the morning she had trouble waking up. It had been a sleepless night and she was not rested now. Dutifully she made Steve's breakfast, dutifully, she sat down at the dining room table with an Eiffel tower of manuscripts waiting to be read and judged. She drank her coffee. She stared. She drank another cup of coffee.

'I've got to do something.' she said aloud to the empty air. 'I've got to do something, or I really will go mad.'

She sat, unable to think of the first thing to do.

Finally she pulled the manuscripts toward her and began reading. But nothing excited her; they all seemed so dull. She stopped reading — this was not fair to the manuscripts or their writers. She had gotten into such a deadly state that nothing could appeal to her.

'I want a baby, damn it!' she said, pounding her fists on the table. 'Everyone else is getting one. Why can't I?'

She rose, restless, and walked through the house. Outside the day glittered with cold. Inside, the air seemed expansive with silence, except for her footsteps, her breath.

'Well, that's it, I'll just sit here and go mad,' she said aloud, and plopped down where she was, on the third stair of the staircase.

She had no idea how long she had been sitting there when the doorbell rang, so near to her — just a few steps across the hallway to the front door – that she almost screamed. It was the mailman with a small special delivery package from Julia.

'Open immediately!' it said in bright red letters on the brown wrapping paper.

Sara thanked the mailman, then carried the parcel to the dining room table and sat down with it. Inside a small box she found a tiny oval rock, a not particularly pretty or unusual one, and a plastic sandwich bag filled with tiny brown – what? Nuts? Seeds? Dry oatmeal? She unfolded Julia's note.

> In the seventeenth century, they believed that 'The seeds of *Docks* tyed to the left arme of a woman do help Barrennesse.' I looked it up in the dictionary – 'dock' is one of several coarse weeds of the buckwheat family. Then I remembered that my mother – and you know what an intellectual snob she is – took wheat germ for a long time trying to get pregnant with my brother. So this mishmash is wheat germ mixed up with ground buckwheat noodles – the closest I could get to buckwheat seeds. I wonder why it should be tied to the *left* arm.
>
> The pebble is for you to use in the bath. 'To cure sterility, in Shetland in the nineteenth century, a woman washed her feet in running water in which an egg-shaped pebble was placed.' So tie this stuff to your left arm, put the stone in your bathtub, take a nice long bath, and there you are, all knocked up, I'll bet my medicine works at least as well as Dr Crochett's hanky-panky.
>
> I love and adore you even if you are insane, and I've sent a decent Christmas present to you and Steve in a separate package.
>
> Love, Julia

Sara studied the box. For the first time, here were some ancient cures for infertility that she could actually do something with. She'd never tried to find wolf pizzle, and she'd never sit over a bowl of steaming garlic – but this she could do.

'Oh!' she exclaimed, standing up suddenly, wild with energy. For she had a thought – why stand in a bathtub with this one egg-shaped stone when she was so close to the ocean, which had to hold billions of egg-shaped stones. All those pebbles. Why there must be more than billions – in the ocean there must be trillions, more than could be numbered, more than all the stars in all the galaxies!

Hurrying, she dressed warmly, piling a wool sweater over a flannel shirt and leg warmers over her jeans. With a piece of Christmas ribbon – she paused a moment, considering just which color was right, and decided on green, of course, for fertility, for life – she tied the baggie of wheat germ around her left upper arm. Then, careful not to knock it off, she pulled on her parka. She jammed a wool cap on her head, pulled on her thickest gloves, grabbed up a pair of wool socks, slipped into her boots, and ran out to the car.

There could be people at the Jetties Beach, or at least out in the harbor, scallopers and fishermen going out or coming in. She headed to Surfside Beach on the Atlantic Ocean side of Nantucket. And she was in luck – no one else was there. She ran down the long slope of sand to the water's edge. It was not windy today, so that the waves seemed to dawdle in, taking their time, lolling about on the sand. Good. She wouldn't have to worry about being knocked over or dragged under.

Sara kicked off her rubber boots and walked into the water. The cold was so intense and painful that it was like putting her feet against burning irons. Immediately she felt the instinct to jump back, to jump out, but she gritted her teeth and walked farther into the waves. She leaned over and, taking Julia's peeble from her pocket, tossed it into the water next to her feet. She stood there then, letting the icy waves surge around her feet and ankles. She looked out at the navy blue waters to the horizon, then up to the winter-pale sky where the sun rolled overhead like a primitive god, hunting her eyes with its glare.

'All right,' she said aloud. 'Here I am. Look.' The ocean was alm today, but even so the waves rolled with noise, a steady booming that drowned out everything else. 'I SAID HERE I AM!' Sara shouted. 'WITH MY EGG-SHAPED ROCK AND MY DOCKS TIED TO MY LEFT ARM AND ALL MY PRAYERS AIMED AT EVERY SINGLE GENERATIVE FORCE IN THIS WHOLE FUCKING UNIVERSE! SO DO SOMETHING! GIVE ME A BREAK!'

She began to shiver. Her feet hurt unmercifully. In the warmer months, after a few moments in the water, one got used to the relative cold – but this was too cold. This was painful.

Perhaps if she walked. The quote Julia had sent said 'washed.' All right. Although she had no soap – but there was sand, the old primitive matter for washing. Pushing up the sleeves of her parka and sticking her gloves in her pocket, she leaned over and scrubbed at her feet with the sand, with small egg-shaped pebbles. Her hands contracted with the cold.

Standing up again, she noticed a portly woman bundled in layers against the winter wind, walking along the beach toward her, her black Lab dog dashing and yelping joyfully.

Shit, Sara thought. She felt intruded upon.

'Are you all right?' the woman called, approaching Sara.

Actually, no, Sara wanted to reply. *Actually I'm insane, demented, absolutely berserk.*

'Just fine,' Sara called back cheerfully. Sticking her hands in her pockets, she turned in the opposite direction and strolled along casually, kicking at the water with her feet as if she were wading in August warmth. She racked her brain but could think of no rational explanation to give the older woman for standing barefoot in the freezing water, so she just went splashing on, until finally she was shaking with cold.

She stepped out of the water then, sat down on the sand, and drew on her wool socks. Oh, the ecstasy of warmth. She looked out at the ocean. *All right*, she spoke silently to the ocean, to the natural force that ruled the ocean and all other universal forces. *I've done my part. Now you do yours.*

When she got home, she took a long bath and drank cups of

hot herbal tea, trying to ward off a cold. And when Steve got home for lunch, she attacked him. She made him gobble his lunch, then dragged him into the bedroom and attacked him. It could still happen, the timing could still be okay. He staggered off to work, exhausted but happy. Sara lay in bed, full of his seed, and fell asleep.

'I've got a wonderful Christmas present for you, but you've got to leave the house to get it,' Sara said to Fanny. They were sitting in her blue living room, an applewood fire blazing next to them, the animals nearly comatose from the heat.

Fanny set her teacup down gently in its fragile saucer. 'Sara,' she began.

'No, I won't take no for an answer,' Sara said. 'It's a beautiful day, the streets and stores are glorious with Christmas decorations, and you are coming with me if I have to wrestle you from this house.'

'What an inelegant image,' Fanny said, smiling faintly.

Sara could tell that Fanny was displeased. Really pissed, though she'd never use that word.

'Fanny, you're going to England next month. Now really, be sensible. Do you think you're going to waltz out the door, onto a plane, and through all of London when you haven't left this house for four years? You'll be so shocked – so disoriented – it would be crazy. You've got to go out a few times before then, test the water, get used to it. Now come on, you know I'm right.'

'I can't go out today. My hair is a disaster,' Fanny said. A tiny strain of petulance streaked her graceful voice.

'I know,' Sara said. 'But you can put a hat on over it. And that's part of my gift – we're going to get you a new hairstyle. We're going to a beauty salon.'

Fanny rose, indignant. 'My hairstyle is perfectly fine. There is *nothing* wrong with my hairstyle. I've had it for years.'

Sara was silent, letting the expression on her face say: Precisely. That's just the point.

Fanny began to do her slow, fluttery pacing around the room. She changed tactics. 'Sara, dear, this is thoughtful of you. I can certainly see that. And undoubtedly you are right. I *should* go out a bit before I go to England. Like practising. And I will. But not today, not so suddenly. You've rather sprung this on me, you know.'

'Fanny,' Sara said, '*you* know it wouldn't have worked any other way.'

Now Fanny was trembling with anger. 'And it is not working now!' she said. 'I will go out of this house when *I* decide to, not under anyone's pressure.'

'There's more news about *Jenny's Book*,' Sara said. 'Interesting news. Quite a bit, actually. And I won't tell you until you're at the hairdresser's with me.'

'Fine,' Fanny said. 'Don't. I can always call my agent.'

'He won't tell you. No one will tell you. I've talked to them all and they agree with what I'm doing and they've promised not to tell you.'

Fanny flushed with anger. She turned her back on Sara and walked toward the door at the far end of the room. When she turned her back to Sara, she had tears in her eyes. 'This is blackmail,' she said.

'So, call the police,' Sara said cruelly. 'You would have to let them come in the door to talk to you, to *see* you.'

Fanny turned her back again. Sara rose, went toward her a few steps, and said in a conciliatory voice, 'Fanny, please. Think a moment. If it's this hard for you to go out with me, just to a hairdresser, just think how hard it will be to go to England. You'll be paralyzed; you won't be able to go. You'll miss everything. Fanny, this is like – like learning to walk again. You've got to take this first step.'

'All right,' Fanny said, her voice low. 'Let me go change my clothes.'

Sara knew that if she let Fanny out of her sight she would probably barricade herself in the bedroom for the next twenty years.

'No,' she said to Fanny. 'You're fine. Your dress is fine, your makeup is fine. All you have to do is put on your coat. I rented a car in Hyannis and drove up here so that you wouldn't have to deal with a taxi driver. Just me, then the beauty salon, filled with women who no matter what their age couldn't hold a candle to you.' As she spoke, she could almost see the tension ebb from Fanny's body. 'Fanny, I know just how you should have your hair cut.'

'Cut?' Fanny asked, her hand reaching for her hair. 'Why should I have my hair cut?'

'Because you look like you're ready to sing opera,' Sara said. 'You have beautiful thick hair, but when you wear it piled up like that, you look older than you should. Grandmotherly. I've even talked with the hairdresser about you, and we've agreed on something that would be marvelous for you.'

'I can't have my hair cut short,' Fanny said, her confidence returning slightly on the wings of her inexorable powers of judgment. 'It would not be sensual, feminine, to have my hair cut short.'

'It won't be *short*,' Sara promised. 'It will be elegant. Not faddish, though. Classic. Even sexy. But very simple.'

Fanny came back into the room. She put her hand up to her hair. 'I haven't had my hair styled in *years*,' she said.

'Remember how luxurious it is?' Sara said seductively. 'How good it feels to have someone else wash your hair and massage your scalp? This is a very good hairdresser we're going to, the best.' She was close enough to Fanny now to reach out and gently take her hand. Fanny's hand was silky and plump. Carefully, as if she were leading a wild colt who would bolt at any startling movement, she urged Fanny toward the living room door and out into the hallway.

There stood the gruesome Eloise. For one wild moment Sara feared that Fanny would fling herself at her housekeeper, crying for protection, while Sara attempted to wrestle her away.

Instead, Fanny said, calmly, as if she were asking for more tea, 'I'd like my coat, Eloise. The mink. Please find my gloves, too. The brown suede lined with cashmere. I'm going out.'

Except that her eyes bugged out of her head, Eloise expressed no surprise. She only nodded and, eyes bulging, went off to fetch Fanny's things. Fanny looked at Sara, and to Sara's immense surprise Fanny snorted, the only way she could let out her suppressed laughter. So Sara knew it was going to be okay. Fanny was going to be okay.

Sara had parked the rented sedan right in front of Fanny's house. Fanny made her way to the car with her shoulders hunched forward and her head bowed nearly into her chest, as if she were a criminal averting her face from a hungry press. Once in the car, however, she seemed to relax. After adjusting her scarf so that it curved in concealment around her face, she turned her head toward the window, then faced front.

'I'll never forgive you for this, you know,' Fanny said as Sara started the car.

Sara grinned. 'Yes, you will,' she said. She tried to keep the triumph from her voice. 'I think you will.'

After that they rode in silence – until Fanny began to notice the sights they were driving past. 'Oh, look at that,' she said. And, 'Oh, I had forgotten that.' And, 'The river looks like gunmetal today.' Sara knew Fanny was not talking to her. She was talking to no one, she was expressing delight and amazement at the buildings, trees, railings, churches, colleges, bridges, parks, sidewalks – all the outside world that she had not seen for four years.

CHAPTER ELEVEN

'God, Sara, look at you,' Steve said.

It was New Year's Eve. They were getting ready for a huge party that the group was going to at a local hotel and restaurant, a champagne dinner at nine and then dancing in the hotel's grand lobby.

Steve had worked late, because it was sunny and warm, then came home exhausted and fallen asleep for a few hours. Now he was just coming from the shower, naked, his hair damp, smelling of shaving lotion.

Sara was standing by the bedroom dresser, putting her earrings on. She was wearing a dress that her sister had worn in college, when dresses like this were called 'semiformal'. It was an old-fashioned dress that had come back into style and would always be alluring: simple black taffeta, strapless, with a full poofed skirt that swung just below her knees. The waist was very tight. The top was very low, so that her breasts swelled upward from the curving bodice. She was wearing high black heels and rhinestone earrings that fell in sprays from her ears. No other jewelry. It was a fabulous look and she knew it.

But she hadn't expected Steve to notice it. He was so zonked out these days with his work, either tired or worried, he scarcely noticed her at all, and she didn't mind, she had some idea of what he was going through, because she was so engrossed these days in setting down the guidelines for the new Heartways House series. Some of the financial pressure had eased with the big checks they had received for Christmas from both his parents and her mother. Still, they had to be careful and hardworking. One of the reasons she had decided to wear this dress tonight was that it meant she didn't have to buy a new one, or wish that she *could* buy a new one.

Now that Sara had so inadvertently captured her husband's attention, she basked in it, pleased. She turned slowly in front of him, holding the skirt. 'You like it?' she asked.

'I like you,' Steve said. 'You are the most beautiful woman on the planet.'

'Oh, Steve,' Sara said, and felt tears of joy rush to her eyes. In the early days, when they had just met, he would say things like that all the time, but it had been years since he had said anything so extravagant.

He started dressing, in gray flannels, a pink button-down shirt, and his navy blue blazer, then sat down on the bed to put on his shoes. 'When was the last time I wore this blazer?' he asked. 'It seems like ages.' Abruptly he looked up at Sara and asked, 'Do you ever think about how different our lives could have been if we'd made different choices? For example, if I'd kept on teaching at the prep school. Then I'd be wearing clothes like this every day.'

'Then you never would have met me!' Sara said. She sat on the bed and leaned against the headboard. It was unusual for Steve to be so talkative. Probably the fact that he had tomorrow, New Year's Day, off was helping him relax. Whatever the reason, she was happy; she loved talking with him. She loved knowing what he was thinking about.

'Well, then, if we hadn't decided to come to Nantucket. Would I still be working for Masterson? Or would I have decided to go out on my own in Boston? And if we hadn't moved, you might be senior editor at Walpole and James now.'

'I'm not sorry we came here, are you?' Sara asked.

'No,' Steve said. 'I love it here. And in spite of my anxieties, I think my business is going to make it. And I think I'm going to make a difference – infinitesimal, but real – to the way this island looks. No, I'm glad I'm here. But when I see you looking the way you do now, Sara, I wonder if . . . if you ever have doubts.'

'None,' Sara said honestly. 'I love it here. The only thing that bothers me is that I feel guilty about this trip to England. I hate to think of being away from you for a whole week. It doesn't seem right. Sure you don't want to come with us?'

Steve laughed. 'Do you know what I'm planning to do while you're gone? I'm going to buy eight big cans of chili or beef stew and eight pints of Häagen-Dazs and several six-packs of Michelob and eight packages of pretzels, and every night when I come home from work I'm going to sit in front of the TV and drink beer and eat my stew and ice cream and veg out. When I want to get wild, I'll have another beer and some pretzels. I'm not going to answer the phone or go to any parties, hell, I may not even shave. I'm really going to be a slob.'

Sara laughed. Then, 'You know,' she said, turning aside, 'I'm having my period again.' She waited for him to speak. When he said nothing, she said, her voice surprising her with its bitterness, 'Why don't you say something? Sometimes I feel lonely, trying to have a baby and grieving when I don't.'

'Sometimes I feel lonely, too!' Steve said, his voice raised. 'Sometimes I think that baby's all you care about – it seems to be just about all you think about.'

'Oh, Steve,' she protested, turning to face him.

'No, wait,' Steve said. 'Listen to me. I've got a lot on my mind now with my business, problems with the bookkeeping, supervising all my men, making decisions I'm not used to making. And sometimes when I try to talk to you about it, I see you sort of fade away from me. I mean you sit there looking at me and nodding, but I know you're thinking about that baby.'

'If you were in my body,' Sara said, 'if you knew what it was like to wonder what every little twinge meant –'

'But there's more than that, Sara,' Steve said, putting his hands on her arms. 'Don't you see, there has to be more than that for us. Sure, I want to have a baby, and we will, but I also want to build up my business and my reputation, and I want to make a difference to this island and the way it develops. And I wish I had someone who cared about it to really listen to me. If you can't focus on me now and then, on *me* just for a few minutes – well then, what's our marriage about?'

Sara put her hands on her husband's chest and looked up at him. 'You're right,' she said. 'I'm sorry. I think I've gone a

230

little bit mad. And I do think of you, you know – I keep feeling that I'm failing you by not getting pregnant.'

'Sara, believe me, I'm glad we don't have a kid right now. I don't think I could handle it. It's fine with me if you don't get pregnant for months.'

Well, it's not fine with me! Sara wanted to scream, but a warning voice inside her said: *Haven't you been listening to Steve?*

'Is there something wrong?' Sara asked. 'Are you having any special problem?'

The look on Steve's face was a gift. 'No,' he said, 'No one special problem – it's all one giant headache.' He began to elaborate on his problems with a house he was restoring at 'Sconset. Sara listened, responded, asked questions. Suddenly they realized they were late for the dinner-dance, and they rushed out the door, still talking. As they entered the restaurant Sara felt Steve's arm around her shoulders, keeping her close to him. It was as if they had just finished making love – which, in a way, they had. She felt closer to him than she had for a long time, and more in love.

The Harbor House was glittering with holiday glamour. In the middle of the dining room a vast Christmas tree, dripping with decorations, towered to the arched ceiling, flashing its bright lights through the room like a lighthouse beacon. The group had its own long table at one end of the room, and everyone was there: Pete and Carole, Wade and Annie, Sheldon and Jamie, Mick and his newest girlfriend, the nymphet Cindy, Bill and The Virgin, and another couple, Watson Marsh and Eileen O'Hara, friends of the Clarks who had come to celebrate the holidays on Nantucket. The meal was delicious, and everyone drank champagne and ordered more champagne; then the band started playing and everyone danced and drank champagne. The room was filled with people and music and laughter under the crepe-paper-garlanded lights.

It was after midnight when Sara and Annie staggered off to the bathroom to repair their makeup. They had just plopped down on the long pink-cushioned seats when Carole and Jamie came in with the new woman, Eileen.

'What a little whore!' Eileen said. She was crying, and her mascara had streaked two black tracks down her face. She collapsed on a bench next to Sara. 'What a cunt!'

Two women in their sixties looked askance at Eileen, who did not notice them.

'I know,' Carole said, 'I know, Eileen. I'm so sorry.'

'What's wrong?' Annie asked.

'Watson's gone off with Mary,' Carole said.

'What?' Sara asked, amazed.

'Yeah,' Carole said. She and Jamie both scrunched down on the other pink sofa.

Sara saw the look Carole gave Annie. It was the look of conspirators, of tired and depressed conspirators.

'Carole, I don't understand,' Sara pressed.

Carole sighed. 'I hate telling tales. But surely you've noticed by now, about Mary, I mean.'

'She's a cunt,' Eileen said. 'She's a horrible, trashy little piece.'

'Do you know our secret name for her?' Jamie said. 'We call her HBO. Home Box Office. Because she'll take her box into your home, into your husband's office, anywhere.'

'Would you all please tell me what you're talking about!' Sara shouted, exasperated.

'Now, look, Mary's my friend,' Carole said. 'And she's a marvellous baby-sitter. No one in the world could be better with children. And she's not an *evil* person. She's just got this thing about men. It's like she has to prove to herself, and everyone else, I guess, that she's irresistible to men, that she can get any man she wants.'

'I think it's because Bob is such an *asshole*,' Jamie said with drunken emphasis. 'I couldn't live with that man.'

'She was that way before Bob,' Carole said. 'She's always been that way. I feel sorry for her. It's like an obsession with her, she's got to get every man she sees interested in her.'

'My God,' Sara said, musing aloud, 'I thought she was just that way with Steve. Chasing him, I mean.'

Carole looked at Sara. 'Well, she is *especially* that way with Steve. I think she was really in love with him at one time. I don't know if she'll ever get over the fact that he didn't love her. But that's not why she acts this way. She acted this way before she met Steve. She just has to get every man she meets interested in her, even if it means taking off her clothes in public.'

'*And* sticking her tongue in his ear while dancing with him in front of his girlfriend,' Eileen said. '*And* taking his hand and putting it on her breast. *God*, what gall she has! She's as pregnant as a kangaroo and she's still vamping around.'

'Well, her stomach isn't sticking out *that* far yet, and her boobs are enormous these days,' Jamie said. 'As anyone can plainly see in that dress she wore tonight.'

Eileen began to weep. 'I just can't believe it,' she said. 'I just can't believe it. I can't believe Watson would go off with her. We've been together for four years and nothing like this has ever happened. *I'm* the one who wouldn't get married, I said it was an outdated institution, an anachronism, but now I wish we were married so I could sue the bastard for a divorce.'

'He's drunk,' Carole said. 'I haven't seen Watson this drunk for years. He usually doesn't drink much, that's part of the problem. And cheer up, if they do try to do anything, he probably won't get very far, they say that when men get drunk they can't get it up.'

'Watson could get it up if his brain was in a coma,' Eileen said. 'But I just don't understand how he could go off with that bitch.'

'It's that old sweet and innocent and helpless act,' Annie said. 'She's pulled it on all our husbands. And everyone sort of puts up with it because her own husband is such a gorilla.'

'God,' Sara said. 'I wish I'd known all this before now. I've been making myself miserable the past year. It seems she's always asking Steve to take her home and then telling him how unhappy she is, as if he's responsible for doing something about it.'

'Well, she really is unhappy,' Carole said. 'That much is true.'

233

'Well, *I* don't have any sympathy for her,' Eileen said.

'I don't, either,' Sara said, realizing as she spoke that she, too, had had more than enough to drink. Otherwise she never would have admitted how she felt about Mary. 'I don't like her, and I don't think she likes me.'

'Of course she doesn't like you,' Carole said. 'She hates you. You "got" Steve. He married you. She'll never forgive you for that. And of course she's jealous of you for everything else. Your glamorous life.'

'Glamorous!' Sara said. 'My life isn't glamorous!'

'Oh, give me a break,' Carole said. 'Of course it is. You go up to Boston all the time, you're going to *London* this month, you get to swish around in high heels and silk while we're all squeezing into last year's jeans.'

'It's true,' Jamie said. 'You're so lucky, Sara. And I'm jealous of you, too. Don't get me wrong, I don't hate you, I like you, but I feel so sort of pitiful around you sometimes, when I've got baby goop stuck to my old shirt or when I see a new dress I'd like and then realize that not only can I not afford it but I wouldn't have any place to wear it if I could. That's usually when I run into you, like last week, when I saw you in the A&P. You were wearing high heels and that red cape and you said you had just flown in from Boston and were in a terrible rush, picking up something for dinner. And *I* was wearing my old saggy sweater and had the baby sniveling away in her carrier. The high point of my day was getting *out to the A & P*! As much as I like you, sometimes I hate you!'

'Well,' Sara said, 'I envy you all your babies,' but when they groaned and said, 'Yeah, well, when you have your kids, you'll understand what we're talking about,' she did not pursue the subject. She could not make herself vulnerable to these women yet; she would rather have their envy than their pity.

'I'm sorry if Mary hates me,' Sara said. 'But I don't see what I can do to make her stop. I've never been unkind to her.'

'You can't do anything,' Carole said. 'Mary's like a child in some ways. Maybe that's why she's so good with children. The best you can do is just to ignore her, I guess. Don't take it

234

personally. In a way it's not *you* she hates, it would be any woman who married Steve.'

The group of women filed out of the ladies' room back into the main lobby, where, they had forgotten, a party was going on. Sara sat down with Steve and told him what had happened. They watched as Eileen drank the coffee served to her, as she gathered up her things to leave. Just as she was going out the door, they saw Watson come in. The group could not hear what was said, but they could see what happened: Eileen drew her hand back and slapped Watson as hard as she could across his face. Then she stormed out the door.

'Jesus Christ, what was *that* all about?' Watson said, crossing the room to their table. The imprint of Eileen's hand was red on his face.

'Watson, you ass, you went off with Mary,' Carole told him.

'Well, Jesus, Carole, all I did was drive her home. She said her husband had already left and she didn't feel well. What was I supposed to do, say, "Sorry, baby, walk"?'

'You were gone an awfully long time,' Carole said, skeptically.

'Yeah, well, we sat out in the car for a while and talked. She's pretty unhappy. Her husband sounds like a louse. Jesus, I can't believe Eileen would get so upset! What does she think I was doing?'

'You could have told her you were leaving,' Carole said. 'You could have asked her to come with you.'

'She was dancing,' Watson said. 'She was having a high old time on the dance floor. Besides,' he added, looking sheepish, 'Mary was really upset. She said she needed to get away before she started crying. She was almost in tears. In fact, she was in tears by the time we got out to the car.'

'Poor Wittle Baa,' Jamie Jones said drunkenly. 'Poor baby.'

'Well, you'd better go find Eileen and explain all that to her,' Carole said. 'She can't have gone far; she doesn't know Nantucket that well and I'm sure she couldn't walk to our house from here; she'd get lost. Listen, Watson, you probably did the right thing, but you should have checked with Peter and me. I mean, this is an old routine Mary pulls and there isn't a wife – or lover – around who hasn't gotten upset over it. Mary's a real manipulator. You were only being kind, but she was being sleazy. You've got to let Eileen know that nothing happened. Let her know that you only felt *sorry* for Mary. I mean, I know it's awful that Eileen slapped you, but she thought you deserved it.'

'Why don't the three of us go find Eileen?' Pete said. 'We should be getting home anyway; it's late.'

With that, the party broke up. Sara rode home in silence, leaning on Steve's shoulder as he drove. She grinned nastily in the dark: there would be a perfect moment in the future, she knew, when she could tell Steve that poor little Mary was known among the wives in the group as HBO. Then she sobered, thinking: perhaps the men called her that, too. She felt sorry for Mary now, and in that pity was a great relief.

Earlier that night, when the women had gone en masse to the ladies room, Sara had overhead Jamie and Carole wondering aloud to each other just how much their husbands had had to drink.

'Oh, Jamie,' Sara had said, 'I don't think Sheldon's drunk. I sat next to him at dinner.'

'You don't understand, Sara,' Jamie had said. 'Shel will seem perfectly sober – he'll *be* perfectly sober through a whole lot of drinks, and then suddenly one too many will set him off. And we never know what that one too many is. He's an alcoholic, you see,' she added in a matter-of-fact tone.

'I always know the minute Pete's had too much,' Carole had sighed. 'His actions change completely, instantly. Dr Jekyll and Mr Hyde. God, sometimes I get so sick of it. If it weren't for the kids . . .'

The women continued to talk. Sara combed her hair and put on fresh makeup, listening all the while to the talk going on around her. She realized why these two women had a special friendship, why they went off together one night a week without asking other women in the group to go with them: they were attending Al-Anon meetings. She was so glad to know that! Not that their husbands had problems with alcohol, but that the tie between the two women was one that she couldn't share – thank heavens. It was not that they were leaving Sara out of something because they didn't want her company.

'I sometimes feel that I'm no more mature than I was in high school,' Sara said aloud. 'I sometimes feel I have the mentality of a teenager.'

'Hey, great,' Steve said. 'Wanna drive out to the Jetties and park in the car and neck?'

'No thanks,' Sara said. 'It's too cold. I've grown up enough to appreciate the comforts of a bed.' She looked over at Steve and grinned. 'But I'll put my hand on your thigh and blow in your ear if you'd like.'

'Is that what you used to do to all your boyfriends when you were a teenager?' Steve asked.

'I don't know,' Sara said. 'That's so long ago, I can't remember.'

'Make up your mind, lady!' Steve said. 'A moment ago you were saying –'

'I know,' Sara said. 'I know. I'm too tired to be intelligent now. Too foggy with all that champagne. I'm going to feel awful in the morning.'

'It is morning,' Steve said.

And it was, very early morning. When they walked into their house, they walked arm in arm through darkness, while overhead stars burned and glittered in celestial celebration of another new year.

Morning.

Three-fifteen in the morning, and outside the windows a blaze of splendid blue sky, streaked with flame-tinted clouds. Below them the world slowly whirled.

Really it was eight-fifteen in the morning, for they were almost in London. The stewardess was quietly making the rounds, giving passengers warm rolled-up towels and trays of breakfast with steaming coffee or tea. Time had lurched for the people on this plane, and skipped a beat, but their bodies were still stumbling along on the old time.

In the seat next to Sara, Fanny still slept a deep and dreamy Valium sleep. Sara had no idea how many pills Fanny had taken before she got on the plane, just as she had no idea how many Fanny took just to get through a regular day. She decided to let Fanny sleep until the last moment, to let her sleep until they landed, if possible, just in case Fanny was nervous about landings. Although it seemed it wasn't accidents that worried Fanny — it was always, and only, the judgment of people.

Fanny did seem to be weathering her reentrance to the world well. Sara had nursed her along this past month and watched Fanny grow more confident with every step, just like a child. First she had taken the author to have her hair styled and tinted to hide the streaks of gray. The hairdresser, a handsome young man, had been suavely flattering to Fanny, and her hairstyle had turned out a smashing success. Sara watched while right before her eyes, Fanny's fear of judgment shrank as her vanity caught fire again and leapt up, making her eyes blaze, her skin glow. She had not lost it, the old powerful taste, the craving, for the admiration, and the envy, and the homage paid to her by others' eyes.

The next day Sara took Fanny shopping for new clothes. Again, the outing was a success. The saleswomen were honestly impressed with Fanny's figure and posture, and the new fashions and colors Fanny tried — brighter, more vivid, than the pastels she usually chose — were flattering. Fanny needed everything, business suits (which looked amazingly sexy on her full figure), dinner dresses, walking shoes and slacks for their spare time in London. At one point in their shopping tour, to Sara's amazement, Fanny said casually, 'Why don't we stop in here and buy you a mink, Sara?'

'What?' Sara had asked, almost laughing with surprise. To say something so casually!

'Well, you've admired mine so much, and it does make one feel so elegant to wear mink. Besides, they're warm. It's practical.'

'Fanny, I can't afford a mink coat,' Sara began, but Fanny interrupted her.

'Oh, I know. But I can. And I'd love to buy you one for a present. It's only fair, after all you've done for me.'

For one brief second the dream of owning a mink coat glimmered in Sara's mind like a sparkling jewel, and there Fanny stood, her fairy godmother, ready to wave her wand.

'I couldn't let you buy me a mink coat, Fanny,' Sara protested.

'But, darling, you know I have more money than I know what to do with it!' Fanny said.

'I know, I know, but I'm sure now that you're getting out more you'll find all sorts of things to spend your money on,' Sara said. 'Fanny, it's incredibly generous of you to suggest it, but really, I can't let you do it. And don't worry, I shan't embarrass you in London, I won't go slouching around behind you like a poor country cousin.'

'Oh, my dear, you know it's fine with me if you do!' Fanny said. 'It will only make *me* look better!' She laughed heartily.

Jenny's Book had come out in the States this week, and Walpole and James had thrown a publication party for Fanny – the first party she had been to in five years. Sara had scheduled the party before the London trip so that Fanny could have a trial run-through. For most Americans a London party would be a momentous occasion; for Fanny it would be overwhelming.

The Boston party went well. It was crowded with journalists from Boston and New York, other writers and editors and agents, and assorted types who loved the literary world. Linda Oldham had come from Heartways House, delighted at last to be able to meet the reclusive writer. Fanny had worn a simple black wool dress with pearls, had looked smashing, had been charming and witty, and had been much admired, although Sara wasn't sure just how aware she was of her triumph, for she went to the party stuffed with Valium and drank gallons of scotch once she got there. Sara had seldom seen anyone drink so much and stay so sober. She knew that all those calming drugs were fighting against the adrenaline of fear that was shooting through Fanny's veins. Her first party in years! She did beautifully.

Steve had come up for the publication party and afterward he and Sara and Fanny and Donald James went to a small French restaurant for dinner. Sara watched, both amused and impressed, as Fanny set out to captivate both men. Her Kansas drawl grew more lilting and lazy, her vocabulary more ladylike and quaint, her movements more voluptuous, her smile enticing. Sara noticed that Fanny ate almost nothing but drank lots of wine. Sara had never watched a first-class enchantress at work before, and it was a marvelous lesson. How subtle Fanny was, how *feminine*!

As they were leaving the restaurant, Donald James drew Fanny aside and exacted a promise that she have lunch with him when she returned from London.

'I don't believe it. That old nun!' Sara said in the car. 'He's smitten with you, Fanny, you've managed to get even *him* enamored of you.'

'Oh, dear, he just wants to have a business lunch, I'm sure. Find out how London went and all that.' Fanny's voice was smug. She was slowly rubbing her cheek against the collar of her mink.

'Would you like to meet us for lunch tomorrow?' Sara asked as they stopped in front of Fanny's Victorian house.

'Oh, goodness, no.' Fanny laughed. 'Sara, don't you know that I shan't get out of bed at all tomorrow? I'll probably sleep till three or four – the sleep of the just. It takes me a while to unwind,' she added. 'I always did get so excited at parties. I'll probably be up a few more hours, telling poor old dreary Eloise about my triumphs. Then I'll have a very hot bath and a glass of – don't laugh! – cocoa! – and I hope I'll finally manage to get to sleep about three or four in the morning. I've always been this way. It's one of the reasons I stopped going out. Steve,' she said then, 'will you be kind enough to escort me to my door?'

Not until Sara saw Steve assisting Fanny up the winding slate walk did she realize how drunk Fanny was, or perhaps it was that she was drunk and truly exhausted. For her first night out in five years, it had been a strenuous night. Sara saw the draperies parted in the living room and a dark figure watching: Eloise. Then the door opened and Eloise was there, putting her hand under Fanny's arm. Sara could see Eloise's face in the light; she was not smiling, but she looked sane and gentle, just what Fanny needed now, Common Sense embodied. She was glad they could leave the excitable Fanny in such good hands.

As Steve and Sara waited outside Fanny's door the following evening, the terrible fear that Fanny would back out of the trip to London from sheer terror had Sara nearly sick – but at last the door opened, and there Eloise was. Behind her was Fanny in her mink, with an assortment of luggage lined up in the entrance hall. Steve had driven both women to the airport, and bought them a celebratory glass of champagne and kissed Sara and promised that she would return safely and that he would be completely miserable every moment she was gone. They had gone through customs. They had boarded the plane. Almost immediately Fanny had taken another pill and very soon after the plane lifted off, she was deep in sleep.

Now here they were, about to land. In about thirty minutes, the stewardess said. Sara looked at her watch; she would wake Fanny up in ten minutes, to give her time to get oriented and fix her face and hair. She hoped this London trip would be all right for Fanny. Fanny had done beautifully in Boston, and it did not seem to have taken too great a toll on her; in fact she seemed to have taken on some momentum. But London would be different. She had known people in London; she would very possibly be seeing people here that she had known ten and fifteen and twenty years before, when she was young and beautiful. Fanny's obsession with her youth might be ludicrous, might even, on some ethical spectrum, be *wrong*, but she was caught in it, it was her obsession.

Sara was only now, it seemed, beginning to really understand the nature of obsession.

There was her own obsession with getting pregnant. Her life had become emblazoned with her desire so that no matter what else was happening on any given day, that desire displayed itself in vivid colors across the face of that day, obscuring other meanings in her life. It was crippling her. She knew

241

that, and did not know how to change – that was part of being obsessed, after all, not being able to leave off wanting what you wanted.

At least her obsession was helping her see more deeply into others' lives. It was helping her to be tolerant with Fanny. And it was helping her to understand others, too.

She was just now beginning to realize what her mother's life was like, just now beginning to comprehend her mother's obsession, and was sobered by what she had come to understand. When she had called her mother to tell her that she was going to London with Fanny for a week, and that once again she wasn't pregnant, her mother said, 'Now, Sara, this may be a blessing in disguise. One's life can be just as important, just as worthwhile, and certainly a great deal more fun and interesting if one *doesn't* have children. Children tie you down terribly, you know, they change your life absolutely and completely, and once you have them all your dreams are destroyed. Your dreams can never ever come true. Well, perhaps when they're grown. Really, if I were you, I'd look on this as a godsend. You're going to go to London! Do you have any idea how much I wanted to go to London when I was your age? And there I was, stuck in the house with two young children and the dishes to do. Not that I didn't love you and Ellie, of course.'

Sara had often heard those words and even that tone of painfully concealed anguish, but had never bothered to interpret it. But now she understood. Her mother had majored in French. She had had dreams of working for the UN, or for some corporation with international offices. Instead she had married Sara's father and spent her life near Boston, providing a warm and comfortable home for her family. She had never made it to France until the past few years, after her husband died, when she went on tours with friends, which could not have been at all what she had dreamed of as a young woman. Sara understood at last that if her mother hadn't had children but had been able to work, to travel, she might have led a happier life.

Sara felt a deep sorrow for all her mother had missed. And

242

thought how wonderful if would be if *she* could have her
mother's obsession – then she would be happy with her empty
womb and childless life, then she would see her infertility as a
blessing instead of a torture. And something even deeper filled
Sara now when she talked to her mother – a sense of pride, of
amazed admiration – for her mother had not let her obsession
destroy her life. She had loved her family and kept them safe
and happy and not run away, not escaped through airplanes or
alcohol, and now when she was free to travel, she was doing
that, enjoying herself, rather than spending her days in bitterness and remorse. *I must learn from her*, Sara thought.

Who did not have an obsession? Julia did. She was still
hopelessly involved with Perry, even though she was hearing
less and less from him these days. Jamie Jones and Carole
Clark were not obsessed, she supposed, but their husbands
were; they were obsessed with alcohol, and that meant that
Jamie and Carole had to live their lives according to the whims
of the obsessions of those they loved.

Sara could only guess at what their lives must be like, and,
knowing Pete and Sheldon, and liking them, she could imagine
how they must hate themselves for their desires and their fail-
ures.

So there were worse obsessions than the desire to be pregnant. There was some comfort in that.

Because she had learned something about other people's
obsessions, she had done something before the trip to England
that she would probably not have done. Although it had been
on her mind for months.

She had called Fanny Anderson's first love, Will Hofnegle.
His name, actually, was Ernst Brouwer – she had learned this
long ago from Fanny. All during November and December,
Sara had dreamed and plotted – wouldn't it be lovely if Ernst
was widowed now, or even divorced, and living alone?
Wouldn't it be interesting if she was to call him and invite him
to the publication party that Walpole and James was giving
Fanny in January? Sara imagined picking Ernst up at the
airport – he would be older, of course, but tall and tanned and
weathered-looking, like a man in a Marlboro ad. And she would

243

take him with her – no, she would leave him with Steve. Because she had to pick up Fanny and personally escort her to the party. So she would take Fanny to the party, and after an hour or so, after Fanny talked to the reviewers and magazine and newspaper people and had something to drink and was relaxed in the company of strangers, then Steve could bring Ernst in. He would walk across the room ... Fanny would look up, see him, smile with surprise ... Ernst would take her hands and look into her eyes ... And violins would appear from out of the heavens to salute this lovers' reunion.

She had called the Kansas directory information and asked for the number of Ernst Brouwer in Centerton. Without a pause, the operator gave her the number, which Sara took as a good omen: he was still there, he was still alive, perhaps he was just waiting for this phone call!

But a woman answered the phone. And when Ernst came on the line and listened to Sara's explanation (she tried to make it sound as if the publisher were inviting *lots* of Fanny's old acquaintances, making it a sort of 'This Is Your Life' party), Ernst had said that he was sorry, but he wouldn't be able to make it. His wife was ill and he couldn't leave her and she wasn't up to a trip back east, and their daughter was expecting a baby any day now. But would Sara please convey his congratulations to Fanny? And he would look for the book, would look forward to reading it. His wife would, too; she had gone to school with Fanny.

Sara had hung up, inordinately disappointed. Perhaps, she told herself, perhaps she wanted too much, to have Fanny not only having a first-class novel published *and* getting out of her hideaway and back into the real world, but also to have Fanny in love again, loved again, which would make Fanny whole. Perhaps she expected too much, wanted too much in every quarter of her life. She should learn to settle for what she had.

She was learning that. Yes, she was learning that. Now, as the plane began to sink downward so rapidly that Sara could feel its descent in her stomach, she felt her own hopes not ascend, but at least stay level. This would be a wonderful week. She loved London. She would be able to visit with old friends in the publishing business whom she had gotten to know during her trips here when she worked for Walpole and James. She would be able to watch Fanny have her literary triumph – and the Shelburne Prize really was a victory. And Fanny would not have won it if Sara hadn't discovered the book and encouraged Fanny and edited it, so Sara could congratulate herself, too. People in the business would know what Sara had done, would appreciate her own sense of triumph. She would not let it matter that she was not pregnant and could not hope to get pregnant this month. She would not let it matter that Fanny would not achieve love as well as fame and fortune. She would try to let go of all desires for what she and Fanny did not have and try to spend one pure week celebrating what they did have.

'Fanny,' she said, leaning over to the woman who still slept soundly next to her. 'Wake up. We're here.'

Lindsay Torrance, Fanny's agent in London, picked Sara and Fanny up at Heathrow and took them to their home for the week: the agency's flat, beautifully appointed and situated in the heart of London, right across from Hyde Park on Bayswater Road. Fanny took the large master bedroom with the queen-size bed and peach-colored silk drapes and duvet; Sara took the smaller bedroom and shared the clothes closet there with the ironing board and other domestic essentials. Both women luxuriated in the warm modern bathroom, which had gold-plated faucets and a bathtub over six feet long. It was quite wonderful – the bathroom, especially, because they found themselves exhausted and needing a long soak in therapeutically hot water after slinking around London in their very high heels.

Fanny took to all the socializing like a duck to water. Like the prodigal daughter returning. They went to lunch with her agent and the other people from the agency, to lunch with the people from the publishing house that would put *Jenny's Book* out in paperback, to dinner with the people who were publishing it in hardcover, to dinner with an aggressive but enjoyable young reporter from a women's magazine, to interviews here and there, to two plays that they crammed into their busy week, and, now and then, they went for long brisk walks in the park, their hands shoved deep into their coat pockets, following the meandering Serpentine, sharing their memories of former days in London. They had tea at the Ritz, and as they daintily munched watercress sandwiches, Lindsay Torrance praised Sara so highly that she felt she was drinking champagne instead of tea. Would Sara ever consider moving to London? Lindsay asked. Or working for Lindsay's agency? She could be based in both Boston and London.

Sara smiled a gentle refusal. She told Lindsay about her project for Heartways House, how she was setting down guidelines for the series and choosing the books, and would be editing them. And she couldn't leave Nantucket; that was her home now, and she didn't want to be away from Steve very often.

'Aah,' Lindsay said, 'too bad. Our loss.'

Later that night, still awake – jet lag had tossed any sleeping routine to the winds – Sara played the conversation back with all the pleasure that anyone takes in being complimented and courted; as if she were remembering enticements from a man who would be her lover. She would not be untrue to Steve, but how sweet to be asked. And, she thought, perhaps this really was her world. It did seem to be the one she was successful in. She was a good editor, she knew, and she was good with people. Perhaps she was meant to be involved in the whirl of literary life rather than in the gentle routine of domesticity. She could not help daydreaming about how different her life could be. Trips to London, tidbits of gossip about scandalous writers consumed over caviar and champagne, silk against her skin as a regular choice, and sophisticated people to admire the way she looked in that silk, the sense of making a difference, of assisting others in a creative and always surprising profession . . . Sara finally fell asleep, overwhelmed by her thoughts.

The fourth night was the night of the Shelburne award ceremony. First there was an enormous cocktail party at the agency's flat, with lots of fine champagne and hors d'oeuvres and crushes of literary people. A dinner in the banquet hall of a famous old hotel and the ceremony itself were to follow.

Sara was as proud of the way Fanny looked for the ceremony as if she had created her herself. Fanny's new hairstyle was a sort of modified pageboy, cut shorter in back than in front, so that the sides hung down in sleek curtains that slanted in toward her face just at chin level, with long bangs that swept slightly sideways. It was a new look, a sophisticated look, and Fanny looked years younger with it. For the ceremony she was wearing a modest, high-collared, long-sleeved silver dress that showed off her wonderful figure. A blue brooch on her shoulder. Sara taught her new makeup tricks: blue eye shadow, black eyeliner, lighter lipstick than she was used to wearing. The final effect was stupendous. Sara knew she looked fine in her red silk, but tonight her own looks almost didn't matter to her, all her pride was centered in Fanny.

Fanny, as the guest of honor, held court in the living room of the flat. She sat in the middle of the sofa, where people could join her on either side, and sipped champagne and smiled and was charming. Sara stayed by the door to greet people coming in, to direct them toward the champagne or toward Fanny. All her worries about Fanny! she thought to herself, secretly laughing, all her fears that Fanny would find her celebrity too much after her years of solitude. She had actually been afraid that Fanny might have some kind of nervous breakdown. And there she was, triumphant, flirtatious, a fish back in water: a charming woman back among people.

A tall, lean, and marvelously distinguished-looking white-haired man was suddenly standing before Sara in the entrance hall. He was wearing a beautiful black cashmere coat and a white silk scarf over a beautifully cut gray suit. Sara sighed with pleasure at the sight of such elegance.

'Hello,' he said pleasantly. 'I've come to see Fanny. I'm an old friend of hers. Randolph Bell.'

'Oh, my –' Sara said, with great self-control swallowing the 'God' portion of her exclamation. Randolph Bell – Cecil Randolph; she knew at once. Fanny's old and greatest love. The aristocrat. The fink. 'How nice,' she said. 'Fanny will be so pleased.' She *hoped*. Fanny might be thrown into a state of shock, misery, insecurity. It was only with enormous restraint that Sara kept herself from asking, 'Did you bring your wife with you, or did she, I hope, die?'

But of course Sara did not, would not, say such a thing. She led Randolph Bell into the living room. Sara's mind was racing; she was wondering if there was a way to break the news of his arrival to Fanny so that she could prepare herself.

But it was too late. Fanny looked up. She saw Randolph. She blushed gorgeously. She gasped, and everyone around her looked up to see what had caused her reaction.

And as Sara stood watching, Randolph crossed the room and Fanny stood up, and they took each other's hands and smiled into each other's eyes and for all Sara knew at that moment a thousand violins did come swooning down from the ceiling. This was indeed a lovers' reunion, even though Fanny and Randolph did not embrace but were content to look at each other, still holding hands.

Very few people, Sara thought, got to have a night like Fanny was having that night. Sara felt lucky just to be able to watch it from the sidelines. With her old lover, her real beloved, watching, Fanny received the Shelburne Prize while a room full of writers, press people, and critics stood applauding.

Fanny rose to take the award, looking, with her sleek helmet of dark hair and her voluptuous figure, a great deal more like Cleopatra than Virginia Woolf. After thanking the award committee, she said, 'But the one person I must thank above all others is my editor and friend, Sara Blackburn Kendall. She discovered this book in its raw, embryonic stage, she persisted in harassing me' – here Fanny threw Sara a smile – 'until I completed it, she helped me form it from a muddle into a formal work with a shape as complete as a vase, and she encouraged me every step of the way. The literary world needs more editors like this, brave people who are willing to inflict their values and judgments on writers, people who act really as midwives to writers. For just as babies might die in their mothers' wombs without the skill and assistance of a dedicated doctor or midwife, just so would *Jenny's Book* have died, never to see the light of day, if Sara Blackburn Kendall hadn't coaxed and pulled and struggled to bring it to life. I could not have done it alone. I did not do it alone. Sara taught me that it is never too late – in fiction or in life – to revise.'

Sara smiled, and then, when asked, stood for applause. She was too drunk on the success of the evening to feel any impact from Fanny's speech, but she held it there, in her mind, in her heart, for her to remember over and over again; to remember and to shape her own life by.

When the ceremony and the festivities were finally over, when the crowded room began to empty, Sara, who had been carefully monitoring Fanny and Randolph, confessed that she was very, very tired, too tired to accompany them to a pub for a little after-dinner liqueur. She could tell only too well how much the two were longing to be alone. And she was tired; she fell asleep as soon as her head hit the pillow.

She did not see much of Fanny after that. They had planned three more days in London. Fanny had more interviews and some book signings, which Sara went to with her, and Sara had several appointments and luncheons with old friends and colleagues. In the evening, every evening, Fanny was busy with Randolph – did Sara mind terribly? For it was obvious that this much remained of the old Fanny – an ability to abandon heartlessly any relationship with any woman in order to be with a man. In this case, Sara didn't blame her, and in fact was delighted to see how easily Fanny went off on her own, not needing Sara's reassurance, not hiding away in her room, worrying about how she had aged.

Still, she was surprised when, the last day they were in London, Fanny came into the little bedroom where Sara was packing and announced that she would not be flying back to the States with her. She was planning to go to Randolph's country house in Sussex, where they had been lovers so many years ago. Randolph's wife had not died, but she had left him; they were divorced; their marriage, Fanny reported, was apparently never any good. Randolph claimed that he had never stopped loving Fanny. 'I wouldn't be surprised if he married me this time,' she said. 'Now that I'm so respectable and celebrated. *And* his dreadful parents are dead! He doesn't have to answer to anyone.'

'Oh, Fanny,' Sara had cried, 'this is a fairy tale! I can't believe it.' She crossed the room and gave Fanny a hug.

'Oh, it's no fairy tale,' Fanny said smugly. 'It's more like a contemporary romance novel, wouldn't you say? I mean, it's very *fleshy*; I don't believe they had lust in fairy tales.'

'But, Fanny,' Sara protested, emboldened by Fanny's high spirits, 'listen. Sit down a minute.' And when the writer had perched on the edge of the bed in the one spot not covered by Sara's tousled underwear and sweaters, Sara took a deep breath and asked, 'What happened to all your fears? Your horrible suffocating anxieties? I mean, I feel terrible even mentioning it, but your feeling that you were old now, and that your looks have changed so much that no one could ever love you – all those fears that kept you in your house for years – what happened to them?'

'Oh, they're still there, my dear,' Fanny said. She picked up a silk scarf of Sara's and began to fold and smooth it with a gentle absentmindedness as she talked. 'Of course they're still there. With me every minute of the day. It's just that I have a different perspective on it now. First of all, as far as my vanity's concerned, well, I won't go into detail but I will tell you that Randolph seems to find me still quite arousing, and the marvelous thing about it all, really, is that when one comes right down to it, one only has to turn off the lights! Then there we are, all alone in the dark, with all that nice soft sensitive loving flesh and who cares what one looks like. Who knows what one looks like in the dark!'

With an abrupt gesture, Fanny put down the scarf she had been playing with and looked at Sara, who sat in the bedroom's one armchair and was looking intently at Fanny. Fanny's eyes held Sara's – how beautiful she was! Sara thought, and when she talked earnestly it was like being given a message from a goddess.

'But really, Sara, I'm being facetious,' Fanny said. 'Or

partly so. What I've learned since I've been here is much more important – shocking, really. You see, Sara, now that I've had a good long look around London and a good long gossip with Randolph, I find that half the people I thought would be here judging me are *dead*! Absolutely under the ground or in an urn on someone's mantel. I don't know how I'd forgotten about that – death, I mean – but I won't again. Oh, I used to play at suicide, but that was only an attempt to get Fate's attention: Look at me, I'm desperate, if you don't change my luck, you won't have me around anymore! A childish ploy. I never seriously tried to die. You know, I don't believe I ever seriously thought I *could* die. And now, to suddenly find that so many people I've known are just *gone*. It's dreadful, I mean it inspires real dread.'

Fanny rose from the bed and walked around the room, clasping her hands in front of her. 'Oh, Sara, in the face of death, all my anxieties seem so petty. Well, they are petty. I would *like* to have eternal youth. But I can't have it, and it seems I'd better stop wanting what I can't have and enjoy what I do have! I know people will still judge me – next week we're having tea with Randolph's sister, and believe me, she'll judge me, what a bitch she is. But I'll be judging her, too. And, Sara, I'm so much braver now, having won the Shelburne Prize, having published a novel. I don't know if I can explain it to you, but I really feel like a different person. I think I even *am* a different person. I am not a farmgirl snubbed by easterners anymore. I am the writer who won the Shelburne Prize. I deserve some wrinkles and gray hair. So many things have changed for me, don't you see?'

Fanny looked at Sara long and hard. She crossed the room, and to Sara's surprise, sat down on the bed across from Sara, right on Sara's neatly folded skirts. She reached over and took Sara's hands in hers. 'And all because of you. Do you hear me? I mean it. All because of you. You pried me out from under my rock and gave me the courage to write and go back into the world – and here I am, and I love it! And I owe it all to you!'

'Well,' Sara began, modestly protesting, 'not all, Fanny.'

The two women looked at each other for a long moment, holding hands. Sara thought: *I love her. And she loves me.* She could see the love in her friend's eyes.

'Do you know,' Fanny said, breaking the intensity of the moment, rising and straightening Sara's clothing as she talked, 'Lindsay Torrance suggested the most marvelous idea for a novel the other day at lunch. About a woman like me, *une femme d'un certain age*, hell, *past* a certain age, who hides away for years, in fear, just like I did, and then comes out and discovers, when she's almost sixty, how much life there is left to live, how exciting life can be! It's certainly a book I could write, and I can't stop thinking about it. But I won't make her a writer who writes a novel, it will have to be something else. I don't know. But I know that will be my next novel. And I hope you'll edit it for me, Sara.'

'You know I will,' Sara said, smiling.

'Oh, my dear!' Fanny said. 'There is so much in the world to want!'

There is so much in the world to want.

Well, that was certainly true, Sara thought as she sat alone on the long flight back to America. It was a morning flight; the stewardesses had served and then removed breakfast trays and the first bustle of the flight was over, everyone was settling down, relaxed by the plane's steady drone.

She had in her lap a manuscript that Lindsay Torrance had asked her to read and give an opinion on. She looked down at the type-written pages, then looked away. Across the aisle, a young mother unbuttoned her blouse so that her baby could nurse. Sara started to look away, then forced herself to watch.

The baby. The soft skin. The bald and vulnerable head. The white blanket. With a squeal and a kick, the emergence of a tiny foot in a tiny blue booty. The tiny body. The enormous trust. The flash of plump bare pink thigh as his diaper was being changed. The satisfied little sounds, and asleep at last, the flushed flawless face the source of perfect peace.

Sara turned away and looked out the window. She wiped the tears from her face. Outside there seemed to be nothing, the morning blue bleached by distance into nothing. Nothing as far as she could see. And that was death, she supposed, that endless empty faded air where nothing could occur. That was what death was like: nothing. And on her other side, sleeping in his mother's blissful embrace, was a child, who was life. Who was everything: noise and flesh and the future. If she could never have the one, and it looked as if she couldn't, still she did not yet want the other. There was some middle ground.

She repeated to herself Fanny's admonition to enjoy what one did have instead of wasting life pining for what one didn't have. If Fate had sent her to Fanny to help Fanny complete her book and thus change her life, perhaps Fate had also brought Fanny to Sara to show her what her life was to be about. Across the aisle, the woman held her baby. Sara held a manuscript. And that was not nothing. She loved her work and never wanted to give it up, and now she was having great success. Perhaps Fate meant for her to put her whole life into her work.

And there was Steve. Always Steve, who loved her and who, she believed, would continue to love her whether she gave him a child or not. They had already weathered so much together: lust and jealousy and boredom and anger and disappointment and hard work and the disgrace of stomach flu, the embarrassment of a night's failed passion, the humiliations of a body's repeated failure to reproduce, hope and failure, achievements in work, carnal unions of such bestial intensity that they hurled each other into the heavens, bodies causing souls to meld. They were on intimate terms now, Steve and Sara, and their mutual misfortune had united them as much as their mutual ecstasy.

This was a great deal to have. Sara looked out at the vapid sky and vowed that if the plane landed safely, bringing her back to the complicated world, she would do her best to love what she had; not to spend her life in mourning for what was not being given.

She would not give up hope, though: but she would not live her life only hoping.

At the end of January, Ellie had her second baby, a little girl whom they named Sara Melinda.

In February, Steve and Sara took a short vacation. Because they needed to be careful with money, they took a super-saver flight to Florida and stayed with Steve's parents. Clark and Caroline refrained from making any comments about grandchildren and, to Sara's delight, asked her opinion about various books they had been reading. It was as if they were trying to say, without words, 'It's all right. We love you as you are.' At the end of February, her period started again.

In March the weather was terrible. The island seemed frozen, encased in gloom and cold. Sara missed Fanny. No matter how hard she worked – and she was working very hard on the Heartways House series – time poked by with frustrating, faltering, slug-ugly slowness. Mary Bennett's baby was born, another healthy boy.

Sara looked out her window at the ungenerous white winter sky and remembered her vows on the plane home from England. So she flew into action: she turned the room that they had planned for a baby's room into a study for herself and Steve. She papered the room herself with a cocoa-brown wallpaper with small white fleur-de-lis and painted the trim a crisp white. She stained the floorboards dark and covered them with a gorgeous white Chinese rug with brown and jade and sapphire petals, a rug that no child could even come near without staining. With the money she was making, she bought a word processor for Steve's thirty-seventh birthday. He needed it for his work, and she used it, too. She found an old walnut desk and an older walnut table at a secondhand furniture store. She sanded and stained them until they gleamed. She hung heavy white linen curtains at the windows. The finished study looked so elegant, so perfect, that she told herself she didn't mind when her period started at the end of March.

In April, for her birthday, Steve gave her a kitten, a tiny fluffy white Angora, so feminine and voluptuous and languorous that they could only name her Fanny. Fanny sat in a white wicker basket on a pink cushion while Sara worked. And in

254

April, Sara's stomach bloated and her breasts swelled and ached and the tears came, and the blood. To cheer herself up, she called Julia.

Two days later, she received another missive from Julia in the mail.

> It is said that Rumanian gypsy women who had difficulty conceiving, at one time made animal sacrifices to the moon. During a full moon two male and female birds and two male and female four-footed animals were buried on a mountain. Libations were poured over the buried animals as a sacrificial offering to insure pregnancy.

'Go for it!' Julia had scribbled on the other side of the Xeroxed sheet. 'I'm sure you can find two dead sea gulls washed up on the beach somewhere. Throw them in a bag, come to Boston, we'll buy two lab rats, chop off their little awful heads, head for the Berkshires and do some full-moon voodoo. I'm ready if you are.'

This time Julia's humor seemed a little off – frantic, shrill. Sara called her friend again. 'Are you all right?' she asked.

'No,' said Julia, sobbing. 'No, I'm not and I never will be in my life. Perry is moving to California with his wife and their entire bloodsucking tribe of kids. It's all over, Sara. It's all over between us. And I swear I don't know what to do. I don't know what to do. You know, I think that if there were some magic, even black magic, that would make him stay with me, I'd do it, I'd kill animals, I'd drink blood, anything, anything.'

'I want you to fly down here and stay with us for a while,' Sara said. 'I want you to come today.'

'I can't leave the gallery,' Julia said.

'Of course you can leave the gallery. Come on, Julia, I mean it, I want you here on a plane today.'

'You're getting to be a real bossy bitch,' Julia said.

'That's what happens to us frustrated barren broads,' Sara snapped back.

Julia arrived as ordered and stayed for a week. The local spring festival, Daffodil Weekend, with its parades and outdoor picnics and displays of millions of daffodils, took place while she was there, and Sara secretly hoped Julia would meet a new man in the crowds of people that came to the island that weekend. But it didn't happen.

'Are you going to be all right?' Sara asked Julia the day she drove her to the airport for the flight back to Boston.

Julia gave her a dead-eye stare. 'No,' she said. 'I'm not. I don't think I'm going to be all right for a long time.' Then she manged a nasty little grin. 'But don't worry about me, kid, you know what they say. I'm too mean to die.'

Why? Sara thought, as she watched Julia's plane lift off into the cloudy spring sky. *Why can't we get what we want? Why can't Julia have Perry for a husband, why can't I have a child?* Julia's plane disappeared from sight, leaving the sky empty, white and blank.

In May, there was good news. Fanny called from England to announce that she and Randolph were going to be married. It would be a small private wedding in the garden at the manor house in the fall. Fanny's great desire now was that Sara be her matron of honor; after all, Sara was her best and really only friend. If Sara and Steve would please consent to letting Randolph and Fanny take care of the financial details they would like to pay the Kendalls' way to London, it was the least they could do. The wedding would be in early September.

Sara sat at her desk, looking out at their backyard, which was splendid with spring, the grass Easter-green, jonquils and tulips and hyacinths sprinkled like colored eggs under the forsythia. The world had done it again, had renewed itself, had given birth to itself. And Fanny had been born again, too, into a woman who was competent and loved and finally even a little wise. All things were possible, Sara told herself. All things were really possible. In spite of her vow, she found herself praying fervently all month, praying to whatever god it was that caused springtime, for surely *that* god would understand her desires.

And at the end of May, in spite of her prayers, the blood came.

In June she had a telephone call from a writer, a man who lived in New York and wrote a weekly column for a major news magazine and summered on Nantucket. He had heard of Sara's work with Fanny Anderson and asked if she would be interested in looking at the manuscript of an old Nantucket eccentric. Sara and the journalist and the old codger had tea together, and Sara looked at his manuscript, which was about life in the early years on the island. The articulate old salt had run a charter yacht service for years and had taken celebrities of every kind out for fishing trips or boating parties and celebrations, so he had memories and tales to tell and his own unique philosophy of life to expound upon in his own unique and crochety and colorful way. In a way he was a kind of genius, and Sara looked forward to editing his book. It would be a lot of work, for he was a more reluctant collaborator than Fanny had been and had to be cajoled into changing certain things. He thought it a disgrace that he couldn't call a famous senator's wife a 'ditzy alcoholic cunt', and so on. It was a challenge for Sara, but one that, if completed successfully, would be a real accomplishment.

At the end of June, her stomach pushed out again, making her silk slacks too tight to fasten. Her nipples stung and her breasts ached. She was zany with premenstrual tension, and on the twenty-eighth day her back began its nasty little evil cramps. The morning of the twenty-ninth day, she walked to town, bought herself four giant-size candy bars and every slick glossy magazine on the news-stand. Then she went home, took the phone off the hook and crawled into bed to dissipate in gloom and chocolate.

The morning of the thirtieth day she was insane, maniacal, furious. Her *damned* body and its *damned* tricks! She knew her period was going to start, she could feel its pressure inside her, burgeoning, hanging, weighing her down. God*damn*, why didn't it just go ahead and start? Why was she being tortured like this? She took a long bike ride to Surfside and back, then to the Jetties and back, and collapsed in a hot bathtub with an aching back.

On the morning of the thirty-first day she awoke to find that her period hadn't started. Her breasts ached. Her back was cramping. She was insane. She watched TV all day long.

On the morning of the thirty-second day, her period hadn't started. She thought she would fly out of her skin. She wanted to be put to sleep.

On the morning of the thirty-third day, Steve said, 'Hey, shouldn't your period be starting about now?'

The grin on his face broke Sara's heart. *He thinks I'm pregnant*, she thought. *Oh, my poor Steve, I'm going to disappoint him again.*

'It's going to start any day now,' she said. 'I'm late, but I know I'm going to start, I've got all the signs.'

'Oh,' he said. 'Too bad.'

On the morning of the thirty-fourth day, she flew to Boston and bought two hundred dollars' worth of new clothes: tight dresses and a clinging, plunging swimsuit.

On the morning of the thirty-fifth day, after a night of tossing and turning and hoping and doubting, after a night of almost no sleep, Sara threw on her clothes and went sneaking off to a pharmacy at the outskirts of town where she knew no one. She bought an Early Pregnancy Testing Kit to use the next day.

Morning.

The thirty-sixth day.

Sara rose stealthily from the bed before the alarm went off so that she wouldn't wake Steve. Slipping silently into the bathroom, she took the kit from where she had hidden it behind the towels.

The kit.

The cup.

The test.

The waiting.

The results: she was pregnant.

Sara stood in the bathroom staring at the stick she was holding, which had turned the most gorgeous shade of blue. She looked up and saw her face in the mirror; it was the face of an idiot, of a religious convert, the face of Saul on the road to Damascus. She put down the toilet lid and sank down onto it and just sat there, holding the miraculous stick in her hand, staring at it.

How could this happen? Sara wondered. How could this be? Why now? Why not earlier? Why never?

She did not know; she would never know. She only knew that she was pregnant at last. She sat, stunned, while the sun rolled higher into the sky, warming the day, sending its radiance into even this small bathroom in this modest house so that the room glowed as if there were riches here. And morning spread its brightness around her world, her town, her house, her life. She felt its glow and promise, and the glimmering beginnings inside her body answering back.

She went into the bedroom. She snuggled back into bed with Steve and curled herself against him, pulling at his body so that he was turned to face her.

'Ummm,' he said lazily.

'Steve,' she said. 'Good morning.'

Infidelities

FREDA BRIGHT

The Petersens – the darlings of New York's most glamorous musical and medical circles. Seth, the golden boy of medicine, for whom the Nobel Prize lies within arm's reach. Annie, a woman with the power and determination to realise her potential both as a singer and supportive wife.

Why then, after 10 years of blissful marriage does Annie feel such an agonising, torturing doubt? There's no smear of lipstick, no stray earring, no furtive phonecalls – nothing to confirm her dread. But Annie knows for certain that their world is falling apart . . .

0 7221 1963 1   GENERAL FICTION   £3.99

FiNE THiNGS

DANIELLE STEEL

Bestselling author of WANDERLUST

Living on the crest of a highly successful career, he was moving too fast to realise that he had everything – except what he wanted most . . .

Sent to San Francisco to open the smartest department store in California, Bernie Fine becomes aware of the hollowness of his personal life. Despite his success he grows increasingly disenchanted with his existence – until five-year-old Jane O'Reilly gets lost in the store.

Through Jane, Bernie meets her mother Liz, who finally offers him the possibility of love. But the rare happiness they find together is disrupted by tragedy and Bernie must face the terrible price we sometimes have to pay for loving . . .

0 7221 8308 9   GENERAL FICTION   £3.50

Deborah Fowler

RIPPLES

A top job as a magazine journalist; a charming aristocratic husband; a beautiful London home, and all the money she could spend – Laura Melhuish had everything a woman could want. Until, that is, she finds that her husband Francis has squandered her wealth on his fraudulent business deals . . . Until a takeover puts her out of her job . . . Until Francis disappears without trace, leaving only ripples on the surface of her life . . .

Alone and carrying Francis's abandoned child, Laura begins to rebuild the fragments of her shattered life. And as she searches anew for love and fulfilment, a challenging world of passion, joy, opportunity and purpose unfolds. But can she ever escape from the bitter shadow of the past . . .?

Also available by Deborah Fowler in Sphere Books:
SOMETIME . . . NEVER
REFLECTIONS

0 7221 3716 8   GENERAL FICTION   £3.50

Danielle Steel

KALEIDOSCOPE

THREE SISTERS, BONDED BY BLOOD, SEPARATED BY FATE . . . COULD THEY EVER FIND EACH OTHER AGAIN?

When Sam Walker returned from the front lines of World War II, bringing with him his exquisite French bride, no one could have imagined that their fairy-tale love would end in such shattering tragedy . . .

And, at the age of nine, Hilary, the eldest of the Walker children, clung desperately to her two sisters – five-year-old Alexandra and baby Megan. However, before the year was out, they too would be painfully wrenched from her tender arms. Cut off from every loving warmth, Hilary swore she would one day track down the man who had destroyed her family, and find her beloved sisters again. But could they risk everything to confront a dark, forgotten past?

John Chapman – lawyer, prestigious private investigator – chosen to find the sisters, embarks on a labyrinthine trail which leads him to Paris, New York, Boston and Connecticut, knowing that, at some time in their lives, the three sisters must face each other and the final, most devastating secret of all . . .

0 7221 8314 3   GENERAL FICTION   £3.50

A selection of bestsellers from SPHERE

FICTION

LORDS OF THE AIR	Graham Masterton	£3.99 ☐
THE PALACE	Paul Erdman	£3.50 ☐
KALEIDOSCOPE	Danielle Steel	£3.50 ☐
AMTRAK WARS VOL. 4	Patrick Tilley	£3.50 ☐
TO SAIL BEYOND THE SUNSET	Robert A. Heinlein	£3.50 ☐

FILM AND TV TIE-IN

WILLOW	Wayland Drew	£2.99 ☐
BUSTER	Colin Shindler	£2.99 ☐
COMING TOGETHER	Alexandra Hine	£2.99 ☐
RUN FOR YOUR LIFE	Stuart Collins	£2.99 ☐
BLACK FOREST CLINIC	Peter Heim	£2.99 ☐

NON-FICTION

DETOUR	Cheryl Crane	£3.99 ☐
MARLON BRANDO	David Shipman	£3.50 ☐
MONTY: THE MAN BEHIND THE LEGEND	Nigel Hamilton	£3.99 ☐
BURTON: MY BROTHER	Graham Jenkins	£3.50 ☐
BARE-FACED MESSIAH	Russell Miller	£3.99 ☐
THE COCHIN CONNECTION	Alison and Brian Milgate	£3.50 ☐

All Sphere books are available at your local bookshop or newsagent, or can be ordered direct from the publisher. Just tick the titles you want and fill in the form below.

Name _____

Address _____

_____

Write to Sphere Books, Cash Sales Department, P.O. Box 11, Falmouth, Cornwall TR10 9EN

Please enclose a cheque or postal order to the value of the cover price plus:

UK: 60p for the first book, 25p for the second book and 15p for each additional book ordered to a maximum charge of £1.90.

OVERSEAS & EIRE: £1.25 for the first book, 75p for the second book and 28p for each subsequent title ordered.

BFPO: 60p for the first book, 25p for the second book plus 15p per copy for the next 7 books, thereafter 9p per book.

Sphere Books reserve the right to show new retail prices on covers which may differ from those previously advertised in the text elsewhere, and to increase postal rates in accordance with the P.O.